USA TODAY BESTS

Dale Mayer

BOOK 4-6

HEROES FOR HIRE, BOOKS 4–6
Beverly Dale Mayer
Valley Publishing Ltd.

ISBN-13: 978-1-773360-51-5
Print Edition

About This Bundle

Rhodes's Reward

Even when evil lurks in the shadows, second chances are possible…

Years ago, Rhodes knew Sienna as a young, gawky girl who was all elbows and carrot-colored hair without an ounce of grace. Despite her clumsiness, she'd had something special about her even then. Now she's all grown up, and Rhodes still can't seem to ignore her. One glimpse has him thinking about a lot more than old times. But, sweet and lovable as she is, Sienna has rightly been called a trouble magnet—even while inside a military-secure compound that should be the ultimate safe haven.

Sienna had an epic-sized crush on Rhodes when she was a kid and he was her brother's best friend. Now he's a grown man, hunky and hotter than her wildest fantasies could have imagined. New to the job at Levi's company, Legendary Securities, she doesn't want to jeopardize her position by spending all her time daydreaming about Rhodes so close to her now and yet still so far away.

When she's asked to help on a mission, she eagerly agrees, hoping to score some points with her employer…except she inadvertently triggers a sequence of disastrous events that no one—even one familiar with Sienna's klutziness the way Rhodes is—could have predicted.

RHODES'S REWARD

Heroes for Hire, Book 4

Dale Mayer

Chapter 1

A SHIT JOB. A shit trip. A shit deal.

But he was home. Thank God.

Tired and haggard, Rhodes Gorman walked in the front door and headed straight for his suite on the second floor. He opened the door to his bedroom, dumped his bags and collapsed fully on his bed. He didn't bother undressing, and the thought of a shower was a lot more than he could handle right now. He closed his eyes to let the world take him away.

But instead his mind filled with the scenes and pain of the last few days. He and Harrison had gone overseas, tracking down a person with some intel. Now they were both home, but it hadn't been an easy job and the trip back—brutal. But they'd made it, and all he needed now was a chance to sleep.

Even with his door closed, he could still hear other people in the main house, the voices filtering through his head. One male. One female. Ice used to be the only female in the group, but that was rapidly changing. In his tired mode Rhodes couldn't understand or identify who that female was. Until she spoke again. Sienna. So she was still here. Good. Saved him a trip to haul her back again. They had unfinished business, whether she knew it or not.

"Why would you want to stay here?" asked the guy.

Who was that? Rhodes wondered.

"Because it's different. I feel safe here, "Sienna said. "I like the people." Her voice had shifted there—softening. "I enjoy the work."

"Safe?"

Yeah, that word caught Rhodes's interest too. But the change in tone at the word *people* was something else altogether.

"Yes, even though the compound has been attacked twice," she said, "everybody handled it so well. It was just like military clockwork."

"That's because it was," the man said.

Whoever the man was, he had influence over Sienna, and from the way she talked to him, she obviously knew him well. There was respect and familiarity in her tone … and love. Rhodes frowned. Who the hell was this guy? Jealously crept in.

"Jarrod, you can't rule my life."

Rhodes's eyes flew open. Jarrod? Jarrod Bentley, Rhodes's navy buddy was here? He'd been gone for two different four-week tours overseas. Planned to come by here each time he returned to the States. The first time he'd talked Sienna into leaving with him. But he was not fully informed. Rhodes heard she was just tying up loose ends to move here. Permanently. Figured Jarrod had come back while Rhodes was gone. Slowly he sat up, his head cocked to better hear the conversation out in the hallway.

He had met Sienna years ago, since he and Jarrod were brother SEALs. But he hadn't recognized her when she first came to the compound. Maybe because she had been a pimply face, awkward-arms-and-legs, bony-knees-and-elbows gangly teenager back then. Not the striking beauty who'd walked into the house with Ice that day. Even though she had said she was Jarrod's sister, he really hadn't made the connection. Not until hours later when he'd caught sight of that long-ago teenager inside the beautiful woman.

And then he didn't know how to bring up their earlier meeting. He'd never forgotten her. In fact, Jarrod had warned him away back then, already seeing Rhodes's interest, but who knew she'd turn out to be such a beauty?

Between the two attacks on the compound, the op in Afghanistan—rescuing Lissa—and then a series of jobs covering for Merk while he was busy protecting his ladylove, Rhodes had been more than a little busy.

With Sienna here, there's no way he would sleep now. Plus he didn't want to miss out on seeing his old friend, Jarrod. Rhodes sat up, then stood, stripped and stepped into the shower.

Soaking under the hot water gave him a sense of renewal. When he was done, he quickly dressed.

Nobody was in the hallway when he walked out. At the kitchen, he stopped to see Alfred and found him pouring a cup of coffee, which he handed to Rhodes. "I didn't know if you would choose a shower and some food or just sleep."

"I tried sleeping. That didn't work so well," he joked. "I figured coffee and some grub would hit the spot." He glanced around. "Did I hear Jarrod's voice?"

Alfred nodded. "Jarrod is indeed here. He came back to check on his sister."

"Rhodes?" The man's voice came from behind him.

Rhodes spun, and sure enough there was Jarrod. The huge carrot top had been a new recruit when Rhodes had joined Levi's SEAL unit. For some reason Jarrod and Rhodes had become great friends. He put down his cup and greeted his long-time buddy. "What the hell? I go away and come

won't let us."

Rhodes studied them, seeing the same closeness he'd noted a long time ago. "I met you way back when, you know?"

She shot him a shuttered look and nodded. "I remember."

"I didn't at first," Rhodes said in confession. "Besides, you've changed a lot," he said in an admiring tone. "You used to be this gangly teenager—all elbows, knees and freckles, with red hair going everywhere."

Jarrod snorted. "She still is." But he wrapped an arm around her shoulder and hugged her close. "Now, if she would stop being so damn independent and let us know when she gets into trouble, it'd make us all happy."

"You're always so busy," she said quietly. "Besides it wasn't anything I couldn't handle."

Jarrod turned to her and, in a much harder voice, said, "Ice found you at the gas station with a backpack, sitting under a tree, lost. You had no place to go. You were out of money and had no wheels. How was that 'handling' the issue? The least you could have done was call. We would've been happy to help."

She stared at the table but didn't answer.

Rhodes understood. Independence was a hard battle. When life beat you down, you didn't want anyone to know.

"At least Ice was the one who found Sienna," Rhodes said calmly. "We're not axe murderers. Once she got here, we were quite happy to invite her to stay."

Other thoughts rippled in his head, but to add more was taking the chance he would just piss her off. She shot him a grateful look, and he realized he'd said the right thing. A good thing. He glanced at Jarrod and got a nod of approval from him too. Rhodes sighed. This family stuff was rough. He was an only child, and his parents had retired to Tucson, Arizona where they liked to do morning brunch beside the pool with the rest of the retirees who lived in the complex and then play Scrabble and other board games in the evening. They were happy, so he was too. He'd been a very late-in-life child for them, and his decision to join the military was one they both approved of. He didn't see them very much, but called them often.

"Besides, Sienna has taken over the office work. And if you try to take her away from us, Stone may have something to say."

"Stone?" Jarrod asked with a frown.

"Yes, office work was his punishment whenever he pushed his recovery too much. We're always building new prototypes for that leg of his. Somehow he'd keep his stump more or less sored up. And that meant office work—and a lot of it."

Jarrod gave a subtle laugh. "I keep forgetting he's missing a leg. He's adapted so well," he said in admiration.

"It was a hard adjustment," Rhodes said in a low voice. "He never let anybody know, but it wasn't easy on him."

Jarrod nodded. "I don't imagine it would be." He studied Rhodes's face. "And you're okay? I heard the whole unit got blown up. But when I realized you were all ambulatory and then created this company together, I figured you were fine."

Rhodes said, "I'm fine now. Merk and I were injured but not anywhere near as badly as the other two. For us it was a couple broken bones. We were in traction for a while, lots of soft tissue damage, bruises on the liver, things like that."

"Sounds horrible," Sienna said.

Rhodes caught Sienna's sympathetic look. He quickly turned away. Sympathy was the last thing he wanted. Although his gaze kept straying back toward her, he realized he deserved a special reward for keeping his hands to himself. Because dammit she was hot.

He swallowed hard and turned as Alfred walked in at the right moment, carrying a plate of roast beef, gravy, and veggies and put it down in front of Rhodes.

"Alfred, this looks delicious," he said in relief. "I didn't realize how hungry I was until now."

"Just leftovers. They all had it last night."

"Wow, they actually left me some?" But he was already busy with his knife and fork, cutting into the moist tender meat. He put the first bite in his mouth and closed his eyes as he chewed. "Oh, my God, this is so good."

Jarrod said, his voice envious, "You guys are so lucky to have Alfred." He turned to his sister and said, "So that's the real reason you want to stay here."

Sienna laughed. "Alfred is a dream. If he were thirty years younger, I'd consider going after him myself."

Rhodes smirked. "Do you think we haven't thought of that? I don't twist that way, but I might consider it for a man who can cook like this. … *Hmm-hmm.*"

SOMETHING WAS JUST so damn attractive about a man who enjoyed his food. But he wasn't *eating*; he was savoring every bite. Rhodes had come to her house a couple times with Jarrod way back when. Once, when Sienna had lived with her brother, Rhodes had spent five days at their place. She hadn't taken her eyes off that big tough badass male. And yet he'd never once made her afraid.

In fact, the longer he'd stayed, the more she'd followed him around just to be in his presence. He oozed confidence and power. Back then, she'd felt ugly and awkward. To make it worse, she'd been fascinated by him but clueless as how to deal with it. Now, of course, she understood so much more.

They were both adults, free of relationships and living in the same place.

She couldn't help but consider it. She again dropped her gaze to the table and played with the coffee cup in front of her. Odd to realize that, after all these years, the attraction was even stronger. She daren't let Jarrod know because he'd fight tooth and nail to keep her away from Rhodes if that's what she was staying for.

And Rhodes was only a small part of it, though he definitely factored into it. No way would he seek her out if she left. But while she was here, she could see if there was something to the attraction or not. She needed time to let Rhodes get past that code of honor that said friends' little sisters were out of bounds. And Rhodes was the kind of guy who would see his good behavior as part of his honor system. Unlike a lot of men who would look upon her as prey, Rhodes would see her as untouchable, someone to protect while her brother wasn't here.

A tiny smile played at the corner of her mouth. Or maybe it wouldn't be an issue … if he found something he wanted badly enough.

"You okay, Sienna?"

She stopped and turned toward Jarrod. "Sorry, was lost in my thoughts for a moment there." She stared directly into her brother's eyes, knowing perfectly well that if she didn't pass this test, her life could get very difficult.

He searched her gaze for a long moment, then as if satisfied, he turned back to Rhodes. "So catch me up on your ops over the last year," he said.

Sienna sat quietly and listened to the two men share the events they'd gone through over the past twelve months. She wanted to hear as much as she could, but at the same time, she had work to do. Sienna stood up, patted her brother on the shoulder and said, "I'm not sure when you're leaving, but I have to get back to the office."

He reached out and caught her hand and said, "I leave in the morning."

She bent down, kissed him on the cheek and gave him a quick hug. She stepped away and tossed back, "I'll let you two old ladies sit here and gossip." She smiled at Alfred as she filled up her coffee cup, then headed to the office.

She still didn't understand everything that went on at Legendary Security, but she was starting to. Her first few days here had been hairy, but it had given her an interesting insight. Initially it had been unnerving, wondering what she had gotten herself into and with whom, but then she quickly realized how much and how well they took care of not just her but the entire place.

And how similar they all were to her brothers.

There was a certain freedom in being here. In an odd way she hadn't been free for a long time. She'd also met a kindred spirit here—Katina, Merk's partner, who was also an accountant. Not a programmer like Sienna was, but still Katina understood the financial world. And she'd been to hell and back herself.

In Sienna's case it wasn't her job that had done her in, but the people around her. She'd worked for an independent contractor looking into a series of banking irregularities inside the programming, hackers stealing within the system.

Very detailed work. And a special niche career.

She found what she thought was proof and handed it over but hadn't realized that her lover was part of the same criminal organization. When things had blown up, and the dust had settled, she'd been blamed for all kinds of things, like sleeping with the enemy. She'd lost everything, including her good name.

She'd walked away and started fresh.

Now nobody knew who she was, what she'd done, and where she'd gone. She told Jarrod some of it, but outside of it being a bad deal, there was no going back.

In fact, compared to what Lissa and Katina had been through, Sienna's life was bland and boring. Sure, she'd lost her job and had been betrayed by her lover, and was pretty damn sure her boss had been involved in the whole deal too, but all that was mild when compared to their lives.

Back in the office she settled down at her desk, pulled out her cell and checked the time. She was surprised it was so late already. She buckled down and started on the bookkeeping.

Compared to what she used to do, this was incredibly simple. But the mindlessness of it was also a joy. She didn't have to study lines of endless code or worry and fret over patterns she could see but not yet understand. She was fine not having to dig and follow trails and puzzles in order to ferret out the information needed. No subterfuge was here, and that alone was a relief. When her phone rang an hour later, she didn't think anything of it. She picked it up and answered, "Hello?"

"Sienna?"

"Yes, who's this?

"Bullard."

She sat back with a grin. "Hey, Bullard. Normally you don't call me directly."

"Nope, I don't. But this time I have a question for you."

"What's up?" She tossed down her pencil, leaning back in her chair. She liked Bullard, from the little bit she'd seen of him. He planned on coming back soon. She looked forward to that.

"You used to troubleshoot financial systems—banking software, accounting discrepancies—didn't you?" His voice gentled. "I remember Levi mentioning something like that."

She frowned. "I *used* to do something like that," she said. "I don't anymore."

"Any reason why?"

"Yeah, it didn't work out so well," she said in a dry tone. "Sometimes keeping your nose clean is better than digging for dirt."

He gave a bellowing laugh. "So true. But the business we're in doesn't keep our noses very clean. If I sent you some files, could you tell me where they're from?"

"Not necessarily," she said with a frown. "What type of files? And what do they have to do with my skills?"

"It's a little bit confusing. A friend, part owner of an African bank in Ghana, has found some discrepancies in their accounting. He has someone in mind who could be responsible, only that employee's son has worked with them for about a year as well, and both family members make up their IT department, doing all the upgrades and tweaks to the banking software. So he's reticent to have those guys look at the problem in case they are involved. He sent us access to the back end and several sheets found in the old man's desk. Only my computer specialist isn't accessible, and we aren't making heads or tails out of this."

In spite of herself she was intrigued. Impulsively she said, "Feel free to email them to me, but that doesn't mean I'll help."

"Done," he said triumphantly.

She rolled her eyebrows as she realized the email sat in her inbox, staring at her. "Is this something Levi knows about?"

"He's been giving me a hand on this case."

She nodded. "In that case, I'll look."

"Can you do that while I'm on the line?" he asked hopefully.

She double-clicked on the email and then opened the attachment. Instantly the lines of code appeared. She leaned forward to study it. "Do I get any contextual reference?" she said with a laugh. "This means nothing with so little."

"Money, drugs, and/or weapons," he said succinctly. "We think money is siphoned from a bank here in Africa, then transferred into a US account, where it's used for drug deals and buying weapons—to ship possibly back over here again. The trail led to Dallas."

"Oh." She winced.

She studied the figures, rapidly scanning the columns, her mind quickly interpreting the data. "Okay, so these are from the back end of a banking program. They are transactions, but very little information is here."

Silence came first. "Wow. That was fast."

"Fast but useless," she said cheerfully. "You need more data than this, a lot more."

"Did you check the second attachment?"

She quickly opened and scrolled down to see a PDF of spreadsheets, potentially from a ledger book. What he'd given her was just a drop of water in a missing lake of knowledge. She took a couple minutes to assimilate the information, then said, "I need so much more, preferably the program itself."

"It's all about the gold standard."

She returned her attention to the code. "Right, I can see it now." Indeed, on the last page she found one of the identifying banks, a small regional bank in Ghana. She continued to peruse that line of code. "This is old COBOL code. With a lot of updates …" Her voice petered off as she studied the subsequent lines of code. "Interesting. It's quite an antiquated system. I've seen a lot similar to this, but still wince every time I find some."

"Wow, again so fast. No wonder Levi hired you."

"No, he doesn't really know I can do this type of work." She laughed. "My skills are not a highly prized skill set in the world of private security companies."

"You'd be surprised. But for Levi's company, he's more interested in security on the human level. Mine on the other hand, is more interested in software security. So, any programmer who can see what and how code has been hacked, … that's worth a lot."

She shook her head, even though he couldn't see it. "Nah, I'm sure your guys would've figured this out. I might've gotten it in ten minutes, but they would've in twenty."

Bullard laughed. "We've had it for hours and had no idea what we were looking at." He added, "If you find anything else, please give me a ring back."

"The snippets aren't enough if you want me to see exactly what the developer has done," she said. "I'll need full access."

"Not sure that's possible. My guy sent me several videos

of code streaming. I can send that to you. What we're really looking for is a connection to the spreadsheets and some explanation as to what they mean." He quickly said good-bye and hung up.

She studied the sheets on the screen but really needed them as a hard copy, so she clicked on the correct icon and pulled them from the printer. She wanted to study the code, but had her own work to finish first.

She settled back to her usual job. She had tons of bookkeeping transactions to enter and then papers to file. By the time she was done, she felt like she'd accomplished something.

Levi stepped into the room as she put away folders. She glanced at him and said, "Bullard called and asked me to look at some code snippets he had for a banking scheme."

"Good. I told him you might help."

"I just printed the sheets off, actually." She pointed to them on the side table. "But they are nothing that I need."

He looked at them. "He sent them to me too."

She finished clearing off her desk and said, "I'm putting in a shorter day because Jarrod's here."

Levi waved a hand at her. "I don't care how short your day is. When the work's done, it's done."

She laughed. "In this job the work is never done. There's always something for tomorrow." She quickly told Levi what she'd said to Bullard. She liked the way Levi's eyebrows shot up and how he studied the pages, as if seeing what she said. He'd have to know programming for that. But with Levi, who knew the extent of his knowledge. He might understand a dozen languages—even computer ones.

"Nice."

Bullard's email came in just then with more attachments. She quickly opened the first and clicked on the video. Instead code streamed on her monitor. Her gaze danced across letters and numbers she was very familiar with. She opened up the other two, both shorter.

"Interesting." Levi studied the monitors behind her. "Does the code mean anything to you?"

"Maybe," she said, her focus intense, all three videos running at the same time.

She sat back and pursed her lips. She could see the transactions running through the code and accounts, but at the moment, it meant nothing to her. At least not yet.

"We'll be late for Alfred's dinner if we don't get going." She grabbed up the sheets and stacked them on her desk. They would take a lot longer. While the remnants of code still whispered through the back of her brain, she headed to the doorway.

"I'm right with you." Together they walked downstairs. "Are you okay that Jarrod visits?" Levi asked. "With the two attacks here on the compound, it's natural for all of us to call family when someone could be in trouble."

She gave him a shuttered look. "Yet—twice—nobody considered asking me beforehand."

He grinned. "That's family. It often takes somebody else to point out what we should've done in the first place."

She rolled her eyes at him, stepped into the dining room and sat down at the table. Jarrod came in with a bunch of the other men, taking a spot beside her. Instantly the room filled with boisterous conversation. Once Alfred carried in platters of food, the conversation slowed down. She caught Rhodes eyeing the roast pork coming his way and smiled. He looked like he planned on having the whole thing.

She glanced around the room, unable to hold in her

smile. How lucky that she'd landed here. She could have ended up so many other places. But Ice had been a godsend. Sienna focused on the table and served herself some food—and froze. She slowly raised her head to stare out the window on the far side. There was just something about one of those lines of code, … and now she understood.

With her mind spinning, she realized something else. She'd seen similar entries in one of the classic textbook cases she'd been taught years ago. She pulled out her phone and quickly hit Redial on Bullard's number.

"It's Sienna. The program is converting currencies and rounding them up and down. I won't know for sure unless I have access to the entire system, but at a guess, I'd say the fractional differences were moved to a third account. Fractions of a cent add up damn quick and are almost impossible to trace like this."

The entire room froze, and maybe she shouldn't have made the call in the dining room. She lifted her gaze and caught sight of Rhodes. He frowned at her.

But Levi leaned across the table and said in a hard voice, "Sienna, are you sure?"

Slowly, she nodded her head, hearing Bullard's exclamation on the other end. She answered, "I'm as sure as I can be without having access to the program. But a developer would be doing this. The code is robust but antiquated. A programmer would need to know COBOL and the more modern languages. It's been heavily upgraded and patched but still based on that system."

"Why is that?" Rhodes asked.

"Because it's too expensive for most institutions to change from the original, and as it is robust, it's a great foundation block. Then, like any old infrastructure, it needs updating, debugging, and constant testing. Myriad third-party products support these issues, but again you need a good developer who understands COBOL in the first place. Or several, depending on the size of the bank, the job done originally, and the maintenance." She glanced around the table. "Whoever is doing the tweaks on their end, chances are he's older and looking for a way to retire. And he's likely been doing this for a long time …" She added, "He's not making much off the system initially but over time …"

"Oh, very nice," Bullard said. "I'll be in touch with the bank and get back to you."

"Wait," she cried. "I haven't looked at the spreadsheets yet. I don't understand the connection to the code."

"Maybe there isn't one, but we're hoping so." He chuckled. "After this I'm expecting great things from you." And just as quickly he was gone.

She groaned. "Great."

But she got no help from the others. They were too busy grinning at her.

Chapter 2

SIENNA WOKE THE next morning tired and achy. Instead of enjoying a peaceful dinner last night, the place had erupted with questions and phone calls. She hadn't meant to create such a stir, but when she had connected the sequences in her head, she realized she could look at them in a completely different way. And apparently, that made a difference. She still had to study the spreadsheets …

The group had discussed the issue at length even though she'd said, "I could be wrong."

"But you could also be very right," Jarrod said, sounding impressed. "I didn't know that was the kind of work you did."

"I was doing all kinds." She smiled at him. "It was fun until it blew up in my face."

"Time to tell me exactly what went wrong," Jarrod said in a hard voice.

"It's over." She shrugged. "What difference does it make?"

Katina reached across the table and covered her hand. "I've been there, and it sucks," she said. "But it's much better if these guys know exactly what happened to you in the past."

Sienna frowned. "It's just so … embarrassing." The last thing she wanted was to air her dirty laundry in front of anybody else.

"Give."

Her brother had always been like that. One to bark out orders and expect her to follow. She glared at him. But his expression never eased. She threw up her hands and said, "Fine, I was part of a criminal investigation into a leg of the Mafia. Hard to believe they're around, but they are."

Katina gasped in horror.

"Anyway, while I was looking in the banking transactions to prove they were involved in money laundering, I didn't realize who and what they were after until finding all the information. And my current boyfriend at that time was actually part of the Mafia family." She winced. "It all went south. My bosses said I was sleeping with the enemy, that my information was tainted, so the case was thrown out. I lost my job and good name." She glared at everybody. "Embarrassing enough?"

Jarrod reached over and grabbed her hand, tugging her into his arms for a hug. "You didn't know who he was. That's a heavy weight you had on your shoulders."

When he released her, she said, "Everybody just likes to have a scapegoat. I was it. The stupid thing is, I'm pretty damn sure my boss was part of the same family. I think I was given that job specifically because I was in a position that would compromise the case."

She fisted both hands and stretched them back out again to make them relax. "But it really makes you reassess who you can trust in this world."

"And there is not one person at this table who has not already had to reassess that exact same issue," Jarrod said quietly.

"We were all betrayed by somebody we trusted," Rhodes

said. "Maybe we were foolish to trust in the first place. For some of us, the betrayal was more serious than for others." Rhodes shook his head. "It's a hard lesson to learn but better to know."

"Did you go to the police and report what they did to you?" Katina asked Sienna.

"The police were all over me by that time. I'm lucky I wasn't charged," she said in a low voice. "There was talk of it. Only because I gave as much evidence as I could, was I able to walk away. As it is right now, everybody walked, because whatever I found was supposedly tainted." She lifted her gaze and said, "It was pretty humiliating at the time. I felt so stupid. I had no idea my boyfriend was involved."

Katina patted her hand. "And it doesn't matter. That's all in your past. Time to face forward and forget about him." She gave a lopsided smile. "These guys are good at helping you do that." She linked her arm with Merk. "Merk helped me out of my jam."

"Nobody can help me out of mine," Sienna said. "It's done and gone. The aftermath was pretty rough, and the fallout was terrible. I would have kept falling, but Ice found me, and I am very thankful for that," she admitted. "I couldn't do anything to undo it, so I just moved forward," Sienna said. "We've all come to crossroads in our lives where what we used to do isn't what we currently do." She shrugged. "Honestly, I'm going to enjoy my new life."

Levi wrapped an arm around Ice's shoulder, tucking her close.

Sienna could certainly understand why Ice was happy. As much as Sienna hoped for the same, she wasn't at all sure it would happen.

Abruptly Levi asked, "Did you like that kind of work?"

"Yes," she said. "I did. It was fun to chase the trails. Sometimes it was also frustrating because it would just end, and I had nowhere to go. I had to wait until something else happened. But often I could keep tracking and find out more."

"I have to admit, I would've enjoyed going farther into that field myself," Katina said. "The little bit I got involved with was interesting, but also unnerving."

"If it was directed at you, then it would definitely be. But I was going after criminals—at least I thought I was." Sienna shook her head. "I'm honestly not sure who I was chasing now. Because if my boss was involved, … who knows." She turned to gaze at Levi and realized he was studying her thoughtfully. "What are you thinking?"

"Sometimes we get asked to look in to things like that," he said. "I haven't had anybody I could put onto cases involving that level of programming before now. Money trails we've looked in to tended toward offshore accounts. Certain ones can be very time-consuming. I'm wondering if it's something you want to get away from completely or would like to get further into."

She hesitated a moment. "I'm not sure that's what I could do. I specialized in banking programs. I'd have to know that it was completely legal before I would venture into it again. I got off lightly, considering. Not sure the law would let me go so easily a second time."

"And yet you helped out Bullard," Ice said.

Sienna's lips twisted. "Yeah, he caught me in a weak moment. He's very persuasive."

At that Ice laughed out loud. "Oh, he is indeed. He also has a greater variety of work and would have more exposure to cases like this."

"I'd be fine as long as it wasn't something I'd end up in trouble over," she said finally. "That part wasn't fun."

"I so understand." Katina laughed. "Like you, I don't want to end up in something that is dangerous. I was already kidnapped and someone tried to kill me over the mess I got involved in."

Sienna's gaze widened. "Oh, my situation wasn't anywhere near that bad. I can't imagine what you went through."

"Well," Merk added, "you may not have known how bad it was because you were the one set up to take the fall. In this case, Katina wanted the others to." Merk's explanation brought a laugh from everyone.

"I wish I'd thought of that, but I didn't even see the danger closing in around me," Sienna said. "I don't think like that. I thought I was a happy-go-lucky person, and pretty intuitive. Only I didn't really know the kind of people I was working with. I'd never come up against individuals like that before."

"How long were you with your boyfriend before this all came apart?" Katina asked.

Sienna hugged her coffee mug. "Honestly, not long. I can see now he set me up, targeted me. He'd probably researched me beforehand, so he knew what I liked, what buttons to push. It was a pretty fast whirlwind romance. About three months, maybe four, that I'd known him."

Rhodes nodded. "That sounds like about the right time frame. A con of that magnitude would require at least three months to set up. Obviously, they had enough in place for you to take the fall."

"Doesn't matter anyway," she said. "My reputation's in tatters, and I certainly won't be working in that field anymore."

"Unless you want to do that kind of work for me," Levi said. "I already know how the story played out and understand."

And she had no doubt he meant it. "Why don't we leave it at that? If you get something across your desk that might involve matters like this, I could look." But she didn't really expect anything to come of it.

Until the next morning when Bullard called her again. "I have another bit of code for you to look at."

She leaned back in her chair, rubbing her temple. "Have you talked to Levi about this?"

He laughed. "Of course I have. Levi and I are working on the case jointly."

There really was something magnetic about that voice of his. But she was immune to smooth talkers. "Okay, send it over."

She hung up and returned to the accounts she was setting up for the business. Levi had done a decent job, but some fine-tuning would make it work that much better. She was busy with the forms when an email alert sounded. She checked and saw Bullard had sent four more videos. He really wanted answers.

She downloaded the videos and brought them up on the double monitors. She split the screens so all four played at the same time. All codes were again similar to what she had looked at the day before. She read them over, but at first glance, they didn't appear to mean much. Same program but with newer updates. She studied the stream for close to half an hour.

Levi walked in. "Are those Bullard's files?"

Without lifting her head, she said, "Yes."

"Okay. How about letting Katina help? She has quite a photographic memory. It's one of the reasons she was so instrumental in putting the company she was working for behind bars. When she found access to information, she memorized the material."

Sienna looked up at him in surprise. "You know, that could be very helpful." She motioned at the fourth video and said, "This is different."

He stepped over to stand behind her. "Different how?"

"The others are all very similar to the first ones he showed me. This set of code is replicating, so everything it does, it does twice. Like a mirror image."

She minimized the other videos and opened the fourth in full size. "It's not active. It's like a copy."

"Why?"

She shook her head. "I don't know, unless they are making changes, yet wanting to keep a master. They appear to be working on the code, but I can't see the extent of the tampering."

He tapped a finger on the far column and said, "Good. Bullard can go back to the bank and tell them that."

"Good." She smiled. "If that's all then …"

"Can you track who is doing this?"

"Maybe. But not from here. And Ghana has their own specialists. Didn't he say there was a Dallas connection?"

He stepped away from the desk and said, "Looks like it. They're waiting on results from the bank investigation."

She nodded, but her gaze was still on the monitors. She heard Levi leave as quietly as he had appeared. She quickly brought up several of the programs she formerly used to hunt through databases. She'd caught glimpses of accounts. *Would it help to know what the transactions were?* She'd spent a lot of time doing this before. Very quickly she picked out one of the Swiss banks. Of course that made it even more difficult because those were much harder to get information from.

She kept digging and found several were running through France, and others through Hong Kong. She focused on the latter. Of course, a lot of offshore accounts ran through Asia.

RHODES AND MERK looked up when Levi walked into the kitchen. "What's up?"

"Bullard sent Sienna several videos tracing code from a different bank. She thinks the code has been tampered with."

"Is this Bullard's case or ours?" Rhodes asked.

"Both. There is a Dallas connection here."

"Wow, a shared job. That'll be a first."

"True, but it's good for both of us. Bullard has a lot of work over there, and we have a lot of over here, but obviously, if we can pool our resources on some jobs, it's major. He's also asking how the new security systems he installed are working. Anybody have any criticism or questions on them?"

Rhodes watched as Merk shook his head. "It's fine at the moment," he said. "Until it's put to the test, we can't know how the complete system works."

"I was kind of hoping not to have to stress it that bad." Levi sat down at the table and said, "Logan and Flynn are taking on a West Coast job. We have a couple special people to be escorted back to Texas, with any luck we'll be out and back faster than expected."

Rhodes nodded. "Anything from here I can help with?"

Levi glanced at the two of them. "Bored?"

Merk nodded.

"Bored," Rhodes confirmed. He wasn't so much bored as preferring a way to get out of the house while Sienna was here. Since Jarrod left, Rhodes saw himself in the brother role. And that wasn't the relationship he wanted. A break would be good.

"Bullard has located five addresses," Levi said. "One in New Mexico, four in Texas, the farthest up in Dallas."

"Addresses regarding what?" Rhodes asked.

"Connected to the banking fraud case Sienna is looking at right now," Levi said. "Several Texas addresses were on a sheet found on a bank employee's desk. Check out each one very carefully. Approach with caution, but we must confirm if these are safe houses, terrorists' hideouts, or just holding properties."

"Exactly what kind of a case has Bullard got going on?" Merk asked.

Levi looked up and said, "Arms dealing and money laundering. Plus, it looks like a bank employee might have been pilfering a bit off the top. At least if Sienna is correct. Who knows what else."

Rhodes's face went on lockdown. "Like hell. Sienna shouldn't be working on anything to do with that." Then he stopped himself. In the office, work was a hell of a lot less dangerous than being out in the field. She'd be safe here. He stood up. "I'm in."

Merk said, "Me too."

Rhodes asked Levi, "Driving or flying?"

"Driving." Levi stood up and walked out the kitchen. "Be ready to leave in an hour."

Merk and Rhodes looked at each other and smiled. "I guess he knew our answers already," Merk said.

"It's sure better than doing security detail," Rhodes said,

heartfelt. "He's been getting a lot of requests by these West Coast entertainers."

"Hell, I've had enough of that. He needs to hire guys just for that babysitting stuff if that's what he's doing now. It's probably very lucrative and could keep the company in ready cash while we do the other jobs." Merk rapped his knuckles against the kitchen table and said, "Meet you back here in forty-five."

Rhodes headed up to his suite, happy to leave again. He'd just worry about Sienna if he stayed here. Packing for him was a five-minute job. Too many years being ready to leave at the drop of a hat for him to live any other way. He was back down in thirty, walking into the kitchen to see Alfred had a picnic basket half-full already. "Alfred, you are a godsend."

"Yep, don't you forget it." Alfred quickly added homemade cookies and banana bread in clear plastic containers and then tucked in several large thermoses. "I suspect you both won't be more than two nights, and you'll be stopping at hotels anyway, so this should do you for the bulk of the trip."

Rhodes picked it up, grabbed his own bag and headed out to the truck. Considering the mileage they had to cover, he figured the smallest of the trucks would be easier on gas.

Merk already had the same idea as he had it warming up. He nodded at Rhodes. "Throw your bags in the back. Ice is bringing us the paperwork, and then we're gone."

Rhodes loaded the basket into the small back storage compartment of the extra cab and tossed his own bag in the back of the bed. It was a nice sunny day. No reason not to haul the luggage outside. Within minutes they were off. He checked the GPS. "It looks like we're three hours to the first address."

"Did you hear any whispers as to what might be there?" Merk asked.

Rhodes brought up his cell and punched in the address. He also checked the notes Levi had sent. Each location was registered to a different name. But as they had checked farther back, each had been under one company.

WHEN THEY PULLED onto the street of the first house, they drove past it slowly. It was a rundown large brick two-story house, comparable to the rest of the block. Nothing untoward, nor odd looking. An abandoned-looking vehicle was parked in the driveway. An alleyway was down the back.

Rhodes carefully drove to the rear and parked just behind the house. Merke and Rhodes got out and walked the alleyway carefully. Merk took several pictures of the area and this part of the house.

As he took the second one, Rhodes saw a curtain pull back and then quickly fall away again. "Somebody's in the top second room," he said to Merk.

Merk nodded. "I'll go around front and see if our presence here has pushed anybody out the door."

Rhodes nodded as he headed in the opposite direction to the neighboring house. From his view, the derelict-looking house appeared empty. He quickly hopped the fence and ran up to the back so he could peer at the house from the relative safety of this one. But with nothing showing as out-of-place or unusual, he continued around to the front.

He took several photos from this viewpoint. No windows were on this side. He quickly slipped through the hedge and crept up to peer around the front. Just as he caught sight of the car in the driveway, the engine turned over, and it immediately backed down to the street and took off away from Rhodes.

He caught sight of Merk at the far end of the driveway. As the car drove past, Merk turned and quickly snapped a photo. With any luck he got the license plate. They should have grabbed it as they drove past the first time. He'd taken pictures but hadn't zeroed in on that. He packed his camera in its case for the time being and slung it crosswise on his chest.

Rhodes slipped around the house and went to the back door. He knocked, but there was no answer. He pushed open the door and called out, "Hello, anyone here?"

Again, no answer. But he had seen somebody upstairs. Was that the person who had left? A few minutes later Merk joined him at the doorstep. "Any reason to go inside and check?"

The two looked at each other. They had no legal right to enter. But this was looking more than slightly suspicious. Deciding to take a chance, they went in, weapons in hand. The downstairs looked completely uninhabited. No furniture was in the living room, outside of a single chair and a footstool beside the fireplace. The kitchen cupboards were bare, and the fridge was empty. Obviously, nobody was living here.

Merk and Rhodes swept upstairs and found one room with a single bed, the other two were empty. The hall bathroom was as well. The en suite bath had a toothbrush and toothpaste, but that was it. The sinks were dry; the bathtub was too and looked as if it hadn't been used in a while.

They had no idea who was here earlier, but as he hadn't

hung around, they were short of getting answers. They ran lightly down the stairs and stopped at the door to the garage. At the count of three, they opened it and swept inside. They found no guns or other weapons.

But there were explosives—dynamite.

"Shit." Merk quickly phoned Levi while Rhodes retrieved his camera from its case. By the time they had it all cataloged, they'd been here way too long.

Levi would call the police and somehow let them know what was inside the garage.

BUOYED BY THAT success, they hopped into their vehicle and headed to the second house. This time they knew better and quickly approached to take images of the entire place, including any nearby vehicles, no matter how inoperable they looked. None were found under the carport or in the attached garage. They entered through the backyard once again and did a full sweep of the house. Nothing. Back in the truck, Rhodes called Levi. "Levi, the second house is completely empty, no sign of anyone or anything. No one has lived here for a while."

"Good to know. Head off to the third location. You're making great time. See if you can get this next one done before nightfall."

BY THE TIME they hit the third house, darkness had settled in. That was both good and bad. They needed light to search the place, and if no lights were on, it would be obvious when somebody turned them on. This two-story house was surrounded by trees on a large lot. The house was on the small rise of a hill and appeared to have a walkout-style downstairs. Neighbors were all around, but again it was a heavily treed area, so nobody could really see anyone or anything.

Merk and Rhodes parked on the shadowed shoulder of the road farther up and walked back. No vehicle was parked in the long sweeping driveway. Nobody answered their knock at the door either. The garage was unlocked, so they slipped inside and found an old car.

Frowning—because this looked much more like a broken-down antique than somebody's driving vehicle—they went out the side door and around the back. There, with the sun setting, they were running out of natural light, and none were on inside to see. If they could get in and out now, they could look around without having to turn any on. Just as they approached from the back, they heard a door bang. They froze. With a glance to each other, they carefully slipped around to the side of the house and waited. A lone man walked onto the porch and lit a cigarette.

Rhodes studied him. He was dressed all in black and wore combat boots. From the buzzed head and tattoos, he could be anything from ex-military to a white supremacist. Rhodes dismissed the military angle as the man was unshaven and looking more ragged and violent than Rhodes would have expected.

When the man finished his cigarette, he tossed the butt onto the wooden deck and walked back inside.

Another point against him. Lit cigarettes and wood were not a good combination, and he hadn't stomped on the butt and ground it out. Neither did he separate the filter from the end. Sloppy. He was leaving DNA for the police to collect.

Merk motioned from the far side of the house. Rhodes

waited, watching as Merk snuck up to the deck, came around the side and reached for something, then disappeared back the way he came.

Rhodes quickly assessed the rear of the house. Good. They could gain interior access via the windows, but still there was no sign where the smoker had gone.

They returned to their vehicle and called Levi.

"Don't go into the house," Levi warned. "We'll put a tag on that address. But given what you said, chances are he's guarding something."

Rhodes happened to agree, but that didn't mean the guy was a criminal.

He and Merk grabbed a hotel room for the night. Their motto when traveling was easy. *Get in, get out, get home.* With any luck they'd drive into the compound tomorrow night and not too late at that.

At the hotel, they quickly downloaded and sent off to Levi all the images they had collected, including the ones Rhodes had taken of the militant-looking man smoking on the back deck. Maybe with the new facial-recognition programs they might identify him. Rhodes wasn't sure if a terrorist bombing was something Levi was looking for, or Bullard for that matter, but the fact that he and Merk had found a house with a cache of explosives was bad news no matter what country they were in.

RHODES AND MERK were up and on the road well before dawn to make the trek to the next location on their list. They stopped at the fourth house early enough that the neighbors weren't up and around yet. This time they parked around the corner and entered through the back alleyway. The rear of the house had a large porch that hid them from view—of the neighbors at least. As Rhodes went to open the door, they realized it had already been broken into. Taking a picture of the busted lock and doorframe, they pushed it open and called out, "Anybody home?"

"Hello, is anyone here?"

With a glance to each other, they both pulled their weapons and moved in, one high, the other low. They swept the first floor, moving in tandem. They knew the drill. No one was prepared to take a bullet at this point in his life. The downstairs was completely empty. But somebody had broken into the house for a reason. Unless they'd come in to clean it out.

They moved upstairs and found it completely empty as well. The staircase to the attic wasn't latched. They looked at each other, and Rhodes lowered the access. Merk went up first. They stopped in the empty attic and looked around, puzzled. Something had been here. The place was spotless, no sign of dust collecting, like the cleaning service had come through, or this had all been emptied recently. At the far side of the attic were bags of some sort. The two studied them carefully before going closer.

The odor hit them first as they approached.

They found two dead men. Both wrapped in clear plastic and tied up with ropes. From the decomposition already working and the fluids filling the corners of the plastic, the dead men had been here for at least a few days if not a few weeks. Careful not to disturb them, Merk and Rhodes combed the rest of the small room. Nothing else had been left behind.

It would be damn hard identifying their faces through the plastic. Rhodes took pictures anyway and sent the images to Levi. Rhodes didn't know what the hell was going on, but it was a damn good thing somebody was checking out these houses. Back outside again, they took several deep breaths of fresh air and waited for Levi to get back to them.

"Levi?" Rhodes asked as he answered his phone. "Not exactly what we expected to find."

"Definitely not. I called the cops there. Stay at the scene. Explain that you're working for us, and you were looking to speak with the inhabitants of the house. Don't give them any details, just direct them to me. Say that you found the door ajar, broken into, and went in to investigate."

"What about the house with dynamite?"

"The police raided that house. You can watch it on the news," Levi answered in a laconic tone. "Some good media won't hurt the local police."

Rhodes laughed, but he wasn't at all impressed with having to wait for the cops or the upcoming explanations. He and Merk sat down on the back porch and did as instructed. They'd been in this situation before.

When the cops arrived, he and Merk answered what few questions there were and quickly showed the men the bodies. After that, they were escorted off the property and asked to wait for investigators to question them.

The wait was just long enough that by the time they hit the road again, it would be lucky—if not impossible—to make it home tonight. They still had one more address to check out.

"Damn," Merk said. "I told Katina I'd be home tonight for sure."

"There is no *for sure* in this business. Particularly with Levi."

"Dynamite and dead bodies? Who would have thought?"

"And what's the connection?"

THEY WERE STILL several hours away from the fifth house. Of course, this was the furthest away.

It was late afternoon when they pulled up in front of it. After what they'd found at the first and fourth houses, they had no idea what to expect here. When a family with small kids came out the door, playing in the front yard, they wondered if they had the wrong house. They double-checked the address with Levi, but sure enough a family lived here.

The three little kids all appeared to be under six years old. Mom and Dad were here, as was a puppy. It was the epitome of the happy American family.

Merk and Rhodes drove around the neighborhood, took a few pictures and headed along the back alley. This wasn't what they were expecting.

On Levi's instructions they were given the okay to head home. Damn good thing. They were more than ready to return.

Chapter 3

WITH MERK AND Rhodes both gone, Sienna found the house quiet and lonely. She and Katina naturally gravitated together. In fact, Katina came into the office to help out. She was a fast learner. And her memory was a huge help.

When Sienna got up this morning, she'd found Stone and Lissa had returned from a visit to Lissa's parents. An olive branch of some kind was being offered in exchange. Sienna didn't know the full story, but Lissa appeared to be a little happier about her parents. Then again, she had Stone at her side. And he'd make anybody happy. That man looked like a great big teddy bear and obviously adored Lissa. She was lucky.

It made Sienna sad in a way.

Here it was, fast becoming couples' land. Between Levi and Ice, Stone and Lissa—and now Merk and Katina, the last pairing that had happened while she was gone tying up her former life—she was feeling a little lost and lonely. And that was stupid. The time for that was when she'd been hitchhiking her way across the country, figuring out what her purpose in life was.

Not now that she was here with a job and a beautiful place to live with a very decent paycheck. Who knew how life would end up? She had never expected to be here, particularly finding out they were friends of Jarrod's. There was something very synchronistic about that.

In particular, seeing Rhodes.

Now that she'd handed over to Levi whatever information on the banks she had found, she returned to the basic bookkeeping and office work that in a way she loved. Although it was mundane, dull, and boring, she could blindly do it, dreaming about everything else in the world. When she heard someone at the office door, she looked up to find Katina.

"Do you realize that none of us have any hobbies?" Katina asked. "Nobody here plays music, seems to paint or draw, or do anything along those lines. I wonder why."

Sienna smiled. "Do you have any?"

Katina slumped in her chair. "No. But I plan to. I always wanted to play the guitar and learn to paint. But it's probably a good thing I don't learn the guitar for your sake's, and I doubt I would do very well painting because I really can't draw." She laughed. "I do like to garden, but have you ever seen a place lend itself less to a garden? This is a cement compound."

"True enough, but you can certainly do a lot with planters. Imagine great big cedar ones all over the place. It would really warm up the compound." She nodded toward the door. "Talk to Alfred. He seems like somebody who would love to have a garden. Particularly if it was an herb one."

Katina brightened. "That might be good for me. I never had a place where I could grow things before. I lived in a small apartment."

"And how is it working out for you and Merk here?" Sienna asked carefully. "And if it's too personal, I'm sorry."

There was silence for a minute as Katina studied Sienna's

face. "Are you asking because of Rhodes?" Her tone was light, humorous.

Sienna felt the heat wash up her neck. "Is it that obvious?"

"It has been since the two of you met. Everybody's noticed," Katina said, her grin wide. "Sparks. But it seems like very controlled ones."

Sienna gave her a look. "My brother and Rhodes are friends. That means I'm a no-no to him."

At that, Katina laughed. "Well, you just have to change his mind. You're an adult, not a little sister anymore, and Jarrod can butt right out. You get to make these choices on your own."

"Yes, except Rhodes will never see me as anything but Jarrod's little sister."

Katina leaned forward and whispered, "Take him to bed. He won't know what happened to him."

At that Sienna snickered. The idea appealed to her. Yet she didn't want to mess things up with Rhodes or her life here. Especially if her relationship with him wouldn't be a long-term scenario. That would just make working together very uncomfortable.

And that was the last thing she wanted. This was his work and his home. She was the newcomer. She didn't want to upset the apple cart just because she was attracted to him.

"I can't do that to him. He'll think it's a mistake later and hate himself."

"You worry too much. Rhodes is a big boy. Besides, once he chooses, it'd be a decision forever. His loyalty is something else. All of them together have formed a family network here that I've never seen anywhere else. It's really wonderful for them."

Katina looked out the window, seemingly someplace far off. "I had worried I wouldn't fit in. That I would be the interloper. Or that I would in some way disrupt that sense of family." She glanced over at Sienna and said, "You were even here before me. But what I found is that the family unit expanded. It's elastic. It opens and closes as it needs to. And now I feel like I belong."

"That doesn't mean there's anything between Rhodes and me."

"Of course it doesn't. But if you don't work toward that, there never will be." With a cheerful smile, Katina stood up and said, "I'll head down and see if Alfred needs any help in the kitchen." She glanced around the room and added, "You don't need me, do you?"

Sienna shook her head. "No, I'm almost done with the paperwork. The guys should be back soon anyway. Apparently, they had quite the trip."

"That's true. They found dead bodies." Katina shuddered. "Kitchen and office work is much better suited for me." She gave Sienna a beaming smile and left.

Sienna watched her walk away. Katina was just so cheerful and upbeat. She was fun to be around. Sienna hadn't considered herself gloomy, but she'd definitely lost a lot of her bounce when her former job fell apart.

The phone rang. Bullard again. "Hello, Bullard. Now what?"

He laughed. "Do you think I only call you when I need some help?"

"Of course you do." She looked around the empty room, tilted her chair back, kicking her feet up on the desk. "It is what I expect."

"Not everybody in the world is out to use you," he said

in a cheerful tone. "Lots of good people are in the world too."

"Those good people would use me too," she said drily. "Back to business. What do you need?"

He laughed. "Nothing. I wanted to give you an update. The first bank found their employee—the older guy I was telling you about, the IT manager, who will be retiring soon. He started pilfering off the top. He confessed readily. Trying to save his son, who could be involved in something much darker as he's the one who had the spreadsheets."

"Were they working together?"

"Not according to the father. His son is completely innocent if you listened to him."

"I doubt it." She laughed. "But the father almost got away with it." She stared at her desk. "I caught some account numbers on the code you sent. The transactions were all international."

"That makes sense. I'll let you know when any of the other banks get back to me." His tone turned calm. "I owe you one." And he hung up.

She was still smiling when Levi walked into the room. He raised an eyebrow and asked, "What's up?"

She quickly brought him up to date on Bullard's case.

"This is really good work, Sienna."

"I didn't do anything. It was easy stuff." She shrugged self-consciously. "That part was just luck."

He laughed. "Something's only easy because you're good at it." He headed to his desk.

She studied him as he sat down again and asked in a low voice she hoped was calm and disinterested, "When are the guys getting back?"

"They're on their way now."

She nodded. "Right. Going to be late then." She looked over at him and asked, "Do you have any other work for me right now?"

"No, you've done a ton already this week. It's much appreciated."

She shut off her computer and stood up, saying, "In that case, I'll see if I can round up a cup of coffee."

She wandered out of the room and headed toward the kitchen. The compound was huge, and a dozen or so people lived here. There wasn't a whole lot of social activity in this remote area, but when she had a chance, she did take trips into town. She didn't want to feel like she was forced to stay in the compound. Because she wasn't. She had gone with Katina, and sometimes Ice, to watch a movie or two in town, plus lunch outings and shopping. Sometimes the guys joined them. But her needs were minimal, and it was senseless to pay for a meal when Alfred was such a good cook.

In truth, she was bored. And she hadn't expected that. Although she'd settled in here, with her brother leaving, there was a sense of loss. It was compounded by the fact Rhodes was gone these last few days. Then again, he didn't really see her when he was here.

She wandered through the kitchen now with a cup of coffee in hand and headed out to the garage. She didn't know very much about electronics. Harrison was bent over a laptop, swearing. She stepped up beside him and said, "What's going on that has you so upset?"

He looked up at her with surprise and then grinned. "I'm not upset. This is actually fun for me. I like to see what people have hidden on their laptops and what they were doing with secret files they thought were erased. People always presume that, if they delete something on their computer, or damage the hard drive, it's gone." He shook his head. "And it isn't."

She nodded. "Same thing with code." She frowned, looked at the mess, and asked, "Is there anything I can do to help?"

He looked over at her and said, "If you're serious, yes. Try to sort through all the different cables and set up bins for each type. Sometimes I have to hook up multiple units together, and if we don't have an orderly system, it can take time to find what I need."

She walked over to what appeared to be a brand-new storage system and asked, "Do you need things in any particular order?"

"If you use those bins, we can move them around to suit us."

Taking a closer look, she realized the plastic boxes detached, so as long as she stuck one thing in each, he could organize them as he wanted. She turned her attention back to the large workbench completely covered with cables.

She sorted through what she could in the stash and put the obviously distinct ones into the top three empty bins and then separated the remaining pile. She found everything from standard-issue cables to printer cables to a bunch of cut wires and big long ribbons of cloth-looking cables, plus a rat's nest of who-knew-what. These were hubs, but she had no idea if they were to come apart or not. She set them off to one side to ask questions later and quickly delved into the big snake pile on top.

She knew software. This venture into hardware was different.

When the big double doors opened behind her, she turned in surprise. Sure enough it was Rhodes and Merk, driving the small truck. They pulled up, parked, and she just barely caught sight of Katina as she raced around to dive into Merk's arms. As he held Katina tight, Sienna's gaze bounced to Rhodes and off again. It was enough to see him studying her.

She quickly turned back and nudged Harrison to let him know the guys were here. And then she said, "I didn't know what to do with the rest of the stuff." She pointed out the items still on the desk. "I did get the others in the bins."

"Wow, this looks great," he said with a big smile. "What a huge help." He glanced at the desk and said, "Okay, these guys we can do this with." He quickly separated off the rest of the electronics, and as she watched, he tossed things into different bins.

She could have done that but not without knowing what he wanted. When she turned around, Rhodes was still glaring at her. She glared right back. "What the hell's wrong with you?" she snapped.

"You," he roared.

She fisted her hands on her hips and studied him. "Now what?"

"You've already put in a full day. What the hell are you doing out here helping Harrison?"

"Whatever I'm doing is my business," she snapped. She glanced over at Harrison, but he had wisely stepped out of the way and was busy washing up.

She caught sight of Katina and Merk, both hiding their grins as they walked toward the door. Katina called back, "Rhodes, we held dinner for you, so it's time to wash up and come in."

As they disappeared, Harrison went in right after them, leaving her and Rhodes alone in the garage.

"Look at you, covered in dirt."

She glanced down and smiled. "But it's honest dirt. And it will wash off. Just like I will. It's just jeans and a T-shirt. I can get changed easily enough." She tried to brush off her clothes, but it was pretty ineffectual. She shrugged. "And it doesn't matter. Dinners waiting, so let's go."

Rhodes stepped toward the main door, then turned and said, "Does that mean you haven't eaten yet either?"

She glanced down at her watch to see it was seven o'clock. "No, I haven't. I guess I have been out here for a few hours with Harrison."

"So, as soon as your brother disappears, you stop taking care of yourself?" he asked.

She gasped. "That's so unfair." She fisted her hands on her hips again—which seemed to be the stance she preferred all too often when facing him—and said, "It doesn't matter if he's here or not." She hopped onto the step in front of him so she could meet his glare head-on and said, "Just because my brother is gone doesn't mean I need another man to step up and take his role." She turned her back on Rhodes and stormed inside.

She headed into the kitchen to wash up. When she went to the long dining table, the only open space was near Rhodes. Like hell she wanted to sit next to him. But everybody was already in place, so she took the empty spot without being rude or causing a scene, which would draw even more attention to her and Rhodes. She sat down beside him and completely ignored him for the rest of the meal.

HE HADN'T MEANT to snap at her. But they'd driven like crazy to get home when they had. And he'd been looking forward to seeing her the whole way. Only to find her with Harrison. But seeing her work herself to the bone drove him crazy. He should've realized she needed other interests and had likely been curious about what went on here.

Besides, Harrison would've accepted any help coming his way. When he got into a project that had anything to do with electronics, they lost him for hours. That was both good and bad. But Rhodes couldn't stop wondering if something was going on between Harrison and Sienna. He gripped his fork a little too tightly and stabbed the chunk of roast beef a little too hard. *Ease back, buddy. Ease back*. Rhodes also really liked that she stood up to him.

Still, he was coming on a bit strong. She was right. She had older brothers, and she didn't need Rhodes watching over her too. At least not in that role. But the only one left to him was as a friend, and he didn't want that. He wanted so much more.

He deliberately avoided looking at all the couples at the table. It was increasingly obvious that Levi and Ice's company had too much in common with Mason's group. And they'd all be angry if he said something about it, but…it was pretty hard not to think about it.

Because he was one of the men without a partner.

Sighing, he finished off his plate and pushed it back. "Thanks, Alfred. As usual that was fantastic."

Other voices joined in with their appreciation. Rhodes slipped off the bench, grabbed his plate and carried it into the kitchen. He rinsed it and loaded it in the dishwasher himself, grabbed a cup of coffee, stuck his head into the room where he had been sitting and said, "I'm done for the night. See you in the morning." And he turned and walked to his suite.

It was early, but that wasn't the point. He just needed time alone, away from the others. In his suite, he quickly unpacked, had a shower and set up his laptop. He had research to do to see how much the news had come up with on the nameless bodies he and Merk had found. Two dead men had put a huge damper on the trip, because no matter what one thought about criminals, they had been a father, brother, husband, and/or son to somebody. And people somewhere would be in pain right now for the loss of those men.

There was also no proof they were the bad guys either. For all Rhodes knew, they were innocent.

Very strange indeed. Unless the house was being used for drugs versus dynamite, and something went wrong. Maybe the thieves had a falling out, and those two men were left behind. They could be brothers who own the house and were taken out as a point of convenience.

Sometimes life just sucked.

He quickly checked the news media, pulling up the local newspapers, but found no mention of either man.

This was an odd case. They weren't seeing the whole picture, and he didn't like that. He wanted to know more, do more. He wanted closure, and how the hell would they get that when it wasn't their case?

At a knock on the door, he stood up and opened it to find Levi.

He leaned against the doorframe and said, "We got two identifications on the men found."

Rhodes straightened. "And?"

"They were cousins. Both with ties to the drug trade. Neither seemed to have any connection to the house or to Bullard's bank fraud case."

"Odd that they would've been found there then." Rhodes frowned. "Obviously, there is a connection as he gave us the addresses."

"Not if there was infighting among the thieves, and these two lost the argument."

"Anything's possible." Rhodes added, "What about the raid on the house with the dynamite?"

"The police tracked down the owners, currently living on the West Coast. It was a rental unit. They have no idea what was going on there, and they don't have any answers."

"That wouldn't have been a pleasant surprise for them to hear either. So, no answers there." He studied Levi and said, "I don't like only getting bits and pieces about this job. We got a house with explosives, a different residential address a long way away that probably housed drugs but had two dead men. What's the connection? Is this our job, yours, or Bullard's? And how does any of this pertain to the code that Sienna was looking at?" He threw up his hands in frustration. "At least in a normal job that's fully ours, we have all the information. We have the targets. We know what's going down. In this case, it feels like we're subcontracting to Bullard."

"And we are. It's new. It's different—and maybe it's not something we want to do a lot of—but we are closer to the Dallas bank than Bullard. We're the locals here. The same holds true vice versa. At any future point in time, when we need some information that he can access easier than we can from here, then we'll subcontract to him."

"I understand that in theory. It just feels … odd. Make that wrong." He gave a Levi lopsided grin. "You know how I like to have a target."

Levi laughed. "Sure you do. Maybe you should go to the

fitness room and work out some of that frustration."

"That's not a bad idea actually. My own research on the men to see if the media had picked up a trail didn't find very much on anything."

"Several jurisdictions I know of were working on this. But nobody has any information to help."

"What were the names of the cousins?"

"Martin and Jeremy Lewis." Levi smacked the wall and said, "I'll be in the office for the next hour if you want to talk." And he turned and walked away.

Rhodes wasn't sure what the last line meant, but figured it was probably an open-ended comment. Still, Levi's suggestion about a workout was a good idea.

They'd put in a large fitness area soon after they got here. He quickly changed into a muscle shirt and shorts, grabbed a towel and water bottle, then headed to the lower floor. The fitness room was across from the medical center. Thankfully, *that* area was clean and empty. They'd christened that room already many times over.

He walked in, dropped his towel, and headed for the free weights. He did his upper body exercises for a good ten minutes, then had the feeling he wasn't alone. When he turned, of course, it was Sienna.

She was doing floor exercises, completely ignoring him.

Well, he could do the same. He quickly did another set, put his weights down, stretched out his muscles and caught sight of her in the mirrors. She was now doing push-ups. And man, could she move. He prided himself on a perfect push-up, but when it came to a woman's form, she was knocking it to the floor. He wanted to stand here and admire her, but that wouldn't do his own workout any good. Besides, she was damn prickly, and he was pretty sure she didn't like anybody watching her.

He returned to his upper body weights. By the time he focused on her again, she'd left. It had been a perfect opportunity to apologize, and he hadn't taken it. That was the problem with apologies. They really needed to happen on the spot, before it spun into bigger arguments over nothing. Now he was frustrated again.

He walked to the floor area, dropped to the mat and did fifty push-ups. Then he added another twenty-five, just a single left-hand version and then twenty-five more on his right. Still needing more, he flipped onto his back and did one hundred crunches.

By the time he was done, he felt a little on the mellower side again. As he stood and walked back out, towel slung around his neck, he caught sight of Sienna in the medical clinic. She was wandering through the room, studying everything. He watched her for a long minute before stepping through the doorway. "Do you have any medical training?"

She shot him a look, then shook her head. "It's really not my thing." She waved her arms at the clean cabinets. "It's like some kind of big mystery happens here. I'm fascinated and repelled at the same time."

He grinned. "I don't think you're alone in that."

As she walked toward him, as if intending to step past him to head to her suite, he said abruptly, "I'm sorry."

She turned and looked at him. "What for?"

Uncomfortable already, he bristled. "For acting like your older brother."

"Well, that's one brotherly thing you didn't get right. Jarrod would never apologize." She grinned. "However, apology accepted. Just don't do it again."

He rolled his eyes. "You don't make it easy."

"And I don't intend to either." She walked away, then turned and continued walking backward as she asked him, "Any news on the men you found?"

"Cousins. Last name Lewis, first names Martin and Jeremy. Both with connections to the drug trade."

She froze. Her gaze widened. "Those were two names I connected accounts to." She frowned. "I forgot to give that to Bullard."

"What?" He took several steps toward her.

She spun around and raced to the stairs, calling back, "I have to talk to Levi." Then she was gone from sight.

Like hell she would keep him in the dark. He picked up the pace and raced up the stairs behind her.

Chapter 4

"LEVI?" SHE STOOD hesitantly at the office door.

Both Ice and Levi had their heads bent over blueprints of some kind. She knew they had plans for an expansion to the compound but didn't know what that entailed exactly.

Levi looked up and smiled. "What's up, Sienna?"

She ventured inside a few steps and said, "Rhodes just told me about the cousins found dead in the house. I'm pretty sure those were the two names I deciphered from the code and spreadsheets Bullard sent."

Levi's gaze widened. "I wondered why they sounded familiar. I couldn't find anything that would give me a reason to confirm that though." He stood up straight, walked to the table where she had placed the codes with her scratch pad of decoded names. He tapped the second line and said, "You're right. J. Lewis, M. Lewis. Also, the initials R.F."

"And those names had the lower figures by them," Sienna said. "It's potentially a smaller deal. Of course, this is just supposition until we get more answers."

"But we can also track a lot of information about those cousins now ourselves," Ice said.

She walked to a desk in the far corner. Sienna recognized it as the one she usually used, but as they all shifted, depending on who was here and who was gone, she didn't know if anybody had a dedicated computer.

Ice sat down, opened the laptop and said, "I'm not as good as some of the guys, but I'm learning."

Levi grinned. "We don't do anything illegal," he explained to Sienna, "but we do have access to a lot of databases, including police files. And if we can't get enough information on our own, we have friends in places who can."

"No arrests on either name," Ice said. "But we have sealed juvie files for both."

"I'm not surprised. We won't get those unsealed."

"Don't need to," Ice said simply. "The fact that they even exist means their teenage years were something of a life of crime."

"Any other members of the family?" Levi asked.

Sienna waited, wishing she could be more involved. Then realized she had access to some of that information as well. She went to her laptop and turned it on. Within minutes she said, "Martin has a brother. Both parents are still alive. Jeremy has a sister, and his mother is alive. The cousins were raised next door to each other."

She studied the addresses in front of her. "The families actually own their houses. Maybe they had money or came into some. There are no mortgages on either."

"So both men were raised with lots of family, good values, and obviously not a poor living area if the parents owned their houses," Ice theorized.

"I can't confirm that about the neighborhood," Sienna said, "but it wouldn't be too hard to double-check. Not that it helps much."

"There's often no reason why some kids go south like that," Ice said. "Also, maybe they just went into that world to make money, and that's how the parents paid off their houses." She looked at Levi. "About time to bring in a few of our connections, pass over some of this information and see what they might have to offer."

"Or call Bullard first," Sienna said. Both turned to look at her as she smiled. "Or not." She raised her hands and shrugged. "Don't quite know how all this works. But normally we would get as much information on our side before offering any to somebody else."

Ice laughed. "I like the way you think."

Levi checked his watch and said, "Perfect. It's about six in the morning over there. I'll call Bullard now." He pulled out his phone, turned to look at Ice and said, "I'll let you talk to him."

In a surprise move she reached up and kissed Levi on the cheek. "You can talk to him, sweetie." She walked from the room. "It's getting late. I'm headed to our suite."

Sienna shut down her laptop as she heard Levi talking to Bullard and with a small wave, turned and walked toward the office door. And that's when she saw Rhodes, leaning against the doorway, arms crossed. She glared at him. "Did you hear the whole thing?"

He raised his eyebrows at her tone and said, "Sure. Why not? I didn't interrupt or have anything to add."

His words were correct, and his voice was level, but the glint in his eye made her suspicious.

She brushed past him. "Levi's talking to Bullard now. So, if you want to talk to him about this, you'll have to wait."

"Are you heading to bed now?"

An odd tone was in his voice. She turned to look at him. "I'm going to take a shower."

"Ah."

She stopped, pivoted to face him fully and glared at him. "What does that mean?"

He raised his eyebrows once again.

She shook her head. "Don't raise your eyebrows like that. What do you mean?"

"Nothing. I should take a shower too." He whistled as he walked past her and tossed back, "Too bad we can't have one together and conserve water."

And then, just like that, he was gone. She made her way into her suite and slammed the door, locking it behind her. She leaned against it. Then slowly sank to the floor.

Because now the only thought in her head was of the two of them, making passionate love, bodies twisting in hot water, completely into each other.

Damn him. Now she needed a cold shower.

THAT WAS MEAN of him. Yet he grinned. *Too bad.* She was just way-too-damn distracting. He should have spoken to Jarrod when he was here before he went off on another mission.

Jarrod had to know his sister hooking up with someone here was a possibility. There were several single men. Attraction happened. And way too fast in some cases. He headed to his suite and stripped to get into the shower. He laughed again at his comment and the look of shock on her face. He stepped into the water, then realized though he had said it as a joke, his body was already thinking about the two of them in the damn water. And his body wasn't taking no for an answer.

He was forced to turn down the temperature to cool himself off in order to get through it. By the time he wrapped himself in a towel, dried off and stepped into the bedroom, he was pissed at himself. By teasing her, he was teasing himself, and that was the last thing he needed. He glanced at the time and realized it was still pretty early. He put on his sweats and a T-shirt and headed downstairs to watch a movie. The living room was empty, and that was the way he liked it. He turned on the monster seventy-two-inch TV. The one thing they all agreed on when they decided they needed a TV was that they would buy the biggest and most badass one they could find.

He grinned as he checked through the movie listings until he found a hard-core action flick. Before pressing Play, he walked to the kitchen to grab some popcorn. He put the bag in the microwave, poured a shot of whiskey and when the microwave finished, carried the drink and popcorn back into the living room and stopped. He was no longer alone.

Sienna had the remote, checking out a chick flick on the screen.

"Ah, hell, no," he said. He put down the popcorn and his drink and said, "No chick flicks allowed in the house."

She turned, one eyebrow raised, and said, "As a man you're afraid of romance. Or maybe it's sex."

He glared at her. He remembered all the comments he'd made way back when about her temper. Obviously, he had pricked it well tonight. He decided to change his tactic. He bent in front of her and kissed her. "Anytime you want somebody to warm your bed, you just have to say so," he said. He snatched the remote from her hand and immediately flicked it back to the movie he had set up.

"Besides killing, is there anything else you guys like to do?"

He hit Play, and the movie started immediately. He

knocked her around, he'd have taken care of the guy immediately.

Rhodes settled back to watch the movie, happy she had stayed with him. She moaned after a couple action scenes and groaned at a couple dumb one-liners, but hey, he didn't put this movie on because he was concerned about the eloquent conversation between the characters. It was exactly what he needed to escape. And the longer they sat here, the more she relaxed. Eventually her legs stretched out beside him, not quite touching, not avoiding him either. But she was totally at ease, and that's what he wanted.

At one point, she pulled her feet up and accidentally touched him. "Sorry," she muttered.

"Doesn't matter. The couch is huge."

At that, she stretched out her legs. There wasn't quite enough room, so he picked her feet up and put them on his lap. "Just leave them here. You'll be more comfortable."

At that she tucked a pillow under her head and turned her attention back to the movie.

By the time the credits rolled through, he was grinning like a fool. He always liked those movies. A large group of men going after the bad guys, along the way rescuing the damsel in distress. Just like his life. He shut off the TV and turned to ask, "What did you think of it?"

And stopped. She'd fallen asleep. He shook his head. He didn't even know when she'd nodded off.

He got up, took his empty glass and bowl into the kitchen, rinsed and loaded both in the dishwasher, and came back out, wondering what he should do with her.

He checked his watch. It was 10:30 p.m. Definitely time for her to go to bed. He reached out a gentle hand and tried to shake her awake. She body-rolled with his movements but never woke up. He frowned and gave her a harder shake. She mumbled, tried to turn over, but the couch wasn't giving her any room. Finally, in frustration, she fell back asleep.

He didn't think he'd seen anybody sleep quite that way. But he had an easy answer. He reached under her body, picked her up in his arms and quietly walked to the elevator, hit the button and stepped inside. He could feel his muscles work as he had lifted her, but thankfully everything seemed to be going just fine. His original injuries caused him some concern, but this last year with heavy training, he was back into his prime condition again.

On the second floor, he walked to her suite and had to shuffle her in his arms to get her door open.

Thankfully, she'd left it unlocked. He nudged it wider with his foot, and walked carefully over to the bed. Then he frowned because of course, it was made. He pulled back the covers and sheets and laid her down. He quickly took off her shoes and stopped, staring at her shirt and jeans. If he undressed her, she'd be pissed. But how could she get a good rest if he didn't?

He decided to go for it, taking off her jeans and T-shirt. Tucking her under the covers, he folded her clothes nicely, leaving them on the other side of the bed. At the door, he turned off the light, glanced over at the sleeping beauty and whispered, "Good night."

She didn't respond. Just snuggled deeper into the covers. He shook his head at her ability to sleep so deeply, so fast. He'd had high hopes for sleep himself. Now he wasn't so sure. Instead of pictures of great action scenes dancing in his head, he would see a model-perfect body twisting beneath him.

By the time he made it to his suite, he contemplated another cold shower.

Chapter 5

WHEN SIENNA WOKE up the next morning, she twisted uncomfortably, wondering what was pulling at her ribs. She rolled onto her back and realized she was still wearing her bra. She struggled to remember last night, anything past the movie and sitting on the couch with Rhodes. She threw back the covers and, relieved to see she still wore panties, headed to the bathroom, took a quick shower, dressed in fresh clothing and headed out. She snagged her cell phone as she left, checking the time. It was only 7:30.

She wouldn't be the first downstairs. She wasn't sure Alfred ever slept, as he had to get up at some godforsaken hour to bake those always fresh cinnamon buns and other goodies he offered them.

Sure enough he was there, as were most of the men. "Don't any of you guys sleep?" she asked in a half mumble. She headed for the coffeepot and poured herself a large mug. Turning around, she sat down at the table. She'd had lots of sleep, but her body said it wasn't done yet.

"What's on tap for today, Levi?" Rhodes asked.

"How does Sienna feel about discussing some of this with the DA's office in Dallas?"

She stared at Levi. "Me?" she squeaked. "Why should I go?"

"Because you can explain the codes and names you found."

"Wouldn't it be easier to do that on the phone?" She'd never done any fieldwork. Even with her old job.

"Possibly. But Rhodes needs to check out a couple more places."

Her heart sank. At the same time, her nerve endings came alive. She was going with Rhodes? That would not be a good thing. Especially if that meant a night at a hotel. She dropped her gaze to her coffee mug and lifted it to take a sip. In her mind, she thought it was foolish. "How many hours are we talking?"

"If we leave now, we might get back tonight," Rhodes said quietly. "Otherwise, we'd have to stay overnight. It also depends on what kind of trouble we run into."

Immediately she shook her head. "Remember, I don't do trouble."

Everybody at the table laughed.

"Easy for you to say," Rhodes quipped, "considering you came here through trouble. But when it happens, nobody's ever prepared for it."

She really didn't want to, but she wasn't sure how to come up with an excuse not to. She also didn't understand what the point was.

Ice walked in then, sitting down at the table. She looked over at Sienna. "Did Levi ask you?"

"If you mean about seeing the DA, yes, he did. But it doesn't make any sense to me."

"Don't know if you heard that they found more pages of code, but they don't really understand what they're looking at. There has to be a reason these sections were printed off. This time there are names."

Sienna immediately shook her head. "They will have a whole team of specialists more capable of sorting through that paperwork than I am."

Levi nodded. "Maybe we should say they don't have anybody they trust. They're afraid some of those names on that list are coming out of their offices and higher up."

"Oh." Her shoulders slumped. That she did understand. It made sense then. Betrayal happened at all levels. And often those were the hardest to prove, the higher-ups. And they often had to bring in somebody from an outside firm to handle it.

She considered the risks, realized that Rhodes would be there with her, something she desperately wanted, even if it was really bad for her, and nodded. "Okay, let's hope we can be back tonight."

Ice immediately shook her head. "That won't happen. They have meetings set up for you today and tomorrow."

Sienna raised her gaze to study Ice's expression but found only sincerity in hers. "Remember, you guys, I haven't had any field experience. This could be a really bad deal for Rhodes."

They all snorted. "Rhodes says he's up for it."

She glanced at Rhodes to see him studying her intently. She didn't know what was going on in the back of his mind, but she knew something was—a challenge and something a whole lot warmer. And she'd never backed down from one of those yet.

"Then I guess I'll pack an overnight bag."

Alfred walked in carrying a large platter of food. "You can pack a bag after breakfast. The food is hot and fresh. Eat first." He placed the food down in front of her.

Within seconds they were all eating.

Only it was a little hard to get her food down. Suddenly she was uneasy. Her tummy queasy. She only ate a little bit, but of course Alfred noticed.

"I'll pack you some food to-go." He bustled away to the kitchen.

"I don't mean to be a problem," she murmured.

Merk laughed at that. "He loves to mother us. So, let him. He sent a huge basketful of food with Rhodes and me the last time we took off."

She stood up and filled her coffee cup. "I'll be back in ten."

She headed to her suite. It was the first chance she'd had to relax after becoming the center of attention down there. She didn't know what was going on in Rhodes's mind, but she was afraid of what that meant. Because, if it was what she thought it was, she wanted that too. Was it so wrong? No, but she wasn't ready for another relationship, and if it went wrong, she'd screw up her perfect job here. Not to mention she'd have to find a new place to live. No, it was too early to risk this. She liked it here and didn't want anything to mess that up.

In her suite, she pulled out her bag and quickly packed a few pieces of clothing. As she stared at her worldly possessions, she realized even though she'd been here for close to a month, she hadn't increased her material possessions at all. She didn't have any more clothes. She had the same few pairs of jeans and underwear, and she hadn't done laundry either. Now she didn't have time to do that. There was no sense fussing. What she had would have to be enough.

Resolute, she turned, checked out her suite and felt an odd sense of good-bye. Although she'd left the compound before to come back again, there was a sense of detachment this time. And she didn't like it. She'd found a home here—she'd made herself a place. She wanted to keep it. But times were changing, obviously.

She turned out the light at the bedroom door and headed downstairs, running into Ice in the garage. "I don't have a ton of clothes to take with me," she confessed. "Even when I was gone, I hadn't bothered shopping for more. That sense of only having what I can carry still applied back then, and I can't seem to shake it even now."

Ice patted her shoulder. "Dallas has lots of malls. It's a shopping mecca. You can run into a store to collect what you need."

"That's fine as long as jeans are okay," Sienna said. "If you're expecting me to wear some kind of professional outfit for this deal, we have to shop first."

Rhodes walked into the kitchen, wearing jeans and a shirt the same color as hers too.

She smiled. "Okay, so maybe we're a matched set."

"Absolutely," he said, picking up her bag, then motioning toward the truck. "We're taking the same small pickup as last time." He tossed her bag behind the seat, turned to accept a basket of goodies from Alfred and said, "Come on. Let's go."

"No, I need coffee first," she said. "Let me grab a travel mug." As she headed toward the coffeepot, she found Alfred had two big cups and a thermos there waiting. She turned to find him right behind her. She threw her arms around his neck and gave him a big hug and kissed his cheek. "Thank you, Alfred. You're the best." She grabbed the coffee and ran.

RHODES WAITED FOR her to get in and place the coffee

mugs in the cup holders. When she didn't reach for her seat belt immediately, he said, "Buckle up."

She shot him a look but did as told.

When they were finally out of the compound, heading toward the main road, he turned to look at her. "Are you sure you're okay with this?"

She huffed beside him.

He didn't know any other word to describe it. It was like a half-snort, half-sniff, and it made him smile. "I'll take that as a yes."

Nothing but silence was her response. He shrugged. *Whatever.* They had a long way to go. It would be easier if they got along during this trip, but if not, well, he was a pro. He could handle it regardless.

After a few minutes, she turned to look at him. "Did you set this up?"

He turned in astonishment. "Hell, no."

In a small voice she said, "Oh."

"I have better things to do with my time than take cold showers in the evening," he said simply. He laughed at that. He could feel her shocked stare, but he wouldn't elaborate. Not after their conversation last night.

He drove steadily for several hours. When they came to a gas station, he pulled in and filled the tank. She hopped out and cleaned the windshield wipers, surprising him.

When he was done, she walked over to him. "Want me to drive for a bit?"

"No, I'm good. If you want more coffee or something, you can get whatever inside."

She shook her head. "No, Alfred sent lots of coffee. I do need the washroom now. Who knows when we'll be taking another break."

He paid for the gas, took the receipt, pocketed it and hopped into the truck to wait for her. He reached across and opened the basket, grabbing a handful of sandwiches from Alfred. She was right. When would they stop again? While he waited, he devoured one sandwich and was busy working on the second when she returned.

She took one look, raised her eyebrows and said, "Are you leaving me any?"

He motioned at the basket. "Help yourself."

They both ate while he returned to the road and kept going. He checked his watch. "We should be at the Dallas city limits in another twenty minutes."

"Fine. I still don't understand why I had to come."

"Sure you do." He glanced at her. "Besides Levi's probably checking out how you handle yourself. Are you afraid of getting involved in something like you were before, or are you really against fieldwork?"

She thought about the question for a long moment. "I don't know what it is. I guess I thought I'd closed that door and walked away from it. I hadn't really expected to open it again, not in these circumstances."

"Fair enough." He put on his signal, changed lanes and pulled over to the exit ramp. "We don't come across this kind of problem very often."

"If it's tracking money, it'll be in every case."

"True. Levi often handles that, and Harrison is a whiz on computers, as are you. I do a lot of that kind of work too. But none of us have the same level of skill you do. Maybe if you could teach us, we wouldn't need you to do it at all."

"Coding isn't something you just pick up," she said quietly. "Not at this level. Besides I don't know many languages. I specialized in banking software. That's it."

She seemed to brighten up after that. He had to wonder if she'd told him everything that had gone on. Did anybody really know the whole story? Or did she keep some of the darker stuff to herself? It took him back to that whole ex-boyfriend-who-had-been-a-drinker thing. He hadn't questioned the scenario originally. But now that he watched her reaction to it all, he was starting to wonder.

But he kept his concerns to himself.

He pulled out the address for where they were going and punched it into the GPS. He could've done this a long time ago, but now that they were heading into town, he'd get a better reading. He followed the instructions to the DA's office and pulled in the adjacent parking lot. He shut off the engine and turned to look at her. "Are you ready?"

"As ready as I'll ever be." And with that she opened the truck door and stepped out.

Chapter 6

SHE TOOK A deep breath and followed Rhodes into the big government-looking building. For some reason, she expected the DA to have an office in a much smaller, more private setting. She didn't know if this was normal or just set up for today. Rhodes seemed to know where he was at least.

At the DA's office, they were seated in a small boardroom at a table, waiting for the meeting to start. A few minutes later, a tall, very lean-looking male walked in. He seemed in his late fifties, with an air of cool competence as he joined them. He shook their hands and introduced himself. "I'm District Attorney Robert Forrest." He nodded as a second man joined them. "This is Bobby. He'll help you with whatever you need. He'll get the box we have collected."

Even though the two names were similiar—one was just a shortened version of the other—she worried she'd mix them up, her nervousness getting the better of her. Even gaining strength from Rhodes's presence wasn't helping much.

Robert immediately got down to business. He pulled out the sheets forwarded to him. She recognized her handwriting on one.

"Now I understand you guys know of these two men." Robert pointed to the mug shots of the cousins.

Rhodes nodded. "Yes, that's them."

"Good. And you?" He turned to look at Sienna. "You're the one who pulled the names from this series of spreadsheets, is that correct?"

"Following the pattern I saw in the software code, the banks stopped the employee who'd hacked their system. These sheets were found in his possession," she said. "Those are the names the code decoded down to."

She was very careful to say she hadn't been the one to do anything. But at the same time, Robert didn't seem interested in placing blame or giving credit.

Again, he nodded. He opened his briefcase and pulled out several more spreadsheets. "Having seen this work before, potentially you could find more information in these?"

She pulled them toward her and looked at the first one. She quickly scanned the seven sheets. "They look to be similar, yes."

"Do you see any other names?"

She frowned. "Potentially. If they decode down the same way as the other sheets, then yes, that's easy to do." She wanted to say it would be easy to have them done without her being here, but she didn't. She glanced over at his briefcase and asked, "Is there a scratch pad and pen I could use?"

Instantly both appeared in front of her. She picked up the pen, grabbed the first spreadsheet and very quickly had the first ten lines listed. She went back to the spreadsheet, noting the repetitions within the lines. On the fourth page, she came to a new name. She wrote that down, and her system continued, and soon she had them all down on the sheet of paper in front of her. She turned the pad around, pointing it to Robert so he could read the names.

He stared, and some of the color washed out of his face.

She glanced at Rhodes. Had he noticed how nervous she was? She hoped not. Once again, she didn't have an explanation for her feelings. He reached across and grabbed her fingers and squeezed them reassuringly. She relaxed some and asked, "Is that what you were expecting?"

The DA sat down in the chair heavily. "No. It's worse than that. Some of these names are pretty high up in the city."

"But there's no proof they've done anything. That's the problem," she said quietly. "Without tracking these accounts and the banks that have been hacked, there's no way to see just where they lead and what's been done under these people's names. For all we know, their identities have been stolen, and they aren't involved at all."

Robert looked at Rhodes and said, "I spoke with Levi about this. I believe your other man, Bullard, is involved on the banking end. This case is obviously global. My concern is less about the hacking and more about drugs and arms dealings in my city. But we'll obviously look in to all of it."

The door opened, and Bobby walked in, carrying a file box. He placed it beside the DA and took a seat at the back without saying a word.

The break was good timing as far as she was concerned, considering the DA's stand on his city needing to be clean. She kept her opinion to herself, but couldn't help thinking that nobody wanted to have this garbage in their area. Yet, if it were pushed out beyond their boundaries, they were fine. But it wasn't prudent to open that discussion.

"What you really mean is, we can't have it at all," Rhodes corrected. "Doesn't matter if it's in the cities or somewhere else, it will filter into the cities eventually."

Distracted, the DA said, "Yes, of course." He looked back at Sienna. "What do you need to get proof?"

"I'm not sure. I'm a programmer. But without access to the banks in question, I only have the spreadsheets to go on." She motioned to Rhodes. "He will be more help at this point. Or Levi's team at home."

"As I said earlier, some of these names are very high profile." He turned to look at Rhodes. "We can keep you out of this and the courts if we have actual physical proof. But if the methodology of how we got this information should ever be questioned, you might be required to come in as a witness."

She slumped in her chair and shook her head. "My reputation won't stand up in court."

Silence filled the room. His gaze narrowed, and he shot her a look. "Just what does that mean?"

She glanced over at Rhodes and shrugged. While she listened, Rhodes gave a short explanation of her history.

"As an end result, her name was muddied from all this."

The DA tapped the sheet of paper in front of them, then the box, and considered the issue. "I guess it's down to finding any hard facts, so it's not your word against theirs."

"Most of these people won't have very much registered under their names," she said. "If they're doing investment banking, offshore accounts, or anything like that, we'll find it with enough time. However, usually companies are involved, not an individual person. Shell corporations have doctored books to hide the profits that are moved. They wouldn't list arms dealing anywhere, unless they have legal licenses to do so."

"Sounds like you are the person I need right now," the DA said. "You specialize in banking security, which means you understand money." The DA pointed at one name on the list. "Find out everything you can about this man."

She looked down at the name. *J. R. Wilson*. She frowned. "Wilson's a very common name."

"He also owns and runs a company—a huge charity for refugee camps in the Middle East."

She slowly raised her gaze and said, "Which *is* perfect for gunrunning."

"Exactly." He gave her a quiet nod. "He also has headquarters in Dallas and Ghana. That's the connection to the African banks."

She looked over at Rhodes. "I don't know how long we're expected to be here, but I could get started now."

"Anticipating that you'd be willing to stay here and begin now," he said, "I have a brand-new clean white laptop. Every step you make will be tracked." He patted the box beside him. "And this holds everything we have on the company."

She looked from the box to the laptop and nodded. "It's the best way."

All gazes were on her, but still she hesitated.

In a low voice Rhodes whispered, "You don't have to."

She gave him a veiled glance, took a deep breath and opened the laptop. "How can I not?"

RHODES WATCHED HER. She'd been put in an awkward position she hadn't been ready for. He understood the DA wanted as much information as he could get from her, given any names on her decoded list were in this office, understanding there would be even more problems using those people in this investigation.

Bobby got up and walked to a coffee service on the sideboard. "Can I get anyone a coffee?"

"Yes, please," Rhodes answered for the two of them.

Bobby turned to look at Robert. "Do you want a cup?"

The DA shook his head, his gaze intent on Sienna. Rhodes wasn't sure he liked that either. She'd been put through enough for doing her job. She'd come here to work for Levi with a completely different expectation, and she had every right to avoid the same murky water she'd traveled before. Still she'd agreed. Stepping up when the need was thrust upon her.

On the other hand, she was gifted, had something everybody needed, so it was hard not to utilize her skills.

"I'll be nearby if you need anything else," Bobby said before leaving.

Two hours later, while the DA worked on his files here with them, she said, "Do you have a printer?"

Rhodes, sorting through the contents of the box, glanced at her. She looked a little pale. Then again, she hadn't had lunch either. Her breakfast had been various contents of Alfred's basket earlier. Or was her expression something more?

He had one hard-bound ledger in his hand. He opened it to find what looked like standard accounts. The interesting thing was, it was a paper copy. Didn't everyone do digital accounting these days? Still, it wasn't illegal. Unless they were keeping a second set of books. He replaced it in the box.

Robert lifted his head and stared at her in surprise. "I guess the laptop isn't connected to that printer, so email it to me and I'll print it."

She hesitated, and Rhodes understood why. "Robert, do

you have a small printer she could hook up here?" he asked. "To keep everything completely separated."

Robert stood up and said, "I'll go see." He buzzed for someone to come help but after five minutes with no answer, he got up and walked from the conference room and left Rhodes and Sienna alone.

Rhodes placed a fresh cup of coffee in front of her. She looked startled for a moment and accepted it gratefully. She picked it up and hugged the hot cup close to her.

Concerned, he asked, "Are you okay?"

She took a deep breath and nodded. But she didn't say anything. When he saw her white knuckles gripped the cup, he realized something was even more wrong than he expected.

"Can you tell me?" He glanced around the room and realized it was quite possible the room was bugged. It shouldn't be, but they had been led to this room in particular. Although they hadn't been left alone until he requested a printer, that didn't mean everything they said wasn't being taped and/or recorded. He could send her a text asking what was wrong, but if anybody saw them doing that, their phones could be confiscated before they left.

Feeling protective, he made a sudden decision and said, "Let's go back to the hotel. You can work there if you feel up to it. But really, you look like you should probably lie down."

He studied her face, and in truth, she did look ill. Her skin was white, and her forehead was moist, as if she had a fever. He frowned, walked over to the door and opened it. As he stepped into the outer hallway, the DA approached, accompanied by Bobby, carrying a small printer. Rhodes quickly explained the problem, motioning toward her.

Robert frowned. “Damn. Well, I guess you couldn’t stay here much longer anyway. The office will close soon. Although I thought maybe we could keep working into the evening.”

“We have a room booked for the night,” Rhodes said. “Let me take her back so she can lie down. She might just need some fresh air. She also hasn’t eaten since morning. If she feels better, we can come back.”

The DA hesitated and glanced at Bobby, who shrugged. The DA turned back to Rhodes and said, “Take the laptop and box. If she feels like working, she can do so from there.”

That was the best news he’d heard yet. Not giving anybody a chance to argue, he pointed at the printer and said, “Her reasons for needing that still applies. May we bring that too?”

Without a word Bobby handed it over.

Rhodes had his arms full. He laid the clean laptop inside the box and stacked the printer on top. With all that under one arm, he very gently snagged Sienna’s elbow and lifted her to her feet.

“Come on. Let’s get you into the room so you can lie down.”

She gave both men a half-hearted smile and murmured, “Sorry.”

“Don’t be,” Rhodes told Sienna. “I hadn’t expected we’d be in the office that long. If I’d known, we’d have stopped for lunch.”

As they walked out and went to the elevator, he wasn’t sure if she was acting or really was sick, but her footsteps were getting fainter as they went along. By the time they got to the elevator, he was half supporting her, and now he was really worried.

The elevator was full. He got them both inside and down to the ground floor. Outside, still not knowing if she was physically ill or not, he led her to the truck and quickly got her inside and buckled in. On his side, he put the laptop and box in the backseat and hopped in. He considered whether anything had been placed inside his truck to monitor them.

And realized someone could have put a tracker on their clothing. He knew all too well how gifted some sleight-of-hand people were. It was also quite possible the laptop had something going on in it which she hadn't shared. Levi had already reserved the hotel suite for them. As Rhodes drove, he contemplated the options.

First was to get her safely inside. He quickly shifted her to the hotel room and had her stretched out on the bed. He made several trips back to the truck to grab their overnight bags and the box that contained the laptop and printer. On his last trip, he picked up the basket of food, the electronics from the compound, and the dashboard box where he had stowed his weapons—not allowed in the DA's building. Inside the room, he turned on the meter to see if any unexpected electronic devices were in the room. He did a full sweep, then came back to the clean laptop. Instantly the laptop caused the meter to buzz. He stared at it in shock.

She nudged him with her foot and said, "Exactly."

He lifted a finger to his lips, fished his phone from his pocket and stepped outside the hotel room. Still not happy with the distance, he walked to the parking lot where his truck was. There he stood and called Levi. He quickly explained what was going on.

"What? The laptop was bugged? That the DA gave you? You sure it wasn't just the fact that the document was being tracked?"

"No. She saw something. She immediately became ill or faked it. We're at the hotel now, and the new testing device Bullard sent us tells me the laptop is bugged. They know where we are. It doesn't change the fact that she needs a laptop to work on."

"Did you bring yours?"

"I've got the one that comes with the truck."

"See if she can use that. She can log on to the main server here. We need to get to the bottom of this and fast." Levi hung up, leaving Rhodes staring at the empty truck. He had taken the company laptop up to the hotel room with the other stuff. He walked back to the room, picked up the laptop from the DA's office, brought it back to the truck and locked it behind the driver's seat. Then back in the hotel room he once again tested for more electronic devices. The sweep was clean this time.

Laying down the testing kit, he said, "Okay. Now we can talk." He sat gently on the bed and leaned beside her, looking down at her. "First off, are you really sick? Or is this just a pretense?"

"Both," she said. "When I realized that laptop was recording our voices, I realized I was right back into the same damn thing I was in before. And that's when I felt sick."

"Right. Levi says to use my laptop to do whatever work you need to. Their laptop is locked in the truck."

She gave a sigh, rubbed her eyes and shifted her position so she was propped against the headboard.

"What else did you find?"

"The initials R.F. again."

He studied her as she tried to figure out who R.F. was.

"The DA's name has both those letters."

"Ah, hell." That was not good.

"Exactly. Either he wants this information so he can bury it or to figure out how to better hide his tracks, or there's a completely different R.F."

Rhodes reached for his laptop, flipped it open and placed it on her lap gently. "One of the hard rules of this kind of work is the fact that there's only one way to know how bad a scenario can get. You have to keep digging through the surface for the meat underneath. Just because R.F. is there, doesn't mean it's the DA's name being referenced."

"Three names were decoded. Or rather three sets of initials, because three of those patterns were just numbered accounts, which we can't easily access to find the corresponding names, and then we have the initials R.F."

He nodded. "We'll go on the assumption the DA's a good guy. But we won't take any chances, and we'll always keep in mind, if we find any proof he's not, it's an entirely different story."

"Then what do we do?" she cried. "He's the DA."

"That's easy. We go above him."

"And what if above him is corrupt too?" she asked, her voice bitter. "That's what happened to me. And when it all came back down, they blamed everything on me."

"I won't let that happen. You won't be too involved. You've been asked to come in and help out, that's it."

"In theory I understand that. But my heart still tells me to get the hell out and run in the opposite direction."

"You could look at this as an opportunity to leave all that behind. Because as soon as you step up and face it, it helps put your life back in control, like you're no longer a helpless victim. That you are the one with the power to turn it around."

She stared at him, fear in her gaze.

He tugged her into his arms. "Take it easy."

"It's not that easy …" she began.

He just held her close, feeling the trembling inside, even though she was doing her best to hide it. So strong, and yet so fragile. "Of course it's not. You were railroaded last time. That's not the same thing here. But you do have the ability to put some of these people—who have been doing this for a long time—in jail. And maybe you won't find anything. You won't know until you start looking."

"He wants me to look into the company books, but …" she reached over and lifted the same ledger he'd looked at in the office, "the tears from missing pages look suspiciously like the scanned pages Bullard sent us with its ripped edges."

"What are you saying?"

"I'm saying, the DA didn't give me the information I needed, but whether that was an oversight or deliberate, I don't know. There should be all kinds of information online and on paper to back this up and the accounting program they used on the laptop, but the only thing loaded here are the company books."

"We have to trust somebody." He opened his phone and quickly phoned Robert.

"She says she's missing a lot of information here. So, she can't check through the code to see what might be there. Are you sure it's all here?"

"Did she check the box? The answer is yes. It's all there, or it should be." There was a pause in his voice. "What do you mean, that's not all of it? I had our department look. I'll check with them to see if they still have anything." The DA's voice sounded muffled. "I'm walking over there right now.

I'll call you back in ten."

Staring down at his phone, wondering if he should notify Levi, Rhodes said, "Several others had the information first. He's gone to see if they still have any of the material. He thought it was all contained in the box and laptop."

She patted the box and said, "Not even close to what I'd expect."

His phone rang almost immediately. "My men said they put everything in the box. However, they digitalized everything first so we do have copies."

"Send us a digital copy via Levi. We can compare what's there versus what's in the box." His voice deepened as he added, "You might want to consider somebody in your office carefully removed a few things."

"That would be too obvious surely. John's the one who scanned in everything. Sending it now." And for the second time the DA hung up on him.

The email came in moments later, routed via Ice. Rhodes brought up the scanned ledger from the DA and flicked to the back. It was missing the same pages. He glanced at Sienna. "It does have missing pages. So quite possibly the scanned ones Bullard sent you belong in this ledger."

"So the question here is, how did those pages end up in Ghana and the ledger in Dallas?"

They smiled at each other. "J. R. Wilson," they said at the same time.

"This is great evidence of his involvement."

"Or someone who works for him," she corrected. "And guys like him are slippery. If they can pin it on someone else, they will."

"As you already know," Rhodes said quietly.

Chapter 7

"AS I ALREADY know," Sienna repeated his statement. "Yes. I thought I knew my coworkers. But they fooled me." She shook her head. "What is there for food?" She reached up a hand and rubbed her temple. "I'm feeling better. I don't know if it was the air conditioning there or the damn coffee, but I was pretty nauseated."

"We can order in, or check out the hotel restaurant."

Sienna glanced at the paperwork and laptop. "I'm not comfortable leaving this material here without us. So, delivery or room service."

He studied her for a long moment. "I saw a little Italian place around the corner when we drove in. Would you be okay if I left you long enough to get two dinners?"

"That would be perfect." She smiled at him. "And I really love Italian."

"I think you just love food of all kinds." He got up, turned to look at her and said, "Do not let anybody inside. And don't answer the hotel phone." And with that he started to leave, only to stop at the doorway, pivot and walk back. He leaned down and gave her a long, hard kiss. As he lifted his head, he whispered in a dark voice, "Stay safe."

When she could breathe again, she found him gone.

She leaned back against the headboard, grateful for the moment alone to catch her breath. He was a hell of a kisser.

And he cared. She smiled, knowing that regardless of this op or any others to come, she'd been right to accept Levi's offer.

Considering her growling stomach, she was also grateful a meal was coming but was a little more concerned about the fact that information was missing. It had all the hallmarks of someone laying the blame on her. Again. What she had was a clean set of books. And a ledger with some of the pages missing. All it did was make her suspicious. She wasn't an accountant per se. She was a programmer. She flicked open the laptop and looked at the company books again. It showed the last three years. It would take time to go through the multiple entries, so she picked a place to start. She flicked back to last summer and read through them, finding a lot of stationary and supplies, food, shoes, and clothing.

Then it was a charity. Was it asked to buy the stuff, or was it supplying it? It took her a while to figure out the pattern, but then it hit her. Way too many shoes were headed to Africa. She quickly highlighted every entry. And then every one listed as clothing. The figures were astronomical. Unless they were clothing thousands of people in a shelter or village, she didn't understand how these numbers could be so high. They were listed as expenses, and that didn't make much sense to her either because the company was running in the black. There were cheaper ways to buy things like this, she was sure.

As she searched for shipping and/or handling fees, something to ascertain that these products had actually been moved overseas to help somebody, she slowly got a picture of the company. Bringing up a webpage, she quickly researched the business, realizing they were indeed, digging wells, setting up schools, and supplying clothing to the villagers. They were proud of the fact they had put running water into four separate villages so far.

And everything made sense, except for the shoes. Every time she saw a picture of anybody at these villages, they were barefoot. On the other hand, most people wouldn't even blink if they were sending shoes over because, of course, they went together with clothes—but really only to the Western way of thinking. Many people in Africa didn't wear shoes by choice.

On a sheet of paper, she quickly jotted down some notes. The DA could easily ask for answers to some of these questions. As she kept searching through the months, going by location, most of the products had gone to the four villages. Which was all fine and dandy, but she didn't understand where the money was coming from. All these charitable donations originated overseas, and most of them were labeled in code. Invoice numbers with a single letter behind them.

And a few of them were suspiciously familiar.

But when she went to the box, nothing backed up those single-letter references. There had to be another set of books or something that tracked all these invoices. Everything cross-referenced. Business was all about checks and balances. And if this charity went through an elaborate scheme to hide money, it sure as hell wouldn't have done a sloppy job of it. Not at this level. She needed access to the bank's program. But if the company was smart, they'd have used multiple banks. Sure enough, a few months later, invoices showed up.

She continued through six more months, but it was mostly a repetition of the previous ones. The company appeared to be buying shoes and clothing from those going out of business and shipping them to several villages. Which made sense as to the quantities purchased—but not for the prices paid—except by now they should have warehouses of merchandise somewhere. Were they planning on stockpiling for other villages? She shook her head. There had to be an easier way.

But it wasn't her job to judge the validity of a company. Or how well it was run or the business practices behind it. All she knew was the banking program had been hacked and somehow involved this company.

As she moved forward within the books, she could see the company's focus had changed. Instead of clothing, they now bought tools, seeds, and small equipment. She approved. Much better to allow the villagers to help themselves than to just keep doling out charity.

Slowly she gained an understanding of the company's business practices.

When the hotel room door opened, she looked up with a start.

"Sorry it took so long," he said. "I would've called, but they said ten minutes, and instead it was twenty." He closed the door behind him and placed the bag on the bed. "They gave us several dishes and said we can make up individual plates."

She carefully replaced the material in the box, followed by Rhodes's laptop, and walked over to the bed. As she pulled out the dishes, the smell hit her. And that's when she realized just how absolutely, horrifically hungry she truly was. She hated to say that even her fingers were trembling.

"What's the matter?" He studied her with concern. He walked closer and picked up her hands, frowning. Then lifted one to his lips.

If he intended on that calming things down, well, it wasn't helping. But she also wasn't sure she wanted to move so fast. She'd been sucked into a whirlwind romance the last time. She wanted to go slow and make sure she knew who Rhodes really was. Attraction was one thing. But she didn't want an affair. She was hoping for the whole shebang.

"I guess I'm just really hungry," she said, loving the concern but not wanting him to worry. "And my blood sugar drops more and more lately, particularly if I don't eat on time."

"Are you diabetic?"

She laughed and pulled her hand free. "It's more than likely my iron is low. The doctor said I am not taking care of myself."

She sat down on the bed, grabbed a paper plate and dished up one-third of each of the three dishes. For the next ten minutes, there was silence as she ate. She lifted her head to see him thoroughly enjoying his meal too. He was an easy companion. Quick with decision-making, but happy to get her input, like dinner. "This is really tasty."

He nodded. "It smelled wonderful when I walked in."

"I just have no idea what it is."

He laughed. "Well, obviously, it's pasta. Some Italian-sounding name. But what I remember, they had roasted vegetables and a breaded meat."

At that she laughed. "I figured that much by myself."

He reached over, grabbed the receipt stapled to the paper bag and handed it to her. "Here, maybe it'll make sense to you.

But the items were written in Italian. And not much of it made any sense. She tossed it on the bed and said, "Doesn't matter. It's delicious."

"Did you find out anything while I was gone?"

"They made some bad business decisions early on. They

should have warehouses full of clothes and shoes by this point, but finally they now supply tools for these villages they're working with," she said. "They brought in fresh water for the people and have been teaching them how to garden for themselves."

"I approve of that."

"I do too."

"But what about warehouses full of clothes and shoes?"

"Honestly I have no idea. But they have all these purchases for them."

"Let's hope they were reasonably decent purchases, and they have handed them all out. What about income?"

"Most of it is donations. When the money comes in, and they have it sitting there, then they spend."

"Well, that makes good business sense. Most of us can't do it any other way."

"Exactly. So far I've not seen anything terribly odd."

"So that's good then. Finish so we can go home."

She shook her head. "Not quite."

He lifted his head and stared at her. "Sorry?"

She glanced over at him. "It's too clean."

Chewing, he slowly lowered his plate and studied her face. "So you suspect something is wrong here?"

"Let's just say I have questions. If the DA can get the answers, then potentially we're in the clear."

"If there's no profit—which, from what I understand you're saying, the money comes in, and they spend it all—so it goes out again."

"I'm sure buying the farming tools is good, but I can't guarantee what they're listing is actually what they're purchasing. Ten thousand shovels are listed in separate entries, but were that many picked up and delivered?"

"How big are the villages?"

"Isn't that the question?" She smiled at him. "Ten thousand shovels isn't a lot when you're talking about several being outfitted. It all depends on what they were doing and the population of the able-bodied individuals in each. We don't have facts and figures on the villages, and we don't know if they are buying that many because they got a better deal, and they'll always need them down the road."

He nodded. "I can see what you mean. What about the owner?"

"Nothing. No dividends were paid to him, and he's not withdrawing cash in any way, shape, or form."

"So he's clean. And that's who the DA wanted you to find more information on?"

"Yes and no. How he made his money is something I'd like to know."

"He shouldn't be making it from a non-profit charity."

"He probably draws a salary if he's working for the charity full time. The statistics of what those CEOs earn running some of the major charities across the states are pretty scary. A lot of them are making seven figures."

"That doesn't sound very charitable to me," he said with a frown.

"A lot of times the charity doesn't get the money it needs. It's too busy paying its staff." She shook her head. "A couple employees in the lower salary range are making less than fifty thousand a year."

"So they're handling all this themselves from this end."

"But I'm not seeing payments to any staff over in Ghana where the warehouses are. So, either they're all volunteers, they're dealing with another company. or are paying out cash. And maybe I need to access the banking software. They could be moving money that way in the background. Still, it gives me hope that we might leave tomorrow."

He took another bite and nodded toward the rest of the food. "When we're done eating, we can give the DA a call and see if he can get the answers for us."

"I was hoping you'd say that. I don't want to return to his office. Something is wrong there, but I can't put my finger on it. I just get nauseated and this closed-in feeling. I don't know what the hell made me sick, but I'm really not signing up for more of that air."

"And yet, I wasn't sick and neither Bobby nor Robert had any symptoms."

She nodded. "I can't explain it. But I had to listen to my own body."

"It could be just a case of nerves," he answered quietly. "Reminding you too much of your former job."

She nodded and turned her attention back to her plate.

When they finished dinner and cleaned up, he pulled out his phone. "Robert, she's gone through several months of the accounts and has a few questions. She can talk to you about them directly." He handed the phone to Sienna.

In a businesslike voice, she brought up the few questions she had about the company books. When she was done, she said, "Other than that, I'm not seeing anything at this point. It lacks information. These are very simplistic books. Only two people work for the company, and the person you asked me to keep an eye out for, J. R. Wilson, is not mentioned in any way. Some odd things are going on in the way the charity is run, but nothing that references him."

"I can call and get some of these questions answered," he said, but his voice was distracted as if buried in work. "It might not be until tomorrow morning."

"Let me know if you find anything else."

When she hung up, she handed it back to Rhodes. "He wants me to keep looking." She tapped the box and said, "I think Bullard should run this name for us. He could figure out if there's any property in Africa registered in the charity or owner's name, or even a family name."

"You think he's invested in Africa?"

"It would make sense, as that's where his charities are operating. Not to mention the warehouses."

"That's a call I can make." He opened his phone and said, "But I'll do it outside."

When he left again, she buried herself back in the laptop. The one thing about code she loved: everything was tracked.

"BULLARD, SEE IF you can find any information on a J. R. Wilson. He's a person of interest on that banking fraud case. We're currently in Dallas to see the DA. Checking out the charity he owns and runs here."

"*Wellness for Everyone*?" Bullard asked. "It's always been a bit dodgy. One thousand and one charities are here, everyone supposedly wanting to help." He paused then added, "But I can tell you that name comes with a warning."

"So we do have the right man?"

"I'll do some digging on this side, but I wouldn't be at all surprised."

Rhodes thought about that for a minute and said, "There was something in the early years about ordering clothes and shoes, but we're talking about hundreds of thousands of dollars' worth."

"It's possible it's legit," Bullard said carefully. "But not very probable. There's no point in buying clothes when a lot comes from the Western world and other countries for relatively small money, if not outright free. Just pay the shipping."

"According to Sienna, it's like they're stockpiling warehouses full of them."

"And if it is warehouses, it could be full of something completely different."

"And then it stopped. Instead the company bought tools, farming equipment, things like that."

"Which is what we would expect. And on the books it sounds like they had initial good intentions, making some bad decisions, and then quickly moved into an area more helpful for the people. But was it really clothing and shoes, or something else?"

"And of course, we didn't see any addresses where any of this stuff is stored."

"Actually I think I have an idea about that. But no way in hell can you get a warrant to go in and look. Not there." His voice slowed. "Given the connection, I think I'll send somebody around to do it. If I thought guns were in those warehouses, I'd be all over it."

After hanging up, Rhodes walked back into the hotel room to give an update, but instead of finding her back at work, it looked like she'd nodded off. Her eyes were closed, and her steady deep breathing came from her chest. "I'm not asleep," she whispered. "Honest."

He laughed. "Put it away. Tomorrow will come soon enough. We're waiting on Bullard to get back to us." He quickly explained their conversation.

She rolled over and stared at him. "It will be interesting to hear what he finds." She closed the laptop, tucked it into the box, replaced all the papers and moved it to the hotel desk. Then she returned to the bed, folded back the covers and crawled under them.

"Aren't you getting undressed first?"

"Too much work to do still," she muttered. "Besides, I won't get much sleep tonight. This is just a nap."

"It's almost nine o'clock. Better to sleep through the night."

She frowned, and he could see the ideas warring in her expressive face. Finally, she threw back the covers and growled, "Fine."

She grabbed her bag, pulled out some clothing and a small case and walked into the bathroom. When she returned fifteen minutes later, he was sitting on the bed with his laptop open, taking notes of what had happened during the day.

She was dressed in shorts and a tank top. She stumbled to the bed, threw herself under the covers, turned out the light on her side and muttered, "Good night."

He grinned. He never thought he'd want somebody who was prickly, but he liked her just fine. More than actually. He'd hoped for a little more interaction tonight, but given her state and the fact he'd already gotten a terrific response from his earlier kiss, it wasn't the time. … She had to move at the speed she was comfortable with. He wanted her for a long while, not just for a good time. But he hoped for plenty of those through the years too.

"If only Jarrod could see you now," he muttered, laughing, but then remembered what her last lover had done to her. Well, he was no friend to betrayal, having experienced more of his own than he wanted to. But he'd made peace with it. Now he needed to help her do the same with hers.

"If you tell him, I'll be in a shitload of trouble."

"Would he really be upset?" Should he tell her about his conversation with her brother? Or wait until she was awake. The last thing he wanted to do was get involved in a discussion that would potentially upset her. She needed a good night's sleep. Today had been tough enough on her. Besides, they had time. And the journey was all that much sweeter, knowing where they were going.

"No idea. Not ready to walk in that direction. The less he knows, the better. Same for his job. If I don't know he's going out on dangerous missions, then I don't worry. If he doesn't think I'm involved in something that'll mess up my life again, then he won't worry. It's a good deal all around."

"It's a bad one because it leaves you standing out in the cold alone."

"I'm used to it." On that note she pulled the blanket higher on her shoulders and sank deeper into the pillow. The conversation was over.

Chapter 8

SHE WOKE UP suddenly. Lying quietly in the center of the bed, Rhodes was atop the bedding beside her. His eyes were wide open. She leaned up on one arm only to have him immediately raise a hand to stop her from moving. Quietly she sank back down again and waited.

A shadow crossed in front of the hotel room window making her blood run cold. Outside their door stretched a lengthy deck that ran along the front of several hotel rooms. They were all separated by small fences, but in theory, anybody could hop across if they wanted to. She caught her breath again as the shadow retreated across the window once again. She waited anxiously for Rhodes to make some kind of move. But he didn't. Neither did he relax.

She was rather desperate for the bathroom. Didn't know if she dared take a chance. Finally, he dropped his hand, turned to look at her and said, "It's clear."

She raised her eyebrows but took his words at face value. She threw back the covers, slid off the bed and walked to the bathroom. Maybe it was nerves, maybe it was the stuff she'd been working on, but her sense of unease grew. After washing her hands and returning to the bedroom, she worried if she'd fall asleep again. She checked her cell phone to see it was four o'clock in the morning. She glanced over at him and said, "Do you think that shadow had anything to do with us?"

"Yes."

That was it, short, terse. A typical Rhodes's answer. He'd been a lot more amiable years ago. But then they hadn't been in danger back then. He had also been teasing and kind to her as a gawky teenager. She punched up the pillows against the headboard and crawled under the covers, then sat and stared at him. "Do we need to leave?"

He shot her a sharp look and shook his head. "Not yet."

She waited. But he didn't elaborate. "Are we waiting for something?" she asked in exasperation. "Are we waiting for this to get worse, for somebody to charge into the room and actually attack us?"

His gaze never stopped moving around the room as he checked out something. She didn't understand what he was looking for, but it seemed he was mentally cataloguing the contents of the room, wondering how fast they could get out.

"You want me to start packing?"

"How long would it take you?"

"Right now, running on adrenaline, five minutes."

His eyebrows shot up. "Make that two." He walked into the bathroom and closed the door.

She bounded out of bed and quickly got dressed. She hadn't brought much in the way of clothing with her, and had already packed the DA's material with Rhodes's laptop and the ledger inside the box of documents. So, it was complete and ready to go. If anybody was after her, chances were more than likely they'd want the ledger. Sienna knew something fishy was going on in those accounts, but they had to have the proof. The DA needed a forensic accountant to look in to this deeper. If they had digital copies of all the documents, it didn't really matter if the box of papers was stolen or not. But it would be much better to have it all.

Still there was no understanding the criminal mind these days. By the time Rhodes came out, she was putting her shoes on. She said, "I'm ready."

His gaze searched around the room, and he nodded. "You have stuff in the bathroom."

She walked in, packed the few toiletries she'd brought with her and added them to her backpack. "So where do we go from here?"

"It's too early to head to the DA's office, but several coffee shops are around."

"Okay. That works for me. Especially if we can bring in the laptop and work."

He glanced down at his watch and nodded. "It's 4:15. With any luck, there's an all-night café close by." He grabbed up his bag. "If I take the box, can you grab your bag?"

She snatched up her backpack, put it on her shoulders and grabbed the laptop, and together they headed out, locking up the hotel room behind them. He went by the registration desk and dropped off the key. Having already prepaid, it didn't matter when they left. Outside he led the way to the truck. There they stowed what they had and were on their way within minutes.

It felt odd to be up so early. Almost as if they were sneaking out of the hotel room so nobody could see them, but it wasn't a clandestine affair she was involved in. It was something a lot more dangerous.

Although an affair would be a lot more fun.

He drove from the lot and headed down the main street. Within minutes they found several good coffee shops. He pulled into the second one and parked. With Rhodes's laptop in her hands and a few of her notes, he locked up the truck, and they went inside to get coffee. "You want to eat?"

She shook her head. "Not right now. It's too early for that."

She settled back into the chair and opened the laptop. She was really too tired to review the material. Wasn't even sure what she'd found at this point. When the coffee was delivered, she closed the laptop again and pushed it off to one side, yawning.

"Did you get any sleep?" Rhodes asked as he reached across and covered her hand with his much bigger one.

She smiled. "Still the big-brother attitude?"

He raised his eyebrows at that. "Hey, I knew you back when," he said with a smile. "Besides, Jarrod's my friend."

"I'm no longer a little girl."

He settled back, gently pulling his hand away from hers.

She was kind of sorry she'd said anything. Something was so damn comforting about his touch. She doubled the cream in her coffee and stirred it.

"Did Jarrod say something to upset you before he left?"

She looked up in surprise. "Hell, no. Jarrod's a good guy. He knows he can trust me to have common sense."

"Have it about what?"

She gazed at him innocently over the rim of her cup. "Life, I guess." She smiled into her mug.

"Why is it I think you're laughing at me?" he asked.

She shrugged. "Jarrod gave me the same old warnings he's always given me. His friends are good, decent men, but they played fast and loose with women, so watch it. But he trusts me to make the right decision for me." She stared at him directly. "I got that warning ten years ago, and again a few days ago."

"Wow, I didn't know he still considered all of us that way."

"I don't think he does, but I think he was so used to giving that warning that it came out naturally as part of his habitual good-byes."

"That makes sense. I don't have a little sister to worry about, but I can see that being a prime concern."

"What he doesn't realize is that I'm an adult, and I won't have an affair with anybody I don't want to have one with," she said a little too strongly.

There was a sudden silence as he studied her. Then she realized she and Jarrod hadn't even discussed something along those lines. It wasn't like her brother was warning her off having sex; he was warning her off the men at the compound. That they couldn't be trusted to stick around longer than a one-night stand.

She shook her head. "And that's just an overly strong reaction of the younger sister having been told off for years and years on the same issue."

He laughed. "Whatever works."

She smiled. "You always did have that get-along-with-everybody attitude."

"I wondered how much you remembered from back then," he said curiously. "You never say much."

"What's to say? I met several of Jarrod's SEAL friends." She shrugged. "I've seen most of them over the years again too. This is the first I've seen of you since then though."

"Right. You sure don't look like you did back then. Cocky, skinny, braces, and carrot hair." He gave her a lopsided grin. "You were adorable. And are a beauty today."

Her gaze widened in surprise. "Well, I had a hero complex over you back then." She laughed. "I got rid of the braces, but sometimes I still put my foot in it."

He grinned. "I think we all do. That's not a skill you outgrow easily."

The waitress came back and asked, "Do you want to order anything to eat?"

Sienna shook her head. "Just more coffee for me, please."

She listened as Rhodes gave a similar answer. The atmosphere had warmed with their confessions. It gave her hope. She stared out the window, seeing the world around her lighten up slightly. That could've just been because her eyes were more adjusted, but it seemed like daylight was finally kicking nighttime into the background.

"Can we go home today, do you think?" she asked, pulling out a notepad. "I have a few points for the DA to look in to, but there's not a whole lot here."

"In that case, yes, we can go home."

She brightened. "Good."

"Glad to hear you consider the compound home."

"It took a while. After the attacks, I wondered what I'd gotten myself into. But I quickly realized Jarrod knew most of you and that somehow I'd been lucky to end up there. But since then, just sitting back and watching everybody go through their own personal relationship issues, it's been something else to handle."

Rhodes laughed. "Isn't that the truth? Levi and Ice, Stone and Lissa …"

"Merk and Katina," she added with a laugh. "Those two were destined to be together. I can't imagine how they even broke up last time."

"You might've felt differently if you'd been the one in

the Las Vegas wedding."

She grinned. "Good point."

"You are okay staying at the compound?" he asked, his gaze intent, warm.

Warmer than she'd seen before. Instead of making her uncomfortable, she wished they were alone. Still this bubble was intimate. The moment special. She gave him a slow smile. "For the moment. The work is interesting. Lots to learn and do, and I feel safe there."

"All good reasons."

"And, of course, I like the people." She batted her eyes at him playfully. "Some more than others."

OVER TWO HOURS later, Rhodes put down his empty coffee cup. "Let's go." He tapped his watch and said, "The DA's office will open soon. If we get there soon enough, maybe we can leave early. We could be home just after lunchtime."

That brought a smile to her face. He watched as she quickly packed up the little bit of material she had with her, drank the last of her coffee and stood up. "I'm leaving the laptop here while I go to the ladies' room."

He watched her go. That long, lean, gawky body had turned into a voluptuous woman with legs that seemed to never quit.

He wondered if Jarrod really did believe all of them were the *love 'em and leave 'em* types. Rhodes could understand the warning ten years ago, but it hardly applied now. Not with all his buddies getting hooked up, and those relationships made the place sound more like a love compound than an actual security one.

While he waited, he paid the bill. When she still didn't

return, he checked his watch and realized she'd been gone ten minutes. He frowned. That wasn't terribly outlandish, but if she wasn't back soon, he'd bust down that damn door and haul her out. He picked up the laptop and her notebook, pocketed the receipt from the register and made his way to the ladies' room. He knocked on the door and it pushed open easily. The room was empty, as were the four stalls.

He stepped back out again and searched the restaurant. Where the hell was she? He glanced at the window in time to see a small van leave the parking lot. Instantly he knew something was wrong. He bolted outside, checked the parking lot to make sure she wasn't waiting for him, raced to his vehicle, dropped the items inside and headed after the van. He jammed his phone onto the dashboard mount and called Levi. As soon as he came on, Rhodes said, "Sienna's gone missing."

He explained what happened and that he was chasing a white van but had no way to know if it had anything to do with her disappearance.

"Did you check the other washroom? Did you check everyone in the restaurant?" Ice asked. "If the place was busy, she could have used the men's room."

"The restaurant barely had a few people, and all the stalls were completely empty. Something's happened to her."

He knew it inside. His gut clenched. He unlocked his hands from gripping the steering wheel, his knuckles still white. Up ahead he could see the van as it went through several lights. Not giving a shit about the traffic speed, he gave the truck more gas and pulled up as close as he could to the van.

As if suddenly realizing they were being followed, the

van's driver crossed three lanes of traffic and took a left on the next street. It also went through a red light, leaving Rhodes in the middle of the intersection until the cross-traffic passed.

He quickly followed and turned down yet another street. No sign of the van. He drove slowly up and down it, then backtracked, looking for an alleyway, a garage, or something. Only two of the houses had a garage. He went around the back of the place but found nowhere for the van to hide.

Around the front again, he caught sight of one young guy standing outside on the front step. That could easily be him. As Rhodes passed the second house with a garage, he watched a woman and children walk out the front door. Immediately he made a U-turn and headed back to the first house. The man was no longer outside.

Rhodes parked in the driveway so they couldn't leave. He sent Levi a text with an update. He made it look as if he was heading around the back of the house. Instead he backtracked and snuck inside the garage via the side door.

Bingo. There was the van. He opened the doors, looking for any proof Sienna had actually been inside. The last thing he wanted was to barge into a house and terrorize a family who had nothing to do with her kidnapping.

Unfortunately the van offered nothing helpful.

At the back door, he peered through the window but found no sign of anybody inside. There had been a guy on the front step, but Rhodes didn't know where he'd gone. Rhodes opened the house door quietly and slipped inside. Stairs to the second story were right in front of him. With a quick glance around the stairwell, not seeing anyone there, he crept up the stairs.

He checked all the bedrooms, and in the last one he

found Sienna tossed onto a bed. Her mouth was taped; her hands and feet tied. She appeared to be unconscious. Still no sign of the person, or persons, who had taken her. Hearing a sound below him, he quickly hid in the closet.

Two voices traveled up the stairs. "Are you sure we should've taken her?"

"We didn't have much choice. They were heading back to the DA's office. You heard them."

Rhodes frowned. That meant whoever had taken her had been in that restaurant with them. A couple young punks sat two tables over, but he hadn't paid them any mind as they'd been sitting there drinking coffee and playing games on their cell phones. They hadn't shown any interest in her or him. Apparently he'd been wrong. They seemed to know exactly what Rhodes and Sienna's plans were.

"I still don't understand what difference it makes."

"They're afraid that whatever paperwork she has will implicate one of the bosses," the other replied.

"So why didn't we just steal the boxes?"

"Don't be daft. Everything's digital nowadays."

"And so what the hell difference does it make if we have her or not?"

"Leverage."

"Oh."

Rhodes watched through the slats of the closet door as two men walked over to Sienna. "Wake up, bitch."

Sienna didn't make a sound. The same guy hauled his arm back and smacked her across the face. Her head snapped from one side to the other and then rolled gently until it came to a stop. She never made a sound.

"How hard did you hit her?"

Inside Rhodes's anger built. They'd knocked her out,

and now they couldn't even wake her up? As soon as he got her out of here, she was heading straight to the hospital. No matter what she said.

"I didn't touch her. It's not my fault when I grabbed her that she slammed her head against the window. It made her easy to deal with though." The two guys backed up slightly. "You think we should tell anybody?"

"Hell, no. Let's not bring that type of trouble down on our heads just yet."

The two young men walked out of the bedroom when one of their phones rang. "It's the boss," said the kid.

Staring through the slats, Rhodes saw the kid on the phone wore a red shirt and the other a light gray hoodie. Honestly they looked so similar they could be brothers. They were both about five foot ten, skinny, with jeans that barely hung on their hips. Rhodes shook his head. What the hell had he and Sienna stumbled into?

The one in red spoke into the phone. "No, we've got her." He glanced over at his cohort and held up his hand. They high-fived each other. "No problem. We'll take her to the rendezvous point." He looked at his partner as his grin widened. "Sure, no problem."

He clicked his phone off. "We're supposed to take her down to the warehouse."

"Oh, shit. We just hauled her ass up here. Why didn't he call a few minutes earlier, and we could have just kept on driving," the hoodie guy said in disgust.

"Doesn't really matter. What the boss says, we do."

The hoodie guy looked over at the bed and said, "Shit."

Rhodes knew that carrying her upstairs had not been easy for these two scrawny teenagers. He watched as they walked over and manhandled Sienna off the bed to the floor, repositioned their hands and picked her up, slowly carrying her down the stairs.

Rhodes stepped out of the closet and waited until they went around the corner. They'd learn soon enough they couldn't leave without his vehicle being moved. As the guys went to the garage, Rhodes headed out the front door. He called Levi and the cops. He waited until the two had her at the back of the van inside the garage and followed. As soon as they lowered her to the ground, he took out the first one with a headlock. Only there was a brittle snap, and the kid went limp. Checking that he was unconscious, Rhodes dropped him to the floor. The second guy looked at Rhodes in shock.

"Who are you? Where did you come from?" His gaze landed on his partner on the floor, and he screamed. "Oh, my God! Did you kill Joe?"

Rhodes grabbed the kid and slammed him against the van, his arms pinned behind him and his head flattened against the side of the vehicle. "Maybe. Not that I planned it that way. What the hell did you expect when you kidnapped someone? A slap on your wrist?"

The kid started to cry. "You killed my brother."

He struggled in Rhodes's arms, but he seriously had no freedom to move and even less strength. No wonder it had taken the two of them to pick up Sienna.

Rhodes again slammed the kid against the van. "And you'll get the same treatment if you don't shut up."

The kid subsided. Rhodes glared at him as he pulled cuffs from his back pocket and quickly clipped the kid's wrists together. "*Jesus.* Kidnapping is a federal offense. Did you really think you would get away unscathed?"

"We weren't really kidnapping her," the kid said. "The

boss just asked us to bring her down, and she didn't want to go."

"Hence the term *kidnapping*, when you pick up people against their will. You've tied her up, knocked her unconscious, and hauled her out of that restaurant into your vehicle. Where the hell do you think you are going from there? I believe it's jail. If you live that long."

The guy's eyes widened as he stared at Rhodes in horror. "Oh, no, no, no, no, no. No jail for me. I won't survive it."

Rhodes could believe that. "The only way you might cut some of that jail time short, or get into an easier one, is if you cooperate fully."

Immediately the color drained from the kid's face. "You might put me in jail," he said, "but the boss'll kill me if I tell you anything." At the sound of sirens he trembled. "Oh, my God! I'm so in trouble."

"You'll be in even more when the boss finds out you've been picked up by the cops because he'll assume you turned on him. Your life is now forfeited anyway."

He stared at Rhodes, the horror in his eyes turning them almost black. "You don't understand these people. They have very long arms. They can also kill me in jail."

"Welcome to the criminal world," Rhodes snapped. Shoving the kid ahead of him, he quickly hit the button to open the double doors of the garage. And that's when the kid saw Rhodes's truck. "You were already on to us. You followed us from the restaurant?"

"Yes." Rhodes nodded. "I certainly did."

Two black-and-white police cars pulled up behind his truck. Rhodes quickly pulled out his ID and hauled the kid over to one of the men. But he didn't let him go.

An ambulance pulled up a few minutes later. He waited

until Sienna was checked over, then her still form loaded into the ambulance. He hated to leave her, but he also couldn't trust the cops. Before they could take possession of the prisoner, he phoned the DA's office and talked to Robert.

After that, things moved at a slightly different pace. Another vehicle arrived, and the DA himself got out. He took one look at the kid and said, "Take him in for questioning. Rhodes, I suggest you come with us." He glanced at the ambulance, now heading off down the street. "Will she be okay?"

"As for these assholes, he's the one who knocked her out," Rhodes said bitterly. "If you could just leave me alone with him for a few minutes …"

The kid screamed, "He killed my brother. You can't let him anywhere near me."

The DA looked at Rhodes.

He shrugged. "I didn't kill him. Just rendered him unconscious."

The kid stopped and stared at him. "You told me that you killed him."

Rhodes smiled. "I lied."

He got into his vehicle and followed close behind the DA and his prisoner. No way was he letting this kid out of his sight. The DA seemed to understand. They drove to the police station and very quickly were in an interrogation room.

The DA said, "We must handle this officially."

Rhodes nodded. "I agree with that. But I need to know who the hell is after Sienna to put a stop to this fast. Get me a name. I'll take care of the rest." His voice was hard, his glare bitter. He wasn't letting up until he had that name.

Sienna had gone missing on his watch, and he'd never forgive himself for that.

Only the kid didn't want to talk. Between the cops and the DA, he just sat there and glared at them. In frustration, the three law enforcement officers got up and walked out.

Rhodes had been watching from the observation window. He said in a low voice, "Let me talk to him."

The officers immediately protested. Robert smiled and said, "You could scare anybody. Go ahead. You got five minutes. But remember, the entire thing is recorded, so stay on this side of the line. We can't have this case fall apart."

Rhodes walked in and headed straight for the kid.

The kid shrieked, jumped up from the chair and ran to the back of the room. "You can't touch me. The cops will keep me safe."

"The cops might, but only long enough to get the information we want. I already put word on the street you're talking."

"But I haven't said anything," he cried out in protest. "You can't lie like that."

"What universe do you live in, kid? Do you think this is some punk-ass game you played in high school? People are dying here. And you'll be one of them if you don't smarten up."

And suddenly the kid realized he really was in trouble. "You don't understand. If they think I'm tattling, they could kill me."

"And *you* don't understand. The minute you were picked up by the cops, they assumed you *were*, so you're dead anyway. You and your brother, Joe."

The kid walked over to the chair and slowly sank back down. "Oh, my God," he said. "You're right. I have no way out of this."

"Only one—cooperate fully with the cops. With any luck you and your brother will get a lighter sentence, and you might actually still have a life after this. If you don't, well, no promises."

Rhodes turned and walked out, slamming the door behind him. As he left, the kid yelled, "Wait, wait. I want to talk."

He nodded to the cops. "That's your cue." He stormed over to the side window and glared out at the morning sun. He still wanted to wring the little chickenshit's neck.

The DA said, "A little brutal but effective."

That startled a laugh from Rhodes. "Yeah, that's me, right down the line." He turned to study the man they'd come to help. "The files and your laptop are in my truck. I'll get them for you, and then I want to know who ordered the attack on Sienna."

One of the cops came out and walked over to them. "He wants to make a deal."

The DA said, "That's my cue." He turned back to Rhodes. "If you'll bring in those materials, that'd be great. I presume you're heading to the hospital right now?"

Rhodes nodded. "Until we pick up whoever it is that ordered the kidnapping, she's not safe. Not even there."

As the DA walked in to make a deal with the punk kid, Rhodes raced to his truck, pulled out the box of information the DA had given him and carried it to the observation room. As he entered the outer room again, the DA was talking with the police officers.

The DA took one look at the box and smiled. "Okay, we got names and addresses. We're putting together a tactical team to go after them." He hesitated and said, "I know you'd like to, but I can't have you take part in that."

"Damn." He shrugged. "You do your thing. I'll go to the hospital and protect Sienna. I let that asshole get at her once. Can't let that happen a second time."

"You're not responsible for this," the DA called as Rhodes headed to his truck.

"I'm not, but I am." And Rhodes thought, *That's just the way life is.*

Chapter 9

SHE WISHED TO hell the noise—moaning—would shut up. It was really giving her a headache. She shuddered and tugged the blankets higher up on her shoulders. She had no idea where she was, but everything hurt.

"Sienna?"

A gentle finger stroked across her cheek. She struggled to open her eyes. When she finally did, everything was blurry. But the moaning had stopped. Thank God for that.

As she stared ahead, a fuzzy rendition of Rhodes's face came into view. A second later, she could actually see him clearly.

"Hey." He leaned over and kissed her very gently on the temple.

Her eyelids fluttered closed. "What … happened?"

"You went to the washroom in the restaurant and met up with two punks who tried to persuade you to go with them." His tone was dry. He gingerly sat on the edge of the bed and reached down to gently cradle her hands in his.

She stared at him in surprise as the memories tumbled in and around each other. "One wore a hoodie and the other had a red T-shirt on."

He nodded. "Brothers. Just young kids. They were ordered to pick you up, if they got a chance, and they took it at the restaurant."

"And, of course, you rescued me, right?" She gave him a knowing smile. And she was very grateful to have missed the whole damn thing.

"It took me a few minutes," he said gravely. "I saw them take off and gave chase. But I couldn't guarantee you were inside the van. I found it in a garage at somebody's house. When I got inside, you were upstairs tied up on a bed."

She stared at him in shock. "I don't remember any of that."

He bent down and kissed her on the nose. "Good. Another set of nightmares you won't have to worry about."

She rolled over and tried to sit up, crying out in pain. Her hand instinctively went to her head. "Did they hit me over the head or something?" She groaned and realized that the moaning she'd heard earlier was probably coming from her. How embarrassing was that?

Using his strong arms, he slowly propped her up against the pillows. She felt slightly better, but it took a moment for the booming in her head to stop. "Did you catch them?"

He gave a half snort.

She smiled with her eyes closed. "Of course you did." No question about it. She was here with him.

"I captured them. The second I did, I got the police and DA involved. Robert was there when they collected them, to make sure we didn't lose them to a crooked cop, and now they're cutting a deal with him."

"That's actually the best thing we could've hoped for," she said with a smile. "Does that mean we can go home now?" She tried not to whine, but she didn't want to stay. "I really don't want to spend another night in a hotel, worrying someone is breaking in."

"Since you're awake, we won't have to check you into

the hospital, I hope. You're still in the emergency room. As soon as the doctor clears you, I'll take you to the station to give a statement. Then we can leave."

Her shoulders sagged a bit. "That sounds horrible. I was thinking maybe you could just pick me up, put me in the truck and drive me home." Her eyelids slowly lowered again at the thought of all that extra movement. "Everything hurts."

"The kid says he didn't hit you, that you slammed into the window. You were probably fighting them."

"If I did, I must have taken the damn window latch to my brain," she muttered. "I didn't even have much time to react. It just seems like my world went black right away. And if they knocked me out, why the hell does everything hurt?"

He grinned. "You really won't like this part."

When he didn't continue speaking, she finally rolled her head slightly to look into his eyes. "What part?"

"They were both very skinny teenagers, not a pound of muscle between them. They had difficulty lifting you."

She stared at him in outrage.

He laughed. "So I am pretty damn sure they must've dropped you on your butt to shift their grip many times. I was there as they tried to carry you from the bedroom and down the stairs. They might've bumped a few body parts going around corners too." He chuckled. "And before you ask, I had no opportunity to get you away from them without putting you in more danger. The last thing I wanted to do was take them out and have you roll down the stairs and break your neck."

She gave a tiny shrug. "I can understand that but damn …"

He laughed, bent down and kissed her. This time on the

lips. "I'm just so damn glad to see you alive and well," he said cheerfully. "Although I probably shouldn't kiss you with you being Jarrod's sister."

"Would you stop always shoving Jarrod into my face?" she snapped. "He's not here, and he's got nothing to do with us."

"Are you sure?" He stared at her with a steady gaze. "He's your big brother, and he cares about you."

"And you're his friend, and you care about me too." She smiled. "You just won't admit it."

His eyebrows rose at her words. "Of course I do. You're Jarrod's sister."

He had turned the tables on her very neatly. She glared at him. "Is that all I am to you?"

He frowned, his gaze dropping away.

"Right. I'm not. So drop the excuse. My brother isn't here, and he's not my guardian. I'm an adult. I can do what I want with whom I want."

"And what is it you want to do?" he asked, lowering his head to kiss her again.

"Right now I want to feel better." When she could, she whispered, "And that means getting the doctor to give me permission to leave, getting to the goddamn police station, giving my statement and going home."

She shoved the blankets back and slid her feet to the floor. With more bravado than strength, she stood up and clung to the bed rail. "But first I have to make it to the bathroom."

Instantly he was at her side, holding out a hand. Grudgingly she accepted it, and using him as a crutch, made her way to the bathroom. At the doorway, he stopped and raised an eyebrow, looking down at her. She shook her head ever-so-slightly.

Even that little bit of movement made her wince. "I'll be fine."

"You'd be 'fine' even if you're not because no way in hell would you ask for help, right?"

"Right." And she shut the door in his face.

"STUBBORN," HE SNAPPED.

From the other side of the door came her response, "Yep, get used to it."

He shook his head. "No way to get used to that," he called back. He could hear the muffled snort from the inside of the bathroom, and grinned.

He pulled out his phone to check for messages, wondering if he should say anything to Jarrod about his sister being attacked. But Jarrod was on a mission, out of touch. Still, if Jarrod did get it, that would be fine. At least he'd be in the loop. Making a sudden decision he pulled up his buddy's number and sent him a text.

Sister was attacked. She's okay. We're on it.

Instantly a response came flying back.

WTF? Make sure you get the asshole.

Rhodes laughed.

I already did. At least two of them.

Is she really okay? Are you standing guard? I know how much she means to you. It was impossible to miss.

checked that her wallet and its contents were there and slung the whole thing over her shoulder, brushing her hair quickly, which just snagged on the dried blood there. "Let's go." And she walked past him out to the reception area.

There she handed over her insurance card and waited while the paperwork was completed. When she turned around, paperwork and receipts in hand, he held out his, offering support. Instead of putting her arm through his, she slipped her hand into his and laced their fingers.

"Can we go home now?"

"Police station first if you're up to it."

She nodded. "Make it fast."

It was fast but still took over an hour. As he helped her back to the truck, he found the DA's laptop he'd stashed there the night before. Shit. "Robert, she's out of the hospital but pretty woozy. And I found your laptop in the truck. I missed it earlier."

"Can you bring it back before you leave?"

"Yes, we can do that much." He walked around, got in the driver's side and started the engine. "The DA wants me to drop off their laptop. Then we're free to go."

"Perfect." And as if washing her hands of the whole issue, she curled up in the far side and laid her head against the glass. Then she closed her eyes.

He wanted to rush back to the hospital. He understood her point about not staying there, but she didn't look like she was strong enough to have left either. The walk outside had been enough to finish her. "You want to stay in town or are you up for the long drive home?"

"I'll sleep along the way," she said. "That's exactly what I need right now."

It was pretty hard to argue with that. He pulled in the

front of the DA's building and said, "I don't want to leave you out here alone."

She opened her eyes and turned to look at the building, then over at him. With a heavy sigh she nodded. "No, I can't say I want to be alone either right now. But getting up there to the DA's office, … well, that's looking like a little bit too much work."

But she opened the door and slowly got out. He opened the extended cab, pulled out the laptop, then locked the doors. He stepped beside her and said, "Grab my arm. We'll take the elevator straight up."

They walked inside and headed for the elevator. By the time they got to the DA's office, she was looking a little on the weaker side yet again. But as soon as they walked in the office and people stared at her, her back stiffened, and her grip on his arm tightened. She had grit. He loved that.

Robert rushed over. "How are you feeling? I am so sorry we got you involved in this."

"It wasn't exactly the highlight of my day," she said with a wan smile. "But you couldn't have known they would come after me either."

They walked into the office where Rhodes set down the laptop near the box of documents. "Everything she found is still there, and of course, traceable. And the paperwork I delivered earlier."

The DA shook their hands and said, "Much appreciated. I'm so sorry about what happened though." He offered them a chair. "Do you want a quick cup of coffee? Can I get you anything?"

He was going to refuse but Sienna said, "A cup of coffee would be nice."

He looked at her and saw she was determined to make

this as normal a visit as possible. Besides, the caffeine would be good. Neither of them had had a cup in the last few hours.

The DA spoke to somebody just outside the room. He directed them to the chairs in the boardroom around the long table. They discussed the case for several minutes over coffee.

"With the information we have from the young kidnappers, we can trace the people who hired them." He was effusive in his thanks. "I'm just so sorry this has come at the price it has."

Silently Rhodes agreed. But sometimes shit happened. What could you do but reach for the toilet paper?

Chapter 10

AS MUCH AS she hated to admit it, she was feeling the effects of her kidnapping. She didn't know how long she'd been in the hospital, but when she checked the time and saw it was almost four o'clock in the afternoon, she realized just how much longer the day would still get.

But she'd been honest when she said she was likely to sleep most of the way. She was also getting hungry. Maybe that was a good sign. Although she was afraid if she ate anything, it would come right back up.

They had a second cup of coffee and continued going over some of the information they found. She also learned the kids who kidnapped her had made a deal with the DA. She didn't have a problem with that. She was more concerned about getting the people above them. What she didn't want was to have anybody coming after her again.

It was thirty minutes in when the DA stood up and said, "We're very grateful to you, Sienna. I'll let you be on your way. The office is closing in a few minutes too."

An alarm ripped through the building.

She quickly put her cup down and stood. Her hand went to her head as the sudden movement brought on the pounding inside again. "What the hell is that?" she asked. She reached out for Rhodes immediately and found his arm wrapping around her, holding her close.

He looked at the DA and said in a hard voice, "What does the alarm mean?"

The DA's expression showed shock, bewilderment. "I don't think I've ever heard it before, but it's a lockdown."

"Lockdown?" she asked in a faint voice. "As in we can't leave?"

He nodded. His hand immediately went to the phone. Picking it up, he put in a call to security. There was a short exchange. "Security said they've had a viable threat called in from one of the other offices. They apologize, but lockdown mode is necessary until I can verify what's happening."

"Wouldn't it be better if we were all allowed to leave first?" she asked. The last place she wanted to be was here.

But Rhodes made it very clear. "The only reason they wouldn't let us leave is if they're afraid this person would escape with the crowd." His voice fell off as he considered the implication. He looked at the DA, then back outside. "Call security back and see if this person is holding anybody hostage in the building."

The DA immediately picked up the phone again and called security. "This is the DA. I want more details. Specifically, I want to know exactly what the threat is right now."

He stood rigid; his voice never changed, but his gaze immediately zinged to Rhodes. "One gunman or two?"

After a few more harsh words, he hung up the phone. "Two gunmen were seen on the floor below us. Security was called by somebody who saw them on the elevator. The lower three floors have been emptied of employees. Only our security guards are left. We're on the fifth floor. The gunmen were seen on the fourth. No sign of them now. Plus, there's been no contact with or from them."

Sienna slowly sat back down. "Is it me they're after?" She waved her hand at the box of materials on the table. "Or the information you have?"

"Both prisoners, the kids, were taken downtown to lockup earlier. They left maybe an hour ago. But we did it on the sly. Just in case …" the DA said. "If that's who they're after, they are out of luck. If, however, they are after me, or even you two, … then it's not so good for us."

She glanced at Rhodes. "Are you armed?"

He shook his head. "I have weapons locked in the truck."

"He wouldn't have been allowed to bring them into the building," Robert said. "Our security system wouldn't let him pass through the metal detector if he'd been armed."

"Well, it didn't work then, did it?" she snapped. "Apparently we have two gunmen inside downstairs, while the good guys aren't allowed to carry weapons to defend themselves." She leaned her head back and rubbed her face gently. "I knew we shouldn't have come inside."

There wasn't much anybody could say to her. Rhodes reached his hand down and grasped hers. "It'll be fine."

She opened her eyes and stared at him. "How the hell can you say that?"

"Because I'm getting you out of here." He looked at the DA. "Both of you, you're targets." He glanced at the box of paperwork and laptop. "Do you have a place to lock that up safely?"

Robert hopped to his feet, walked to the side filing cabinets and opened the bottom one. They put the laptop in and pulled the paper out of the box, filling the drawer. He locked it up, pocketed the keys and left the empty box with the lid on the table.

With Rhodes ushering them both toward the door, they quickly moved through the series of offices.

Sienna glanced around as she walked. "It looks like most of the people have left already."

"The offices closed a few minutes ago."

"So maybe the gunmen wanted that to be the case."

They shouldn't have stayed for coffee.

Still, it was too damn late. Like so much of her life. She couldn't believe she was in this situation. Talk about going from shit to shit. Still, she trusted Rhodes. He'd saved her once; she figured he'd do it again.

Although that was a lot of pressure to put on one man. And no matter how good anybody was at any point in time, everyone's luck ran out sometime.

THIS WAS NOT the end of the day he'd planned. It wasn't even the afternoon he'd hoped for. They should've just left. In fact, she should've stayed in the vehicle and he could've come back down after delivering the box. But the world was full of *should haves*. Now they were stuck in the building with gunmen. And no way in hell those men weren't after either Sienna, Robert, or both.

He wished he had his weapons though. He'd already have these two gunmen taken out. And Sienna's safety was primary. He needed a weapon, which meant he had to take one off the gunmen. He opened the door to the hallway, calling back to Robert in a low whisper, "How many exits are there?"

"There's the stairs and a service elevator. Plus, the three main ones."

"Where's the service one?"

"We can't access it from here. Have to go to the floor below. This was an add-on to be a rooftop deck and God only knows, a garden, I guess. They decided to close it in for offices. So the service elevator only goes to the fourth."

Rhodes turned and looked at him. "We have to take the stairs or the elevator down one floor so we can grab the service one?"

Robert nodded.

That was the stupidest of all stupid ideas. But Rhodes had certainly heard a lot worse. Development projects had construction issues, all covered up in a pretty layer of drywall and paint.

"Is it safe to leave?" Sienna asked behind him.

"The one thing you can count on is if they're looking for you, they'll go room by room. If we stay here, they would eventually find us."

"I vote for escape," Robert said.

"I do too." Sienna added, "I have no intention of sitting here like livestock going to the slaughter. If they want a piece of me, then they'll have to fight for it."

As much as he liked her attitude, she didn't have enough in her right now to make good on any threat.

"If there's only two, they can't cover all the elevators and stairs. If we get a chance to see just one, I'll take him out and grab his weapon. That'll even the odds somewhat. The intention is to take the stairs down as far as we can go. You ready?" He turned and looked at both of them. When he got a nod from each, he opened the door to the hall wider and slipped out. Quietly he motioned to the stairwell to the left. He raced toward it and pushed open the door. They were right behind him.

No sound came from below. He was taking a risk, but

they had very few options. Moving as silently as they could, the three made it down one set of stairs. Still nobody. Rather than trying for an elevator, considering that Sienna was still strong enough to keep going down the other three flights, he moved them forward, and on they went down to the third, the second, and the first.

Something inside him said it was way too damn easy. At the main floor, he paused and looked through the glass window in the door, where he saw one of the security guards holding a weapon on the rest, who would normally be the last to leave after completing a full sweep of the building.

Shit. This was an inside job. Robert caught a glance at what was outside the window too. His gaze widened, and he shook his head. Rhodes immediately placed his finger to his lips and motioned them to continue down to the parking garage level. They had to get somewhere they could hide.

At least in the garage there would be vehicles. There was only one more floor. He was careful as he peered through the door window. He couldn't see anybody. Taking a chance, he pulled it ajar slightly. No alarms went off.

He pulled it fully open and motioned the other two out ahead of him. They immediately raced to the first vehicle and crouched down beside it. He didn't see anyone standing guard, so he joined them. He didn't know how the underground system here worked, but there must be some kind of a gate to enter and exit through. But they had to get there first. In the background, he heard something that made his blood chill.

"Did that door just open?" someone yelled too damn close by.

From the opposite side, on his right, came the answer.

"I didn't see anybody come out."

From the left again came someone speaking. "You're supposed to stand there, keeping an eye out, making sure nobody escaped."

"I was, remember? Then he sent me over to check out the ramp. Make sure nobody walked in or out." The man's voice was frustrated. "I can't watch everything. What the hell are you doing?"

There was only silence to Rhodes's left.

And Rhodes knew the man was on the move. He motioned for the others to stay low against the vehicle. He peered around the back of the car, his ear cocked, listening hard. He could hear footsteps approaching. Desperate to keep the gunman away from Sienna and Robert, he raced around the car to intercept him.

"What the—"

One solid blow to the throat and the gunman crumpled to his knees. Rhodes caught him as he pitched forward and slowly lowered the man to the ground. Rhodes pulled the semiautomatic weapon off his shoulder and slipped it over his own.

He crept forward to the front of the car and around to squat quietly beside Robert and Sienna.

"Hey, Jimmy, is that you?"

Damn. Rhodes had hoped for a minute's window before the other guy realized his buddy was not answering. Still, Rhodes had a weapon now.

At the sound of running footsteps, he huddled at the front of the vehicle and waited. If he could take out both these assholes, that would give the SWAT team a chance to come in. They needed a clear entrance into the building.

He could see Robert had his phone out, sending a text, alerting the police probably. That was all fine and dandy, but

Rhodes wanted these two out of here before the bloodshed started.

"Jimmy?"

Silence.

Rhodes's muscles tensed as he waited. The second gunman's footsteps slowed, and Rhodes heard the shifting of the weapon in his hands. But he no longer called for his friend. Rhodes heard the gunman's footsteps coming closer, and he counted them off in his head. Three. Two. One. He stood up and fired. One single shot. The second gunman dropped, his weapon banging to the ground.

Rhodes raced over and kicked the second weapon free. One bullet to the upper shoulder, but he was unconscious and bleeding heavily. He dragged the gunman over to join his buddy, then went back and picked up the second weapon. Using his shoulder as a harness, he threw it over his back and went around to Robert and Sienna.

"That's the two who were on guard down here," he said. "Come on. We'll head toward the ramp. With them down, that leaves law enforcement an avenue to get in."

He ushered them quickly through the rows of parked vehicles to the exit. Up ahead he could see one single bar across the road. At least there was no floor-to-ceiling gate at the entrance. They should be able to get out without any trouble.

He pulled them back just as they were about to walk up. "We have to be careful, in case a sniper is out there."

They both froze.

Sienna looked at him. "Is that likely?"

He shot her a look and said, "Would you have thought this building would've been taken over by gunmen? Was that likely?"

Robert made a single call. "We're free down in the parking garage. We've taken out two gunmen watching this entrance. We're standing by the ramp. Not sure if there's any snipers to stop our escape. Vehicles can come in here. It's clear." And he hung up.

Two minutes later a SWAT vehicle came ripping through to the underground parking level. Several men jumped out and raced toward them, weapons raised. Rhodes held up his hands. Robert stepped forward and quickly explained.

As much as he didn't want to, because they still weren't free and clear, Rhodes quickly gave up the confiscated weapons. They were ushered as a group outside to the street level. There they were quickly moved around to the corner of the block where the police had a control center set up.

Sienna clung to Rhodes's side. They were quickly checked over, and when he turned around, Robert was gone.

Realizing the SWAT focus would be on the building, he pulled Sienna farther back out of the way and said, "Feel like sneaking off and getting out of here?"

She looked up at him gratefully. "Can we?" She pointed at the front of the building. "Isn't that where you parked?"

He stared over at the vehicle, then at the surrounding chaos. He made a fast decision. "Stay here."

And he bolted for the truck.

Chapter 11

SHE WANTED TO call him back but knew it would be useless. He was already on the move. Besides, they needed the wheels. But she wasn't sure the law enforcement officers would let him grab the vehicle and go. They were likely to shoot him first and ask questions later. At times like this, it was just crazy out there.

Still, acting like a man who knew exactly what he was doing, he walked over and unlocked the truck, got in, started it up, pulled it forward and around the corner. Several policemen converged on him at that point. When he quickly explained who he was, they allowed him to pass. He pulled up beside her and opened the window. "Get in."

She didn't need a second urging. She raced around to the far side, opened the passenger door and got in. They were moving before she got the seat belt buckled. "Should we tell anyone we're going?"

"Send a text to Levi and tell him to inform Robert we're leaving. Or better yet"—he pulled out his phone and tossed it toward her—"find Robert's number under the contacts and send him a text."

She did as he said. The response came in very quickly. "He says, **Thanks for the update. And a bigger one for the rescue. I owe you.**" She laughed. "There's a lot worse things than having the DA owe you a favor."

She glanced around as he drove the small truck through the city streets. "Should we stay and give a statement?"

"Do you want to? I thought you wanted to get home."

"I want to get home and stay there," she corrected. "If we have to come back to give one, then there's no point in leaving just now." She sat there in frustration. "But then, this might not be settled for hours yet." She glanced at the time and added, "It's almost six o'clock. And we've already been there once today."

"We can go to the police station and do something about it right now if you want."

"It's an option."

She could see him wavering. Sure enough he turned the corner and then several more.

They pulled up outside the station. "Let's go in and take care of our citizens' duty," he said calmly. "After that, we're either grabbing dinner and a hotel, or we're going home. You decide."

Only it wasn't that easy. By the time they walked in and talked to someone, and that person realized they were actually in the building, part of the mess going on downtown, they were quickly ushered into a room and told to wait. Several people came in and asked questions; proof of identity was handed over. And then finally the same man they had spoken to earlier walked in and sat down.

"Rhodes, it's good to see you again." He reached over and shook hands. He turned his gaze to Sienna. "Now, young lady, why is it that you were likely to be one of the targets all over again?"

She glanced at Rhodes and then back to the big man. "Same reason as last time. I was helping the DA gather information for a case. Only I was kidnapped and just released from the hospital. We dropped off the DA's laptop I'd been working on. That's when we found out the building was taken over."

"You've just had a shitty day then, haven't you?"

She laughed. "That's one way to look at it." After that, she was asked a series of questions. She gave the details she could remember. Several times she just said, "You will have to ask the DA about that."

When she finally answered all his questions, he turned his attention to Rhodes. "Now, as I understand it, you have a very different take of what was going on. Let's go through it from the top."

Sienna collapsed back into her chair, tuning out most of the conversation going on around her. After all the questions, it was like the stuffing had been ripped out of her. She should've just stayed in the hospital. At least there she would be resting right now. She was feeling woozy again.

All she wanted to do was sleep. With her head pounding, body aching a whole lot more, she realized a hotel might be the better answer for tonight. It also looked like they weren't getting there any time soon. She glanced down at her watch and saw it was well past eight and she groaned.

She closed her eyes. Tried to silence her thoughts.

"We're leaving, now." Rhodes stood up. "She was only released from the hospital just before three and got involved in that downtown mess within the hour," he said to the detective. "I'll take her to a hotel, get her some food. She needs to lie down."

The detective stood up. "Please stay close. I don't know how quickly we'll get downtown wrapped up, but we'll probably have more questions for you. And I understand that your home is a few hours away. You don't want to come all the way back here to do this again." He glanced at Sienna, who was now shaky but standing valiantly and holding on to the table. "You need to rest."

She gave a half laugh. "I believe I have been trying to do that since I left the hospital."

Rhodes walked over and wrapped his arm around her shoulders. "If you have a card, I'll call you from whichever hotel we're at."

The detective immediately pulled one out of his wallet and handed it to him. "Just send me a text. Let's make sure you guys don't disappear off the grid for a third time."

Sienna stared at him in shock. "Please don't even joke about that." She moved toward the door, but it was suddenly looking very far away. Even with Rhodes's arm around her shoulders, she felt the room spin. "I …" she muttered. She stopped and grabbed the chair for support. She glanced over at Rhodes. "I'm sorry."

She registered his stare of surprise as her knees sagged.

He quickly swung her up in his arms and said, "That's it. Back to the hospital."

With the last of her strength she whispered, "No. No hospital. Just a hotel. Just let me have a bed so I can lie down."

WITH THE DETECTIVE walking alongside him, holding open the doors out to his truck, Rhodes carried Sienna carefully in his arms. "You sure you don't want to be taken to the hospital?"

The detective used Rhodes's keys and unlocked the door. "Head wounds are tricky."

Rhodes said, "Unfortunately, I know that all too well."

He carefully placed her in the seat and buckled her in. He turned and thanked the detective, accepting his keys back. He shut the passenger door and walked around to the driver's side. "I need a place where I can carry her into the room without raising alarms. Any ideas?"

"Several motels about four miles down the road. On the right."

"Good enough."

Rhodes hopped in and turned on the engine. Checking traffic, he pulled out and kept going down the same street. It was getting late, so darkness was falling. He didn't want to be anywhere close to the mess downtown. By now they should have all the gunmen secured, but he wouldn't count on it. Often they would just hold off, wait and see what the gunmen did. It depended whether they had a whole parcel of hostages or not. They didn't have Sienna or Robert now, and for that, he was glad for the decision to pull out.

Life didn't always work out that way.

There were several motels, just as the detective had described. Rhodes pulled into the parking lot of one and went to turn off the engine, but instinct prodded him.

What were the chances somebody might have overheard or that the detective wasn't on the up-and-up? Suspicious by nature, he couldn't quite leave it alone.

He pulled back out onto the main road and found another motel on the opposite side, about two blocks down. He pulled into that one. Leaving Sienna locked inside the vehicle, he walked in and booked a room on the main floor. With the key and receipt in hand, he drove around to the far side and parked outside the room with the coordinating number on the key.

"This is good," he muttered under his breath. "Now for

Sienna."

He got out of the truck and unlocked the room, then returned to carefully unbuckle her. He lifted her in his arms and carried her into the hotel room, laying her down on top of the king-size bed. There hadn't been any twin beds on the main floor, and he wanted to exit fast if they needed to. So one bed was what they had to share. With the shape she was in, she just needed to be comfortable.

Another trip out, and he brought in their luggage and the picnic basket. He quickly locked the truck and then the hotel door behind him. They needed food, or at least he did. She needed to sleep for as long as she could. But when she woke, she would be starving. There was still some of the traveling food from Alfred. But it was looking less than prime.

He opened the night table drawers for any brochures of fast food places close by. A pizza shop was across the street. If need be, he could make a quick phone call and have that delivered. He didn't care how close the place was, he wasn't leaving Sienna's side again tonight.

Chapter 12

SHE WOKE UP several times in the night, and each time she felt a strong hand reach out and stroke her arm. At one point, her arm was tucked under the covers, and the blanket pulled up to her neck. He still managed to find it with a reassuring pat.

"Just sleep. You're safe."

Realizing Rhodes was on watch, she tumbled back under.

When she woke the next morning, instead of feeling refreshed and wide awake, her body was heavy, resisting movement of any kind. It was the first full sleep she'd had since the kidnapping. And therefore, it was actually the day after the event, and everything hurt. She had to go to the bathroom in a big way, but just the thought of standing, let alone walking that far, made the throbbing pound even heavier and harder.

She rolled over slightly to see Rhodes sleeping atop the covers beside her. He was still fully dressed, in warrior mode just in case. A sleeping giant. But all alpha when awake. And she had to admit—she loved that. She lay there as long as she could before her need grew too intense to ignore.

She eased back the covers, slipped out from underneath them and straightened. She caught her breath, but she managed to get to the bathroom. She wished she had something for the pain. She didn't really want to take anything chemical, but holy crap, she hurt. After she used the bathroom, she eyed the shower and wondered. She wasn't sure she could stand long enough for that, but a soak would be lovely. She glanced back into the room to see Rhodes still napping.

Decision made, she filled the bathtub with hot water. Stripping off her clothes, she sank into the warm heat. And that's when she realized she had more than just bangs, bumps, and bruises. There were several scrapes. They stung as she eased into the tub, and it took several moments of biting her lip until she felt she would not cry out. Finally, she lay there totally submerged—the warmth washing over her, easing deep into her sore muscles. This was more like it. She hoped this would give her flexibility to move easier.

Using the soap available, she did a quick shampoo and rinse, being careful with her head wound. Dried blood remained in her hair, but she did her best to get most of it. She soaked as long as she thought she could, then pulled the plug. She stood, still a little wobbly, and grabbed a towel. Dry and wrapped up, she headed back into the main room. It didn't look like Rhodes had moved at all. She was sorry he'd had such a poor night looking after her. A good night's sleep was so necessary for healing.

Taking her bag off to the side, she lifted it onto a chair and selected some clean clothes. She managed to pull on her underwear and then dropped her towel and quickly dressed.

It was light outside, and she was very hungry. She walked back into the bathroom and hung up her towel. While in there, she brushed her teeth, and feeling ready to start the day, returned to the room and found Rhodes sitting up in bed, looking as alert as she'd ever seen him.

"I'm sorry. I hope I didn't wake you."

He bounced to his feet and said, "I've been awake. Just dozing off and on." He checked his watch, opened his phone and made a quick call.

Realizing it was business as usual, and hopeful maybe they could go home, she quickly repacked her bag and sat down on the bed to wait for him.

When he was done, he turned to her. "Robert wants to know if we can meet for breakfast."

"I presume you said yes"—she nodded at the phone in his hand—"especially as the phone call is already finished."

He laughed and took her gently in his arms. "I figured you didn't want to meet him. But if we have to eat breakfast anyway, might as well combine the two." He studied her critically, then kissed her gently on her temple. "You obviously had a good night. You're looking so much better."

"You are definitely right about not wanting to meet him. But if we can meet, eat, and then leave ..." She smiled. "It's the best of both worlds." She stopped and said, "I'm starved."

He shook his head as he reached for her bag. "You're just rushing me along so we can get to the food faster."

She grinned. He loaded the luggage in the truck, came back and went into the washroom. When he returned, he stopped in the doorway. "Ready?"

She nodded. "Absolutely."

They were fifteen minutes away from the restaurant where they had arranged to meet. As they walked in, they found Robert already in a booth by the window. He waved at them, and they sat down on the same side, facing him.

"Good morning, Sienna," Robert said in a low voice. "You're looking much better."

"Then it's a facade," she said with a half laugh. "I woke up this morning to find I had more muscles than I ever remembered feeling before, and every one was screaming."

He nodded in commiseration. "You went through a lot yesterday. Take several days off just to rest and relax."

"That's all I plan to do for the next three days. I'm hoping to go home and crash on my bed and just do nothing."

Robert turned his attention to Rhodes. "I wanted to thank you personally for getting me out of there yesterday." He nodded toward Sienna. "For getting us both out."

"Not an issue. I did what I could." Rhodes laced his fingers on the table in front of him. "How did the armed gunmen situation downtown end?"

"Unfortunately, all six are dead."

"Six?" Sienna shook her head. "I thought there were only two."

"Two on the garage level," Rhodes clarified. He turned to gaze back at Robert.

"Actually, four were in the main building. Plus, the two we encountered on the garage level."

"I didn't kill the men in the garage. I only knocked out one and shot the other in the shoulder."

"Then somebody came along and put a bullet in both their heads," Robert said.

Rhodes sat back. "Which means there was a seventh."

Robert nodded. "That's what we're thinking."

"Wouldn't that be too obvious?" Sienna asked. "Why would he have done that?"

"Dead men don't talk." Rhodes reached over and covered her hands with his.

She sighed and gently unlocked her hands from the fists they'd become and held on to his instead.

Just then a waitress walked by, holding a full pot of coffee. "May I offer you some?" she asked with a smile.

Gratefully, they pushed their cups toward her so she could fill them up.

When done, she motioned at the menus in front of them. "Are you ready to order breakfast?"

"Absolutely." Sienna hadn't even looked at the menu. "I'm starving."

"If you'd like our special, it's a big breakfast. Three eggs, sausage, bacon, ham, pancakes, hash browns, and toast."

"Sounds fantastic. I'll have that." She'd ordered a ton of carbs, but with her energy level right now, that was just what she needed.

"Make that two," Rhodes said. They handed the unopened menus back to the waitress as Robert ordered just coffee.

Feeling much better with coffee in her hand, a meal ordered and Rhodes at her side, Sienna sat back to wait. She just didn't know what she was waiting for.

SO THIS WASN'T just a social call, allowing Robert a chance to give thanks. Not that Rhodes wanted or needed any. And it wasn't exactly doing his job, but if he could help, then he would. He'd been capable of so much more, but he couldn't leave Sienna alone. She'd been through enough already. They'd gotten lucky. He knew that. That didn't mean he would be so lucky at the next encounter. And there would be one with the seventh man still free.

Had the killer seen them? Had he been in the garage level while they'd been there? If so, would he let them just walk away, somehow knowing they hadn't seen him?

He glanced at Sienna. If he brought it up, it was just one more thing for her to worry about. That wasn't exactly what he wanted. But sticking their heads in the sand wasn't an answer either.

Sienna stared right back at him. "Are you going to say it or am I?"

He raised one eyebrow at her.

She looked at Robert. "Chances are very good whoever killed the men in the garage to silence them also knows we escaped. I'm pretty sure his plan is that we don't live to talk about it either."

Instead of answering, Rhodes squeezed her fingers gently. He glanced back at Robert to see him staring at the two of them in surprise.

"Were there any surviving hostages?" Rhodes asked.

"Yes. Our security people all lived through this. Thankfully, the other employees and visitors left the building early on." He glanced back to Sienna. "As you see, the six gunmen didn't shoot anyone." Rhodes laughed. "So there's a good chance nobody's after us at all." But even he didn't sound convinced.

Sierra gave a half snort. "And if you believe that, I've got a bridge I want to sell you."

Rhodes didn't mention the two dead bodies he and Merk had found in the empty house that could possibly be somehow involved too. Probably killed by one or two of the dead gunmen. Just because they didn't kill anybody in the downtown Dallas hostage situation doesn't mean they haven't killed people elsewhere. "The seventh man could have seen all three of us together in the garage," Rhodes said calmly. He turned to look at Robert.

"It would be easy enough to see I was meeting with

you," Sienna snapped. Then she calmed down. "Look, I don't want this guy to come after me, but I'm not exactly comfortable thinking he'll forget about us either."

"He still would have to know who you are," Robert said. "Your names were kept out of the news release."

"Right." After that she didn't say anything else; just sat quietly.

Rhodes glanced back at Robert and said, "Are you planning on staying around? Do you have a bodyguard? Do you have a security detail just in case?"

"Actually, I ran that by the department, but they think the chance of this guy coming after me is pretty low."

"Of course they do. No budget money, I presume."

He nodded. "I see you're familiar with that department line."

The waitress returned with hefty platters of food, then refilled Robert's coffee cup. "I'll be back in a few minutes with your toast."

And she disappeared.

Sienna let the conversation drift around her as she began eating the food.

Rhodes was slower, taking his time. He contemplated how much danger they were actually in. The killer would likely already know who they were, and if not, it wouldn't be hard to find out. But Robert was more likely to be in danger.

The waitress returned with their toast and they nodded their thanks. They quietly ate for several long minutes.

"Do you have the identities of the dead gunmen?" Rhodes asked. "I'm presuming it's got something to do with the case Sienna was helping you with?"

"When I left last night, they were working on that. I haven't seen or heard the names yet. I can forward them to you when I do."

"That would be helpful. At least I can check them off my wanted list," Rhodes said drily. "Plus, it may lead us to the seventh man. What about the laptop being bugged?"

Robert shook his head. "According to Bobby, they couldn't find anything on it. Are you sure your results were right?"

Rhodes shrugged. "No. But are you sure no one in your office took the sheets out of the ledger? Same person could be bugging the equipment in your office."

"We'll open an investigation into the department, but as much as I could hope for answers, I doubt they'll come fast." He then gave them a sober smile. "We're on it."

That lightened the mood, and they finished the rest of the meal with other conversation. As he got up to leave, Robert collected the check and said, "I would like to have you come back to the office and give us a hand with this case, but I understand the need to go home and rest."

They shook hands, and then Rhodes led Sienna out to the truck. He stopped outside the restaurant to look around the area. He could sense nothing wrong.

In a way this was a whole new day. Sienna stepped up beside him, slipping her hand into his and said, "Are we good to go?"

"Yes, we are."

Chapter 13

SHE WANTED TO laugh and crow in delight as Rhodes finally pulled the truck into traffic and took the turn toward home. At the same time she didn't trust it. It was hard not to keep looking behind them to see if they were being followed. So she continued checking the side mirror on her side. But the farther they went, the more she relaxed. After they'd traveled for more than an hour, Rhodes turned to her and said, "Go ahead and have a nap if you want."

She shook her head. "Actually, I slept decently last night." She studied his face and said, "You're the one who didn't."

"I slept enough," he said. "This is an easy drive home."

"Good thing. I'm more than ready to be back there. I hope we don't have to return for court or anything else."

"There's no point. All those men are dead, and we've already given our statements."

"Do you think the killer will come after us, making sure nobody can talk?"

"Anything's possible." He glanced down at the fuel gauge. "We need some gas. I'll turn off at the next stop I see. But there has to be much more at stake to kill all his men. The DA will sort this out."

She nodded. Her bladder needed to be emptied again also. She'd had so much coffee at breakfast, she probably wouldn't need any more until tomorrow morning. Still, the comforting drink would be nice for the rest of the trip.

Up ahead was an off-ramp that headed to a truck stop. Rhodes quickly took the turn, and after driving around, he pulled up to a gas pump and turned off the engine.

She hopped out. "I'm going to find the ladies' room."

He nodded, busy putting his credit card into the machine, grabbing the pump.

She walked into the restaurant area and followed the signs to the washrooms. She was done a few minutes later but took the opportunity to brush her hair and wash her face again. Just being in the truck for that long was making her tired. She didn't want to sleep anymore.

She walked back outside to see Rhodes still filling up the truck and called over, "You want a coffee?"

"Sure."

She turned back into the restaurant and ordered two, and since they had fresh muffins on the counter, she picked up an assortment. They certainly wouldn't stop for another meal after that big breakfast, but having a muffin, you could never go wrong.

After paying for the food, she carried the tray of coffees and bag of muffins out to the truck. Several vehicles were leaving the parking lot, so she had to dodge them before she could cross to the truck. She stowed the cups inside where they were safe and secure. She saw no sign of Rhodes.

She closed the passenger door and walked around to the side. Rhodes had collapsed on the ground, his arms stretched above his head. She dropped to his side, crying out, "Rhodes, what happened?"

But he didn't answer. She shook him gently. He groaned and then opened his eyes to stare at her. Awareness filled his gaze. "Somebody hit me from behind," he said. "I was just putting the pump back, and somebody reached out with a pipe or something and smashed me in the head. I went down, but I don't think I lost consciousness." He slowly sat up.

"Did you see who it was?" she asked, hating to think they'd been followed this far. She bounded to her feet and turned to see if anybody was still around. But of course, they weren't. They would've taken off immediately. She'd seen dozens of vehicles leave.

As she looked back down at him, she found Rhodes standing again, holding on to the side of the truck for stability. Instantly, she wrapped her arms around him to help. He turned and leaned against the side panel, taking several deep breaths, his arm holding her close. "I didn't expect that."

"Neither of us did." She glanced around again, wondering if she should call for help, then realized that was foolish. She faced him. "You want to call the police?"

He snorted. "Hell, no. But you're driving." He pulled the keys from his pocket and handed them to her. Then he slowly, using the truck bed for support, walked around to the passenger side. After making sure he was settled, she opened the driver's side and hopped in, turning on the engine. "I have no problem getting us home," she said, "but I'm worried about your head."

"Don't worry about that. I'm pretty tough—hard to crack."

"Yeah, but the headache that comes afterward will just about kill you." She carefully drove out and took the ramp leading them back onto the main freeway. "You might as well relax and rest," she said. "We've got a couple hours to go." She couldn't stop herself from looking over at him in worry. "But please don't sleep. You're never supposed to after a head injury."

He shot her a look and said, "I won't, nor will I pass out. But until my blurry vision restabilizes, I'm not the one to be driving."

She winced at the thought. "How about you try to text Levi and tell him what happened. No way in hell this was an accident."

"Well, if it was deliberate, they did a poor job," he said, "because they left me alive, and that's always a mistake."

"Maybe they didn't have the right man."

"More than likely too many people were around, so he couldn't get you at that time." He pulled out his phone and sent off several texts, starting a flow of discussions as his phone buzzed and beeped multiple times during the next fifteen minutes. That was good. She wanted the whole damn team involved in this. Somebody had attacked one of their own, and that couldn't be allowed to happen.

She would get him home to the rest of the team so they could all help. This was so far beyond her. She didn't do trouble. She'd told them that already.

Driving carefully, she kept the truck moving steadily toward home. The last thing she wanted was another incident. But thankfully it was a straight and quiet drive—too quiet. She kept checking on Rhodes, but he looked awful, collapsed against the passenger door. By the time she took the turnoff and drove past the small town close to the compound, she could feel the tension keeping her body rigid. She was so damn sore now it was nearly impossible to drive. A headache was starting again, but as she glanced over at Rhodes, leaning back with his eyes closed, she knew she was better off than he was. As she pulled into the compound and parked, turning off the engine, she muttered, "Instead of the returning heroes, we're a sorry pair."

"We're fine. We survived. That's what we do."

She turned sideways to look at him. She was aware of the others coming out of the compound, racing toward them. "Is that really the bottom line here?"

He reached up with a hand and gently stroked her cheek. "There's no way I'd let anything happen to you," he whispered. "You'll be fine."

"Is that what you think this is all about?" She shook her head. "You're a fool."

"I promised your brother I'd look after you," he said, opening his door.

She froze. "I make those decisions myself. I understand wanting to keep an eye out to make sure I don't get hurt unnecessarily, but don't you dare sacrifice yourself to save me."

She opened her door and hopped out, finding Ice standing there. Her intense gaze searched Sienna from top to bottom.

"We'll unload the truck," Ice ordered. "You get your ass up to bed."

Sienna gave her a wan smile. "And here I thought I looked pretty good."

Ice snorted. "Move it."

"Only if you insist Rhodes goes to."

Ice gave a clipped nod. "That's exactly what'll happen."

Hoping Ice was serious and not willing to argue anymore, Sienna made her way to her suite. She sat on the bed, kicking off her shoes, when Levi came up, carrying her bags. Stopping in the doorway, he dropped them to the side, looking at her. "Will you be okay here alone?"

"I'll be fine," she whispered. "The drive back was pretty nerve-wracking. I kept worrying he was hurt more seriously than he was letting on."

"That's Rhodes. Hell, it's any of us in that same situation. We hate to be injured in the first place. We never admit to it being as bad as it is."

She stretched out on her bed and moaned as her head sank into the pillow. "You'd better check him over then because, as far as he's concerned, it's nothing. But I believe he was out cold for a few minutes."

"Will do." And he closed the door gently behind him.

That's the last thing she remembered as she closed her eyes and let the world disappear.

RHODES SAT DOWN at the kitchen table. As much as he wanted to crash, that wouldn't happen soon. A slew of communications continued since he'd arrived home. And he was feeling relatively fine. Not that Ice listened to him. She checked his head wound and clucked like a mother hen. Something he'd never heard from her before.

"You sure you didn't see anything?"

"You should ask Sienna that. She came around with coffees right after I hit the ground." He raised his gaze to look at Levi. "She might've seen the vehicle as it drove off."

"According to her, you were actually unconscious for a few moments," Levi said.

Rhodes frowned. "I don't think so. I could still hear the vehicles driving past."

"Any chance it was a punk just looking to steal your wallet?" Stone asked from Rhodes's side.

Rhodes shrugged. "You know how I feel about coincidence…"

"The same way we all do," Stone interrupted. "She's kidnapped. You both get caught up in a hostage situation. You take out two men in your bid to escape, and both are found with a bullet to the head, execution style, and the next morning you're attacked at a gas station as you leave town." Stone shook his head. "Sloppy."

"Exactly. And now we know for sure someone is after us. I did warn Robert that somebody would likely come after him, as it had been well-reported in the news how he had escaped the attack on the building. His office in particular."

"So somebody knew you two were there as well?"

"Anything's possible. SWAT and dozens of cops were around. Honestly, I didn't see anybody suspicious, but people could've talked, or placed bugs in the conference room or DA's office. Several of the hostages were released afterward. Maybe one of them said something. There should be cameras in the parking level."

"They were shot at," Ice said. "We'll find out."

As the conversation dwindled, Rhodes looked around at the rest of them. "If you guys don't mind, I'm going to crash." He stood up and walked to the doorway, his hand instinctively reaching out to grab on the frame. The room was circling around him.

He could hear the cries behind him. The next thing he knew, Stone had his arm wrapped around Rhodes's rib cage, supporting him.

"Easy does it, buddy. Let me give you a hand."

Muttering his thanks, and using Stone for support, they got into the elevator and went to the second floor. There Stone helped Rhodes into his suite. He made the last few steps to the bed and sank down into the waiting softness. He kicked off his shoes and stretched out, then said, "Turn out the light, will you? It's killing my eyes."

Instantly the room darkened. Stone stood at the open doorway, and Rhodes knew what the problem was. "I'll be fine. Come back and check on me in an hour if you want. I just need to rest." He rolled over to his side, punched the pillow under his head and closed his eyes.

He vaguely heard Stone's heavy footsteps as he walked away while hushed voices remained outside in the hall. That was fine with him. His friends had his back.

Chapter 14

SIENNA WOKE TO talking in the hallway. She froze, terror turning her blood cold until she identified Levi and Ice's very distinctive voices. She had yet to recognize everybody by just hearing them speak.

"He's still sleeping."

"Was he responding when you spoke to him?" Ice asked, the concern in her voice evident.

It took Sienna a few minutes to figure out they were talking about Rhodes. She sat up slowly, slipped on her shoes and walked out to the hallway. "How is he?"

Ice spun around, walked over immediately, her hand capturing Sienna's. "How are you feeling?"

Sienna smiled. "The sleep did me good. I feel much better. I'm worried about Rhodes. Should I have taken him to the hospital?" She clung to Ice's hand. "He was pretty resistant to the idea of going anywhere but home. I suggested we call the police, but he didn't like that either."

"No, there was no point in this instance," Ice said. "He's got a concussion, so we just wanted to keep an eye on him."

"Is somebody standing watch over him all the time?" Sienna frowned as she walked toward his door. She knew Rhodes slept solid. "I'd like to stay with him if that's possible." She turned to look at Ice.

"We're all checking on him pretty closely. Nobody needs

to be here full time." As if seeing something in Sienna's face, Ice rushed to say, "If you want to stay for a while, that'd be okay. You can let me know if his condition changes."

Sienna nodded. "I'll do that." She looked around and said, "I'll grab my laptop and a cup of coffee then sit with him for a while."

"I'm heading to the kitchen, so I'll bring you a cup. Get your laptop or whatever you need. I'll meet you back here." Ice turned and left with Levi.

Sienna returned to her suite, right next door, grabbed her sweater to ward off the chill she still felt and pulled out her laptop. She wasn't useless here. Robert was supposed to send the names of the men who had been killed in the hostage situation. And right now she really wanted to know if those names matched up with any of the ones she'd found. She grabbed a power charger and headed over to Rhodes's suite.

It took a lot of effort, but she moved the big chair closer to the bed so she could sit down and put her feet up, then she plugged in the laptop and turned it on. When Ice came in, Sienna was already researching the news articles to see what coverage there had been regarding the attack on the DA's office.

She smiled up at Ice and said, "Thank you." She nodded at her laptop. "Did Robert send you the names of the dead gunmen?"

"I believe he sent them to Levi." Ice put the cup of coffee on the night table beside Rhodes's bed. In a low voice she whispered, "Why?"

"I want to check their names against the spreadsheets."

"Good idea. I'll email them to you." With one last glance at the two of them, she backed out of the bedroom, disappearing around the corner.

Sienna opened her email program, and within minutes she had an incoming one from Ice. Sienna clicked on it, bringing up the names. She glanced through them, but they meant nothing to her. She popped each name separately into Google to see what kind of history would come up. Then she copied them over to her notes on the case and searched the spreadsheets she'd created.

And came up with nothing.

Damn it. She'd been so sure something was here. Some way she could make sense of all this.

So far she drew a blank. But she wasn't ready to give up.

An hour later she wasn't getting anywhere. Except tired. She closed the laptop, slipped down in the chair and closed her eyes.

A gentle touch on her foot woke her up a few minutes later. She glanced over at the bed to see Rhodes there, a smile on his face, his hand around her foot. She gave him a lazy grin and asked, "Is this how you spend your days, just lazing about in bed?"

"Well, I would if you joined me," he said lightly. "That sounds like fun."

He stroked her calf. But she didn't want to let him know how his words affected her. She gave him a light sneer and said, "You think too much of yourself if you believe you can keep it up for days."

With a glint in his eyes he turned his gaze to hers. "Is that a challenge?"

She laughed. "It so isn't."

He propped himself up on his bed, his fingers lightly drawing a pattern on her foot, around her ankle and slowly up her calf. "Anytime you want, … sweetheart."

"Yeah, what about Jarrod?" she reminded him. Her gaze was sharp as she studied his face, looking for any sign of change.

But there was none. Jarrod's name didn't appear to make any difference to Rhodes.

"If and when we have a relationship, your brother will accept it," he said. "Trust me."

She opened her eyes wide and stared at him again. "Okay, if you say so." She dropped her feet to the floor and stood up. "I'll let the others know you're awake." She grabbed her coffee cup.

As she went to step through the door, he called back. "Wait."

She turned around to face him, one eyebrow raised. "What do you need?"

"You."

His voice was so low and soft she almost didn't hear it. Frowning, her eyes searching his, she walked back into the room and sat down beside him on the bed. "What did you say?"

"You heard me."

She continued to study his face, but his gaze was clear, with a glint of humor, but also something else. Sincerity? Passion? She reached up to stroke his cheek, her thumb drifting down to gently follow the curve of his lips.

He grabbed her hand, held it to his lips and kissed it. Then he tugged her slowly toward him. When her head was just above his, his hand slipped up to the back of her neck and he pulled her all the way down and kissed her.

"Yes, I mean that." When he finally released her, he whispered, "We've been dancing around this for weeks. I figured one of us had to make that move to cross the divide."

Still dazed from the touch of his lips and the heat coursing through her system, she asked in confusion, "Divide?"

"Your brother. You seem to think he'll have a problem if we have a relationship."

"I figured you thought that," she corrected him, her breath catching in the back of her throat, but that look in his eyes, … she was drowning …

He flashed a wicked grin her way and said, "I might have, but I already spoke to him about us."

She gasped. "You what? Why?"

"So we'd have this out of the way. Because he warned me off when I first met you. I had to let him know I couldn't follow that dictate now. You matter too much. He knew it already—we just needed to clear the air."

She studied him carefully. "So what does that mean now?" she teased. "Do we go for coffee dates? Or are you looking for something else?"

"I'm not looking for anything," he said. "I've already found something special. I guess I want to see where we take it."

He reached up and captured her cheek. With his thumb running across her lips, he tugged her down a little bit more as he rose up on his elbow and kissed her again. "Why don't we try? Why not give us a chance? That same chance we've always wanted to be given." In a voice dark with passion, he dropped kisses on her chin, cheeks, and eyebrows. "Say yes," he whispered. "To this. … To us. … To right now."

It was what she'd wanted. All she had wanted. She leaned closer and kissed him ever-so-gently and whispered, "Yes."

He pulled her down to the bed with him. She let out a startled cry.

Rolling her over flat on the bed, his body covered hers, and his lips crushed hers. She had only nanoseconds to understand how quickly their positions had changed. The insistent prodding against her pelvis had her blood pulsing though her body; liquid pooled between her legs.

Dear God, she wanted him. She just hadn't expected this right now. They'd spent two nights in a hotel already, and now they were home, and she was wrapped in his arms in his bed. Just where she wanted to be.

It wasn't that it was bad timing but … She wrenched her mouth free and whispered, "The door."

Rhodes stared down at her in confusion, already with passion clouding his vision. He glanced at the open door, back at her, and was up off the bed, walking toward it.

She laughed and watched as he stuck his head out in the hallway, then closed the door and locked it. As he turned to face her, she scrambled to her knees and waited for him to come to her.

Only he didn't. He stopped in the middle of the room as if to give her a chance to change her mind.

He opened his mouth to say something and then closed it. And she understood. It wasn't that he was uncertain, but he was unsure about her. She gave him a slow dawning smile of passion and heat. She grabbed the corners of her T-shirt and pulled it over her head, dropping it to the side. Then she stood on the bed and took off her jeans. Standing before him, long and lean, in just her panties and bra, she waited to see what he'd do.

He caught his breath, then galvanized into action. He stripped right down to his skin.

Slowly he walked toward her, his erection standing proud. She dropped to her knees, her legs suddenly too weak to hold her.

He swept her in his arms before she could lie down again and tugged her close. Hot flesh seared and stoked the fire within. Brushing his lips against hers, he whispered, "You're still wearing too much."

Her lips tilted into a smile as she kissed him back. "I think you can take care of that." And she kissed him passionately, pouring out all the loss, loneliness, and desire she had kept reined in for the last couple months.

She had tossed and turned at night, deciding whether to stay, because of him, or if she wanted to be a part of this whole unit. That he was here was definitely a plus. If he wouldn't be hers, then it would be hard. And if he had other women, it would be damn-near impossible. It wasn't what she wanted for her life, for herself.

But this was absolutely what she wanted. Cool air swept between their heated bodies as he stepped back to drop her bra onto the floor. Instantly she was crushed against his chest, the cool skin of her breasts pressing hard against his muscled chest. She stroked and caressed, her fingers frantic as they explored.

"Slowly," he whispered. "We have lots of time."

She slid her hands up to grab his face and study the look in his eyes. "You don't think they'll come looking for you?"

"They'll come. They'll see the closed door. They'll assume I'm in the shower, or we're busy."

She winced.

"Don't worry about it. They already know."

Her lips twitched. "And here I thought I'd kept the secret to myself."

"Yeah. I've been teased about it already several times." He slid his hand down to her butt and pressed himself tight against her, his erection hard against her belly.

And she wanted so much more. She rose on tiptoes, her hands around his neck, and hooked one leg around his hips. She slid her hands down to stroke his heavily muscled backside. He kissed her again and again, his hands exploring. He wasn't heading toward the finish line. He was slow, methodical, and careful. Cherishing her body, needs, and emotions.

When he drew back from his heavy passionate kisses to now trace a line down her throat to her collarbone, his tongue tasting, exploring, and loving, she opened her arms and fell backward on his bed and laid there, her legs wide open and welcoming.

He leaned over her but paused, taking a moment to just stare. "Oh, my God, you're so beautiful."

She shook her head. "As long as you think so."

He bent over, dropping a kiss onto her ribs, his finger stroking down the valleys and hollows of her body. He knelt between her legs, gently cupping her breasts, exploring her belly and long legs, slowly dragging his fingers up the inside of her thighs. He slipped one long finger underneath the edge of the elastic on her white cotton panties, gently stroking, teasing. With his other hand he slipped his fingers into the top, sliding them to the side. She gasped and twisted on the bed.

"You're still wearing too many clothes."

He shifted, then drew her panties down and off. She watched as he stared at her. He swallowed hard. She worried something was wrong, but then he whispered, "And you've got red hair below."

In an unexpected move he slid his fingers through the bright curls and moistness, sliding one finger right inside.

Her hips rose up as she cried out in surprise. Immediately he added a second, gently coaxing.

"Jesus, Rhodes."

And with his thumb he found the tiny nub hidden in her soft folds. She cried out again as he gently teased and tormented her.

She couldn't take too much of that. She wanted him inside her. "Rhodes, come to me," she demanded.

Sienna wrapped her legs tightly around his body, and with powerful thighs, drew him toward her. He slid his hands upward as he licked, leaving a moist pathway on her ribs, stopping to suckle one breast, then moving to latch onto the other nipple, giving it his full attention. By the time he rose up to capture her mouth, she was trembling.

He looked down at her, his hands holding her head in place, his voice as dark as midnight as he whispered, "You're mine."

And he entered her all the way.

Pinned beneath him, she was lost in a fury of sensations as he slowly seated himself deep, then moved inside her. With her long legs wrapped around him as hard and tight as she could, he took her to a place she'd never been—then tossed her off the edge into a kaleidoscope of exploding nerve endings.

Dimly she heard herself cry out, but it was distant, as was the sound of his own as he joined her floating in the cloud of sensation.

Tears tugged at her eyes. Emotions at her heart.

The sense of completeness, oneness, at her soul.

When he slipped to one side, cuddling her close, he whispered against her ear, "Are you okay?"

And she whispered, "Never better."

RHODES TIGHTENED HIS arm around her, a smile on his face. This was an unexpected pleasure. As much as he'd hoped to get here, he hadn't thought to do so this fast. Then again, they'd been dancing around this for weeks. Such a joy to hold her in his arms. She shifted her position slightly, snuggling close.

He should get up and talk to Levi and the others about any further developments. But he didn't want to move. He figured by now somebody would've been alerted to the fact that his door was now closed. He and Sienna would be given some time together, but there was no guarantee of how long. Of course no one would know for sure until he and Sienna showed up, and it was written on their faces.

"I guess we should get up?"

He hugged her gently. "Can't say I want to."

"No, can't say I do either." She puffed out a heavy sigh. "But we should find out if Levi has any news. I'd like to know who attacked you at the gas station."

A laugh rumbled up from his chest. "I'm less concerned about that than I am making sure the Dallas police found the man responsible for the attempted hostage taking."

"Any chance they were the same?"

"Only if it was yet another hired gun. And that's possible."

She raised herself up on her elbow and looked down at him. "What do you mean?"

"If there was one man who hired the attack on the DA's office building, chances are he still had a different person go in and shoot the men in the garage. And that same man could've followed us out of town and attacked me at the gas station."

"But we didn't see anyone tailing us," she said, staring down at him.

"No, but it was a long drive and a lot of traffic."

She sagged back into his arms. "So easy to be a criminal in this world. We make it too easy on them."

"Another reason we're never out of work," Rhodes said quietly. He sat up gently. "Stay here. I'm taking a quick shower." He glanced at his clock and winced. "I'd coax you in there with me but for the time."

She chuckled. "Next time."

He lowered his head and grinned. "Glad to hear there'll be one."

He kissed her with enough passion that her arms snaked around his neck to tug him back into bed. He pulled free and escaped to the bathroom, regret in his heart. *Later.* He'd hold her in his arms all night. That was the only thought which kept him walking in the direction of the bathroom.

Standing under the water a few minutes later, his mind returned to his attacker. Chances were good, if he'd been followed to the gas station, they were all the way to the compound too. He figured Levi and the others would've considered that fact, but it was tearing him up inside and would until he brought it up to them. The last thing they needed was another attack there.

He also needed to contact Robert to see if there was any news on his end and to give him an update. Rhodes's head still ached, but he carefully soaked it under the hot water. Using a bit of shampoo, he cleaned his hair. By the time he was done, dried off and stepped into his bedroom with a towel wrapped around his waist, he found his bed made and Sienna sitting in the chair where she'd been when he'd woken up, now with her laptop open, checking her emails.

And she was fully dressed.

Too bad.

"Find anything?" He leaned over and kissed her on the forehead. She smiled, snagged a hand around his neck and pulled him down for real one. When he finally straightened, his blood was boiling. "Hold that thought," he said, his voice hoarse. Shaking the shreds of passion back to where they belonged, *for now*, he quickly pulled clothes from his dresser and got dressed. Finally he turned around and asked, "You ready?"

She took a deep breath and let it out very slowly. And she grinned. "Sure. What's the worst they can do? Fire me?"

His eyebrows shot up. "We are both consenting adults, and every one of them saw this happening."

She shrugged. "Maybe."

He clasped her hands in his, tugging her forward. "It'll be just fine."

Chapter 15

SHE PLASTERED A smile on her face and asked a question as they approached the kitchen. "Do you think we'll have to go back to Dallas?"

"I doubt it." They walked in, smiled at everybody, and filled two cups of coffee, while still talking. "No need for us to drive up there again."

On that note he turned to face Levi and asked, "Any update?"

Levi shook his head. "Nothing worthwhile." He studied Rhodes and asked, "How you feeling? You took quite a blow to your head."

"It doesn't appear to have broken the skin though, right?" Sienna asked, worriedly studying his head. She turned to look at Ice. "It's just like a concussion, correct?"

More comfortable now, Sienna walked around the table and sat down across from Rhodes, beside Ice.

Sienna looked at Rhodes critically and shrugged. "Obviously whatever it was didn't hold him down too long. If it'd been me who had been hit on the head …" She shrugged. "I probably wouldn't be awake for days."

Rhodes glared at her. "You *were* hit on the head and knocked unconscious—and I tried to get you to stay in the hospital—remember?"

She winced, feeling foolish, Rhodes's injury having superseded her own. "I … forgot."

"Well, I haven't. And I'll have enough nightmares from that one time already, thank you very much."

She laughed. "I'm not planning on getting kidnapped or hit on the head again anytime soon."

Rhodes turned to look at Levi and Ice. "As we must have been followed to the gas station, and that's where I was attacked, have you considered we could've been all the way here too?"

"Stone is in the control room right now. He's been searching for any kind of traffic or suspicious activity around us."

Rhodes smiled. "I figured you were on it, but because we didn't talk before now, I wasn't sure."

Sienna felt her jaw drop as she glared at him. "And you didn't think to mention that possibility the whole time I drove home?"

"Would it have done any good?" he asked bluntly. "You were doing what you could to get us here. That's what counted. And you were doing a damn good job at it. If we'd needed more support from the team they'd have come and helped us. But we didn't. We were good. *You* were great."

"I just do not think the way you guys do." She slumped back onto her chair and rubbed her temple. "I told you I don't do trouble," she wailed.

"Good thing." Ice smiled at her and patted her hand gently. "You went through enough yesterday. The wounded leading the wounded home. We're just grateful you both made it safely here."

"What now then?" Sienna asked. "Did you get to update Bullard?"

"I spoke with him not long ago, told him what happened to you and Rhodes. He's got some men heading over to check the charity run by J. R. Wilson. Bullard says just his check of the exterior of the warehouse is suspicious as hell. And he wants to have a better look."

"Can he do that?" Sienna asked, looking from Levi to Rhodes and back again.

The corner of Levi's mouth kicked up. "This is Bullard we're talking about. And Africa. Although there are rules everywhere, some over there are slightly different. At least for him."

She wondered about that. But Bullard had a lot of connections. And he wasn't green in this field. Whereas she was. She relaxed some at those thoughts.

Lissa walked in just then. She beamed when she saw Sienna and rushed over to hug her. "Oh, my God! Are you feeling okay? I couldn't believe it when Stone told me what happened." She crouched down beside Sienna and gently cupped her cheek. "I'm so sorry this happened to you." And in true Lissa form she wrapped her arms around Sienna and hugged her again.

Sienna pulled back slightly, wondering how she got so lucky as to find not just these men but these women as well. "I'm fine, honest. It was a bit rough yesterday morning. The worst part was, according to Rhodes, the two guys who kidnapped me were young teenage punks and could barely carry me, so they basically dragged me down the stairs. When I woke up, I had more spots that hurt than I thought were possible."

Lissa winced. "That sounds absolutely horrible."

Sienna grinned. "Yeah, that wasn't the highlight of my day. Neither was finding Rhodes knocked out on the ground." She cast a teasing eye across the table. "No way could I lift him. I was ready to call 911 to get somebody to help me load the lug."

Everyone laughed. She looked over at Levi. "Any update on the men who kidnapped me? I understand the attack on the DA's office probably took precedence, but it would be nice to hear of those two men's fates."

"They will be put away for a long time for hurting you," Lissa said loyally. She sneaked into a spot between them, the three women now sitting together.

"Robert said they were still talking, giving up names," Levi told her. "With any luck this issue will be over soon."

"Except for the last guy who killed everybody," she said bitterly. "I'll sleep well tonight if they have number seven in jail too."

"You'll sleep just fine regardless," Rhodes said calmly. "Everyone is out looking for the man. He's got to be on cameras somewhere in the building. They will find him. Don't you worry."

"Except he followed us to the vehicle and gas station."

"But we don't know if it was him or just someone he hired," Levi said.

"So that makes it better?" Sienna slumped in her chair. "That just means there are more assholes out there gunning for us."

"But you're safe here." Alfred walked in then. He took a look at Rhodes and Sienna and said, "Glad to hear you two are back home. If you want to clean off the table, dinner will be ready in about thirty minutes."

Sienna straightened. "Oh, great! I'm famished."

Rhodes laughed. "When are you not?"

Lissa confessed at her side, "I'm looking forward to the next meal too."

Merk called out from the doorway, "Are you ladies ever *not* hungry?"

Sienna grinned at Merk and Katina as they walked in, holding hands. She turned toward Levi and said, "You should change the company name from Heroes for Hire to Heroes from Heaven."

An immediate shocked silence was broken by a giggle, coming from the most unexpected person. Ice couldn't hold back.

Levi stood up, raised his chin and glared at her, but no heat was behind it as he said, "The company's *name* is Legendary Security. The Heroes for Hire was just a nickname. And it sure as hell won't be Heroes from Heaven." He snorted. "Bad enough everybody around here is pairing up. It's like a bloody love nest instead of a compound." And he walked out.

Ice tried to get to her feet, but was laughing too hard. She turned to look at Sienna and said, "Oh, I've wanted to say that for a long time." She reached over and gave Sienna a big hug, "Good for you." Then she got up and followed Levi.

Rhodes shook his head. "That's just demoralizing, that's what that is."

"What, *heroes*?" Sienna asked. "Heroes for Hire makes sense, and you guys bash that name around lots too."

"Yeah, Heroes for the Heart has been mentioned too, but Heroes from Heaven?"

"Well, I think it's a lovely name," Lissa said with a smile. "And I might just keep using it."

"Not if you don't want an all-out war," Rhodes warned. "As a joke that's one thing, but don't ever mean it."

Sienna looked over at him. "I guess this is some kind of an ego thing?"

Lissa looked at him too. "Because Heroes for the Heart sounds lovely too," she said. "You know that, right?"

Stone walked around the table, bent down and kissed her. "You are lovely. But there's no way in hell I would allow a name like that. This is not a romantic retreat here."

Sienna batted her eyes at him. "But it could be."

"Ha." Stone flashed a grin at her. "Not everybody gets to spend the day in bed, you know?" He turned that knowing look on Rhodes before flashing back at her. "Must be nice to have your own hero from heaven." And he headed to the kitchen to give Alfred a hand.

Beside her Lissa giggled. She leaned close to Sienna and whispered, "Don't tell him this, but we spent a lot of days in bed."

The two women chuckled. Rhodes stood up. "Okay, my turn to leave now."

Sienna quickly but gently kicked him under the table. "You can't. You're helping us clean the table and get ready for our meal. Alfred said the food is coming."

She and Lissa both hopped to their feet and cleared the cups and collected the miscellaneous dishes. They walked into the kitchen, loaded the dishwasher and came back with a big white tablecloth.

By the time the table was set, Alfred brought out the food. The rest of the gang slowly drifted back into the room. Nothing like a meal to bring a family together. And she realized that was what this really was. And she was so blessed to have joined it.

WHEN HE LEFT the military, Rhodes hadn't expected to end up in a scenario like this. The men he worked with here were his family. They'd been brothers in arms in the military and best friends. Ice had naturally joined them, and Rhodes had never felt like he was losing any part of Levi because of his relationship with Ice. And as they'd all slowly come together with their own partners, Rhodes realized just how special this truly was. With the increasing number they had here to actually maintain a positive happy family, well, it was something out of his experience.

What would it be like to have their numbers grow further? There were other men, like Logan and Harrison, who had moved into the compound and who knew if Flynn would as well. He'd done well protecting Anna and her animal shelter when he'd been given the chance. The team had discussed Flynn's execution of that job, and it had been a group decision to bring him on board. Flynn was a character, and Rhodes looked forward to seeing him again, and Rhodes was also dying to meet Anna, as Flynn had a lot to say about her. The last words out of his mouth on the issue had been, "Good riddance."

Katina, who'd overheard Rhodes laughing at Flynn, instead of being upset, had just said, "It'd be interesting to get Anna's take on this."

Maybe they would now. As Katina was hoping to have her friend visit her at the compound.

Rhodes suspected Flynn wasn't anywhere near as untouched by the Anna experience as he tried to make it sound. And Rhodes had to admit that finding Sienna made him want the same opportunity for all his buddies.

Alfred sat down at the head of the table as always, with Levi at the other end, and said, "Bon appétit."

They all dug in. Rhodes didn't know what the name for this concoction was, but it was meat and vegetables smothered in one huge flaky pastry, and it was freaking delicious.

"Bullard phoned," Levi said when everyone had refilled their plates and sat back down again. "They're going into the warehouse tonight."

Silence. Rhodes glanced over at him and said, "Wish I was there."

"He'll go in with a tactical team and will let us know what they find."

"I'm surprised it wasn't some kind of joint effort with us."

"If we had confirmation they were the ones responsible for the goings-on here, then it would have been. But we don't have that yet."

Rhodes glanced at Sienna to see her gaze down on her plate. "It'll be fine," he reassured her.

She lifted her face to his, then swept her gaze over all the people seated at the table and said, "These men are killers. One got away, and we know the charity has offices in Dallas. Is there no way to see what they're doing here?"

Rhodes caught Levi's look as he studied her. He chewed methodically as they all considered the issue. "Find proof they are involved, then we can."

She stared directly at Levi for a long moment. Then nodded. "I'll work on that after dinner."

Rhodes turned to look at her, a question in his eyes. But he thought better of it. Maybe she had a few tricks up her sleeve they didn't know about. He was willing to give her the benefit of the doubt. Maybe she was just reaching, hoping she could find something to put this nightmare to rest. For that he couldn't blame her.

Chapter 16

AFTER DINNER, SIENNA grabbed a cup of coffee and made her way back to her desk in the office. It was late; she was tired, but her mind buzzed. Surely there was more information to find. With no one around to hear her, she freely talked to herself out loud. And that made her feel better as she went over what she knew so far.

She brought up her notes on her laptop, refreshed the page, then walked to the table where the spreadsheets still lay. Pulling up a chair she grabbed a blank notepad and emptied her mind. She studied the number and letter combinations. It might be names and numbers, but there had to be more to be found here. It would help if she had more sheets, with more data and options, easier to confirm too, because she'd have a larger sample to work with. She took the complex number and letter combinations and wrote down the information she had already decoded with the letters on the side. Then she took a look at the numbers lined up. Was it also in a pattern, or were they something simpler? Like an invoice number, purchase dates, or could they be random? "No, not random," she whispered. "It's too specific to be."

There had to be a pattern. It didn't mean she would know what it was. Then she turned to look at the spreadsheets Bullard had sent. These papers had been found in the young IT guy's desk. She'd started with the first but hadn't caught anything. Just more numbers. This time just straight numbers and columns. The final column appeared to be monetary amounts—a decimal point two digits in from the right. But no dollar sign. And for this level she doubted anybody dealt in change. But accountants the world over kept precise track of every transaction. She put that page down and picked up another.

By the time she had the third one, an idea sparked in the back of her mind. She grabbed her notepad and tossed around codes, numbers, and ideas. Finally she sat back and noticed it had been over two hours, and she had a glimmer of truth in her hand. But she needed Bullard to confirm. She also needed to review the names she had gathered so far, including the six dead gunmen.

She got up and walked back to her laptop. She'd noted the various people her decoding had brought up. She added the six people from the shooting in Dallas, wondering if she should pull up Robert's name too.

She went back to the spreadsheets, checked every one that had an R.F., considering the numbers behind it. If he was involved—and that was a small *if*—he was the only one she knew of who might confirm some of these numbers.

What if these were bank accounts? What if they were payments into one with his name on it? She had several from the Swiss bank.

Back at her laptop again she printed off every Swiss bank account. Then with a highlighter, she quickly cross-checked them and found nothing. Now that was wrong. She knew something had to be here; she could feel it. And then she saw it. In an attempt to confuse the account numbers, the first and last characters had been switched. And with that knowledge, she quickly decoded all the bank account numbers in front of the initials. Now she needed somebody to confirm the name on these accounts.

"This is it," she said jubilantly.

"This is what?" Rhodes asked.

Surprised, she looked up to see him leaning against the doorjamb, watching her.

"I think I solved it."

He came around to look at the data she had.

She quickly showed him how the accounts unscrambled onto the scanned ledger sheets with the ripped edges. "I think these are the accounts and names they belong to." She sat back. "And I can't let go of the idea that R.F. is Robert Forrest, the DA."

Rhodes shook his head. "No, I don't think so. R.F. could mean a lot of people. He'd been with us. He had ample opportunity to set us up or to get rid of us himself."

She frowned. "That's true," she said slowly. "And if he had hired somebody to go in the building when we were there, it would've been a simple enough case to have taken us out. He had a cell phone with him." She shrugged. "I wasn't making him be the bad guy. I was just fitting the name to the R.F. initials."

"*Robert* is only one of the many possibilities."

She nodded. "And that takes us down a rabbit hole because there's probably hundreds, if not thousands, of potential combinations."

"Hundreds of thousands." He tapped the papers on the table. "But this is interesting, and very good." He glanced down at her. "We can ask Bullard if he knows any of these people on his end. And we can also get somebody here on ours, someone a little higher up, to help us out and get some names for these accounts."

"In fact, that is something Robert could probably do for us, right?" she asked drily. She glanced down at her watch. "It's seven. Probably too late to call him now."

Rhodes laughed. "We could certainly email him. If he's working, then he'll be on it and answer pretty fast."

With him sitting beside her, she quickly typed up an email, documenting bits and pieces that she'd found. She hit Send.

He held out a hand and asked, "You ready to leave the office now?"

Her laptop dinged immediately. She sat back down and looked. "It's Robert."

She heard Rhodes's heavy sigh beside her and realized he probably had different plans for her this evening than what she was currently doing. She smiled. Now *that* she could get behind. Still … "Let me just see what he says."

She brought up his email in response. There were only two words, *thank you*. She sat back, stared at them and shrugged. "Just because I'm excited about it, doesn't mean anybody else is."

He chuckled. "And Robert is probably way too tired to deal with any of this."

She winced. "I had to stay behind and handle a lot of late nights in my former position, so I understand how overwhelming it can be." She sat there and stared at the thank you for a long moment. She didn't like it.

"I haven't had any contact or dealings with him in the past, but this seems way too simplistic for an email from him. And no capitals."

He stopped and stared at her. "What are you talking about?"

She shrugged. "I asked a bunch of questions, gave a lot of information." She turned her gaze to him and asked, "And all he says is 'thank you'?"

She scrolled down to his signature, just below the message. And above the signature was an odd series of digits, numbers. She sat back and said, "Whoa."

He walked around and asked, "What?"

She pointed out the code on the bottom. "This helps." She turned to gaze up at him. "It's the same code I had explained to him earlier on the accounts."

He stared at her, then the email, pulled out his phone and tried to phone Robert. She waited in her seat, studying the code, her blood running hot at the thought of somebody going after the Dallas DA. But of course, that could've been because they'd gone after Rhodes and her.

"Why didn't we check on him before?" Her body was tense as she waited for Robert to pick up his phone.

But his phone rang and rang. Finally it went to voicemail. Rhodes didn't leave a message. He turned it off and said, "I'll find Levi."

She closed her laptop, tucked it under her arm and raced behind him. "Any idea where they are?"

"Last I heard, they were talking with Alfred in the kitchen area." They ran down the stairs and burst into the kitchen. All three people turned to look at them.

"What's up?" barked Levi.

Sienna opened the laptop, hit the button to bring it out of screensaver mode and showed him the email with the little bit of code on the bottom. "If I decode this like for the other accounts to get names," she said, "that particular line of code reads *help me*."

THE DISCUSSION WAS hot and heavy as they decided the best way forward. Harrison came in from the other room where he was watching a movie, snagged up the laptop with Sienna's permission and checked to see where the message came from.

"It was sent from his house," he announced ten minutes later. But he glanced at his watch.

"That's … several hours' drive away," Sienna said. "We should call the cops and have them go by his house."

Ice said, "We already contacted somebody there. But they'll check first if he's being held hostage. If they just knock on the door, there's a good chance they won't find out anything or will get a bullet through the door themselves."

Rhodes knew the truth was hard sometimes, but Sienna needed to understand these people were dead serious and had long-reaching arms.

Levi's phone rang. He pulled it out and said, "It's Robert." He waited a second for silence to follow, then held it to his ear and asked, "Hello, Robert, that you?"

Rhodes watched Levi's face as his gaze hardened. It zinged to Sienna and if possible, became even harder.

"I heard you. Where do you want to make the exchange?" He turned and faced Ice. "You are where? Almost in Houston?"

Rhodes waited and realized exactly what was happening. He checked his watch, mentally ran over the weapons they had ready and the men available. The plan of action would be determined by wherever the exchange was because Rhodes had no doubt they had Robert and were looking for Sienna too. Levi would have said, *in exchange*, but in reality, one of them was likely already dead. Which meant they were all leaving and Sienna would stay here, where she'd be safe.

Levi closed the phone. "A hotel on the other side of Houston. They've come into our neck of the woods. An hour." He stared at everybody at the table. "This will take every one of us. We're to meet in the parking lot."

Rhodes pursed his lips. "That's still pretty public."

Harrison snapped, "Even worse, he could have a dozen men hiding inside the hotel rooms with sniper rifles already in position now."

Levi nodded. "He said Rhodes must come too."

Rhodes crossed his arms over his chest and said, "I wouldn't have it any other way."

"No way you're going," cried Sienna. "He wants to kill you."

Rhodes turned to stare at her. "No way in hell you are."

She stuck her chin out at him and said, "We have to stop them and help Robert. These bad guys think they can just take out a DA now?"

"Five minutes ago you thought that DA might *be* the bad guy," Rhodes said calmly. "And you're not leaving. You're safe here. That's the way you'll stay."

"And no way are we getting Robert back if they don't see me there." She added in a low voice, "Or you, for that matter."

He opened his mouth to order her to stay when Levi stepped in.

"You know she's right, Rhodes. She has to be visible—not accessible. We can protect her. But we have to do this. We'll need all hands."

"One hour's not much time." Rhodes stood up. "We must get there earlier and park somewhere else."

"We need a plan," Ice said as she stood up, facing them. "I can fly several into town but where to land and have wheels there?"

Levi studied her. "If we take the helicopter, we're likely to trigger an alarm, and it's not worth it. We'll be faster driving. It's only thirty minutes out."

"We do need a plan," Rhodes snapped. "But let's make it while we're driving. Because there's just no time otherwise."

"We'll take three vehicles," Levi said, standing up. "Everybody gear up. This could get ugly so come fully armed. Ice with me, Sienna with Rhodes."

Stone walked in just then and asked, "Do you want to leave somebody here or not?"

"I'll stay," Alfred said. "I'll be in the control room with Lissa and Katina." He nodded to the women. "Sienna has to go. Otherwise, I would have kept her here too."

"We leave in five."

Everybody scattered.

Rhodes kept his gaze on Sienna. She clenched the laptop, her knuckles white. He told her, "Grab a sweater. Don't know how late this night'll be. We'll take the same truck as the last time. Be there in five." He waited, watched her nod before she bolted from the room. He turned back to Alfred and the other two women. "Use the satellite and see if you can find the hotel. You start searching now, you might be able to give us the heads-up as to what is waiting for us."

"We'll be up there in five minutes. As soon as you're all off the compound, we're in lockdown."

Rhodes gave him a curt nod and headed to the truck. On the way, he stopped at the weapons room. They had depots all around the compound with a full armory downstairs. He pulled out several handguns and put one into his shoulder holster, then tucked a spare in his ankle boot.

He grabbed the keys and raced to the truck. Now all he needed was Sienna and they were gone. As he shifted the truck into Reverse to back up, the passenger door opened, and Sienna hopped in.

She quickly buckled up and said, "Let's go."

She slammed the door shut; he hit the power locks and ripped out of the compound. Levi drove with Ice, Harrison rode in the back. Stone drove the third truck carrying Merk. The full team.

Every one of them ready to kick some ass.

Chapter 17

THE TRIP WAS fast and furious and done almost in complete silence. At least for the first five minutes. Then Sienna ran communications between Ice and Rhodes. By the time they hit the outskirts of the city, the plan was for Levi's team to meet up two blocks on the other side of the hotel. They were running ten minutes early as Rhodes pulled in to rendezvous with Levi and the others. Rhodes grabbed his phone and called Alfred. "What did you see?"

Rhodes held the phone slightly away from his ear so Sienna could hear.

"Two snipers, one each top right second floor and top left third."

She stared at Rhodes in horror.

"What's in the parking lot?"

"One dark sedan," Alfred said. "Quite possibly belongs to Robert himself."

"Did you recognize any faces?" Rhodes asked.

"No. But we're running what we have through facial recognition. Can't get decent images yet."

"Okay, we're a couple blocks away, about to set plans into motion." He turned to stare out the window.

"One more thing," Alfred continued. "Bullard checked in. Warehouse was full of weapons. He sent a warning. Now that the cache has been seized, the police are all over J. R.

Wilson's ass." He paused. "In other words these men are prepared to do anything to get away."

"Got it. We'll call with an update as soon as we can. Record everything, will you?" He pocketed his phone, turned to look at Sienna and asked, "You ready?"

She let her breath rush out and said, "At least for this part."

The plan was simple. The other two vehicles would park here, and the men would take positions inside and out of the hotel. Levi, Rhodes, and Sienna would appear for the meeting. Simple with not a whole lot of options. Only this time they were going in Levi's truck, just the three of them driving in to the hotel parking lot. She stared down at her hands, not surprised to see the fine tremor working its way through her fingers. This was not exactly how she'd expected to spend her evening. She just hoped to hell there would be a night after, not the endless one she suspected was the plan for her.

She ran her fingers over her face to still the panic erupting inside. They all had weapons, and for the first time, she wondered if she'd rather have one too. She was completely defenseless. She understood the risks of arming an untrained person. Maybe Rhodes would teach her. She really didn't want to be in this kind of situation again and not have any skills. She knew Ice was hell on wheels with many weapons. Wouldn't it be nice if Sienna could at least learn some of that?

Also, considering her free time while living and working at the compound, maybe she could convince somebody to give her some martial arts practice—something she'd really like to get back to. Maybe she hadn't forgotten all of it. Surely if she got into a wrestling match with these guys, it would come back to her.

The vehicle was parked in front of the hotel as they had been told. Levi drove around until he was facing back out again, and pulled up at a cross angle to the vehicle.

Nobody moved.

"Do I get out?" Sienna asked in a low voice.

"Not yet. Wait until we see Robert, alive."

The passenger and driver side doors of the sedan opened. The man on the far side got out first. She didn't recognize him. The driver hopped out, and she didn't recognize him either. They were followed by two more muscle men.

Then the rear passenger door was opened on the far side. Robert got out. A very disabled, bloodied Robert. She caught back her small cry. "Oh, my God. Did they have to hurt him like that?" She opened her door and stepped out.

And then she stopped when she saw the man walking toward her. "Bobby?" She stared at the man who'd brought her coffee, delivered her the printer she needed, and anything else for those hours she'd been at the DA's office. And something else clicked. *Bobby was short for Robert*, and she sighed. "R.F. by any chance?"

He looked at her in confusion. "What are you talking about?

"Your last name, does it start with an *F*?" she snapped as she walked toward them.

Rhodes walked at her side, his arm holding her back. She could feel her anger rising inside. These bullies with a need to inflict pain on everybody had to be taken down.

Bobby frowned and replied, "Yes, but how the hell would you know that?"

She snorted. "You really are stupid, aren't you? Did you have to hurt Robert? Did you break his bones just for your own satisfaction?"

"I had to do what I had to do. With Wilson's operation now compromised, and you two meddling into things, I had to make a run for it. The gunrunning was a great way to make cash. The drugs were ugly but necessary. I've wanted to get out for a long time. Now I have to. The only way to do that is to make sure I don't leave any threads behind. And that means the three of you."

"Sorry for upsetting your plans." She gave him a saccharine smile to let him know she was anything but. In truth, she wanted to reach out and smack him, but Rhodes was being very particular about keeping her at his side. She didn't understand why, but he was too strong for her to argue with. She shot him a harsh look as if to tell him to leave her alone. She had another question for Bobby. "How did you lose the pages from the ledger?"

"Shut up, bitch. You think you're so smart, but that had nothing to do with me. Goddamn J. R. Wilson. He didn't even notice after a meeting at the bank in Africa. That man's a mess. That stupid IT kid ripped out the ledger pages, then tried to blackmail us. We didn't even have a solution worked out for him yet. Hopefully you'll nail his ass to the wall too," Bobby snapped. "Not that it matters to you. You don't know anything."

He raised his hand to the sky, instinctively she ducked.

And he dropped his arm as if he were starting a race.

Rhodes held her tight against him. And she realized he'd been expecting snipers to fire. She straightened and faced Bobby. With more bravado than she felt, she sneered. "What exactly is that surprise you've got for me?"

He glared at her, raised his arm and dropped it once more.

Nothing happened.

"Missing something?" Rhodes asked.

Levi, now standing on the other side of Sienna, said, "We thought we'd even the odds and take out your snipers."

Bobby's face hardened into a cruel laugh. "You didn't think I came with just those two, did you?"

Instantly gunfire erupted all around them.

Rhodes grabbed Sienna and tucked her behind the truck. She dropped to the ground instinctively.

"Roll under," Rhodes ordered as he pulled out a gun and fired over the truck bed. Shots came from the left and behind.

"Shit."

She twisted underneath the truck to look at him. "Rhodes, you hurt?"

He shifted into a squatting position and fired again.

"Stop right there," Bobby snapped in a hard voice. And he had a rifle aimed right at Rhodes's back.

"Stand up slowly and throw the gun on the ground."

Shit! … She didn't know what she should do. She watched as Rhodes slowly straightened. All around them the gunfire slowed down.

Levi yelled out, "Leave my men alone, and I'll leave yours alone."

"Like hell. This is the asshole who knocked out my men in the garage. I had to shoot them because of him."

Rhodes snorted. "You were just looking for an excuse to kill them anyway."

"They were sloppy. Stupidly so." The rifle butt jammed in Rhodes's back this time, making him gasp.

And that was when she saw the gun tucked into Rhodes's boot. His pant leg was caught over the top of it.

But Bobby didn't know. She heard him say something else but her gaze was on that handle. Her hand snaked out, lifted the gun free. She was under the truck, no one the wiser. *Yet.*

Except for Rhodes. He knew what she'd done.

She stared at the gun in her hand.

Beside the truck, so close to her, Bobby said, "Get down on your knees, asshole."

She watched as Rhodes slowly lowered to the ground beside her. And realized she didn't have time for decisions here. She flipped sideways so she could see the man, lifted the gun and pointed at his chest.

Then pulled the trigger.

The sound of the gun firing echoed in the silence.

For a long moment no one moved. Bobby slowly sank to his knees and fell over sideways. Rhodes spun, kicked the gun away from the man, then turned and dragged her out from under the truck, pulling her to her feet. He grabbed her, held her tight against him and whispered against her ear, "Thank God, you're safe."

She threw her arms around his neck and held him close. "You mean, thank God, you're safe." With a half laugh, she pulled back, placed her hands on his cheeks and kissed him hard. "When he put that gun to your back and told you to go down on your knees …" She kissed him again. "I was so scared."

He stepped back and glared at her. "What were you thinking?"

She laughed. "That I didn't want to lose you." And she again hugged him tight. Over her shoulder she could see Levi, standing guard on two other men. The two other compound vehicles raced in and came to a sudden stop. Everybody hopped out.

Ice raced over to Robert, leaning against the car. She had her med kit with her but called out, "Somebody call 911. Robert needs an ambulance now."

Not that they needed to worry. All the gunshots had alerted somebody. Sirens already raced toward them. But that would be the cops, and they needed medical help for Robert. Sienna pulled out her phone and quickly dialed it in. She patted Rhodes on the shoulder and walked over to help Ice. She crouched down in front of Robert, now lying on the ground with Ice beside him.

"Robert, how you feeling?"

He rolled his head to look at her and said, "You got my message, I see."

"I did. But this asshole phoned Levi anyway within a few minutes. Still, you gave us just that much of a warning."

He closed his eyes. "Good. I worked with Bobby for ten years. Ten long years and I had no idea."

"When you're back on your feet, you can rip his sorry life apart. He's dead, so he won't be going to jail. But a lot of other people were involved in this mess. Like J. R. Wilson. Bobby's statement should help to nail his ass to the wall."

Robert gave a broken laugh. "I can't wait."

Rhodes came and collected Sienna as the cops came roaring into the parking lot. Levi stepped forward and quickly explained the issue. Including the identification of Robert as the Dallas DA. At his name the place erupted into organized chaos.

The ambulance arrived five minutes later. While she watched, Robert was quickly loaded into the back of the vehicle and driven off. She turned to face Rhodes. "Should somebody go with him?"

Rhodes shook his head. "I believe he has a married

daughter in this area. The police will be calling her. She'll likely make it to the hospital shortly after the ambulance."

Sienna said, "I hope so. At times like this, nobody should be alone."

The last thing she wanted was for the man who'd done so much for his city to recuperate on his own. As she glanced back at the cops all around the place, she realized it would be another long night. "I guess there's no chance in hell we'll get to bed anytime soon, is there?"

"Nope. It'll be a while."

AND HE WAS right. It was. But it could've been so much worse. Still, it was another three hours before they drove into the compound once again. Alfred and the other two women met them at the door.

Alfred took one look and said, "To bed, all of you."

Rhodes wouldn't argue with that. He was beat. But he made sure he didn't go alone. He grabbed Sienna's hand and headed for the elevator. At his suite, he didn't even give her a chance to comment as he dragged her inside. He closed and locked the door and said, "Sleep. All I need is sleep."

She stood in the middle of the room and watched as he stripped down and collapsed on his side of the bed. She took off her clothes, tossed them on the floor and crawled into bed beside him. He lay there, resting. She reached up and kissed him. "Thank you for being you."

His eyes popped open. "You're welcome, but that's a very interesting thing to say. I'm nobody special. I'm just me."

"That's not true. You're a hero to me."

He winced. "Remember, we don't use that word."

She reached up and placed a finger across his lips. "Levi can say whatever he wants. But for me, you're my hero and always will be." She threw her arms around him and kissed him hard, pressing her breasts against him, her hips cuddling his growing erection.

When he finally came up for air, he brushed his nose against hers, his heart swelling with an emotion he barely recognized. "Have I told you that I love you?"

Her gaze widened in delight. She shook her head. "No, you haven't. But it's a damn good thing because I love you too."

Their gazes locked and slowly he turned his head, his warm breath washing over her as he whispered, "Maybe I was a little too quick to say I needed sleep."

His hand slid down her back to cup her butt and tug her hard against him. "I think sleep can wait a little longer."

And he lowered his head and kissed her, knowing for the first time what it was to make love to the woman he loved. He was a one-woman man, and Sienna was his. Forever.

Epilogue

"HEY, ANNA," FLYNN Kilpatrick said as he walked up to the pallet of dog food she was unloading. "I just came from Levi's compound. Figured, since I was in town, I'd give you the good news in person."

She straightened, brushed the hair back off her face. "Hi. That's a crazy place to be these days. Katina told me about Rhodes and Sienna. I'm going down there this afternoon if I can get away."

"Good." He reached down and hefted several bags over his shoulder, walking inside to stack them in the shed. "But I wanted to tell you that the last of the men involved in Katina's kidnapping have been locked up. We heard this morning. Even better, several are talking, and the DA is expecting everyone to go away for a very long time."

"Great," she said with a big smile. "I'm so happy to hear that. I'd hate to have anything else bad happen to Katina."

"Merk won't allow it." He grinned at her. "Looks like the two of them are fairly matched up."

"They matched up a long time ago. They are just now realizing how perfect they are together."

Flynn laughed. Anna had told him a little bit about Merk and Katina's relationship. He'd heard the rest from the guys. It was all good. As a matter of fact, it was looking damn rosy around the compound. He'd been there just this morning. He heard about all the chaos with Rhodes and Sienna. But he'd been out on the West Coast with Logan on a short job for Levi and had missed all the fun. Typical. But damn. Rhodes and Sienna—who knew they were a thing?

"That is great. Thanks for stopping by," she said. "I know how much you were hoping to get hired into the company."

He was indeed. And this next job would be short and sweet. With any luck he'd get over to Saudi Arabia, handle this problem and get back home again. The timeline was tight, but that was the way they liked it. And he wasn't going alone; his buddies—Logan and Harrison, were going. That worked for him. He'd left his jacket at Anna's to give him a reason to come back. But as the good news had come in, he hadn't needed it – this time. Now he had an excuse to stop by after his next trip.

He wondered if she'd seen it. He'd hung it on the back of the door. Hopefully obvious enough for a man to see and understand but not so obvious that Anna would see.

He brushed the dirt off his hands, checked out the shed's roof and realized the dog food would be nice and dry here. He closed the door, snapped the simple lock closed. Then he picked up the empty pallet, moved it to the stack with the others behind the shed. "Anything else?"

She shook her head but kept her face away from him. "That's it. Thanks for the help." Her voice was overly cheerful and bright as she turned to face him with a big smile. "I appreciate your timing for a visit. I have to admit, it was great to have your muscles for the couple weeks you were here. This last week, well, I missed that."

"You need to get yourself an assistant. You know that, right?"

She laughed. "I need a lot of things. But it all takes money."

He nodded. "Just don't be thinking about hiring that Jonas character."

She glared at him. "You won't be telling me what to do any longer, thanks. You can leave again now." It was said in a joking manner. They'd done a round or two about Jonas, a guy who kept coming on to her.

"I can't believe you actually dated that guy."

"It was hardly a date. I ran into him at the mall, sat down and had a coffee with him," she protested.

"In Jonas's mind that was a date. Obviously, as he's come around, what? Five times since I've been here? He's bad news. Stay away from him."

"He's not that bad."

"He's worse," Flynn countered. For the weeks while Flynn had been guarding over her, he'd watched her, lived with her, inhaling the scent that was so Anna. And not touching her. But now he was leaving. But not without a taste of her. Especially when he wanted so much more …

Before she had a chance to protest he tugged her into his arms and said, "There's really only one way to say good-bye." And he lowered his head and kissed her.

Only neither expected the flash of passion that threatened to consume them both. Fireworks exploded in his head. And damn if he didn't hear music.

Anna broke away, gave him an uncertain look, then headed inside her house.

Leaving Flynn wondering what the hell just happened.

FLYNN'S FIRECRACKER

Heroes for Hire, Book 5

Dale Mayer

Chapter 1

HE DAMN WELL better be there. Anna Burrows whipped down the road, turned into the compound and braking hard, stopped abruptly in front of the garage. Part of her was absolutely ecstatic to see Katina, while another was equally so to see Flynn. But the biggest part of her was furiously angry with him. And she planned to take a strip off his hide. If he wouldn't stand still long enough for her to do that, she would rip into him one way or the other. She hopped out and slammed her car door. Several men stood in front of the garage, and a few more came out to see what the commotion was. Then she caught sight of Flynn. She snagged his jacket from the passenger side, stormed up to him and slammed it against his broad chest.

"Did you really think I wouldn't know?" she yelled into his face. "You did this on purpose. Why? Why would you do that?"

His face split into a huge grin. And his eyes danced with joy. She knew she had made his day, but this was way too damn serious to let him walk all over her.

A joke was one thing. But this was beyond that.

She shoved her face into his surprised one. "Well, it didn't work, asshole." She turned and marched back to her car. Then she grabbed the plastic bag from the dashboard and held it up for everyone to see.

By now there had to be half a dozen men about. All of them big badass-looking dudes. But her gaze was locked on Flynn. He was the one who had made her absolutely bonkers the last few weeks. She knew she'd been nothing but a job to him, all the sadder for the type of reaction he'd gotten out of her, but even then he hadn't been able to keep it totally professional.

From the first moment he'd stepped on her property, he'd set her ire exploding into the sky. And it hadn't calmed down yet. She shoved the bag in his face. "And if this is yours, I'll call the cops again and see if it's covered in owl blood—one that was killed last night and left gutted on my back step. And, lo and behold, this bloody knife was in your goddamned jacket pocket *in my kitchen*."

With fury riding her like she'd rarely felt before, she pulled her arm back and smacked him hard across the face.

Absolute silence filled the air.

Then she heard a gasp. "Anna?"

Katina came running. As soon as Anna saw her best friend, she burst into tears. The two women fell into each other's arms. Not one of the men said a word.

Finally, when she had calmed down enough to stop crying, Anna hugged Katina again and said, "I'm so sorry. But I had to come and tell him that I knew what he did."

Katina shook her head. "Something's wrong, sweetie. Flynn might be a lot of things, and I certainly don't know him as well as the others, but I do know the type of man he is. He'd never hurt an animal."

Anna lowered her voice and whispered so the men couldn't hear. "What about a woman? As in my heart?"

Katina pulled back to stare into her friend's eyes and must have understood as she didn't say a word, but Anna saw the question in Katina's gaze. Anna shook her head.

"I'm sorry," Katina whispered. "I was hoping things would work out better between you two." At that Katina turned and stepped in front of Anna, fisted her hands on her hips and glared at Flynn. Then she took one step forward and poked him in the chest. "If you hurt one hair on any of her animals, or on Anna herself, and let me add her heart to that list too, you will answer to me." She glared at him, almost eye to eye.

Behind her, Merk said, "Easy, Katina."

Without breaking her stare on the shocked man in front of her, she took one step back and reached out a hand. Anna grabbed it immediately. Katina wrapped her arms around her friend and said, "Come on inside. We don't need to be around him."

She shot a look at Merk that had him holding up his hands and saying, "It wasn't me."

Anna nodded her head in defiance at him too. As the two friends walked inside, Anna whispered, her voice loud enough to carry backward, "Is that Merk?"

Katina nodded.

"Well, now I understand."

FLYNN STOOD IN complete shock. He'd only returned home earlier this morning, from a quick job Levi had sent him on. He'd been looking forward to seeing Anna as soon as he could get the time.

However, this was not the homecoming he'd envisioned.

Very few things in life could shut him up. A woman's tears made him blubber apologies left, right and center, but her anger—that unjustified and unprovoked attack just now by Anna—well…he didn't have a clue what to do about it.

The other men surrounded him.

"Flynn, what the hell was that all about?" Levi asked. His tone was hard and uncompromising.

Flynn looked at Levi and said, "Shit, I'm not sure."

"Even if that knife was used on that animal, we know it wouldn't have been you wielding it. But, for the record, could you please state that?" Merk asked.

"I have never in my life intentionally hurt an animal," Flynn said, shaking his head in bewilderment. "Yes, this is my jacket. And yes, that's my knife. But I thought I lost it at her place."

Stone leaned against the garage doorway. "She mentioned calling the police once already. So I'm assuming she found your jacket with the knife in the pocket afterward."

"Right, but I didn't gut any owl." Flynn couldn't tear his gaze away from the doorway the women had disappeared into. Sure he'd left his jacket in her house on purpose. But in the kitchen. And *that* he could explain, if he ever got the chance. But he really didn't want to do it in front of all the guys. As for both his personal and professional life—although the lines had blurred many times in her case—he'd prefer to keep them as far apart as possible otherwise. Particularly as the former wasn't exactly headed the direction he wanted it to go and maybe never would now.

He ran his hands through his hair and rubbed his face. "When she calms down a bit, I'll talk to her."

"When she does, we *all* will," Levi said. "She's made this public, and made accusations. We have to get to the bottom of it."

Flynn looked at Levi and nodded. "We can do that." Inside his heart was sinking. Damn, he really wanted to be a part of this unit. He didn't need this. But it was so typical to finally make headway in his life just to have something blow up and, literally, smack him across the face. "I have no idea what she's talking about, but I had nothing to do with killing an animal."

Stone punched him on the shoulder. "We know that. We just have to convince her."

From a few steps away, Merk said, "You're also missing a very major point here. Not only did somebody have access to her house to put the knife into your jacket pocket, chances are good he knew exactly what would happen between you two by doing this. So what you need to ask yourself is, who the hell hates you enough to set you up for this?"

Flynn stared at him in shock. "No one. I made a lot of enemies in the military. Hell…" He looked around at everybody, his arms outspread. "We all did. But nothing at this level. This is…" He shook his head. "I'd never hurt an animal."

"So what happened hits you at one of the most painful levels possible?" Stone asked. "Interesting."

With a sinking heart Flynn knew he'd have to apologize, somehow convince Anna he had nothing to do with this, and then get to the bottom of it. These guys were right—somebody was pinning this on him.

"I need this sorted fast," Levi said. "We have three jobs, people." They were just setting up all the teams to head out. "With this coming down on you, Flynn, you have to stay local."

"Oh, hell no. I was so ready to go off on another job."

Levi nodded. "Understood. Depends on what we find out." He nodded toward the inside of the house. "So the sooner the better. You ready?"

Flynn felt as if he were being led to the slaughter. He took a deep breath. "Damn, yeah. I guess I shouldn't have left my jacket there."

"In her kitchen, I believe we heard her say," Merk said, one eyebrow raised.

"Not by me," Flynn said, one hand up as if swearing to God. "As much as I tried, I never quite got her there. But she has an asshole hanging around. He's trying to start a relationship, yet she's been saying no all along. He's just not listening. He saw me around the place a couple times. I figured if I left my jacket someplace—like, in her *kitchen*—then he'd believe there was more going on between us, and he'd get the hell out of her life. Honestly the guy is messed up."

"Enough to kill an owl and pin it on you?" Stone asked, turning to face him.

Flynn frowned. "Maybe. But I assumed he loved animals too. He was always talking to them." Flynn stared at the doorway again. He was a huge animal lover. He'd enjoyed helping Anna at her place. The few weeks he'd been there had been an easy job, which gave him a chance to indulge in his love of animals of all kinds. To think of somebody going in there, killing even an owl, well, that was heartbreaking. That it had been left on her doorstep was disturbing. As a threat, it said the killer could get to an animal anytime, as well as Anna. Flynn wouldn't be happy until he resolved this, as much for her as for him. The last thing he wanted was to start his career at Legendary Security with a tainted history.

He knew Katina and Anna had been best friends for a long time. He didn't want anything to get in the way of that. But he had high hopes for Anna himself. He'd met very few women who faced up to him, and who got his emotions rocking and rolling like she did. There was a whole lot more to their relationship that he was only starting to figure out. He had tried damn hard to get her into his arms and still planned for it in the near future, but he had come to realize she wasn't the one-night-stand or easy-on/easy-off type of affair. And that was a good thing as he wasn't either, but it did mean he had to slow down.

She was the type you took home to your parents and married for life.

That had set him back just enough to reconsider his own long-term plans.

When Levi had a quick second job available for him, Flynn had jumped at it, thinking distance would help him put his relationship with Anna into perspective. Only problem was, he left four days ago and was home again this morning, with her right back into his life. And from what he could see—in his heart—she'd damn near made herself a permanent home.

Too bad she didn't look interested in spending any time there, as she'd just proven.

No, he was better off alone. Damn. Even though she was a bit volatile, he had liked her all the more for it.

Chapter 2

SHE SAT INSIDE the massive kitchen beside Katina with a hot cup of coffee in her hands. She could feel her rage and pain fading. She'd needed to vent. At someone. She hoped she'd chosen the right person. She certainly was justified with the jacket mess. Only she didn't know for sure if he'd killed the owl. If he had, what was to stop him from attacking her other animals? That inherent threat scared her. These animals didn't deserve this shit. Why would anybody kill them so unmercifully? She shuddered.

Katina reached an arm around Anna's shoulders and hugged her again. "It'll be okay. Just take it easy."

Anna raised tear-stained eyes to her friend and said, "Why would anybody hurt an animal?"

Katina winced. "We know that many people would say it was only an owl, but it was so horribly…" She swallowed hard.

"It had been gutted. Essentially there's no rhyme or reason."

"Often we can do nothing about it but catch the assholes who did this and put them away."

Anna had been trying to find good homes for the animals at her shelter, but in the meantime, they had her to look after them. And maybe that was why she felt so bad. What if this guy came back? She'd never thought Flynn did this, but she'd lost it when she'd found the bloody knife. The guilt just ate at her. She was alone again since Flynn left. Permanently, just over a week ago.

It hadn't taken long for the reality to set in. He'd been a huge help getting the backlog of work done, and he also maintained a steady presence there. One she'd been happy to have. Also, the extra hands made the work go so much faster. Without him there now, all the chores fell once again on her shoulders. She'd become used to having his assistance. She wasn't sleeping well at night now either. She thought there had been an intruder the night before, but then realized it was probably just her nerves. Now she had to rethink all of this.

But she hadn't called the cops last night. She hadn't done anything because she had nothing concrete to tell them. But she'd called this morning about the gutted owl. The police came and took notes and pictures. She'd given a statement, and they'd left. She had no idea if they gave a damn. After all it was *just* an owl.

Feeling sorry for herself, she'd had a crying jag in her bedroom, and only then did she realize Flynn's jacket was on her chair. It hadn't been there earlier. It was hanging on the back of her door, and she'd smiled when she'd first seen it there—right after he had left her, his job done—knowing he'd come back for it. But she wasn't smiling now. She didn't even know how it had gotten in her bedroom because he had been gone for over a week and sure as hell hadn't spent any nights in there with her. But it was definitely his. And when she had picked it up, the knife had fallen from the pocket. One with dried blood.

Even now she couldn't quite explain to herself why she hadn't called the police again right away and shown it to them. Instead, she came racing out to the compound. And now that she was thinking straight, something even more horrific gripped her throat. If that knife had been used to kill the owl, then the asshole had been inside her house, her bedroom. And placed the jacket on her bedroom chair.

Dear God, had he been in there while she was asleep?

"Do you think whoever killed that animal was inside your house?"

Anna stared at Katina. "He had to because I found that knife inside Flynn's pocket, and the jacket was in my bedroom." She gripped Katina's hand hard. "I just don't know if he was when I was there."

She cast her mind back over the most recent time line. "The dogs were fine last night when I took them for a walk at eight, and when I went to bed at eleven, there was nothing wrong, no sign of a disturbance. But between then and six this morning, the owl was left, but the dogs didn't kick up a ruckus." She shivered. "I just can't stand the thought of somebody hurting my animals."

She lifted her coffee cup and took a sip, sniffling back the tears. When she heard loud sounds—signifying the men were coming inside—she stiffened and hugged the cup a little harder.

Katina gripped her fingers with her own. "Don't worry about the men."

Anna shot her friend a look. "How can I not?" She shook her head. "I wasn't exactly a calm, rational female when I got here."

"And you had good reason to be upset." Alfred walked over at that moment and put a plate of tarts down in front of the two women.

Katina gasped in surprise. "Alfred, these look absolutely

delicious."

"When life gets us down, sometimes we all need a treat." He disappeared with a quiet smile.

Anna watched him go. "How come all the good men are in that age bracket?"

"In Alfred's case I'd take the jump," Katina said with a laugh. "If Merk wasn't around, that is."

Anna slid her friend a sidelong glance. "You guys tying the knot again?"

"Quite possibly. He hasn't asked me officially. Afterward I'd have to answer, officially, and we would then make plans—officially." She shrugged. "We haven't gotten that far."

"I'm really happy for you. Obviously you were meant to find each other again."

"I wish I didn't have to be kidnapped or tormented like I was to make that happen."

"But you did what was right, and that's what counts."

The two women shared smiles. They'd been friends a long time. They had a damn good idea of just how rough the world could be. Especially when it came to two women alone. Anna's mother was alive—if that was what you called somebody who spent a lifetime in and out of jail. They'd parted ways when Anna was sixteen. She'd had a really rough upbringing, and maybe that accounted partly for why she would go off the handle at times. One of the biggest things that burned her ass was injustice. She was always there for the underdog. Which was how she got herself into so much trouble.

And why she helped the animal world.

The shelter was a full-time job in all ways but income. She was constantly looking for ways to increase the donations and took on other small jobs to help out. Yet it was hard to keep the money rolling in. She worked as a dog walker and did any number of other odd errands to pay the bills, but every month there seemed to be a shortfall. She had a couple companies that donated a lot of the cat and dog food. But the vet bills were getting pretty rough. She'd wondered about putting herself through school and becoming one herself just so she could look after the animals.

The men arrived and took seats on both sides of the big table. Anna glanced at Katina, who smiled brightly at everyone. Anna really hadn't had a chance to look at any of them, other than Flynn. Now she felt really bad because Levi had sent Flynn to watch over her when Katina had become a target. And instead of actually thanking him for looking after her, she'd flown off the handle at Flynn.

Always wanting to own up to her mistakes, she straightened and whispered to Katina, "Which one is Levi?"

Katina looked at her in surprise, then as if she realized Anna didn't know any of the men, set out to do introductions. One by one, when the man's name was called, they nodded their heads at her.

She realized they all looked at her a little strangely. "I'm sorry for the explosive entrance," she said. "Waking up to find the gutted owl on my doorstep and Flynn's knife in his jacket pocket in my bedroom appears to have sent me over the edge. I'm not normally this volatile, but I care about animals greatly, and it's really unnerving to think that the asshole who did this"—she couldn't help glancing over at Flynn—"had not only been in my house but in my bedroom."

Several of the men straightened as if they hadn't quite made that connection. And of course, why would they? She hadn't given them all the information. She turned to the man Katina had introduced as Levi. He was studying her with a different expression, but didn't appear to be mad, although from the look in his eyes, she wasn't exactly sure what he was feeling.

Hurriedly she said, "I never got a chance to thank you for allowing Flynn to look after me and mine while Katina was in trouble."

"And yet, as soon as we remove Flynn, you get into your own?"

She shook her head. "Well, not quite. He left, what? Seven—eight days ago? He stopped by once, but this just happened last night."

Silence reigned as the men looked at each other. Levi nodded. "But if somebody had been watching the place, they would know you were no longer around. So if you were out of the picture, why put the knife in your pocket to firmly put you back into the picture?"

Silence.

One of the other men, a monster of a tank, leaned over the table and asked Anna, "Did you tell the police about the knife?"

She shook her head. "No. They came this morning and spent a short time there. When they left, I went into my bedroom, and that's when I saw the jacket."

"And you didn't call them again?"

She shook her head. "No, but I should have. For some reason I came racing here instead." She made a funny face. "Like I said, I don't normally fly off the handle like this."

An odd snort came out of Flynn's mouth.

She glared at him. "Although some people do seem to prick my temper a little more than most."

One of the men on the other side of the table, she thought his name was Rhodes, spoke then. "Flynn's like that. He does it to more than you, believe me."

"Hey, that's not fair." Flynn laid his hands on the table. "I didn't do anything."

"But somebody went to a lot of trouble to make it look like you did," Levi said. "We need to know why. And if it's connected to anything else."

"To anything else?" Flynn asked. "What do you mean?"

"You were looking after Anna because of Katina's kidnapping case. It's possible that whoever is implicating you now could be a part of that case in some way."

Katina straightened beside Anna. "Oh, please, don't say that. I thought for sure we got everybody."

"And given the time frame, chances are we have. However, that doesn't mean it isn't connected to something else. Not only did Flynn leave your place, he then hooked up with Logan."

Levi turned to stare at a different man, leaning against the kitchen wall, one Anna hadn't seen before.

"Logan has been attached to several of our cases, so it's possible Anna and her shelter were just caught in the crosswinds of something much bigger, deeper, and uglier."

Levi turned to study Anna.

She gave him a small smile. Her only thought was *holy shit*. She didn't know this man, but he seemed to be searching her, studying her, like he knew something she didn't. It was a daunting feeling.

Just as she was about to nervously ask Levi what was the matter, one of the most strikingly beautiful women she'd ever seen walked into the room. Levi lit up. The woman sat beside him, smiling directly at Anna, and said, "Hi, I'm Ice."

"Hi, pleased to meet you."

Obviously Ice and Levi were partners. There was just something about the way they sat together, not to mention they were perfectly matched, like a tight couple. Fascinated, Anna watched as they appeared to have a low conversation, almost in code as they finished each other's sentences.

Finally, Levi turned back to Anna. "As much as we hate to dig into your personal life, we have to ask a few questions."

She straightened and frowned at him. "What does that have to do with this?"

"Is there anybody who hates you enough to do something like this? Any neighbors who hate the fact you have the shelter and maybe want to shut you down? Do you know anybody who would be angry enough at Flynn for being in your life that he might find this an avenue to turn you away from him?"

Her jaw dropped. Slowly, she pulled herself together. She considered the questions for several moments. "I've never heard any official complaints, but I know several of my neighbors weren't too happy with my animal shelter. I do have a large piece of land on the outskirts of the city, and most of the properties there are almost as large, so there's distance between us. I get a lot of traffic through my place, but it would be hard for my neighbors to have any grounds for complaint as it's not steady.

"I don't think we ever truly realize who might hate us or just dislike us. As far as I know, there's nobody with a grudge against me. I haven't had any major breakups, put anybody in jail, nor had arguments with anybody to that extent. So that shouldn't be a concern. As for anybody who'd be angry at Flynn being there, well, it only makes sense that I would have somebody around the place to help out. I have in the past. Flynn was only there for a few weeks." She frowned at Levi. "I'm not sure what you're getting at."

From the far side of the table Flynn said, "He's asking about past boyfriends who might think I was somebody you were hanging out with."

She sent him a frown. "As you well know, I don't have a boyfriend, so it's not an issue."

"And what about Jonas?"

"What about him?" she snapped. "We only met for coffee once at the mall, then he started hanging around the place because he's lonely. I don't think he has many friends, but we didn't have a relationship."

"He's not taking no for an answer," Flynn reminded her. "I sent him away that day, remember?"

She stared at him for a moment, and then her confusion cleared. "Sure, but that was only one time. He was just trying to see me. You know he comes around now and then. I figured he was harmless. Whatever mood you were in, you didn't want to let him in."

"Well, maybe it was because he was high. He was completely stoned out of his mind and shouldn't have been there."

She shrugged. "That's not unusual apparently. He's like that most of the time he's been around the house."

"He was also very angry at seeing me there."

"Well, you were inside my house."

Silence.

She slumped back into her chair. "He was upset because he saw you inside my house and figured you were my new boyfriend." She looked at the men at the table. "So now you're all considering it was Jonas who killed the owl, and placed a knife in Flynn's jacket pocket to incriminate him, so I'd be angry?"

She looked around at all the faces and added, "Right, of course. But that wouldn't work as I do know who Flynn is inside." She dropped her head in her hands. "If I hadn't been so upset and scared, I wouldn't have said what I did in the first place."

Glumly, she stared at Flynn. "For the record, I don't believe you had anything to do with killing that owl. I saw you work around my animals. You're just not that kind of a guy." She stared down at the table. "Now I feel like an idiot."

Katina, still sitting beside her, said, "No, it was fear. And coming here was right. You came here to get help. Whoever it was thought they'd set Flynn up and got the opposite reaction to what they expected. The good thing is, they don't know about it."

Anna turned to frown at Katina. "I don't get it."

"They might have thought you'd fly down here and break it off with Flynn. But instead you came to be safe, and get help. So instead of breaking up with Flynn, all you've done is get his attention to help solve this for you." Katina smiled. "The opposite reaction. But still the right thing for you to do."

Feeling like a fool and wishing she could just leave now, Anna muttered, "It doesn't feel like it."

Just then Alfred arrived bearing platters of big sandwiches and wraps cut in pretty little pieces.

Hurriedly, Anna stood up and pushed her chair back. "I'm so sorry. I didn't mean to intrude on your luncheon."

Katina stood up beside her. "Don't worry about it. You're welcome here."

"No, that's not necessary."

The two wrangled back and forth until Flynn stood up and roared, "Sit down."

Silence. Again.

Anna glared at him. "You're not in my house on Levi's orders, so you don't get to boss me around any longer."

In a low deadly voice, he leaned across the table, his large hands flat on the surface, and snapped, "Sit down, damn it, or I'm coming over there and making you."

"Don't you dare threaten me," she growled right back, leaning over, her hands near his on the table, shoving her face in his. "Just you try it."

Then she heard it. A snicker. Then a choked laugh. And suddenly the entire group at the table erupted in laughter.

Mortified, she sat back down and buried her face in Katina's shoulder. Arms came around her, and she realized her best friend was laughing too.

Such was her day.

AS THE LAUGHTER broke out, Flynn sat down with a hard bump. How nice that he and Anna had provided entertainment for the crew. It wasn't exactly how he wanted to introduce them to her. She really was special. He had hoped that having a break from each other would make her seem less so in his eyes. New attractions were always deadly. He wanted some time away to ensure what they had was potential enough to go after.

Her accusations had stunned him. Her apology just now only slightly less so. He glared down into his coffee cup, wondering how long it would take for this hilarity to die down.

When the laughter finally stilled, Levi spoke up. "First thing is to get the knife to the police. Should be simple enough to test it to determine if it was used."

Logan, sitting opposite Katina at the table, said to Levi, "We can test that here, you know."

Levi tilted his head at Logan.

"It's really simple to determine certain things about blood," Logan said. "But our sampling must be small so the police can have the rest for whatever tests they have to do." He nodded toward Anna. "If you want to come with me after lunch, we can see what our testing kit can find."

"Thank you," she said in a neutral tone.

Flynn studied her downcast head. This had been a tough morning for her. He couldn't imagine the shock of finding the bloody knife in his jacket pocket. He knew it was his, just as he did that he'd lost it; therefore, he hadn't been the one to bloody it. Not this most recent time at least. It may have some on the blade, but it could be human, and it would be a degraded sample—something from a long time ago during one of the more ugly missions he'd been a part of in the Middle East. He'd cleaned his knife, but the best labs could always find evidence—and they would find something.

Still, it was bothersome. He hated to think of her all alone in that place with a madman running around killing animals. It was a very small step from that to humans, as he knew all too well. Nothing like being in the military—particularly when he'd been over in Afghanistan and Iraq—to shake his belief in humanity.

The atrocities he'd seen had been shocking. He had no problem with animals being killed for food, but he hated to see them starved, abused, injured, or toyed with. It was one of the reasons he'd been so happy to help Anna. It gave him a chance to reconnect with the animal world he'd missed so much.

And for that he was grateful.

Stone, who had been quiet up until now, asked, "Any chance the man who did this was either the previous owner or neighbor?"

Anna frowned at him. "It's possible, but I don't know why now though."

"But it is a line to tug," Flynn said. Not that he had the time. He was supposed to be heading out of town. At least he'd really been hoping to, but according to Levi that wouldn't happen now.

"First things first, let me take a look at the blood on the knife." Logan glanced over at Flynn. "You still have it?"

Flynn pulled the bag out of his pocket and handed it over.

Logan stood up and said, "With any luck I've got five minutes to set up my tests before you guys eat everything. The actual results take longer." He turned and disappeared out the door they had come in.

Stone stood up, picked up his cup of coffee, refilled it at the sidebar and followed Logan.

Flynn watched as several of the women got up and went to the kitchen to help Alfred bring out the rest of lunch.

The others stayed seated at the table and talked about opening a lab in the compound, but they needed the money set aside for it before doing so. Expansions were expensive, and all kinds of equipment were needed. Apparently, a morgue quickly became a hot topic as well. From what he'd heard about the attacks on the compound so far, he conceded that would be a need. Though a large walk-in freezer would be a better option.

After lunch, several people headed back to whatever they were doing before the interruption.

The place was large, and well over a dozen people were in and out on a regular basis. He was one of the newest and still finding his own place. Having Anna storm in this morning had just added to his problems. But he was more concerned about her.

Katina still sat very close to Anna, their heads huddled together as they talked. He wondered what it was like to have a friend like that.

Guys had buddies. They hunted, fixed cars, and barbecued together with a case of beer open beside them as they talked about everything, but nothing personal. These two women shared such a special bond. And he wondered how that worked for them.

He got up, refilled his coffee and sat back down across from Anna. When he noticed hers was empty, he winced, stood again and poured a cup for her.

She raised her eyes to him. "Thank you."

"Just relax," he said. "We'll get to the bottom of this."

Logan came back in, his face grim and his voice hard. "I heard you say that." He shook his head. "But it's a whole lot more serious than that."

Levi came in from the kitchen. "What did you find?"

"The blood in the bag and on the knife is not animal. It's human."

Anna gasped, her hand covering her mouth.

He held up the bag containing the knife for everyone to see. "And it's covered from one end to the other."

Flynn's stomach knotted. He turned to Anna's pale features.

Logan continued, "I don't suppose you found a dead

body—other than the owl—on your property, did you?"

She shook her head, saying, "No."

"Did you even look?" Flynn asked.

"Why would I?" she cried. "I found the owl and was so upset, it never occurred to me to keep looking. And then I found the knife in the jacket. Obviously I assumed you used it on the owl."

Flynn looked to Levi. "Definitely past time to call the cops."

Levi nodded. "You'll need to take her to the station and hand over the knife and jacket."

He nodded as he stood up, looking at Anna. "Are you ready?"

"For what?"

"I'm taking you to the cops in Houston." He glanced at the others. "And then I'll go back to her place to see if we can find a body."

She let out a hoarse cry.

"You want company?" Logan asked. "I got nothing better to do today, and I would like to see how this goes."

Flynn nodded.

He and Logan had been buddies for a long time. He wouldn't mind having him come along. Something was seriously off, and he knew better than most how important it was to have someone he trusted to watch his back.

Chapter 3

ANNA HUDDLED INSIDE her jacket. She was grateful she'd thought to grab one. She couldn't believe the sudden turn of events, and was really not looking forward to a trip to the police station. Then somehow going home with Flynn on one side and Logan the other was completely the opposite of what she thought would happen this morning.

To find out the knife was covered in human blood changed everything. She cast her mind to what she thought she'd heard last night and everything she'd seen this morning, but there had been nothing to indicate an injured human was anywhere around. She just couldn't believe this.

They made the trip in complete silence. As they entered the city, Flynn turned to look at Logan and asked, "How about a change of plan? We should check on her place first, make sure there isn't something else to find, and then report to the police."

"Good idea," Logan said. "We'd look pretty stupid if we take a knife in, then go to her place and find a body."

She shrunk down into the seat a little farther. The last thing she wanted was to find anything else dead around her place. At least she had a decent security system. But what good was it when an intruder could shut it down, like this one must have? The cost of running the place was so high she was barely limping along. She had several acres here in what had been the outskirts of Houston, only the city had grown up around her—increasing her taxes and utilities. How could she set up security for the entire place? It would cost a small fortune.

Flynn drove into the driveway and parked off to the side. Stuck in the middle, she had to wait for the men to get out first. She hopped down, walked up to the front door to unlock it, only to find the door was ajar.

"Shit."

"Shit what?" Flynn stepped up and seeing the door open, pushed her out of the way and pulled a weapon from his back pocket.

She'd almost forgotten about the fact he carried. Sure this was Texas, and she should be used to it, but there was something about the way he wielded it. He was a man who knew exactly what to do with that weapon. And wasn't scared of doing what needed to be done.

It wasn't comforting before, but now it was downright soothing.

Both men had their weapons out and walked into her house quietly. "Stay here," Flynn whispered.

She made a face. She wasn't stupid. She would let them go first, but no way would they keep her out for long. She was terrified of what might happen to her animals in the back.

After giving them a long moment, she peered around the corner into the front hallway and living room. It seemed normal. As upset as she had been when she left earlier, there was a chance she forgot to shut the door.

She walked in and followed the men as they searched the entire downstairs. She shrugged. Nothing appeared to be wrong or out of place. "Maybe I forgot to lock up," she said.

She walked to the kitchen's back door. It was closed, the lock in place. She opened it and went toward the animals in their kennels. With her heart pounding, she walked through the shelter, checking all the cages, finding everyone safe and sound.

She turned to face the men and realized only Logan was here with her. "Where's Flynn?"

"He's gone to check the rest of the house."

That made sense. "All the animals are here and accounted for."

She walked to where the dogs were kept. She hated to leave them for very long. As soon as she got home, she would move them out to the yard for a few hours to get some exercise.

There was Jimbo, a big golden Lab, and Duggy, a pit-bull/Doberman cross that needed freedom more than the others. She also had two small dogs, which was a blessing. She quickly shuffled the bigger ones and their pens, letting the animals out back, and they jumped and played with each other. She smiled. It was one of the reasons she did this, and a way she could find homes for them.

She took the remaining dogs and moved them to one of the smaller pens. She had four cats in residence right now. She shifted them as well. Something she normally would've done this morning.

The playhouse was in a separate room where the cats could sprawl out for most of the day. After finding the owl this morning, she'd put everyone back in their cages. Maybe a foolish thought, but now they could return to the play area.

It took a good ten minutes to shuffle everyone around. Several other animals were at her place right now, and one was a huge bunny named Bugs. But he lived outside in a pen—as long as the weather was warm enough for him. She checked and found him nibbling on grass.

That left the snake, in a glass terrarium for now, safely sequestered from the hamster in a large cage off to the side. He was snoozing in the sawdust. Happy.

"Good. Everyone here is fine," she said to herself. She turned to find Logan, standing guard. She winced. "Are you actually playing bodyguard?"

He gave her a flat stare. "Until we figure out what the hell's going on, yes. You won't be alone until then. And there's nothing playful about this."

She nodded and brushed past him. "I'm heading back to the house then."

"Wait. How much of this is your property, and is there somewhere else we should look for a body?"

She froze. "I have four acres here," she said. "You want to check everywhere? Just stay out of the dog pen. They don't know you. Other than that, do what you want."

Flynn spoke from behind her. "What about the food shed?"

She turned to stare at him. "What about it?"

"Have you been inside it this morning?"

She shook her head. "No. I don't need to. I have dog food inside."

"Then Logan'll stay with you in the house, and I'll check the rest of the property."

He glanced at Logan, and she saw as they exchanged looks.

She threw up her hands. "Fine, we'll go together." She led the way to the back and opened the double doors. "I get a lot of food donated by companies. I keep most of it in the shed."

"Is it locked?" Logan asked.

"Yes," she said. "I have to. I can't afford to have any of it go missing. It's expensive enough to keep this place up."

"You need better security here," Flynn said from behind her.

Immediately her back stiffened. "So you said, more than once." She took several steps toward the shed, adding, "As I said before, there isn't any money to upgrade."

At the shed she stopped and stared at the busted lock. "Ah, hell. It's been broken into." She'd just die if all the food was gone. There was over a year's supply stored in there. She wouldn't be able to replace it.

Her shoulders were grabbed roughly, and she was jerked back several feet. "We'll go in. You stay out of the way."

She shot Flynn a fulminating glare, but he wasn't looking her way. Instead, he and Logan were communicating in a way that was all too easy to understand. As she watched, Flynn gave a nod to Logan to open up the door.

With her gut wrenching in fear, she waited, her arms across her chest as she chewed on her bottom lip. This was one of the easiest, most accessible places on the property.

And she hadn't really considered it that way before.

Logan pulled open the door, and both men jumped in, weapons out.

When would this nightmare end? When Flynn had stayed at her place to keep an eye on her, all she'd been able to think about was the day he'd finally leave. He'd been such an irritant in so many damn ways. Yet, he'd also been fun, bringing a lot of laughter to her world. When he did leave, all she could think about was an excuse to see him again.

But today hadn't gone the way she'd hoped. She'd just been so angry and upset that she hadn't been able to think straight. Now he was here, coming to her rescue yet again, and all she wanted was for him stay.

"Anna?"

She was startled back to the present and walked a few feet forward to peer into the darkened room. "What?"

Flynn's voice was somber and hard. "We found what we were looking for."

She couldn't see anything with the two men standing in front of her. She pushed her way in between them. The shed wasn't that big. On the floor between the full racks of pet food lay a man, collapsed on the floor.

FLYNN WATCHED HER face, seeing the shock as emotions swept over her. She clapped her hands over her mouth, and tears filled her eyes. He had a sinking feeling in his stomach. "You know him?"

She raised her gaze to him. "You do too."

He pulled out his keys with a small flashlight at the end and turned it on. Focusing on the man's face. "Hell, that's Jonas, the asshole that's always after you. The damn stalker."

"Whoa," said Logan. "Her stalker ends up dead on her property. And the knife likely used to kill him ends up in your jacket pocket in her bedroom." He shook his head. "This is not good. Someone is pinning this murder on you, buddy. Who the hell did you piss off so bad they want to lock you up for twenty years?"

"No one. Hell, I haven't pissed anyone off lately. Not so they'd do something like this," Flynn protested.

"Except me," Anna muttered. Flynn gave her a sharp look, and she had the grace to look ashamed. "Okay, you have a tendency to rub people the wrong way. But that's no reason to set you up for murder." She turned to look around the small room. "What really concerns me at the moment is, to set you up, what other evidence is here adding weight to that?"

"No idea. But I didn't do it, so it doesn't matter what the hell they find. It just means I have to clear myself."

Logan said, "Hey, buddy. I know that's how it's supposed to work, but too often the cops just look at the surface. They get easy evidence, and that's it. Slam dunk. You're locked away as a murderer."

Flynn glared at him. He crouched beside the body. "He looks like he's been shot."

"Except his arm is cut up pretty bad too," Logan said, pointing to the dried blood on the dead man's sleeve.

Flynn exchanged a hard glance with Logan. "I have an ugly suspicion as to what knife might have caused that injury too. It would explain the human blood on it."

Logan held up his hands. "I know you wouldn't do something like this. We'll help any way we can. This is bullshit. I know it. You know it. But we still have to call the cops."

"I'll do it," Anna said, pulling out her phone. "It needs to be me."

Flynn pulled out his. "Do it," he barked at Anna. "I'm calling Levi."

Logan held up his phone. "Good idea. I'm calling my father. I think we might need everyone in on this deal."

Chapter 4

ANNA STARED AT the officer standing in her kitchen. "I'm sorry. Did you just say I need to leave? I don't have any place to take the animals. This is a shelter. They are here because they require someone to care for them in the first place."

"It's now a crime scene. You can't be here."

"No," she protested. "The shed is a crime scene. That has nothing to do with the animal shelter or my house."

"And yet, we think it's related to the owl being killed. The knife was found in your bedroom in a jacket pocket. Therefore, evidence is tracked to the house."

"You don't understand. I have no place to go." She stood and looked out the window at the animals. "And there are no other shelters around that can take them. That's the reason they're here."

The police officer walked several steps away and pulled out his phone. She didn't know who he was calling, and didn't care. Somebody needed to solve this. How long would her place be a crime scene? Surely a day was enough for them to get whatever evidence they needed.

If they left the animals, she could come back and feed them. Maybe she could stay somewhere for the night. She just didn't know. Often the police wouldn't let people back into their homes for days, if not weeks. That couldn't happen here. It was her home. Surely something could be done.

So far Logan and Flynn stood quietly at her side. They answered all the questions they'd been asked, but hadn't offered anything extra. She understood how Flynn felt. At the moment she was feeling pretty damn antagonistic toward the police herself.

Then she remembered that Jonas's mother was alive. That was one thing about Jonas always coming around and making a nuisance of himself—he'd talked. A lot. She knew how hard this news would be for his mother. Nobody should lose a child. Now that he was dead, she was sorry for not having treated him nicer. But he'd become difficult, a pain in the ass, someone who wouldn't take no for an answer.

But she had never wanted him dead, just to go away and leave her alone.

She deliberately kept her gaze from zeroing in on his body, instead looking at the back window of the shed. She couldn't help worrying that she might need access to the food stored there. Damn, what was wrong with her? Someone had been killed in there, and all she could worry about was the animals.

That was typical. The donation money had slowed to a trickle, and she was in dire straits. The last thing she needed was something like this. It was hard to get support for the animals at any time. If anybody thought a murder investigation was going on at the shelter, the money would completely stop.

Morose, she sat at her kitchen table, drinking coffee, waiting for the police to go through whatever it was they needed to. There was no point in fighting it. She'd given them access to the entire property. She wanted them to do their job.

The officer came back and told her, "We need the property for twenty-four hours. When it's time for you to work with the animals, an officer will be with you at all times. You can't stay here overnight, but during the day, you can be here for the animals. After that time, we should be done, and you can have the place back." He stood and waited for a response.

What choice did she have? This was the best she could get. She gave a curt nod. "I will be here from seven in the morning to seven at night. At that point, I will leave." He frowned, and she shook her head. "There are dogs to feed and walk, cats to look after, as well as cages to empty and disinfect. There's food to sort and medicine to give out. There are phone calls to make, etc. This is a business, and it's a charity. I need people to understand it's still operational."

He turned and walked away. She sank back into her chair. "That went well."

Flynn spoke from behind her. "Where are you going overnight?"

"I want to sleep in the cages with the animals," she muttered. "I don't really want to leave them alone."

"The police won't let you do that."

She propped her elbows on the table and dropped her chin into her hands. "Of course they won't. That would be too easy. I have no idea what I'll do. How's that for an answer?"

She stared out the window, wondering what the hell happened, and how she would get past this—then chastised herself for being selfish. She knew Flynn was in bigger trouble. Yet he had people backing him. People he could trust to find out what was going on and make sure this didn't have a long-lasting impact on his life. She was in the same boat Katina had been in before, and now understood why she was with Merk at the compound.

In fact, it wasn't that far away, but still she wouldn't impose on her friend any more than she had to. Mentally she went through a list of people she knew, wondering if anybody would be generous enough to offer their couch for the night. But the list was short, and the answers were no by the time she got to the end of it. No way could she justify staying at a hotel. She needed money for her own electricity, phone, and water bill. She would not blow that kind of money on a hotel.

So maybe she would have to spend the night in her car.

Logan appeared at her side. "Levi said you're welcome back at the compound until the police are finished in your house."

She turned to stare up at him. "Why would he even offer?"

Logan laughed. "He is a very generous soul. You're also friends with Katina. And obviously you have some kind of an oddball relationship with Flynn. Love and murder, perhaps?" His tone was teasing, yet with the threat of darkness and all that had already happened …

She winced. "The murder, yes, but the love … I don't think so."

"Hey, how do you know? Give it—me—a chance," Flynn said, his wicked grin flashing.

She shot him a look and laughed. "Flynn, you've probably left a wrecking-ball-size pathway of broken hearts in your life. I have no intention of becoming part of that."

Logan laughed. "Flynn's all talk but very little action."

"Hey, that's not true. All the girls love a hero."

At that Logan really laughed. "Don't let Levi hear you say that. He's got this thing about that term."

Flynn frowned at him. "What? Hero?"

"Yeah, that one. Ice made a joke about Heroes for Hire being the company name. And the subsequent women who have joined us at the compound have come up with versions of their own to go along with it—much to Levi's disgust."

Flynn laughed. "Oh, my gosh, that's rich. And it's actually a very good name."

"Levi doesn't think so."

Flynn grinned. "No, Legendary Security is way better than that. But as a nickname, it's perfect."

"That would make you a hero," Anna said.

"We tried that once, remember? Didn't work out so well. And you don't have the money to hire anybody, so there is no Hero for Hire here."

She got up and walked to the teakettle, filled it and put it on to heat. Inside, her mind was churning options.

The last thing she wanted to do was go to the compound. But there would be a hot meal and place to sleep overnight. She just loathed the thought of leaving the animals behind. She stared out at the dog runs. "I can't leave the animals alone. What if somebody comes back to kill them?"

"Didn't the police say they would be here overnight?"

She shook her head. "I don't believe that's what they meant. I think they just wanted to have access overnight, not that they'd be here or have guards on duty, keeping an eye on the place. I doubt they have money for that. Nor do I have it to hire somebody to look after the animals or stay in a hotel."

"You won't be. You'll be staying with us," Flynn said.

"And if I don't want to?"

"Then it would mean the two of us having a very uncomfortable night here."

"You'd stay with me?"

"Yes, but I can tell you that because it's a murder scene, the police will be back and forth searching the entire house looking for fingerprints, so the animals will be safe tonight."

She hated to be persuaded, but also knew she needed sleep. "Can I come back early in the morning?"

"Yes."

She checked her watch. It was already after seven. "It'll take me at least an hour to finish with the animals tonight."

"We can help too," Flynn said. "I'd like to be on the road in an hour."

She blew the hair out of her face. "Well, we'd better get busy then."

She started with the dogs, the two men beside her. They walked all of them at the same time for a good half hour. That cut the time way down for her. She struggled to take that many dogs at once, particularly when Jimbo, the big Lab, was rambunctious and tended to tie up all the leashes. Flynn took Jimbo on his own; she took the little ones, and Logan took the pit bull, Duggy.

Thirty minutes later they came back, putting the dogs into their cages for the night. With help, she fed and watered them, gave each a good cuddle, and then turned to the cats. She studied them inside the playhouse and said, "I can leave them all in here. We'll move the litter boxes, food, and water in there too, and they'll be fine."

They did everything needed for the cats, then she turned her attention to the outside pens with the hamster, rabbit, and snake. The hamster needed clean bedding, fresh water, and food, as did the bunny. The snake, well hidden in his habitat, always scared her when he revealed himself. She tossed some live crickets into his terrarium and slammed the lid shut.

By the time they were done, the police were still all over the place, now under outside lights. It gave an eerie look to everything.

She walked back to the officer she'd spoken to earlier. "We'll be leaving now. Please keep an eye on the animals for us."

He nodded. "They'll be fine. We still have hours ahead of us here. It's doubtful anybody else will come back tonight. If they do, they'll get a bit of a surprise."

"Let's hope they do, and you guys catch them. I won't sleep well knowing somebody put a dead man in my shed. Or killed an owl as a twisted message."

"Where exactly was the owl?"

She pointed to the back step. "It was dismembered and left on the step."

"What dogs are here now?"

"The two big guys are in the back. Normally the two little ones are in the front, but I have them closer to the bigger dogs now. Although in the front they'd notice everything from birds to intruders." She winced. "So maybe it's safer for them to be in the front."

"They'll be fine. See you in the morning then."

With the two men at her side, she was persuaded to head back to the vehicles. She was taking her car; she wanted full autonomy to leave in the morning. Otherwise there was a good chance Flynn would stop her.

She got into the driver's side, and as she put the keys in the ignition, Flynn slipped into the passenger seat beside her.

"You can ride with Logan, you know? I'm perfectly safe."

"But I want to ride with you," he said. "Besides, I need to explain something."

She shot him a shuttered look as she pulled out onto the street. Logan was ahead of them. She planned to follow him right back to the compound. She worried that Levi hadn't been given an option about her staying there. It may be that Flynn had somehow pressured Levi into letting her come back. She'd made quite a scene this morning. She wasn't sure she was even welcome.

"Explain what?" The truck ahead of her took several turns and then turned onto the highway. She followed him, and within seconds they were heading down the main road toward the compound. It wasn't a very long drive, but it was one she didn't remember well.

"My jacket."

"Was it?" She looked over at him in surprise. "I thought you were explaining something about the compound."

"As much as I love being part of that place, it's impossible to explain," he said with a laugh. "I'm still figuring out exactly how it all works."

"You sure I'm welcome?"

"It was Levi's idea."

She shrugged. She needed to be happy with that, though she wasn't. She still felt like he had been pressured into it. "What about your jacket?"

"I left it on purpose."

"What the hell did you do that for?" She stared at him in shock.

"Two reasons. One, if Jonas came into your house—your bedroom—he would see it and realize you are in a relationship, and maybe leave you alone."

"Jonas doesn't go into my bedroom. Never even went into my house." Then remembering Jonas lay dead in her shed, she added, "And obviously it's way too late to worry about something like that now." She still didn't quite understand Flynn's meaning. "What do you care if Jonas thought I was in a relationship?"

"Jonas was damn creepy. Any woman should have been terrified of him."

"Well, now that he's dead, I don't think it's an issue."

"At the time I didn't realize his demise would happen quite so fast. And I was more concerned about you."

"Well, thank you for that, but it was completely unnecessary."

There was an odd, uncomfortable silence, and then she remembered he said he had two reasons. "What was the other?"

When he didn't answer, she studied his profile as he stared out the passenger window. "Well?"

FLYNN NEVER BEAT around the bush. He was a straight shooter. He prided himself on that. And when he first opened his mouth, it was with the full intention of telling her more about his jacket. But it just felt odd now. The timing sucked. And he was really big on that too. It seemed like lately everything he did was out of sync with what he should've been doing.

The best time of his life was when he had been an active SEAL. But even then, the timing had sucked. He'd been in Afghanistan, and his orders at the time would've been completely normal and fine, if he had been in the right place. But he'd lagged behind, and gone into a village to help somebody on their way back when nobody would help them. He'd stayed longer than he should. When he had explained it to his CO, he'd been reprimanded. When the orders came through that they were pulling out, and he needed to leave those children in trouble, it went against his better nature, and in his ire, he disobeyed direct orders.

His famous Irish ire. That damn temper of his got him in more trouble. He ignored the orders to return to camp. Instead he helped set a broken leg and then assisted the injured mother with carrying the children back where they would be safe. By the time he made it to camp again, he was in deep shit.

If there was ever a black day he remembered, it was that, and no one wanted to hear his side. It didn't matter that he was doing a good thing. He did not follow orders. The other guys didn't sympathize. In fact, several of them got really angry.

But his CO was an asshole. It didn't matter how good a job you did sometimes anyway. So Flynn had spent a year traveling, "finding" himself. It didn't all suck. It was a great year, but the thought that he'd been having a midlife crisis already at thirty wasn't something he was proud of. But he was lost. Angry, disbelieving the sudden turn of events, and it had taken a long time to get back on his feet.

But now he had a shot with Levi's company, and didn't want to lose it. This was what he was geared to do. Born to do. They were all former SEALs. He knew that would change over time. A lot of other really good men were out there who he knew would like a chance to join. But Legendary Security was a fledgling company, and Levi could hire only so many people at one time. Yet his company was growing. Flynn had no doubt in a few years, this would be *the* company, and he wanted in now.

So when Levi had asked Flynn to look after Anna, the answer had been an instant yes. He'd jumped at the chance and would have done it for nothing, like his official job interview for Levi, so Flynn had been delighted when he was paid.

But nothing had prepared him for meeting Anna. Or for the attraction. It wasn't all one-sided either. He lived large. And he loved well but was looking for something so much more. In Anna, he'd found it. Only they'd argued—a lot. And he'd loved every minute of it. When he'd been told by Levi it was time to pack it in, Flynn had been disappointed but accepted that the job had come to an end. When it came time to actually go, he'd had a hard time leaving things the way they had. So he had left his jacket behind on purpose.

"Are you going to tell me?" she asked. "Is it some deep dark secret you don't want anybody to know? What? Have you been holding a candle for me?" She sneered. "I know that's not true."

He glanced at her. "I guess I deserved that."

She frowned and stared at him.

And he knew she didn't understand. "Because I did leave the jacket behind for a specific reason. It gave me an excuse to come back and see you." He gave a heavy sigh. "And maybe I was staking a claim. So that if any man went inside, he'd see it and know my clothes were there first."

Her gaze widened, and she jerked her attention back to the road. She didn't say anything for a long moment. He slunk back into his seat prepared to sit in silence until they got to the compound.

"And why did you want to come back and see me? All we did was fight."

"Not quite," he said quietly. "Or have you forgotten the kiss?"

"I haven't forgotten *anything*," she mumbled.

He grinned at her emphasis on *anything*. Maybe this wasn't as much of a lost cause as he was afraid it was. He certainly hadn't misunderstood her response to their passionate kiss, but it was something they hadn't gotten a chance to talk about, until now. Leaving the jacket behind was his way of saying, *I'm coming back*. Apparently, she got the message.

As they entered the compound, she slowed and came to a stop in the middle of the road. She looked over at him and said, "Where should I park?"

He pointed at a spot between two of the company trucks. She pulled up and shut off the engine. "It feels weird to be back so soon."

"It shouldn't. It should feel just about right." He gave her a warm grin and exited the car.

As she got out, she turned and asked, "Do you think it's related to that night the dogs went crazy?"

He frowned.

"You know that night …"

He realized several of the men in the garage had turned at their arrival. Of course she chose this moment to bring up what should have been a private conversation.

He thought back to the night in question, realizing he didn't remember much about it, but there had been a ton of barking outside. "You're thinking there was an intruder then?"

She shrugged. "I don't know. It just was an anomaly, and now something else has happened, so I have to wonder."

"What was an anomaly?" Levi asked, approaching.

Flynn winced. Great. Now Levi would think Anna was better at this job than he was. But no way in hell was Flynn walking into a new company, a new job, lying about something. "The night before I left her place, we heard something. It wasn't very much, but it set off the dogs. We didn't find anything at the time though." He glanced at Anna and added, "She's wondering if someone had been checking her place out even then. But what for?"

He motioned her to enter into the garage, and from there he'd take her into the kitchen and find her a spare bedroom. "Now with the killing of the owl, well, that only makes me more concerned. The only reason to do that is to terrorize her."

Levi nodded. His gaze was assessing as he watched Anna walk into the kitchen, and Alfred took over from there. Flynn and Logan remained in the garage, knowing Levi had more questions.

"Do you think she's hiding anything?"

His question was directed at both Flynn and Logan. The two men looked at each other.

Flynn said, "I don't think so. I worked with her for a couple weeks. What you see is what you get. She has a temper, loves to argue. She's passionate about the animals. But I don't think she's deceptive. I never saw any instance where she was lying, and she doesn't use feminine wiles to get her way—she's direct." He shrugged. "I think she's very honest. And she's just horribly upset and shocked by what's happened."

"And I'd have to agree, from the little bit I've seen of her," Logan said. "She's had a particularly tough day. The cops are all over the place. The animals are upset. And, of course, she knew the dead person."

"How well?" Levi turned to face Flynn.

"Not well. They met accidentally the first time, and she was nice to him. He started coming around all the time after that. Being more of a nuisance than anything. She felt sorry for him." He opened his arms. "You know how that goes. He kept coming around, hoping she'd change her mind."

"Was he violent?"

Flynn shook his head. "He never laid a hand on her. He seemed to always be high, coming on or going off from his look. He was fixated on her, obsessed, and if he hadn't died, I'm sure he would have become a much bigger problem. How big of one, I can't tell you."

"We've already done a search on him. Nothing we found changes that. He didn't have a steady job or relationship, but had money. He didn't own property. The vehicle was in his name, but his mother was paying for the insurance. He's done time for small crimes, like petty theft, possession charges, and some breaking and entering, but all on a lower scale."

"So he got himself killed?"

"Or else," Logan said, "he was in the wrong place at the wrong time."

Levi pivoted to look at Logan, then said, "And if we look at that hypothesis, why was he there in the first place? Who needed to take him out because of it? What was the killer doing there?"

Flynn shook his head. "I have no idea."

"How many people knew you were there, Flynn?"

Flynn stopped and looked at the ceiling, contemplating how many actually knew where he had been at that time. "You and your team, Logan's dad, anybody he might have told, Anna, and me. We didn't get out much, just staying on her property. I don't really have friends or family who care. And I wasn't there long enough to make an issue out of it."

"Because what we really have to know here is, why you were set up. Was it to throw deflection from the killer? Or were you the target and Jonas incidental?"

Flynn stared at him as he finally understood. "There aren't too many people who'd go to that kind of effort to set me up."

"How many?" Stone asked from behind him.

Flynn spun, not having heard the big man creep up. Flynn shook his head. "Damn, you're silent."

Stone studied him. "Don't deflect from the question."

"It's just not a pleasant time in my life."

"All the more reason we need to know about it in case it's related."

"Back when I was a SEAL, I went rogue and was booted. I'd do it again in a heartbeat. But at the same time I was kicked out, so was somebody else. He wasn't with me, but he blamed me. I have no idea what reasoning or evidence the military had for their actions toward him."

He stood stiff, not knowing if any of them were aware of the circumstances surrounding him leaving the military. If they were, he hoped they'd understand his position.

"What was the man's name?" Logan asked. "I don't think you told me about that, buddy."

He glanced over at Logan. "Nobody likes to smear dirt. Especially not with a fellow SEAL."

"His name?" prompted Levi.

Flynn considered his options. Then shrugged. "Brendan McAllister."

Instantly, the other men stiffened and nodded knowingly.

"You already know him, I presume?"

"We know him, and you're right," Levi said. "It's not nice to say anything bad about anybody. But if we were, it would be him. He was a lazy lowlife, and he would never have had your back. He was a coward through and through."

Harsh words for a SEAL, for anybody in the military, because if there was one thing everybody needed, that was to know your teammates had your back.

"I heard he was dishonorably discharged," Stone said. "Good thing. I'd have kicked him across the country if they'd given me half a chance."

On that note, Flynn turned to head to the kitchen. Several of the other men joined him.

"I'll get Dad to look into that," Logan said. "He knows his brother. But no two siblings could be as different."

Levi asked Flynn, "Any idea if Brendan is local?"

Flynn stopped. "I don't know."

Logan grabbed his phone. "I'll find out."

"I thought he lived in California," Flynn said. "But that may not have been his choice after he was booted." He pointed toward the kitchen, then said, "I need to show Anna where she will be staying."

"Alfred's got that well in hand."

Of course he did. What would they do without Alfred? Flynn walked into the kitchen to find it was empty. That was also when he realized he'd missed dinner. With any luck some leftovers were in the fridge. He opened the huge double-door appliance, checking to see if he could warm up anything.

As he turned around, Alfred walked into the kitchen, heading for the dishwasher. He pulled out two plates. "I'll have your meals ready in a minute."

"I think Logan's probably hungry too."

Alfred laughed. "Okay, make that three plates." He reached inside the big metal dishwasher and pulled out a third one.

"Anna is in the room beside yours. You'll probably have to bring her back down, otherwise she will not eat. She looks like the kind who doesn't want to impose."

"You got that right."

Flynn was happy to be the errand boy in this instance. He was also delighted that Anna had been put in the bedroom beside his. Alfred was very astute. Maybe he saw something there. Flynn hoped so. But it was way too early to tell.

Chapter 5

THE NEXT MORNING Anna woke up early. It was almost six o'clock. She had a quick shower, got dressed and then made up the bed. With a last glance around the place to see if she left anything behind, she grabbed her bag and walked down to the kitchen. If she was lucky, coffee might be on; if not, she would slip out and head home. The animals needed her.

At the kitchen she stopped to see several people up already. "Wow, I thought I was the only early riser."

With a light grin shining in his eyes, Flynn stood up. "I heard you moving around and figured you'd be sneaking out early."

She glared at him. "I wasn't sneaking anywhere."

"Good, because Alfred's cooking breakfast."

She smiled in delight. "I wish I could steal Alfred away from you."

"Not happening," Levi said, "and you're certainly not the first to try."

She sat down on the far side of the table, watching as everyone came in the room in various states of wakefulness.

When Katina came in and saw her, she dashed over to give her a big hug. "I'm so sorry I didn't see you when you got in last night. I was really tired."

Anna studied her friend. She caught sight of a blush

across her cheeks. She'd let her friend get away with the white lie. If Anna had been sleeping with someone like Merk, she might've had a reason to go to bed early too. She winked at her friend and watched the pink deepen on her cheeks.

Katina smiled. "I was thinking about coming to your place for the day. Maybe I can help out. If nothing else, I can keep you company. It's got to be lonely as hell there."

"We can spend a few hours there, but that'll be all," Merk said quietly. But there was no doubt he meant what he said, and he wasn't budging on the time line.

Katina looked at him and frowned. "Why?"

"Going to Gunner's place. He has information he wants to discuss in regard to Flynn, Logan, and another man named Brendan."

Katina hadn't heard the other news last night.

Neither had Anna. After it was quickly explained to her about this Brendan, she frowned at Flynn. "Why didn't you tell me?"

He raised his eyebrow. "Why would I? That was a long time ago. It's a dead issue."

"Apparently not." She turned to Logan. "And your father confirmed that Brendan is living locally?"

Logan nodded. "Supposedly he's staying with his brother right now."

She dropped her gaze to her coffee cup. "As much as I'm happy he might be a suspect in this killing, it is also kind of unnerving that somebody would hate Flynn so much to kill somebody else." She took a sip of her coffee and added, "How does any of that make sense?"

"We don't have any answers at the moment," Flynn said calmly. "But what you will find is when we do, it will make more sense. Maybe not in the way you would understand, but to the killer, it always makes sense. That's one of the few sad things about people who kill. In their own twisted way, they have a good reason for doing what they do."

"Scary thought." After that, the conversation went to general topics. She watched as platters of sausages, bacon, and eggs came to the table. "Alfred, how can you possibly feed this many people all the time?"

He laughed. "I love it. The bigger this place gets, the happier I'll be." And on that note he turned and walked out.

She raised an eyebrow at Levi. "How big are you planning on making this place?"

"No idea yet," he said cheerfully. "We have lots of room to expand. Depends on the work and need for our services."

She nodded. "It's still empty without animals though."

He laughed. "You're not the first to mention that. Personally, I think all the women want me to bring in a bunch of dogs and cats."

"Well, if that's the case, I do have a few that need homes," she said brightly. "Just let me know, and I'll deliver them personally."

He shook his head. "No way are we going there yet. It would have the workmen in all kinds of chaos around this place."

Flynn raised his head. "Workmen? What's happening next?"

"We're reworking a couple apartments and planning to build a lab. Ice seems to think we need some kind of morgue."

Anna gasped, her gaze zooming toward Ice. "You're kidding, right?"

"Not really. But it could be a cold room for keeping

foodstuffs as well."

"All the health authorities would love that," Anna said with a laugh. "And those guys aren't easy to keep happy at any time."

"Have any of the regulatory bodies made life difficult for you?" Ice asked. "I mean, when we talk about having enemies, very few people actually consider institutions, like health authorities, coming in and closing them down."

"I'm sure groups like that are on some people's list," she said with a smirk. "But no, I haven't had any trouble with anybody."

"Interesting that the best suspect is actually somebody who went to your place as your bodyguard," Levi noted.

Anna glanced at Flynn and quickly said, "That doesn't make him responsible."

"I'm not for bringing him there," Flynn said. "But I might be for pissing him off enough that he wanted some payback."

She leaned forward. "And how does killing Jonas give him that?"

Into the silence that suddenly filled the room, Flynn said, "If I get charged with murder, one I didn't commit, that's a hell of a payback."

"But to kill a man?" She shook her head. "I just don't get that. But I don't live in the same world you guys do. Killing is very alien to me. I'm in a world of saving lives, even if they're mostly four-legged furry ones."

She glanced at her watch and said, "And speaking of which, I need to get going." She stood up and grabbed her dishes, walking into the kitchen. Alfred was there, loading the dishwasher. "Let me rinse these first."

He turned, saw the dishes and smiled. "I'll handle it, my

dear. You take that basket there. It's got lunch and some coffee for you, as well as a few muffins just in case you get hungry. You don't know what kind of mess your kitchen will be in," he rushed to add. "Remember the police were there, and they tore your house apart all day. It could be very upsetting for you when you get home."

"I was trying hard not to think about that." She gave him a sad smile. "It's just work. I can clean it up. I hope the animals survived the night without too much stress. The last thing they need is any more upset."

She walked back into the dining room and picked up her overnight bag she'd dropped in the hallway. She turned to Levi and Ice. "Thank you so much for giving me a place for the night. I need to go and check on the animals."

To the chorus of good-byes, she waved at everybody and headed back through the garage out to her car.

And found Flynn standing at the passenger side.

"What are you doing?"

"I'm going with you," he said calmly. "You have no idea what you're going into when you get home. You shouldn't be alone."

She frowned, realizing she really didn't want to be, but it wasn't good to leave him stuck there. "Don't you want to have your own wheels so you can come home again tonight?"

"You forget several of the guys are going to Gunner's place. I can always catch a ride home with them."

Her face cleared of worry. "I had forgotten. I get to see Katina for a few hours today too." On that much happier note, she got into the car, turned on the engine and waited for him to get in and buckle up, then she pulled out of the compound.

~

DAMN, HE THOUGHT they'd gotten well past that point. But it seemed like she really didn't want him around. Or at least not at night, and that made no sense, considering there had been an intruder at her place, inside as well. He had no intention of leaving her alone in that house, not until this was resolved. The fact that somebody was after him could possibly mean he was putting her in danger. But why didn't this guy face him? There was nothing worse than having an asshole sneaking behind your back, causing mayhem and murder.

He'd had enough trouble living with it in the military as it was. He was sent on missions to ferret out these assholes one by one. But it wasn't something you expected when you hit home ground. And he'd been out of the military now for almost two years.

But apparently, he'd also lost his edge. And that would be a concern. If not to him, then to Levi. If they didn't think they could trust him, then they wouldn't assign him to help out on missions. The others had to know he was there to watch their back. And he had been watching hers.

As the asshole had gone inside her house after Flynn had left, had the killer been watching her place? Had he known Flynn had left? For good? Or had he expected Flynn to be there to take the hit instead of Jonas?

The drive was smooth and fast. When they pulled into the front driveway, cop cars were still parked there. He could almost sense the waves of relief coming off of Anna, presuming the cops had been here since yesterday, so nobody else would have shown up through the night.

He got out, leaving his stuff in the backseat. She hadn't noticed he'd brought an overnight bag, and at the moment, that was fine with him.

He reached the front door ahead of her, found it unlocked and walked in. Nobody was inside. He turned back to her and said, "I suggest we talk to the cops first."

She nodded. "Works for me."

But instead he went to the kennels. Of course she pitched in. Very quickly they had all four dogs moved to the outside pens. After scratches, cuddles, and boisterous good mornings, they turned their attention to the cops and walked around the feed shed.

Flynn watched one man, standing on the far corner, taking pictures of the entire property. He pointed him out to Anna. "Two cop cars are outside the house. There should be at least another man around."

With a heavy sigh she said, "It's a big property. He must be here somewhere, digging into things he shouldn't, most likely."

"There you are."

Flynn turned to see the second cop coming out of the shed. "Good morning."

The cop nodded. "We're almost done here. But while we're working, we don't want you wandering around the property disturbing things."

Beside him, Anna huffed with annoyance. Flynn stepped in before she could say something. "We came to look after the animals. We'll try not to disturb you."

The cop nodded. "We appreciate your cooperation."

"I presume I can go inside and get clothes, etc.?" Anna asked.

The officer nodded. "The house is fine now. That's not where the killing took place."

"Where was he killed?" Flynn asked.

The officers studied them quietly for a long moment and

then said, "Out back of the shed."

Anna slipped her hand into Flynn's. He squeezed her fingers reassuringly and asked, "Was he stabbed?"

"Don't have an autopsy report, but it looks like it from our initial viewing." The officer stepped back and said, "Of course you realize I'm not allowed to discuss anything else in the case." He gave a curt nod and walked back to the shed.

"What could he possibly be doing after all this time in the shed?" Anna asked as they turned away. "Hopefully we won't need to grab any dog food out of there today."

"I filled up all the bins before I left."

"Good. They won't steal any, will they?"

He laughed. "I don't think that's an issue. But grabbing anything with forensic evidence, like blood, they would. On the other hand, they only want the packaging, not the dog food in it."

She shrugged philosophically. "Okay, let's take care of the animals."

Flynn was surprised at how easy it was to fall back into the same routine he'd had for several weeks. They moved down the aisles, cleaning cages, watering, feeding, and changing dishes. Thankfully, there actually weren't many animals.

Then he remembered the cats. As he walked over to the big playhouse, they were all in various states of snoozing. He loved that about cats. The rest of the world could go to hell in a handbasket and they would just lie there and say, *Yeah? And what's it got to do with me?*

The litter boxes, however, was a pretty major deal. They had three in that one room alone. All had to be changed out every morning. He took care of that as Anna filled the food bowls with a mix of wet food and brewer's yeast in some kind of a broth. He knew nutrients were added to it, and apparently the cats didn't mind.

At the sound of Anna and him coming into the room, they all woke up. They twisted around his legs and acted like they hadn't eaten for at least a month. He knew better. This was their daily routine.

He picked up a ginger-colored tom and gave him a hug and pat. The cat bumped his forehead against Flynn's chin over and over again, but his motor was running like a Mack truck. No doubt the cat had kind of stolen Flynn's heart. But no way was he set up to have pets. He gave the cat a kiss, walked him over to the food and dropped him down beside the dish where there was an open space. The diesel engine noise never stopped. But the cat dove in and started eating.

With that done, he followed Anna back into the house. They stopped and surveyed the kitchen. Things were just shuffled about, but there didn't appear to be anything missing. She had a ton of clutter around as it was. And a lot of it had to do with the animals—leashes, collars, and all kinds of doggie and treat bags.

He walked to the coffeemaker and checked to see if she had coffee in the cupboard. Seeing several packs, he opened up the coffeemaker, placed a filter in it, added water, then coffee, and put the glass pot under it to catch the drips. He didn't know how long they would be here, but he assumed he had enough time to drink a pot.

As he turned to see what she was doing, he found her sorting through a stack of mail on the table. "Is that today's?"

She shook her head. "No, these are bills that have been stacking up for a while. They hit the third and final notice before I pay attention."

He winced at that. "That's got to put a lot of stress on

your shoulders."

"Yes, but it's the only way I survive. If anybody gets their money early, then somebody else has to do without, and those really get nasty."

It also explained why there was rarely any food in the fridge, the cupboards were damned near bare, and why she was not so much skinny as borderline scrawny. There had to be a way to get more money to help out at the shelter so she could keep some food on the table for herself.

He studied her clothing. They seemed to have seen years of wear, and even her shoes were cracked with her socks peeking through the front outside seams. He knew she was prideful, but she really needed help. He just wasn't sure he had anything to offer. He wasn't wealthy, and his bank account sure proved it.

But he did know lots of people. There had to be a way to get some interest in this place. Or she would have to disband and find another way to make a living.

Then he realized this wasn't her way to make money. For that, she did all kinds of other jobs. But everything she earned went into keeping this place running for the animals, and all the charitable donations went toward the center.

Shit. With all the cops here, donations would be nonexistent from now on.

She picked up an envelope with no return address and frowned. She quickly ripped it open and out popped a check. She gasped, and sat down in a kitchen chair, hard.

"What's the matter?" He strode across the kitchen floor to study her. She held it up so he could see. It was a bank check for $10,000.

Chapter 6

HER MIND GRAPPLED with the concept of a big influx of cash like this. The number of bills she could pay off, the needed repairs she could make to the shelters, food she could actually buy for her charges—to supplement the free things she received–and the medicine she needed for the animals …

Suspicion ran through her mind, and it was a hard thing to let go of. She took a closer look at the check and said, "I don't know who Goldberg Holdings is."

"Does that matter?" he asked. "It's a hell of a nice check."

She nodded. "It's marked 'donation.' I'll send him a receipt right away."

"It would be more prudent to see it clears the bank first," he said in a dry tone.

She laughed. "Isn't that the truth?" She set the check off to one side, excitement still thrumming through her at all the things she could fix. There would even be enough money left to leave in the bank for future needs for other animals coming to her small shelter. As she tossed bills to one side, she found another envelope. But this time it just had her name and address on it. She pulled it out and asked, "What the hell is this?"

He looked at it and said, "No idea."

He held out his hand, and she dropped the envelope into it. There was something about it she didn't want anything to do with. "I only want it if more money's inside for the shelter."

He gave her an odd look and opened it. There was something small inside. He dumped it into his hand and gasped.

She glanced up at his face to see it had suddenly hardened. "What is it?"

"A SEAL insignia," he said. He laid it on the table with the envelope, brought out his phone and took a picture.

She figured he would send it to Levi. "But why would somebody send that to me?"

"I suspect it was intended for me." He put the phone down and studied the small metal piece. "There's nothing on it that I can see though."

"Why would there be? Are you expecting the sender to sign it?"

He shot her a look. "Wouldn't that be nice?" He looked at the stamp on the envelope. "It was mailed from Houston."

"But it has my name on it. Not yours."

"True enough, but the one man we think could be involved was a SEAL also. As far as I know, he's living somewhere local."

And she realized she'd been really slow to get it. "Of course, you think it's a warning from your friend."

"Not so much that as a statement…*I'm here.*"

She sighed. "You know? It would be really nice if you would take your macho bullshit far away from here."

"It's too late for that. A dead man was in your shed, or have you forgotten?"

Her temper snapped as she said, "Of course not, but that

owl was left as a message for me."

"I'm sorry." He sat back and rubbed a hand through his hair. "I didn't mean to snap at you. It's not your fault."

"Glad you remembered that." She bounced off the chair and walked to the coffeepot, pouring two cups. She brought them back and set them on the table.

"Have you gone through the rest of the mail? Let's make sure nothing else is there before I make a few phone calls."

"There are still some letters in the stack." She shuffled through them. "Electricity, water, insurance, flyer, flyer, flyer, garbage. That's it."

Flynn picked up his phone again and started making calls.

As Anna went back through the mail, she opened the bills, stacking them off to the side. For the first time in ages, they wouldn't cause quite the same pain they had before. Ten thousand dollars would do a hell of a lot of good here. Several of the bills were duplicate notices. She stapled those together within the pile, then picked up the rest of the junk mail and tossed it into the recycling bin.

When he was done on the phone, she turned to him. "Will you tell the police?"

He glanced at her, already dialing somebody else. "What would I say?"

She chewed on her lip as she stared at the metal lapel pin. "I don't know. There's just something…evil about it." She didn't want it in the house. But then she didn't want any of this. "Did you tell them anything about who you suspect is involved?"

Instantly, he shook his head. "No way. I don't have any proof. And if he didn't have anything to do with it, I don't want to ruin his life a second time by sending the police sniffing around his place."

She slunk back down in her chair and tugged her coffee closer. "I guess that makes sense. But it really sucks. What a mess."

"Maybe. Focus on your good morning already. That check helps cover some of the gloom from this insignia."

She stood up again. "On that note, I can go to the office and take a look at where the money will be going. I really needed this check. So thank you very much to whoever Goldberg Holdings is."

She grabbed the bills and her coffee cup, and strode to her office in the back of the house. She didn't know if the cops had been through her whole house or even in her office, searching through her finances or what. If they had, they would have seen a sad sight. Whatever. She somehow suspected they had the right to do what they needed to. With a dead body being found on her property, what else could she say but *help yourself to any information you need.*

She didn't even have a chance to grieve for Jonas. Not that she knew or liked him very much, but he was somebody who had died, whose life had been unexpectedly cut short. And for that, she was very sad. That it happened on her place was horrific.

She added this newest stack of bills to the existing pile and set to cleaning up her office. Nothing like finally having money to clear the debts to completely change her perspective on the business. She went through the stacks of paperwork on top of the big desk and decided to reorder her bookshelves to make space for all the stuff. She quickly set about organizing on a deeper level. By the time she was done, she was ready for her second cup of coffee.

She returned to the kitchen, refilled her cup and went

back to the office. Flynn was still on the phone. Good. Her hands were full with shelter problems.

Anna brought up her Excel sheets and tallied the money she owed. She could do a general expense transfer for some of them and quick payments of other bills online. That would mean a trip to the bank first to make sure the check cleared. But it was the safest route. She didn't have enough to cover all these bills if that check bounced.

She hopped to her feet and walked into the kitchen. "I'm running to the bank to deposit this."

He looked up at her. "Good idea, but you're not going alone. I'll come with you."

"I want to go now, straight there and back. I want to pay off all the bills."

He smiled. "And you look excited about something for the first time."

"Yeah, no kidding."

She grabbed her keys and walked out the front door, Flynn right behind her.

The trip to the bank was fast and efficient. The teller assured her the check had cleared already; they'd checked the sender's bank account, and it was all good. Anna turned around and gave Flynn a huge smile. "In that case, let's buy a few groceries."

He laughed. "We'll do that later. Let's go home, take care of the rest of the stuff that needs to be dealt with, like the police. Then we can shop."

She nodded.

As they walked back into the house, a cop stood in the middle of the kitchen, looking for her. He frowned and said, "Where the hell were you?"

She stepped back at his sharp tone. "I had to deposit a

check in the bank and pay some bills."

That seemed to mollify him. "You need to take a look at something in the shed."

"Fine, let's go."

The three of them trooped out to the shed. Thankfully, the body was long gone. Blood remained on the floor and a couple feed sacks. She worried she'd never get the stain completely out. Even so, her memories would still be there.

The cop pointed out something at the back wall of the shed. "Is that yours?"

She walked toward the rear and saw an old rifle leaning against the far corner. She frowned. "I don't own any guns. And to my knowledge that was never here." She turned to look at Flynn. "Have you seen it before?"

Flynn approached, studied it and shook his head. "No, I don't recall seeing it here either."

"You two sure?"

She nodded yes and turned to the cop. "You should remember if it was here last night. Nobody mentioned it?"

"No, it was hidden under old coats and blankets," the officer said. "It was missed on the first inspection."

She backed away and said, "I presume you are taking it with you."

He nodded. "We will to test it."

"Whatever you need to do to solve this is fine with me." She turned and walked out.

If she could replace the shed with a better storage system, she would do it immediately. She would never be inside it without thinking of Jonas.

"I'M OFF TO finish this paperwork."

He watched as she headed into the office. He'd seen her office many times. Stacks of unpaid bills and receipts were all over the place. She was doing too much on her own, as usual. He followed behind, stopping at the doorway, amazed at how much she had already cleaned up. Nothing like an influx of cash to change your attitude. He would have to thank Goldberg Holdings for the help.

She might be offended if she knew it was Logan's father. On the other hand, she didn't have any reason to know. Gunner had lots of money. And he was big on helping charities. If he had known beforehand that she needed it, he would have gladly helped. He was a big animal lover. So was Logan.

Flynn's phone rang. He glanced down and saw it was Levi. *Finally*. "What's up?" He turned away from Anna's office and headed to the kitchen.

"According to Gunner, Brendan is living at his brother's place, has no job, but is applying. He appears to be diligently establishing a new life. He was really angry but has since calmed down."

"So we're not thinking he's the guy? I'd still like to know where the hell he was these last couple weeks. Anywhere in Houston is certainly close enough to be on alert."

"Understood. Have you found anything else in the house that'll point to him?"

"No, but the cops just found an old rifle in the back of the shed where the body was." He quickly explained the little bit he knew. "It's a little too obvious, considering it hadn't been there before. If someone wants to pin it on me, they'd have to have my fingerprints on the stock."

"Which is not hard to do, as you well know."

His voice turned hard and abrupt. "I know." He stared

out the window for a long moment. "This is really unreasonable though. I mean that's a long time to hold a grudge if it's him."

"But you were pretty damn angry yourself about what happened and how it went down. He's much more volatile. If he still hasn't let go of his anger, I can see him taking time to find a way to pay you back. Maybe he had no idea where to find you and just happened to see you in town. That could have changed things for him."

"It would explain why he was really angry, then disappeared and got angry again. Revenge is best served cold."

"It so is. Watch your back," Levi said.

"Yeah, will do. Levi …" He hesitated. Maybe he didn't want to know the answer to the next question. But it was hard not to wonder and worry if this would end his career with Legendary Security.

"What's up?"

"Will this stop you from hiring me?"

"I already hired you, remember? As far as I'm concerned, this hasn't changed my mind, but we need to put this to rest to free you up so we can send you on missions. There's enough work here for half a dozen more men. I just don't need the baggage that comes along with this case." And Levi hung up.

That was good enough for Flynn.

Whistling, he focused his attention on the kitchen. Quickly cleaning up the mess the cops made, he worked on the rest of the house. When he'd been here before as a bodyguard for Anna, it had been difficult to keep busy, to ignore his cravings for Anna's presence. She became one of those addictive kind of personalities. He knew what she would say, how to get a rise out of her, and when he got that expected response, it would cause some fireworks.

She was fully passionate in everything she set her mind to, which immediately sent him to consider what she'd be like in bed. One kiss was not a seduction. But it was a hell of a start. Now there was much more to consider. Not just how or when to further this relationship, he also couldn't let whoever was trying to ruin her life get a second chance. Her safety had to be paramount. Anybody who killed one defenseless guy already probably wouldn't hold back on killing a woman. And Flynn intended that that would never happen.

Chapter 7

IT TOOK SEVERAL hours, but by the time she was done, she felt so damn relieved and happy it was hard to express. She paid off the very last bill, jotted down the confirmation number on the back of the deposit slip, clipped it together with the bills, and filed them away. She shut down her computer, got up and danced around her office. She was free and clear. She poured every penny of her paychecks into this place, and finally she had some money to help cover things.

It was amazing. The bills were taken care of with just under $1,000. How was it that little of an amount could make such a damned difference? But it had. Now that she had caught up, she could hire someone to fix some of the cage doors. All kinds of little bits and pieces of things needed to be done. She had to find a decent tradesman to help out.

She did have someone in mind, but she should also call the vet and see how much she owed for all the work he'd been doing. Charity was helpful, but people couldn't do it forever. At some point people appreciated getting paid.

She sat back down again, twisted her chair so she could stare out at the huge yard behind her house and kicked her legs up to rest on the windowsill.

Anna sat there for a long moment. For the first time in a long while, she felt peace and contentment. It had been a hard road getting here. And she certainly owed Goldberg

Holdings a huge thank you that she was back on top again, hopefully at least for a full year. She'd probably lost her dog-walking business with the madness of the last couple days.

And maybe this was a crossroad in her life.

She didn't know.

Plus, other shelters were always looking for a place to move animals to. She was a no-kill center, but most in Texas killed thousands of animals daily, all combined. It broke her heart.

So many humans and animals ended up in need because not enough people gave a damn. And for those who did, everybody had their favorite charities. And so many good ones existed and were deserving of the donations, but so was her small shelter. She was competing for dollars among bigger nonprofits. It was hard to get the attention she needed.

Maybe she could look at marketing again, like posting an online ad. Even just having someone hug the animals to let them know they weren't totally alone would be great, which she could accomplish with a visit to a local nursing home or senior center. And that would help the humans there too. On better days she used to take the dogs and cats around to various pet supply stores on weekends. Many of the animals were adopted that way. But there were just so many and the need so great that it often didn't work out.

She hated taking the animals back to their cages. They needed so much more than that lonely space. But at least they were safe while she found homes for them. And they had dog runs and company here.

Yet what she was doing here was barely enough.

"That's a pretty long face for somebody who just got ten thousand dollars."

She jolted at his voice to find Flynn leaning against the doorjamb with a cup of coffee in his hand, staring at her. "Decisions, decisions," she said. "Never easy ones."

"The money wasn't enough to cover what you needed it to?"

"Oh, it is. For the moment it's huge, but I have to think long-term what I should do," she said. "Limping along like this is not a good answer. I could stay and continue as I am. Hopefully better than I've been doing so far."

"With money or time?"

"Both." She stood up and walked toward him. "Are the police still here?"

He nodded. "But it looks like they're packing up."

"Great." She smiled as she glanced around the office. "Things can go back to normal."

"Whatever that means, considering what has happened."

She took a deep breath. "I'm also wondering about selling the property and moving the shelter."

"Why would you do that?" His tone was anything but happy.

"Well, the murder for one," she exclaimed. "How many people do you think will donate money after this?"

"But somebody just did."

"No, the check was sent before this happened. Chances are there won't be more to come." She turned to stare out the window. "It's a large property, and real estate prices have gone way up as the city grew around me. I could sell."

"And do what?"

Her shoulders fell. "Of course that's the problem, because I don't really know what else to do. This is where my heart is."

"Then wait and see. You don't have to decide today—or

this week or month. You have time. This will blow over. And eventually things will return to normal."

She twisted to look at his face. Then asked that one question sitting in the back of her mind. "Do you think he's done?"

Flynn didn't pretend to misunderstand. "There's no way to know. Unfortunately."

"You're thinking this might be related to a previous problem you had in the military."

"Maybe. But no way to know that either," he said simply.

She nodded. "Isn't it ironic Levi sent you to help because of a problem with Katina, and you bring yours here instead?"

There was silence, for longer than she intended. Her gaze intensified. "I'm not blaming you."

"I'm blaming myself." He turned on his heel and stepped back into the kitchen.

Yeah, that wasn't her finest moment. Of course he would take it that way. Maybe she'd intended for him to. Push him away a bit more. But she really didn't like what was happening to her shelter. Although this work was where her heart lay, she wasn't so sure this place was where her future was.

She turned and stared out at the animals, realizing that before when she'd been upset and disgruntled, finding her world tilted, the animals had put her back into balance. And she needed to do what she did best. She went down to spend some time with them.

"NO, I HAVEN'T said anything to her," Flynn told Levi, walking over to the far side of the living room and staring out the front window. The cops loaded the rest of their gear into their cars. Good that they were done. Not so that they were leaving. A police presence was a great deterrent.

"Make it look like you're leaving. If there'll be another attack, we suspect it'll be while she's alone."

Flynn agreed with that. It meant he'd have to stay inside away from the windows and prying eyes. "She might still kick up her heels over it."

"It doesn't matter if she does. She's not safe. I put you there, and we brought this problem to her door. We have to fix this."

"Does Gunner have any insights?"

"Lots. He's tracking down Brendan. But so far his brother doesn't know where he's been today—or yesterday."

"Right." Flynn frowned. "It's pretty damn thin motivation to think he's coming for me after all this time."

"I know." There was a harder note in Levi's tone. "Are you sure you told us everything about your involvement in Brendan leaving the military?"

"I didn't have anything to do with him leaving. I was kicked out because of not following the orders I was given. Brendan was over there at the same time, but I don't know what happened."

"Was he with you?"

"I'm not exactly sure how it all played out. Brendan passed me a message to bring me back to base. I refused because I was busy helping the villagers. I have no idea what Brendan said to the CO. At the time, Brendan had a lot of hard feelings because he felt I got him kicked out. I knew I did myself, and was good with that. But I did talk to the CO and explained that Brendan had nothing to do with me disobeying orders. I don't know why he was kicked out."

"Right. Maybe I can ask someone about that." Levi's voice trailed off. "I have a mission I need you on. Now I'm wondering if maybe it will be safer to send the two of you so Anna gets out of there for a while."

"And the animals?"

"Logan said he'd be happy to step in to stay there and look after them."

"And what if he's attacked instead?"

"Logan would be prepared. He wouldn't come alone, and he's military trained. Like we all are." At Flynn's lack of response, he added, "I know. I'm just tossing out ideas here. Looking for the best way forward."

"That's for Brendan to face me."

"A great idea. But it's not going to happen. As he's already demonstrated."

"One thing I do wonder though," Flynn asked, "is why Jonas was here?" He shifted position to make sure Anna wasn't listening. "I understand he was probably at the wrong place at the wrong time. But what was his reason for actually being here in the first place? And was there something behind the killer picking him? I'd seen Jonas twice the entire time I was here, but Anna said she didn't see him that day at all. What was he doing at nighttime on her property?"

"Do you think he would break in?"

"I have no idea what he was trying to do, or might've thought. I do understand that he was after Anna. But she hadn't given him any kind of encouragement, so if he was here for… The neighbors have a security camera, but Anna's was out."

Levi's tone turned businesslike. "East or west?"

Flynn chuckled. "I can't guarantee that it shows anything."

"But we can't discount it until we've seen it."

After the phone call, Flynn walked outside around the house, to see just what the security feed might have seen. It was pointed at the space between the two properties. But given the angle, it might very well show activity going on in the back of her house. The animal shelters were in the center, while the dog runs were horizontal on the sides. But the shed could possibly be in the viewing angle.

Walking back toward the kitchen, his phone rang. Levi calling him back.

"The police say they've seen it, and nothing was there."

"I was just out checking the angle."

"Stone's actually patching us through. I'll get back to you in a few minutes."

Flynn walked into the kitchen and once again checked the fridge and all the empty cupboards. He went into the office and found Anna gone. From the window, he saw her in the backyard, working with the animals. As he watched, the dogs jumped and scampered as she threw balls and picked up sticks, generally cuddled and played with them. This should be a full-time job for her. No question. But he understood her concerns about staying here.

He wondered if a quiet conversation with Gunner would make any difference. Logan had already gone around Anna as it was. Was the shelter something they could actually help with over the long-term?

What she needed was a couple major benefactors to keep the animal shelter flourishing. Plus, to find more places to give these animals homes. And it could take a while. If a few people would support the place, it would go a long way to add some validity to the shelter. All he had to do was tell a few friends, who'd tell a few more, who'd then tell more. He mentally wrote it on his To Do list. He'd spent a fair bit of time in Logan's home with his family, knew about their love for animals and extensive network among family, friends, neighbors, and businessmen. He'd start there.

Texas had a huge animal problem, and if Anna could do her bit to help out, then he wanted to assist her. Everyone should have lofty goals.

His was to become a valuable member of Levi's company. And to do what he loved. Although he was here, he had a tenuous relationship at best with Legendary Security. Not exactly the start to a great working relationship he'd hoped for. On the other hand, Levi had stepped up in a big way.

And that just made Flynn appreciate him all the more.

Flynn turned his attention back to Anna and decided it was time they went out for a meal. Then they could go shopping for food. He walked outside, headed toward her.

Just as he entered the pen, he heard a sound he'd never forgotten. He threw himself at Anna and dropped them both to the ground.

Chapter 8

"WHAT THE HELL?" Anna rolled onto her back, the dogs all around them barking and yipping. The two little ones tried to clean her face. She wasn't exactly sure what just happened, but Flynn was busy dragging her behind the side of the shed. The dogs followed, jumping, thinking this was a great game. She stared at him in confusion. "What was that all about?"

"I think somebody shot at us," he said in a harsh whisper. "A sniper."

She stared at him in shock. "Who does that? Who lives like that?"

He gave her a wry look and said, "I did. We all did. None of us are looking to do it again now."

She watched as he quickly placed a call. She wondered if anybody else had noticed that sound. She'd heard a boom, but it was kind of a low one. For all she knew a branch had snapped off a tree or something. How he had recognized a silent sniper shot said much about his history.

She didn't understand why someone shot at them, but while Flynn talked to Levi, she had to get all the dogs to safety. Probably moot now. If somebody had actually fired that first shot to kill, chances were very good they could've taken out any of the dogs easily enough. It also bothered her that she now hid behind the shed where Jonas had been found.

Was it the same killer? And how the hell would she get out of the middle of this? Not only did it not have anything to do with her, but somebody had now made it her fight. And that was a whole different story.

"Will do." Flynn turned to look at her. "That was Levi. They're still running the feed on the neighbor's house, looking to find something."

"I doubt they'll see very much."

He nodded and peered around the shed. "If there's any chance of you staying here at all, consider upgrading your system. I can get this one up and running, but you'll need way more than you've got."

"*I* need? You mean, *you* do. This asshole's after you."

"But he targeted your place. Your animals. Your friend."

She winced. "Hardly a friend but okay, I hadn't really looked at it that way."

"And you should. We are in this together now."

"We were from the beginning," she muttered. "How the hell will I ever get my life back?"

He leaned over, studied her face for a moment, then reached down, snagged her chin, lifted it, and kissed her. "We will figure this out. This too will pass. In the meantime, we have to catch the asshole. Then we will make your place bigger and better. Wherever you choose it to be."

She stared at him in wonder. That was kiss number two. Nowhere near as exciting as the first, but the words behind it were so much more reassuring. She waited for something else to happen outside. The silence around them crackled. No birds chirped; not even the dogs barked. In fact, they all lay down beside her, staring at her as if to ask *What's happening?*

Knowing it wasn't the right time, but because of that

kiss, she couldn't resist. "Does that mean you're staying?"

"Yes." That brilliant gaze turned toward her, studied her face, and he smiled.

Not quite the answer she was looking for. But what had she expected? A declaration that he couldn't stay away or something else out of a romance novel? Not likely. She had to remain grounded. "How long until you fix the security?"

"I'll have it done before bedtime."

She knew he was searching every inch of the place, looking for the shooter. But he didn't have binoculars. "Why was the old rifle in the shed?" she wondered out loud. "It really doesn't make any sense."

"So much in life doesn't. The chances are good he managed to get my prints off something and put it on the rifle."

"So that gun is what killed Jonas?"

"That's what I would've done if I was pinning the murder on somebody else. Of course it's a little too neat—placing the murder weapon in the shed where the victim was found. You want it to look like it's been hidden but not so hard that the police can't find it. But that wasn't even a good effort."

"It's a little scary to hear you talk like that."

"Don't worry about it. I never killed anybody who didn't need it." He shifted suddenly and raced around the far side of the shed, calling back in a loud whisper, "Don't move."

She pulled her knees up to her chest and wrapped her arms around them, getting into as small a ball as she could. She was hardly well-hidden. She was alongside the shed where the fence line was. But she was certainly open on that side. One of the dogs crept closer and whimpered. She wrapped her arms around him and pulled him on her lap.

The least she could do was make him feel better.

She thought she had a family for these two small dogs—an older couple whose children had left home, leaving them as empty-nesters. It'd been on her To Do list to call and see if they were still interested. Both dogs were in good health and young, with a lot of happy years ahead of them. They shouldn't be in a war zone, like she was currently living in. As soon as she got back to the house, she vowed to call them.

She glanced at the two bigger dogs. They were definitely much harder to place. It was too bad. Many people wanted a big dog, but by the time the puppy grew up, the owners realized it was no longer so much fun and a whole lot of work and expense. That was the kill age for so many animals. They got dumped at shelters, kicked out of the house and even left somewhere along the highway. It was sad the things animals went through with their owners. Some humans just didn't deserve to have pets.

The minutes grew longer. She kept distracting herself with more thoughts about animals and coming up with ideas where she could potentially find a home for both males. The longer it took Flynn to return, the harder it was for her to not think about him and what he was possibly doing.

When a tree branch cracked close by, she froze. Instantly, the two larger dogs bounded to their feet and barked. The smaller ones came closer to her. She glanced around, but really had no other place to go. She could race to the side of the shed and just keep going around in circles, but that would hardly be the answer.

And suddenly Flynn was there. "Sorry if I scared you," he said.

She bounded to her feet and cried, "Of course you did. You took off and didn't tell me anything, and then you didn't come back for so long only to break a branch before stepping out from behind a tree to terrify us all."

He stared at her, then pushed her back against the shed and covered her with his body. "Where was the crack?"

She pointed wordlessly to the back corner of the building.

He creeped to the far side and peered around the edge. Then he disappeared again.

She was getting fed up with him doing that.

When he came around the same way he'd approached the first time, she sighed with relief.

"Nothing's there," he said.

"And the sniper?"

"No sign of him."

"Of course not." She ran her hand through her hair, staring down at the animals. "I'm not sure I want to leave them out here anymore."

"Do you want to bring them into the house?"

"Will they be any safer?" She looked at him, then back down at the four dogs. It was a precedent she'd been avoiding. "I want to go inside and call someone I had in mind for the two little ones."

"Then let's get them inside."

With him leading the two larger dogs on leashes, she picked up the smaller ones, and they quickly made their way into the back of the house. She stepped inside, set down the dogs and motioned for him to close the door so they wouldn't run out. The dogs set about exploring the place.

She turned, looking around. "It just doesn't feel like home anymore."

"Anytime, when somebody breaks in," he said, "it's a violation that hits the very heart of you."

"LEVI SUGGESTED YOU head out with me. He wants me in another part of Texas to follow up on some inquiries to be made. He suggested it would be a good chance for you to get out of here."

She turned to look at him. "But I can't leave the animals alone."

"Logan said he'd stay."

"And how will that help?"

"It's just one of the many options we were considering. Another was for me to leave but in fact, sneak back inside to help look after the place, which would give the killer a chance to come in, thinking you were alone. But any effort we make to draw him out isn't a guaranteed success."

"Sounds like a guaranteed failure to me. I'm the one who's likely to get hurt."

He shook his head. "I won't allow that."

She sighed. "But this guy came here before and killed Jonas."

"And that brings up another issue. Any idea why Jonas was here?"

She flopped down into the kitchen chair. "I have no idea. Wish I could figure that out. For all I know Jonas was working with this guy."

Flynn had been on his way to the window. He turned and stared at her. "Is that likely? Did he have friends?"

"I think he had a few. But he always talked about this one guy and how the two of them would score big. Then Jonas could donate his share of the money to help out with the animals."

"Whoa. Tell me more. Wait …" He pulled out his phone and called Levi. "Hang on, Anna has something to say." He turned on the speaker, laid the phone on the table and said, "Go ahead, Anna."

"I was just telling Flynn that Jonas said he'd met up with a guy, together they would make a big score, and when Jonas got lots of money, he would help out around my place. I just wondered if Jonas and the killer had been working together."

"Did he give you a description or any way to identify this man?" Levi asked.

"No, not really. Just that he'd met him at the center."

"What center?"

"It's a kind of a community center where people help unemployed individuals get jobs or for retirees to fill their spare time with volunteer work. It's one of those humanitarian places where you can do something to improve yourself."

"Name?"

"I'm not sure exactly. Back on Your Feet or something like that." Her voice trailed off. She shrugged at Flynn. "I'm sorry. I just don't remember."

"Don't worry," Levi said. "We'll find it. We know that Brendan was doing volunteer work. His brother was particularly happy about that."

There was a pause on the phone, as if Levi was writing down notes. They could hear scratching on paper. "I'll give him a quick call. He might even know the name of the center. Good work, Anna. If you remember anything else, let us know." And he hung up.

She glanced at Flynn. "Is he always like that? So abrupt?"

"When it's business, yes. Do you think Jonas's mother would know what the place is called?"

"No, I don't think so. He told me he had a separate entrance downstairs, and his mom lived upstairs. As if somehow that made it different than living in his mom's house."

Flynn grabbed his phone and sent a text. "I'll just let Levi know. I doubt we'll be allowed into Jonas's living quarters, but the police should have gone through it already."

"We can go ask his mom," she said slowly. "I can make up some kind of an excuse. I don't know, maybe he had some pictures or something of mine."

He studied her intently for a long moment and then nodded. "That's not a bad idea." He sent off another text to Levi with an update. Then turned to her and asked, "What about the dogs? Do we leave them in or out?"

"I'd rather leave them in."

"Good call. Grab your jacket. Let's go. We'll stop at Jonas's place to see if we can get in and take a look around. Then we'll head to the grocery store or for a meal first. I've been starving for hours now."

Chapter 9

At Jonas's mother's house, Anna walked, keys in hand to the downstairs living quarters, nodding at Flynn. "Her name is Evelyn," Anna announced. "She doesn't mind us taking a look. She's having a hard time with what happened. She appreciates anybody coming by." Anna was really sad for that. The meeting had been tough as it was. Evelyn had been almost pathetically grateful that someone cared enough to stop by. "She said Jonas had been very odd at the best of times, but the last few weeks he seemed a bit more over the top. She'd wondered if he was doing drugs."

"Did he have a history of it?"

Anna nodded. "He was a regular user, I believe. He offered to share at one point." She shrugged. "It was just part of who he was."

She unlocked the door to the downstairs suite and pushed it open. And froze. The place had been trashed. Everything was upside down and dumped. "Oh, boy."

Flynn stepped in behind her and closed the door. And again he pulled out his phone and called Levi. "We're at Jonas's place. It's been trashed. Don't know if someone was looking for something, but it'd be damn hard to find out what now."

Anna left him standing where he was and made her way into the kitchen. It wasn't as destroyed as the living room.

However, it was a mess with food all over the place. Wow. Did people really live like this? Did Evelyn know? This wouldn't be fun to clean out. Leftover take-out, coffee cups—both empty and not, from various coffeehouses—littered the table. Enough pizza boxes were on the table to feed several men. For a few days.

Carrying on, she pushed open the door to the master bedroom with her boot. Inside was messy, but not like the living room. The clothing was disheveled on the open shelving, but at least it wasn't on the floor. Then her focus landed on the bed. Instantly, she called out, "Flynn, come here."

When she didn't hear his steps, she walked back into the living room to Flynn, standing in the middle of the room, still talking on the phone, and she motioned for him to follow.

"Levi, I'll call you back." He ended the call and asked, "What's up?"

She pointed to the bedroom.

He stepped in, glanced around, his eyes landing on the bed. "Oh."

"Someone has been staying here with Jonas from the looks of it. What's the chance it's the killer?"

"Given this mess, I would have said no. But now that I see that bed … made up military style and damn clean in comparison …" He turned to look at her. "Did Jonas have any military training?"

She shook her head. "No idea."

"This does not match up with the rest of his living space." He turned to look at the kitchen.

She pointed at the coffee cups. "Beside the fact that whoever was here wasn't a housekeeper, the cups came in twos. Not just one set either, but three sets on the table."

"So Jonas and someone."

"Unless Jonas was already dead, and we're looking for two others. But this could be the man that Jonas was talking about."

"Let's hope the police have swabbed this place for fingerprints." But he looked around and saw no evidence a crime scene forensic team had been here. And that made no sense to him. He quickly sent a text to Levi explaining what they had. He took several photos and forwarded them. "We need to find out why not."

"I can ask his mom." She walked back to the front door and headed upstairs. She knocked on the door again to see Jonas's mother. "Here are the keys. I promise to lock up when we leave. But I wonder, have the police not been here yet?"

"Yes," she said. "They have been. They came and got fingerprints from his bedroom and everything up here."

"What? I thought Jonas lived downstairs."

"Jonas *was*," his mom corrected. "But not for the last few weeks. He had a friend down there off and on, one who liked to be alone as much as possible, so Jonas started to sleep upstairs much of the time. I haven't seen or heard anybody down there for days." Tears came to her eyes again. "Everything is just so confusing now. I don't know who it was. But once I told the police another man was living downstairs, they didn't seem too interested. They wrote down the info but wanted to see Jonas's bedroom up here."

"Would you mind if I took a look too?" Anna pulled out her phone and quickly sent Flynn a text, telling him to get upstairs and join her.

At Jonas's bedroom door, his mom said, "You're welcome to look around, just don't take anything."

"Of course not," Anna said with a smile. "I'm sure you want to keep his things."

His mom shook her head. "I have no idea what I'm gonna do."

Anna wasn't sure she should warn Evelyn about the state of the rooms downstairs. As long as it was all part of the crime scene, she didn't think she could do anything yet. Then again the police didn't seem to feel the downstairs apartment was of interest to anyone. She opened the door to Jonas's bedroom and stepped inside.

And it was like a time warp. Posters from *Back to the Future* were on the wall. What looked like high school awards and mementos were all over the shelves.

At the sound of voices she turned to see Flynn talking with Jonas's mom outside the doorway. He stepped inside with a smile for Anna. "Did you find anything?"

Checking that Jonas's mom was down the hallway, Anna said, "It's still like a kid's room."

Flynn stopped and took a good look around and nodded. "Stunted growth?"

"He was immature in many ways. But how much of it was because he was always on drugs?" She opened her arms to the room. "But this kind of explains it a bit. Maybe he did have a mental illness and never quite matured past a specific point."

"Or this is his world before drugs. And the apartment downstairs is his world after." He nodded at the desk that was perfectly clean. "Just think about the apartment downstairs. Often drugs don't affect people in this way, but when it becomes the dominant factor in somebody's life, to the point they're addicted and no longer functioning well in society, often their surroundings no longer matter. What does is getting that next fix."

"He might have been getting to that stage, but I don't know for sure," she murmured in a low voice. The last thing she wanted was for Jonas's mother to hear them. This had to be hard enough without realizing to what extent your son had fallen.

She walked to his night table and pulled open the drawer. She didn't have hope of finding anything important, not once the police had been here. The drawer was empty. The shelf below it was too. She bent down on her hands and knees and checked under the bed. Outside of dust bunnies, it was also clean. She didn't really know what she was looking for, just something that would help her identify who the new person was that had been living downstairs. But then, why would that information be up here? Still she forced herself to go through the motions and checked everything she could.

In the closet she saw one of the coats Jonas wore on a regular basis. She pulled it out and turned to Flynn. "He wore this almost every time I saw him. Odd he wasn't when he was shot."

"So maybe he was living in this room toward the end, if his favorite clothes are here."

She shrugged. "Or he left it upstairs, and his mother hung it up for him."

She returned it where she'd found it, then checked the pockets. She pulled out a crumpled piece of paper—a receipt for fast food from three days before. She handed it to Flynn and went systematically back to the coat again. In the inside pocket she pulled out a small slip of paper, with a phone number and name, one she recognized. She spun and held it up for Flynn. "Is this the guy you were talking about?"

FLYNN STARED AT the note in Anna's hand. Confirmation. Something he hadn't really expected to see. He reached out and took it, looking at both sides. It was torn from a store advertisement, a local one here in town.

He pulled out his phone and dialed the handwritten number on the reverse side. The phone rang multiple times. Not waiting to see if anything else happened, he hung up, then dialed Levi. He quickly updated him, adding, "Can somebody put a trace on this number and see what we get?"

"We're on it," Levi said. "We'll also check the police files for that address."

"Good idea. If there's been any disturbances at that address, the neighbors would probably know something." He stared out the window and said, "I think after I'm done in this room, maybe we'll talk to a couple neighbors here and see what they might have to say."

"Good idea. Touch base in, say, thirty minutes." Levi ended the call.

With a last glance around, he motioned toward the doorway. "Are you ready to go?"

She nodded. "Nothing else of interest appears to be here."

They walked back out, thanking Jonas's mom for letting them see his room.

Back outside, Anna asked, "What was that about going door-to-door?"

"We should check with the neighbors and see if they saw Brendan. Somebody should've seen something."

"Wouldn't the police have asked?"

"Would they? As far as they were concerned, a friend was staying downstairs in the apartment. They didn't seem to care about the other guy. Then again, it's not like the police have much time to worry about this case."

"But we do." Resolutely, she walked across to the first house beside Jonas's mother's place. She knocked on the door. When an older woman came out, Anna quickly explained that she was a friend of Jonas's and wondered if the woman had seen anything suspicious in the last few days.

The neighbor shook her head. "Jonas has always been a bit suspicious on his own. But since he started hanging out with that creep…" She shook her head. "He's just been on a downhill slide. I'm not surprised he was murdered."

Inwardly agreeing with the woman but needing to keep her talking, Anna said, "Have you seen other people around here lately?"

"A black truck. Don't know the man. But it was parked in the front a lot."

"Any chance you know the license plate?" Flynn asked from behind Anna. "Even just a letter or two?"

The lady shook her head. "It always came in the dark and was gone in the morning. It gave me the creeps actually. It's kind of ghostlike."

She gave Flynn a hard glance.

"Nothing good ever comes of people who only come and leave in the dark. Definitely shenanigans going on in that place," he said.

"Well, hopefully that's all over with now," Anna said gently. "The neighborhood should be safe again."

"*Harrumph*. I hope so." And the woman closed the door in their face.

Flynn proceeded to check with the other neighbors, but everybody said the same thing. Large black truck, nobody had seen the license plate. As for the driver, no one saw him.

The only extra information they got was the truck was full-size, solid black, with no contrasting trim, obvious bed liner, or canopy. As far as being helpful, it wasn't much. This was Texas—everyone had trucks.

When they were done and walking back to Anna's car, Levi called. "The phone is registered to Brendan McAllister. And it's a Houston number."

With his breath coming out in a gush, Flynn said, "That's the best confirmation we've had yet."

"This is good stuff," Levi said. "That puts Brendan together with Jonas. We can already place Jonas at the house. If we can place Brendan there too, that would lock it down."

"Do we have motive? Means wouldn't be too hard, as Brendan is a weapons specialist."

"Right. I should phone the cops and see if we can confirm the murder weapon. He's unlikely to be so stupid as to use his own gun, but…" Levi's tone changed. "What are you two doing now?"

Flynn turned to look at Anna. "We need to stop at a grocery store, and then we'll be back at the house."

"Staying there for the night? The others are planning to leave soon. Except Logan, he's staying at his father's for the evening. This would be your last call for a ride home until then."

"Good to know. Thanks. I'll touch base with Logan later." He ended the call and turned to face Anna. "Groceries?"

She nodded. "I'm starved."

Chapter 10

SHE WALKED UP the steps, unlocked the door, picked up the two bags she'd brought from the car and headed to the kitchen. The dogs barked and milled around her in joy. She put the groceries on the table, then reached out to give them each a big hug. "So how was it being inside, guys?"

She glanced around, but it appeared they hadn't had any accidents. For that she was grateful. At least they had each other for company. She could put them back in their cages, but that didn't appeal.

"I'll cook tonight if you want to put stuff away," Anna said.

Flynn nodded and gave her a smile.

She checked the answering machine to find that her earlier phone call had resulted in something very positive. The couple would come by this evening to look at the two little dogs, if that was okay with her. She picked up the phone and called them back. "I'll be here this evening if you can give me a time."

The man said, "How about right after dinner. Maybe six thirty?"

"Perfect." She put away the phone in a much happier frame of mind, then began a chicken Caesar salad for each of them. She snagged the garlic bread, prepped it, set it aside to go in at the end. It would give them some substance to go with the salad.

Flynn was a big man. He had already demonstrated a decent appetite. She didn't have anywhere near the appetite he did, but she was starved. Right now, she could eat both his meal and hers. As soon as she got the chicken breasts in the oven, she called out, "The couple is coming tonight to take a look at the two little dogs."

"That's great," Flynn said. "You should take a walk down there to ensure the cats are okay."

She shot him a horrified look and raced outside.

"Sorry! Didn't mean to make you panic."

"The last thing I need is something else happening around here," she said.

Flynn followed her. "Hey, since Jonas's body was found here, and with the police presence off and on, we probably don't have to worry about Brendan showing tonight. No guarantees, but just saying…" When she nodded at him, he sauntered back to the kitchen.

She arrived at the cages and opened the cat door to find everybody still where they belonged. The four dogs had followed behind her, and the smaller ones barking like crazy. Jimbo stuffed his nose against the glass of the cat door. She reached down and hooked a leash on each of the two little ones and took them out on the small dog run. With any luck they would have a new home tonight. She walked the other two out to the back dog run and set them free. They needed an hour or so to themselves.

None of the animals appeared to be disturbed or upset. She'd take that as a good sign there was no intruder around. The cats would need food soon. As she headed toward them, Flynn was already outside again, saying, "Don't worry about it. I'll feed the cats now. You worry about dinner."

That worked for her.

When Flynn was done, he walked inside, sniffed the air experimentally and said, "That smells good."

She smiled at him. "Just like old times."

"It sure is."

When he'd been here before, they'd taken turns cooking meals. She did a tastier pasta, but he cooked a better steak.

She sat down, checking her watch. "We have twenty minutes to eat before the couple arrives."

"It's all good."

She settled in to enjoy her chicken Caesar salad. She glanced at Flynn to find him halfway through his meal. When she was done, she started the dishes. Before she got the sink filled, Flynn said, "Remember our *old times*? If you cooked, I cleaned, and we switched off as needed. Go deal with paperwork in case they want the dogs tonight."

At that reminder, she headed to her office to grab some adoption papers. There was nothing wrong with feeling positive. It had been a hell of a day already. If she could find homes for these two, it would be perfect.

An hour later, she realized it had been the best day she'd had in a long time. Tears were in her eyes as she watched the couple take the two little dogs out to their car and place them in the backseat.

Flynn walked out and put an arm around her shoulder, tugging her close. "Nice job."

She sniffed and wiped the tears from her eyes. "It's so good to see them leave, going to a good home, but it's also damn hard."

He laughed. "They are yours when they are here. But, like all babies, they have to grow up and move on."

"I really need to do something to help the cats now too.

We're down to just the two large dogs, a hamster, snake, rabbit, and four cats."

"You barely have enough animals to call yourself a shelter anymore. It's a good time to shut it down, if that's what you need to do."

"Now that I have the money, that's not gonna happen," she said robustly, once again buoyed by success. "What I need to do is contact the other shelters and see how many animals need to be rescued before they hit the kill door."

"And then you'll take them in, I suppose," Flynn said with a knowing smile.

"That's what I'm here for," she said. "Maybe with some of that money, I can afford to get an assistant. Someone to help."

"I'm sure you can," he said. "How many animals can you actually take here?"

"With the new pens that I have yet to use, I could probably take in close to forty dogs. The problem is finding homes for them. But they all go eventually. It's just a matter of time. People are always more easily suckered in if they see the animal at events. Those who call me are the ones who have been out looking. I do have a website obviously, and that takes a bit of work too. But now I get to update it, let them know that both little dogs have a new home." She reached up and kissed him briefly on the cheek. "I'll do that right now." And she bolted into the office.

LIKE AN IDIOT, Flynn stood in the hallway, a hand to his cheek. It was the first sign of affection she'd actually shown him since his return. And he was loving it. Obviously, today was one of the highlights of the week, if not the whole month, for her. A sizable check, two animals adopted and she was safe, so far. Plus, the police were done and gone, taking whatever mess they were dealing with. Now if only they could figure out where the hell Brendan was and put a stop to any shenanigans he was up to.

While she was in the office, he pulled out his phone. "Levi, any update?"

"No, I'm still tracking down Brendan's whereabouts. His brother swears he's been at his place for the last two days, but he has a small cottage in the back where Brendan's been staying. So he can't actually confirm that he's been there—in fact, he's hardly seen him for several weeks."

"I can pretty well damn confirm that he hasn't, but was at Jonas's place," Flynn said shortly. "It just feels like he's planning something, but I don't know what it is. I don't want him to target the animals here either."

"No, none of us do."

After ending the call, he walked to the kitchen and put on a pot of coffee. He couldn't shake the feeling that something was brewing in the atmosphere. If he looked at this as Brendan wanting payback, what he had done so far wasn't enough.

Just as the coffee finished dripping, he heard a knock on the front door. He opened it to two policemen standing on the porch. He nodded. "Good evening. What can we do to help you?"

The first officer introduced himself. "I'm Detective Baker. I believe you are Flynn Kilpatrick, correct?"

He nodded. "Yes."

"We need you to come down to the station to answer some questions."

His eyebrows shot up. "Is there any reason I can't answer

them here?"

The two men stepped slightly backward to allow him to step out onto the porch. Baker said, "We would like to see you at the station."

Flynn didn't like the sound of that at all.

"Let me grab my jacket and tell Anna." He didn't give them a chance to refuse.

He turned and walked into the kitchen, grabbed his jacket from the back of the chair and headed to the office.

Anna was working on the computer. She looked up with a big smile. "Hey, do I smell coffee?"

"Yeah, but you'll be drinking alone. The police are here, and they want me at the station for questioning."

Her gaze widened. "What?" She bounded to her feet and raced to the front door. "What do you want with Flynn?" she asked the detectives.

"We just have some questions to ask him."

"Then why the station? You could come in and ask what you need."

Both men shook their heads. "We are requesting his presence at the station."

She crossed her arms and jutted out her chin.

Flynn grabbed her by the shoulder. "Don't worry. I'll go with them. I don't have anything to hide."

"That might be," she said, "but you're not going alone. I'm coming too. I'll drive and follow you." She glared at the two cops. "Make sure you keep him safe. He's already been shot at once. And there better not be one damn bruise on him by the time I see him at the station."

Flynn laughed. "They can't beat me up, sweetie." He bent down and dropped a kiss on her temple. "But it's a good idea for you to follow me there. I don't want you alone here."

She raced into the kitchen and was back out with her keys, jacket, and purse. Turning to lock the front door, she headed to the car as he got into the backseat of the cruiser.

As he sat inside, he watched her follow them down the street. He smiled. He really didn't like this development; it made her worry about him. Well, something was good about that. At least it proved she cared. He quickly texted Levi and gave him an update.

Then he phoned Logan. "Interesting development."

Logan answered, "No worries. We'll send a lawyer over."

"Don't need one," Flynn said comfortably. "I didn't do anything."

"Yes, but somebody's out to get you, so the more support you have at the onset, the less chance you have of anybody pushing your buttons."

"I'm just not sure how much to tell them about Brendan."

"Another reason for the lawyer. We'll meet you there."

Flynn ended the call and stared at his phone. He might have had a crappy time this past year, but he never doubted his friends. It had taken a long time to get to this point with his position at Legendary Security and to where he was with Anna at present. He had no intention of blowing it now. No matter what Brendan might have planned, they'd have to go on without Flynn. Because he and Anna had a future, and it didn't include jail time.

Chapter 11

"YOU CAN TAKE a seat on the side, ma'am." The detective was polite.

She gave him a hard glance and said, "I'd rather sit with Flynn."

"He's just answering questions. You can wait until he comes back out again."

She crossed her arms over her chest and glared at the man on the other side of the desk. "I know you're just doing your job," she said.

"Good," he barked. "Then let us do it. If there's no reason to keep him, then we won't."

She glared at him again until a soft laugh came from behind her. She turned to see Logan. "There you are. You're getting him out of here, right?"

"With you on his defense team?" Logan asked with a chuckle. "I doubt they'll charge him with anything. Because if they did, they'd have to face you. And believe me, that's not what any of them want."

The detective behind the desk muttered, "You got that right."

Logan led her to one of the long benches against the wall. "Let's just sit here and relax."

"How can I possibly do that when they took him in for questioning?"

"Did they say what it was about?" he asked.

"No, but what else could it be other than Jonas's murder?" She let her breath out in a heavy sigh, running her hands through her hair. "The guy makes me nuts. You know that, right?"

Logan laughed. "He has that effect on a lot of people."

She smiled. "But he's a good guy."

"Glad you noticed."

It was the emphasis on the word *noticed* in his voice that had her glaring at him in suspicion. "What do you mean by that?"

His grin widened. "Flynn likes you too."

"Oh," she said in a small voice. "Was it that obvious?"

He laughed out loud. "Your defense of him says a lot."

"You've got to remember I defend the underdogs," she told him.

"That's true. But Flynn really doesn't need anybody to stand up for him."

"I'm afraid he does now. I don't know what the hell that friend of his is up to, but he won't be happy until Flynn suffers for some reason."

"Well, he's not a friend any longer," Logan said. "I'm not sure they ever really were. But they were in the same unit. And when things go bad, they tend to go really bad. Nobody in the military has a weak character, they don't breed them that way. When they find strengths, they hone and sharpen them. So when two military types get on opposite sides of the same bar, it can get ugly."

"He has to really hate Flynn in order to want him to suffer like this."

"I wouldn't be at all surprised if he isn't planning to kill him."

"Oh, my God," she cried. "Really?"

Logan grabbed her hands, already twisted into knots, her nails digging into her soft flesh. "I shouldn't have said that. Just take it easy. We really don't know anything yet."

"No, you're wrong there. We know somebody's setting him up. And with that much hate inside, there's really no way to know when they'll stop. If they're gonna stop. I think you're right. The endgame is to take Flynn out."

"Even if it is, Flynn is not anybody's easy endgame."

"And he's not alone, right?" She stared at Logan as if willing him to give her the answer she needed.

Logan nodded his head. "He has all of Levi's company, me, and my father. And that's considerable. If we have to, we can pull Bullard's team into this."

"Who's Bullard?"

Logan shook his head. "I forgot you don't know who he is. Another guy running a company like Levi's, but they're over in Africa."

"Sounds as if I'd like him if he'd step up and help Flynn out. I don't think Flynn's had so many people stand by him lately."

"No, he hasn't. He doesn't have any family. But I've been his best friend for as long as I can remember."

She nodded. "He's got a chip on his shoulder. That I-don't-need-anybody-in-my-life-because-I'm-doing-just-fine chip."

At that Logan laughed out loud. "I see you do know him, and obviously very well."

His tone held a bit of suggestiveness. She flushed. "Not that way."

"But soon," he teased.

She flushed an even brighter red and glared at him. "Not

likely. The last thing I need to do is spend my evenings sitting inside the police station, waiting for him to come out."

"Especially when you can be doing something so much more fun." And he chuckled again.

He obviously knew Flynn very well too. Maybe too well, from the looks he was giving her. "How long have you known him?" she asked abruptly.

"Decades," he said cheerfully. "We had a few years apart where we didn't have anything to do with each other but hooked up again in the military. That was awesome."

She shook her head. "So you know all about his history with women then."

"Of course I do. Doesn't mean I know the details or about all of them. But I know about you."

She nodded. "Figures."

"Why?"

"Because I have no intention of being yet another little notch on Flynn's bedpost."

"Now that is not something Flynn ever did. He had some short-term romances, but when he's with a girl, he's in 100 percent. That didn't mean it always worked out obviously, as he's never been married. But his relationships always lasted six months or longer."

She turned to look at him. "For real?"

He nodded. "SEALs get a bad reputation. Hell, all military men get a bad name for being more into the wild and crazy one-night stands and weekends," he said. "And I doubt any of us can say that we haven't done something that makes us look back and cringe. But Flynn was much more circumspect. He wasn't into one-night stands—he was into relationships. I give him credit. I thought he was gonna make it with a couple of them. But it's tough being married to a SEAL."

"It's tough being married to any military man," she said. "There is always danger around you. Not knowing if you'll ever come back from the latest mission."

"True enough. And you gotta realize Flynn's doing the same kind of work. Maybe not quite as dangerous. Hell, maybe it's more so. I'm fairly new with Levi myself. But it's the kind of work we used to do. And some of it's hazardous."

"Aren't you the one who looks after the rich and famous?"

Logan gave her a flat stare. "No. I might've done a job or two like that, but that's definitely not where my aptitude lies."

"You sure? You look like the one who prefers to have some of those gorgeous women throw themselves all over you."

Logan chuckled. "Those gorgeous women throw themselves all over me whether I'm looking after them or not."

"Maybe you lost your heart to one of those fancy ladies you were guarding."

She couldn't help teasing him, but she knew that chances were none of it was even true. Until she saw a flush rise up his neck. It was her turn to give him a flat stare and say, "Come on, Logan. Give me the details. Who was she?"

He glared at her. "No one."

She snickered. "Wait until I tell Flynn about this."

He narrowed his gaze, shoved his face a little closer to hers and said in a mock-threatening voice, "You won't say a word to him."

She shoved her face right back into his until her nose was almost touching his. "Yeah, you wanna bet?"

FLYNN WATCHED THE two spit at each other. He couldn't stop grinning. His friends were great. He stood in front of them for a long moment, waiting for them to notice him. When they didn't, he cleared his throat.

Both turned to look up at Flynn, his arms crossed over his chest, a big smirk on his face. "How nice you two are getting to know each other."

"I'm sure she has a crush on you," Logan said with a big smirk. "I told her that she should find somebody else because you're a busy man with the ladies these days."

Flynn's eyebrows shot up.

"That's okay. You don't understand why he's being mean and lying. Logan is missing his sweetheart," Anna said, her voice supersweet. "That's what happens when you're dumped by someone prettier than you." She turned to glare at Logan.

Flynn broke into raucous laughter. "Oh, my God. Seeing you two like this is perfect." He grabbed an arm on each of them, pulled them to their feet and said, "Shall we leave now?"

Anna turned and stopped. "Can you leave? Oh, that's wonderful." She threw her arms around him and gave him a big hug. "I was so worried about you."

"I told you there was no need. It's all fine."

She stepped back a bit and glared at him. "In my world, there's no *all fine.* But I sure as hell would like to get out of here." She turned to look at Logan, saying in a half-grudging voice, "You're welcome to come back to my place for a drink—coffee or something—if you want."

Logan's grin flashed. "Only as long as you don't bring up any more of our girlfriend or boyfriend issues."

She thrust her chin forward. "As long as you don't either."

Flynn snagged each of them by the arm once again and directed them toward the front door. "Damn it, that must've been some conversation while you were waiting for me." They walked outside. "I'm sorry I missed it."

"I could've missed it easily." Anna rolled her eyes. But she was just so damn happy Flynn was allowed to go and there appeared to be no repercussions from the police visit. "What did they actually want?"

They were headed across the parking lot where their vehicles waited. She walked to her car and waited for him to answer.

"Someone sent them a letter stating I killed Jonas."

Her jaw dropped.

Logan exploded with, "Are you serious?"

Flynn nodded. "But apparently the autopsy confirmed Jonas was killed while I was flying home. He was shot by a small caliber handgun. The slices on his arm were inflicted with my knife and more for show than anything else. More forensic evidence to nail my coffin closed. But I wasn't here so the plan didn't work. The same thing for the rifle. Jonas was shot with it postmortem. But it wasn't the murder weapon. They are looking for a handgun for that. And of course, they found a partial print of mine on the rifle." He glanced at Logan and said, "Thank God I went on that trip with you and Harrison."

"Jesus." Logan stared off in the distance, then shook his head. "Somebody has it in for you."

"Not somebody, it's Brendan. I'm pretty damn sure."

"So sure you'll exclude everybody else in that equation?" Anna asked. "Making assumptions is not the best idea."

"No, it's not, but nobody else in my world really hates me like that. And I told the police that this time."

"I think one of the things about it is that we don't often recognize who it is that hates us. The world is full of lies and liars."

"True enough. But most of those liars aren't willing to go through with murder to make a point."

"Aren't the police looking for Brendan? Why aren't they asking him where he was on the weekend Jonas was killed?"

"They are looking for him. And as soon as they track him down, they will ask him just that," Flynn said. "But it appears Brendan is hiding out, and nobody knows where he is right now, including his brother."

"That sucks. We need to find him ourselves."

"That's what I was thinking," Flynn said. "We need to track his credit cards. He has to be paying his way somehow. However, if he was living at his brother's house or Jonas's, that's a different story. So when was his ATM last hit for cash? Does he have a credit card? When was it last used?"

"I believe Ice is getting those answers."

"When we go home, I'll see if I can get more." He glanced at the two of them and asked, "Are you coming to Anna's place?"

Logan nodded. "I'll follow you."

Anna unlocked and opened the car, standing on the pavement, waiting. She turned back to Flynn and asked, "You want to drive, or are you okay if I do?"

"I wouldn't mind driving," he said amiably. "But if it's an issue for you, go ahead."

"I'm tired," she admitted. "If you want to, that would be fine with me." She walked around the car, handed the keys to him and got into the passenger side of her small car.

He walked around, got into the driver's side and turned on the engine. When they were both buckled in, he drove the car out onto the road. Behind them, Logan followed in one of the big company trucks.

"How many trucks does Levi actually have at the compound?"

"Half a dozen by now, I think. Also a Suburban or two and a couple cars."

"I gather business is good."

Flynn laughed. "It is, but one never really knows how good."

"Can't blame him for that," Anna said. "He probably doesn't even know. With so many jobs coming and going, you're really only gonna have facts and figures after a few months. As long as the cash is flowing inward, and you're covering everything, then you're doing fine. To know if there's anything left at the end of the day, well, that'll take a couple quarters to get an idea."

"What was that about Logan having a ladylove who dumped him?"

She shrugged. "He was razzing me about how you and I interact, so I returned it about him being dumped. Got quite a rise out of him too. I think something must have happened between him and a woman he was looking after in California."

"I'll have to ask about that," Flynn said. "Logan doesn't get involved easily."

"Yeah, I got that impression. He said the same thing about you. And that when you do, it's generally for a long-term relationship."

"I try hard. If one is worth starting, I'll give it my all and see how we do." He glanced at her. "How about you? You go into relationships in a lighthearted manner?"

"No." She stared out into the darkness on the other side of the windshield. "But then, I haven't had the number of relationships you have."

"It doesn't matter how many we have." His voice deepened. "When you're in a relationship, you give it your all. There are no guarantees in life, or the future. There certainly aren't any in happiness. All we can do is our best."

She turned to look at him and smiled. "How very true."

He made a couple right-hand turns, then headed out onto the highway. This was one way to get back to her place, probably the fastest. The turnoff was just a mile down the road. Just as they approached it, he put on the signal and slowed down.

Anna glanced behind to see if Logan was there. A big truck was following them, but it wasn't Logan's. "Uhm …"

"I see it." Flynn's voice turned grim and hard. "Hold on."

The truck came whipping right up against the back bumper of her car. Flynn hit the gas, and instead of taking the right turn to get off the highway, he darted between two cars in the second lane, and they moved over to the turning lane on the far side as well. She twisted to look at the truck. It was cutting across too. "Oh, my God, it's following us."

"I think he was running us off the road."

Flynn took a hard corner too fast in front of oncoming traffic, then jumped through the lanes to take the turn on the far side. She gave a small cry.

"Sorry, but I had to get out of there." He whipped onto the first right and took a series of turns, shaking off the tail. Finally, he pulled into a small residential block and parked. The two of them sat there, staring at each other for a long moment. Then both at the same time turned to look behind them. There was no sign of the truck.

"Did I just imagine that?"

He shook his head. "I sure as hell didn't."

"What about Logan?"

Flynn pulled out his phone and called Logan. There was no answer. "Damn it. Best case scenario, Logan followed the truck and is right now tracking it down. Worst, Logan missed the whole thing."

No, that would be that the truck took out Logan first. But he hadn't heard or seen anything happening behind him, so he presumed Logan's luck was still holding. That guy seemed to walk through a fire and come out smiling and smelling fresh as roses on the other side. Flynn had never known anybody else like Logan.

Into the eerie silence she whispered, "What do we do?"

Chapter 12

SHE HAD THE answer to that question a few minutes later. Somehow, from a completely different direction, they arrived at the shelter. Everything looked the same from outside. She had literally grabbed her purse as she'd bolted after Flynn and the police. Now she stared at the house, wondering if the asshole who'd followed them had been here first.

She had to check on her animals. She hopped out of the car and approached the front door. Everything looked the same as she'd left it. She unlocked the door and walked inside with Flynn right at her heels.

She knew he was still phoning Logan. The fact that there was no answer really bothered him. Her too. She'd hate for somebody else to get hurt. She didn't care who this guy was after, he had no business taking out anyone.

She'd left the dogs in the dog run. The house appeared to be fine. Keeping close to Flynn, they walked out to check the animals.

The cats were sleeping, not even noticing she'd been gone, she suspected. The dogs barked as soon as they heard them approach. Once they saw it was Flynn and Anna, they barked in joy, jumping and whining. She opened the pen and walked inside, bending down to give both a cuddle, still missing the little ones she'd found a good home for earlier.

She still had her evening work to do. The rabbit and hamster needed pellets and new hay for their cages. And the snake–maybe Flynn would feed him.

"Let's get this dealt with," she said quietly. "Hopefully by that time, Logan will show up."

"I'm calling Levi first." He walked a few steps away and connected with somebody from the compound.

She turned her attention back to the animals. She had so few here right now. She quickly changed the hamster's sawdust, gave it fresh water and food, did the same for the rabbit and walked into the cat house.

She sat down on the floor, and the cats came over for attention. As much she liked to believe they were fine on their own, they needed human contact just as much as any other animal. She wondered if she were up to having them all in the house. There were four here though. She could consider keeping them, the two dogs, hamster, and rabbit and be done with the shelter. No way would she keep the snake.

Her attitude to the place had changed. Since finding Jonas in the shed, it just wasn't the same anymore. Maybe what she needed was a different location, though that cost money. Not something she had a whole lot of. Her property was worth a lot more now than when she'd first bought it, and the area had grown up around her. It was also a large lot, and the developers would be all over her for it. If she moved out of town though, would it impact how many animals were adopted? She had no idea. It would certainly be a longer trip to the vet, but she didn't have to move that far.

That's when she first realized she was actually thinking of a place between here and the compound. The small towns around it were a lot cheaper. She could sell this parcel and buy something larger and better suited. Plus, set money aside. A lot could be said for being more financially stable. Of course all the cages would have to be rebuilt at the other end. Although a lot of them could be moved too. She could also add a few new pens, bigger and easily accessible.

For the first time she stood back and studied what she'd built here—the pens and dog runs. Replacing the building was one of the biggest concerns, because it had all the cages built inside, plus, she had an examination room in the back and several others for animals recovering from surgeries. To set up something like this all over again would be brutal.

She didn't know if she could do it.

On the other hand, if it was just the property keeping her here, that wasn't a good enough reason. There were better locations elsewhere. She had no place for visitors to come and see the animals; there was no parking out front, which was always an issue. The dogs could use a larger run. If she actually had a property upgrade, she could take in other animals when asked. She was one of the few with a lot of this size. But it certainly wasn't big enough for anything like goats or horses.

She shook her head. This was kind of a crossroad. And all because of Jonas.

Poor Jonas.

On that note she put the dogs on leashes. Flynn was still talking on the phone. She said in a low voice, "I'm taking the dogs for a walk."

She let herself out into the back alley and let the dogs roam. They loved this time of night. She didn't usually take them for too long a walk, not like the exercise they needed being the size they were. But the alleyway ran the full length of several properties on either side. All kinds of interesting smells were here for the dogs to follow.

She walked to the far end, giving them a chance to lift their legs and sniff around, with as much freedom as a dog could have on a leash.

As she walked back toward her property, Jimbo walked along the ditch in the alley on the far side. His head down, that little bit of hound in him had picked up the scent of something. Probably a rabbit or an owl, although Anna wouldn't be surprised at anything. She lived on the edge of the city, and though the properties were big, their owners weren't wealthy. Lots of people dumped their garbage in this alley. She never understood it. There was trash pickup every week. Why throw your shit in the back alley where it would never get collected?

As they approached the back gate, Jimbo refused to budge. She walked over to see what he'd found. If it was a skunk, she really didn't want him to come close to it. A flashlight in its eyes wasn't enough to get it moving. Oddly enough there was something on the ground. It looked like an old rag. She kicked it with her foot, and it flipped and moved over several inches to the side. Something gleamed in the night, but she couldn't see what it was.

She turned to look at Flynn. He stood at the gate, still talking on his phone. She gave a sharp whistle, which caused him to spin and look at her. She pointed at the ground. "Can you bring a light? I need to see what this is."

He unhitched some kind of a tool from his belt, clicked a button and there was a beam of light. He walked closer to her, stooped down on the side of the ditch in front of her. And swore.

"Shit," she said.

On the ground, mostly buried in the dirt and mud, was

a gun. And she had no doubt in her mind it was the gun that had been used to shoot Jonas.

FLYNN STARED DOWN at the handgun and said into the phone, "Levi, one of the dogs just found a gun in the alley behind Anna's place."

"Call the cops. Chances are it's planted evidence, but we have to follow this through the legal way."

"Yeah, that's what I figured."

He ended the call, looked at her and said, "I'll be calling the cops next."

She rolled her eyes and said, "Great. Like I haven't had enough of them yet." Anna took Jimbo and Duggy back into the dog pen.

He watched as she walked through the gate. Then he bent down to study the handgun. He didn't recognize it, thankfully. Although he could have potentially touched this one—several years ago—if it was Brendan's.

On their days off while in the military, they'd often go shooting. As he stared down at the small handgun, he realized it sat in a shitty spot with gasoline, mud, and dirt all around it, so who knew if any fingerprints were left to be found. But if this was Brendan's, then it could be one Flynn had held. Still, the cops knew he hadn't been in the country at the time of the killing.

He quickly called the cops and explained what he'd found.

"We'll send somebody out there within the hour," the dispatcher said. "Please stay with the object."

Right. Like he had nothing else to do. For his own sake, he took several photos and sent them to Levi for backup, and leaned against the fence on the far side. He stared at Anna's house for a long time. And then realized this position gave him a great insight into her life. Because he could see her as she left the kitchen, walked to the office, then into the other room where the dining table was, which meant anyone else could have stood exactly where he was and watched her—and him. He glanced down at his flashlight and checked the surrounding area.

Besides his own footprints, he could tell somebody had stood on the far side. The imprints were deep in the mud. They were also much bigger than his. And there were several cigarette butts around the immediate area.

Brendan wouldn't have been that sloppy. Not unless he thought it was a slam dunk that Flynn would get arrested for this murder.

Still, Flynn would point it out to the cops. And therefore, since he didn't want to trample through it, he waited.

Anna came out the back door. "You coming in?"

He shook his head. "The cops are on the way. I'll wait for them."

She frowned, then nodded. She returned a few minutes later with a hot cup of coffee.

He smiled at her. "Thank you for thinking of me."

As she walked away, she muttered, "I wish I could stop."

"I'd really rather you didn't."

She froze and spun around to see him. "Seriously?"

He nodded his head. "It's why I asked how you felt about relationships," he said, his voice low, deep. "Because I definitely want to take this further and see where we can go with it."

She took several steps toward him and whispered, "So do I. But I just didn't know if you were serious."

He reached out his free hand and gently brushed the stray strands of hair off her face. He tugged her a little bit closer and whispered, "When it comes to *you*, I'm always serious."

With the coffee cup in one hand, he wrapped his other arm around her. He dropped a kiss on her nose and forehead, then unable to help himself, he tilted her chin and gave her a slow, mind-drugging kiss to let her know just how serious he really was. When he lifted his head, she let out a happy sigh and snuggled up against his chest.

He held her close. "We'll get through this," he whispered. "Don't ever worry about that."

"I'm worried about a lot of things right now. And the fact that somebody wants you in jail for life is just one of them. What if he actually comes back and tries to hurt you?" She leaned back to look up at his face in the darkness. "Or worse, kill you."

"I'm not that easy to kill," he whispered, touched that she was so concerned.

"Nobody is invincible, nor can they argue with bullets all the time and get away with it."

She was so serious and sad. He just wanted to wrap her up and carry her upstairs and into bed, show her how good life could be. She'd been through a lot these last few weeks. Months. But there'd been good things too, and she needed to keep that in the forefront of her mind.

"True enough. And I know the danger right now. But my concern is keeping you safe."

She chuckled. "So I'll look after you, and you'll do the same for me."

He barked a laugh. "Sounds good to me."

With her holding him close, the two of them stood in

the alleyway for several long moments. Just as she was about to pull away, a vehicle arrived, headlights shining toward them.

She stiffened. "Are we assuming that's the cops?"

"I'm not sure yet. However, we are expecting them."

They pressed back against the fence. Some shrubbery stood between the two of them and the vehicle, but not enough to hide them if those lights were to shine in their direction.

As they waited for the vehicle to approach, another turned into the other end of the alleyway. This one was a bigger and higher, like a truck.

Anna gasped. "You think that's the one?"

"No idea." Now crouching down very low, pulling her down beside him, he said, "Get to your yard and inside the fence."

She did as he instructed. The truck appeared to be idling at the entrance to the alleyway. And that made it suspicious as hell. The car, on the other hand, was almost where Flynn waited.

But since he didn't know yet who the hell the killer was, he couldn't guarantee the car was anybody they wanted to see either. When it drove closer, he saw it was a cop car. The engine shut off; as were the lights, and two men got out. One was holding a big flashlight.

He shone the light on Flynn. "There you are. I was wondering what the hell you're hiding from."

Flynn motioned to the truck still sitting at the far end. "A truck almost ran us off the road earlier tonight on our way home from the police station. I managed to shake it, but now I'm wondering if that's it again."

The cops turned and studied the truck. The first quietly

said, "I'll go through the backyard and see if I can come up behind it."

He'd already slipped up against the fence. The second got into the driver seat of the car and backed it away. Around the front of the house, he turned as if to take the main part of the road, but instead he pulled a U-turn and went the other way. In the meantime, the first one rounded back to Flynn.

Flynn figured the truck would back out, make a run and disappear before the police car got there.

There was no way to tell how far the cop car would go. Flynn watched its headlights shining in the dark. Then it disappeared. Suddenly, it was up behind the truck which quickly hit the gas and raced forward; the cop was behind it.

The truck blasted past where Flynn and the other cop stood. No way to stop it. However, it slowed as it approached. The driver turned and stared directly at Flynn. And he knew him. It was Brendan. "Shit." He glared as Brendan disappeared in front of him.

"Did you recognize the truck?"

"Yes, it's the same one that tried to run us off the road earlier. And I recognized the driver. Brendan McAllister. He's the man I told the detectives about."

"Good. You let us handle this. We'll get this asshole off the road. And we have more than a few questions to ask, so don't leave."

He didn't know how they would handle it, but the cop car was right on Brendan's ass, sirens going. No way in hell would Brendan slow down or stop. "Even if you have a roadblock somewhere up ahead, this guy will crash through anything in his path."

"Yeah, I hear you." The cop turned back. "We came

here to pick up a gun. Where is it?"

Using the flashlight, Flynn pointed to it on the ground. It looked like it was even more covered in mud now. The cop reached down and with what looked like a pencil, collected it and put it in an evidence bag. He held it up in the concentrated light and said, "This could be the murder weapon."

"That's why I called you."

"Any chance it has your fingerprints on it?" The cop studied Flynn's face intently.

Because of that, Flynn kept his expression easy, natural. "If it's Brendan's, anything is possible. We were in the military together. We often would target practice in the woods. Not only did we need to keep that up for our jobs but it was fun. A great way to pass the time with the guys."

The cop stared from the gun to Flynn.

Flynn felt he had to add, "It's not mine."

"Good enough. You weren't driving the truck just now, so I'll take that as a sign of faith that you're not the guy who did this." He put the evidence in his jacket pocket as another car turned into the alleyway. "Here's my ride. We'll be in touch."

The second cop car pulled up beside them. The cop got into the vehicle, and they drove off. Flynn watched as they disappeared into the night. Good luck catching Brendan. That wouldn't be so easy. In his heart, he knew this guy would get away.

Chapter 13

FLYNN HAD SENT her inside when the police arrived. "Anna?"

"I'm in the office," she called out.

He stopped at the doorway. "What are you doing?"

"Going through the videos for the hours we were gone tonight," she said. "I just want to make sure nothing was touched." She glanced at him and smiled. "Thanks for fixing it again."

"Good idea." He smiled. "And you're welcome."

He was kind of pissed for not having thought of it himself. It just proved when he was personally involved in any case, it would throw him off his game. And he was in this deep, in two different ways—what with avoiding a murder charge, plus, not letting Anna get shot or worse. At the compound they had everything running through video cameras at over a dozen locations. Somebody was always going through them, making sure nothing happened they needed to know about. He should have done the same as soon as they arrived home from the police station.

"I saw him."

She raised her head and studied him. "You saw who?" she asked cautiously.

"Brendan. He was the one driving the big truck."

She bolted to her feet and threw her arms around Flynn.

He hugged her close. "I'm so sorry," she said, her voice muffled by his shirt.

"I am too, but at the same time, I'm relieved. We have the right bad guy. There's no one else out there doing this to us."

"Did the cop see him?"

"The first cop was there with me. The second took off after him. The one seemed to think they'd have no trouble catching Brendan in a roadblock. But I highly doubt it. Chances are he's already long gone."

She pulled back and stared up at him in horror. "Really?"

He nodded.

Just then the doorbell rang. She clung to him instead of stepping away so he could answer.

"Maybe it's Logan."

She gave him a questioning look but pulled back, following him. He opened the door with her standing right behind him.

Sure enough it was Logan.

And he was bearing gifts.

The smell of pizza filled the hallway. She laughed. "Perfect timing. I'm starving again."

He handed her the pizzas and she took them into the kitchen. Thank God he was okay. She had no idea if he just ran off to get the food and hadn't told them, meaning for it to be a surprise, or if something else happened. She brought out plates and poured Logan a cup of coffee, topped hers off, and filled Flynn's also.

Still talking, the men came into the kitchen, laughing and joking.

"I guess he didn't see it then?" Anna asked.

Flynn shook his head. "He followed us just out to the freeway, but since I took the most direct way home to miss all the irritating lights, he actually went into town and ordered pizza."

"Then that was a very slow delivery," she muttered. "We parted ways over an hour ago."

"True enough," Logan said. "But I also stopped at the liquor store and picked up some beer. I figured Flynn could use a little bit of downtime on that whole stress-level thing."

Flynn grabbed a beer, popping off the top. "You're damn right I could. You haven't heard the latest."

When Flynn filled him in, Logan stared at him, his jaw dropping. "You're saying that, if I'd followed behind you, I would have seen the goddamn asshole? Might've been able to run his plates?"

"Yeah. Instead the police are chasing him down. But I highly doubt they'll catch him."

"Hell, Brendan was in the same evasive driving-maneuver training we were. He'll shake that off easily."

Flynn nodded. "I know. I'm expecting him to return. Possibly tonight."

HE EXPECTED SOME kind of response from Anna. When there was none, he turned to study her face. It was white, like ice that had set too long in a freezer. He reached across and grabbed her hands. "I don't want you lulled into thinking this is over. Brendan's actions have escalated. There's almost no time between his various little attacks now. He'll come for the jugular, and we're ready."

She stared back at him mutely.

He squeezed her fingers and reassured her. "Remember,

this is what we do."

She shook her head. "It's what *you* do, not me."

"And that's fine. You just have to trust us."

Logan chimed in. "We have to be on alert and prepared for an attack."

"What kind of an attack?"

"That's the big question. Your security system is back up and running, which is good. But we can't count on that. He took it out the first time. He'll do it again. I did set an alarm for that eventuality. So if the system goes offline, an alarm will sound," Flynn said.

"You can do that?"

"Absolutely. Security systems are way too easy to knock out."

"So we just sit here and wait?" Her voice rose at the end. She pulled her hands free and reached up, giving her face a good scrub. "This is just too unbelievable."

"I think Katina would say that same thing. She went through hell too."

Anna shook her head. "Sure, but she'd seen and done something. I haven't and the animals don't deserve this."

"It doesn't matter who deserves it. This is what's happening, it's what's on the table right now. Don't compare the situation to anyone or anything else. We have to deal with what we have to deal with." Logan's voice was hard. Determined.

Flynn agreed. But he also knew Anna didn't live in the same world they did. Cloak-and-dagger stuff was foreign to her. She dealt with puppies and kittens, and her biggest problem was paying vet bills and getting enough food to feed the animals she looked after. A far cry from his world.

On the other hand, it was a good balance. He saw the

world in a much nicer light when he was around her. Sure, people were often assholes to animals, and for those he'd cheerfully take them out in a dark alley and give them a lesson about how hard the world could really be. But Anna was all heart. She'd spent her life saving animals. She just needed a hand. And as he considered her words from earlier, maybe a move wasn't a bad idea. A little farther out of town would be good. He could see the neighbors not being impressed when she was full with thirty or forty barking dogs. There had to be noise ordinances. She had a business license, but if the city officials ever found a reason to cancel that, or change the scope of the license, he figured they would do it in a heartbeat.

Particularly after this session, her place would be deemed trouble. It wasn't her fault; but his. And for that he was terribly sorry. However, the only thing he could do was get her through this and keep her alive.

Chapter 14

AFTER FINISHING A piece of pizza, she picked up her coffee and walked to her office. "I'll update the website for the other two dogs. See if we can get some interest on Jimbo and his buddy, Duggy."

In truth, she just wanted to return to something resembling a normal life. She turned on her computer and brought up the website. She quickly made the changes, then put Jimbo and Duggy's photos up front and center. She lowered the adoption fee, hoping to trigger some interest from anybody. As soon as she was done, she reached for the phone and called the Rabbit Rescue. She'd been hoping to hand off her rabbit to someone as a family pet. But after a certain number of days, it wasn't fair to keep him in the cage. He'd be much better off at the rescue. There were many acres of land so the rabbits were free to run, and the food was supplemented.

She knew they wouldn't be open at this hour, but she could leave a message. Knowing it was a small business like hers, she was surprised when somebody answered. She explained who she was and what she had.

"My husband's actually in town right now. You want him to run by and pick him up?"

Anna gasped in surprise. "Yes, that would be lovely. Thank you. By the way, do you happen to know anybody who would want a hamster?" she asked in a half-joking manner.

"Well, my daughter is looking for one. I'll tell my husband to take a look while he's there."

At the end of that very happy phone call, Anna got up from her chair and raced out to the kitchen where the men were having a conversation. "Hey, Flynn. A man'll be coming by to pick up the rabbit. He runs a big rabbit rescue outside of town. They're happy to take him."

"Nice. I'm sure the rabbit would much prefer to be free than in a cage."

"I don't know why I didn't think of it earlier," she said. "I was trying to find a family for him, but you're right, free is better."

"It's definitely better," Logan said.

"Also, he'll take a look at the hamster for his daughter."

"So it's possible that, after tonight, it would be down to the two dogs?"

She stared at him in wonder. "Plus, the snake and four cats."

He laughed. "Four is not bad."

Logan laughed too. "I better not tell my dad that you've got cats here. He's quite a feline lover."

She rounded on him. "Tell him. Tell him. Maybe he'll take one or two."

"What's the deal here with the animals anyway?"

She explained how she got them all fixed and kept trying to find homes for them.

"But when you have no animals, then what?"

"I'm wondering if I should sell and move the shelter somewhere else. A place where the dogs would have more room." She winced. "I can't exactly say I'm terribly happy here after Jonas's murder. It doesn't feel like home anymore."

"It's not a bad idea. But a move like that will cost money."

"I know. But the property values here have gone up, and if I move out of town, I might be able to get into a better financial position."

"Did you say this place is paid for?"

She nodded. "That is the one good thing. But all the pens would need to be moved or rebuilt. I'd need a place like this, but better. I'd have to find something within my budget."

The two men looked at each other. She walked to the coffeepot and filled her cup. Money was such a pain in her existence. It wasn't fair. All she wanted to do was to save animals.

She stared out the back. "I'm thinking of bringing the rabbit and hamster inside. I do have traveling cages for them."

On that note, she put down her cup and headed outside. She quickly shifted the rabbit into her arms, giving him a heartfelt cuddle, loving its soft texture and gentle personality. Then she moved him into a smaller cage and gave him a few little treats. The hamster was still in a big cage, and she thought the whole cage could just go with him. She picked both up and carried them in the kitchen, setting them on the table beside the men. "I need to find a home for the snake too."

Logan looked at her with interest. "You have a snake?"

She nodded. "He really should go to a reptile rescue."

"Is there one in Houston?"

"I don't know. I haven't had a chance to look. I just got

him the day before Jonas was killed."

"That's right. He wasn't here when I was, was he?"

She shook her head. "No." She glanced down at the rabbit and hamster. "But with all the successive moving of animals, I'm thinking maybe the snake—with its big slow-healing back injury—would be in a much better place at the reptile rescue."

She gave the men a bright smile, grabbed her coffee and said, "I'll go take a look."

She walked back to her office. She didn't know what had happened to the snake—the first she had had here—but if it had been somebody's pet, she'd want to make sure it went to a better home this time. And a reptile rescue might be the best place for it. If she was lucky enough to have one close by.

She made several phone calls, realizing she was pushing the limit for her good luck, but it was hard to let go of an idea once she sunk her teeth into it.

Her research paid off. She found a reptile rescue and several reptile clubs, and they often kept unwanted animals. She found a couple email addresses and darted off emails, sending a description and photos of the snake.

She'd be hesitant to take in reptiles again without having any idea what to do with them. They would be hard to sell to families. Still, if she could find a place for one or knew who to call when she was given another, that was a different story.

Satisfied she'd done what she could, she stood up just as the front doorbell rang. That should be the man for the rabbit. As she walked to the front door, she found both men waiting on her. Logan was in the corner of the living room. Flynn stood at her side as she opened the door to find a middle-aged man smiling down at her.

"I hear there's a rabbit and hamster."

She welcomed him inside and led the way back to the kitchen. "I've had the rabbit for a couple weeks. It's time for him to find a better place. I haven't had any luck getting him adopted."

"It's one of the reasons we set up the rescue. So often they are just released and become dog food."

She gave him a long look. "I know. It's so hard." She motioned at the big rabbit. "There he is, and he's very healthy."

"Perfect." The man looked over at the hamster and smiled. "Apparently I know a little girl looking for one." Because he was taking the rabbit off her hands to put him in the rescue, there'd be no money exchanged. She smiled. "Well, outside of the hamster's vet fees, he hasn't cost very much, so if you just want to take him for your daughter, I'm happy with that."

The man looked at her, a question in his eyes. "You don't have adoption fees?"

She nodded. "Usually, but hamsters aren't very much to handle anyway."

He pulled out his wallet and gave her twenty bucks. "Buy a bag of dog food."

She accepted it gratefully. "You want a receipt?"

He shook his head. "Not an issue. You okay with me keeping the cages?"

She nodded. "Yes. Thanks for looking after the rabbit. We need more rescues in this world."

He carried both pets out the front door. The whole transaction had taken less than twenty minutes. She'd moved out two more animals. As soon as he got in the vehicle and drove away, she turned to walk back toward the house, Flynn at her side.

"That's two more animals getting homes."

"You've had a great day," Flynn admitted. "I'm so happy for you."

She grinned. She wanted to throw her arms around him, but instead hooked her arm through his and said, "I'm delighted."

He put his foot on the first step, and she jumped quickly onto the step above, intent on turning to give him a quick kiss, when an odd sound came and a harsh burn ran across her arm. She cried out in pain. What just happened?

"Stay down."

She had no intention of going anywhere. But now her arm stung something awful. Lifting her hand, which hid the extent of the wound, she studied it, cataloguing what had just happened. The huge black truck that had tried to run them off the road drove past the house, the driver holding a handgun and spraying gunfire onto the property.

She cried out in shock as bullets rained over them. She crunched up into as small a ball as she could. Dimly in the background, she heard Flynn call out, "Look after Anna."

The big truck roared, its brakes squealing when it picked up speed as it went around the corner. Then a second vehicle raced behind.

Just as suddenly as it had begun, there was silence.

She lay on the porch, controlling her breathing and the urge to scream.

"Are you okay, Anna?"

She turned toward Logan's voice behind her head. He was just inside the house. In a daze she answered, "I think so. Is he gone?"

"Yes, and Flynn went after him."

With Logan's help, she made it into a sitting position. She gasped when he touched her arm.

"You shot?"

She shook her head. "I don't think so."

Up on her feet and inside the kitchen, she stumbled to the table and sat down heavily. With the light she saw blood streaming between her fingers, dripping down her arm. And of course, the minute she saw it, she felt faint. And then the pain hit. She lowered her head to the table and focused on deep breaths. She didn't think the bullet had gone through, but had no way of knowing because she couldn't even see her hand.

"Let me take a look," Logan said.

This will hurt like crap.

He gently peeled away her fingers and put a cool washcloth over the wound. He put firm pressure on it, making her cry out.

"It's bleeding pretty badly. I have to clean it up a bit to see just how bad it is."

"How bad? I presume I'm going to the hospital." She stared out the window at the animals. "The cats and two dogs. Can you handle them?"

"Sure can," he said cheerfully. "Though the priority isn't the animals, but getting you to the hospital."

"True enough, but they have to be scared. There has been an awful lot of noise here. This is not the environment I wanted for any of them."

"And it's not likely to ever happen again. Once we get this resolved, you can go back to that nice peaceful way of living."

"And why is it that it sounded like *boring* was the next

adjective you would use?"

He laughed. "Flynn took the big truck," he said. "You okay if I drive your car?"

She nodded. "Not a whole lot of options."

"Not unless you want to pay for an ambulance."

She snorted. "Not only am I not paying for one, but it's nowhere near bad enough for it. I can probably drive myself, if you want to stay here and look after the animals for me," she said hopefully.

"Not happening. I suspect Flynn will be back fairly soon, and he can look after them."

She had to be happy with that because no way would Logan budge. With her hand again holding the washcloth firm on her arm, Logan reached for her purse, then tucked it over her other shoulder. Afterward he grabbed up her keys, turned out the lights, reset the security and got her to her car in a minute flat. He gently helped her into the passenger side, buckled her in and jogged around to the driver's side.

"You don't have to treat me like an invalid. I won't break."

"But we don't know how long that will hold because right now, you're leaking."

She looked at him, startled, then burst out laughing.

With a big grin on his face, obviously happy he had shifted her mood, he drove her straight to the nearest emergency room.

As he drove, she asked, "It was the same truck, wasn't it?"

He nodded. "Flynn and I recognized the driver. It was Brendan for sure."

"He's really not going stop until Flynn is shot, is he?"

Logan glanced over at her sideways. "And even then he's

not likely to. He's quite fixated on Flynn. Chances are it'll end up with somebody getting killed."

"As long as it's not Flynn."

"Agreed. But I don't want to see you or any of the rest of us hurt either."

She shook her head. "No, that wouldn't be very nice." She stared out the window, a real deep hatred burning inside her for the man completely destroying her life. "I hope Flynn catches and beats the crap out of him."

"You can be guaranteed that we will catch him. If it's not today, it'll be tomorrow."

"He has to be stopped before he hurts anybody else. He just has to." She couldn't live with anything else.

NO WAY IN hell would he let Brendan get away with this. He'd heard Anna's cry of pain and knew she'd been hit. He'd checked it quickly, found it wasn't bad, then raced for the truck. But after that round of bullets hitting the house, he couldn't be sure. He knew Logan would look after her. What Flynn had to do was get this asshole and run him down. Somehow. They had to put a stop to this forever.

Brendan had a head start. Moving around a street corner, Flynn caught sight of the truck several blocks ahead. He picked up speed, catching the light just before it turned red. Then gave chase. The cops would be after both of them. An APB should already be out on Brendan's truck from the last one. He couldn't believe the cops didn't catch him, but then, like Logan said, Brendan had been damn good. It was going be hard to stop him. If Flynn could follow Brendan someplace, see where he was roosting, that would be a different story.

Still a block behind, he watched as Brendan made a sharp left. He followed and watched Brendan take another turn into an alleyway.

That could be good or bad. He drove past it to see what Brendan was doing and saw the truck taking a turn about halfway down, into what appeared to be a backyard.

Flynn quickly pulled off to the side, turned off the engine and lights, and ran on foot down the alleyway. If he could at least find the truck, he would know where Brendan had gone to ground. At the halfway point he slowed, studying each property as he went. These were run-down houses. He'd have to say it was more of a shady area of town from the looks of the backyards, but it could just be a poor one. As he came to an open road, he saw a truck parked halfway in, and it looked like the one Brendan had driven. As he sorted things out, he saw Brendan busy throwing stuff into the back of it.

Flynn stopped and considered his options. It would be stupid to go in without backup, but no way could he afford to lose track of Brendan. Flynn stepped back and pulled out his phone, quickly texting Levi this location. Flynn only had a general guess as to the street he was on. He clicked on his phone's GPS and sent the coordinates to Levi as well.

Still huddled in the alley keeping an eye on Brendan, he sent the next text to Logan. When there was no answer, he frowned. He didn't know how bad things were at home, but he could only hope this wouldn't be something he'd regret.

Levi sent back a confirmation.

Stay there out of sight. Cops are on their way.

He stared down at the message and wondered if that was a good or bad thing. Because if they came in with guns blazing, Brendan would be out of here. And no way would Flynn be able to stop the truck on foot.

Brendan walked to the back of the house. If Flynn could disable the truck, Brendan would be stuck on foot, and it would be a whole lot easier to catch him.

The backyard was a wide open grassy area, and the truck offered no cover. As he studied the neighboring houses, he saw the closest one offered privacy with their fenced yard. He creeped over the back gate of the neighbor's yard to where he could jump the fence close to the truck. He listened carefully and peered through but saw no sign of anyone. Gathering his strength, in one smooth movement he cleared the fence, landing softly on the other side.

He pulled out his knife and stuck it into the tire on the rear right side, then moved to the left and did the same. At least now Brendan couldn't use this vehicle to get away. Inside the garage was a small car. But without moving the truck, no way could he get the car out either. Flynn crept to the front of the truck and stabbed the front tires as well. He stood up to take a look inside the front seat. It looked like Brendan had packed for a long trip.

If he opened the truck door, it would likely sound an alarm, turn on the lights, and all that would alert Brendan. As Flynn peered into the back, he saw duffel bags, several of them. As if Brendan was heading out of town for good. Or at least until he could formulate his next plan of attack.

Well, good luck with that. Flynn planned to have this one locked down before Brendan could make another move.

The back door of the house slammed. Flynn had no place to hide. There was just enough room between the garage and the neighbor's fence to squeeze behind it. Brendan threw another bag into the back of the truck, then stopped and stared. And then he started swearing.

"Jesus Christ, what the hell happened to my tires?" He turned and glared around the yard, searching for the culprit. He ran inside the garage, then down the alley. Finally, he walked back toward the vehicle, shouting obscenities.

Flynn was about to stand up, only to realize the jam he was in. He didn't have any way to sneak up on Brendan. As he opened the truck door, pulling out his bags, Flynn came behind Brendan, grabbed him by the neck and slammed his head into the side of the door. Brendan dropped and rolled, his legs kicking, catching Flynn, and down he went. Brendan was on him in an instant, his hands latched around Flynn's throat.

Flynn tucked his knees up, caught Brendan in the groin while reaching up to press his eyeballs deep into his skull. Brendan roared. But they'd both been trained with military tactics, and it was a fair fight.

Only Flynn had a little more at stake–Anna.

The thought of her bleeding right now was enough to keep Flynn punching and kicking wildly. In the background he dimly heard sirens filling the air. Suddenly, Brendan was hauled off Flynn and held down to the ground.

Guns were pointed at Flynn. He raised his hand and said, "I'm Flynn. He's the shooter."

The cops didn't believe him. "Roll over on your belly with your hands straight out in front of you."

He complied. This would be sorted out with time. The best thing he could do was comply. All he could think about at the moment was that they caught Brendan. Thank God, they'd actually gotten him.

Now to tell Anna so she could rest easy too.

Chapter 15

"ANY WORD FROM Flynn?" Anna asked as she sat on the hard bed in the emergency room.

They were waiting for the doctor to arrive. Logan had told the nurse how Anna had been shot, so she suspected it wouldn't be all that long to get medical attention. On the other hand, this was a big city. Shootings happened almost every single day. She was now a statistic.

"He texted to say he'd run Brendan down to a house. Cops were on the way, and Levi already knew." Logan pulled out his phone. "But there's been nothing since."

"Maybe you can contact Levi and see if he knows anything more."

"Already in progress." Logan nodded, his fingers busy on his phone.

When Logan was finished, he sat back and studied her. "You still don't have any color in your face. How are you feeling?"

"Shaky." She gave him a wan smile. "When we know where Flynn is, I'll feel better."

Just then the doctor came in. "What's this I hear about you being shot, young lady?"

"Shot at," she corrected. "Actually, I have no idea how bad it is."

"Let's take a look."

And he did, poking and prodding. It hurt. She had tears running down her cheeks; she couldn't hold them back. Logan walked to the curtain and stared out toward the waiting room. She figured it was to give her a moment of privacy. All she really wanted to do was curl up on the pillow and bawl.

When the doctor was done, he said, "It could be much worse. The bullet went through the fleshy part of the arm."

She stared at him. "Pardon?" She stared down at her arm but couldn't see anything. "I didn't think I had a fleshy part of my arm," she said in disgust.

The doctor grinned. "Sometimes it's an advantage not being a pure bone rack."

From near the curtain, she could hear Logan snigger.

"Yeah, sure, you're having fun with this. Now you can go tell everybody I'm so fat that the bullet couldn't miss me," she joked.

"I never would," he said. "Besides, the last thing you are is fat. You could easily use another ten pounds."

"I could not. I'm just fine the way I am." She appealed to the doctor beside her. "Right, Doc?"

"I'm not getting in the middle of this one."

She glared at Logan. "See? He agreed with me."

Logan opened his mouth to retort and then snapped it closed and shook his head. "I'll put your lack of logic down to you being injured. Obviously it's a handicap."

She glared at the doctor and said, "You didn't actually tell me how bad it is."

"Nope, I didn't. It'll need some stitches and cleaning. It will be a few days before you can use it at all."

She looked at him in shock. "You know it's my right arm, correct?"

"You know how many people I get through here who tell me something similar?" He picked up his tablet and started to walk away, adding, "I'll send the nurse back in to clean it. Then I'll return to stitch you up."

"I guess that means I'll be here for a while?"

Logan nodded. "I'll step out to make some phone calls." He turned to look back at her and asked, "Will you be okay?"

She waved him off. "I'll be fine. Go find out where Flynn and Brendan are."

When he was gone, the nurse came in. Anna was very grateful Logan wasn't here because she became a blubbering baby. She kept apologizing to the nurse.

The nurse said, "Just relax as much as you can."

Finally the nurse was done. Wiping back her tears, Anna asked, "Can I lie down now?"

In fact, the nurse helped her to lie flat. "I'll give you a shot so when the doctor comes and puts in the stitches, you won't feel it."

"Will it hurt?" She was feeling like a baby. This was so not like her. But then she couldn't remember the last time she'd had any kind of physical trauma. And she would blame as much of this on shock as she could. She felt really woozy too. The pain for the last half hour made her body ache. And she was chilled.

The pain of the needle wouldn't be as bad as cleaning the wound had. The nurse reached down and touched her forehead. "Are you cold?"

Anna nodded, and her teeth started chattering. "It just hit all of a sudden."

"I'll get you a warm blanket. You just lie here and rest."

The nurse took off her gloves, tossed them in the garbage and disappeared. Anna rolled over so her injured arm was higher than her legs and curled up into a ball. And then the tears poured. They were so damn hard to stop. By the time the nurse came back, Anna was shaking from the cold. A warm blanket was draped over her shivering form.

The nurse whispered, "Take it easy. You'll be fine now. This is just shock. Give yourself a few minutes to adjust." Then she was gone again.

Finally her tears stopped, and the shivering calmed down. And warm once again, Anna closed her eyes and drifted off to sleep.

She was awakened rather rudely when the doctor came in and asked in a bright, cheerful voice, "You ready for those stitches now?"

She stared up at him and shook her head. "Is anybody ever ready for them?"

He gave her a quiet smile. "Well, the alternative would be much worse. Let's get this sewn up."

She lay quietly in that position while he went ahead and did what he needed to. Thankfully, it was just a few tugs. Nothing bad.

When he was done, he said, "I'll write a prescription for some pain medication. You need to see your doctor in ten days. If you have any sharp pain, pus from the site, red lines running up and down your arm, or any kind of problem, you get to your doctor immediately. Better yet, come straight back to Emergency." He waited until she looked him directly in the eye before he added, "Do you hear me?"

She nodded. "I hear you."

"I'll make sure she's fine," Logan said from the doorway.

The doctor looked at him. "Are you her boyfriend?"

"No, a good friend."

Logan stepped closer. "Her boyfriend went after the asshole who did this to her."

The doctor nodded. "Good. I presume I will have another body in need of repair soon enough." He handed the prescription to Logan, walked out, calling back, "Glad she has someone looking after her. We all need that."

Logan studied Anna's face as she still lay under the blanket. "Do you need to stay overnight? I might be able to arrange that."

She shook her head. "No, I'll be fine." She looked up at him. "But it's awfully hard to move."

He gently pulled back the blanket and held out his arms. She grabbed him with her good arm and slowly leveraged herself to a sitting position.

Just then the nurse came bustling back in. "Oh, good, you're up. I came to bring you a sling. Keep the arm elevated to take the pressure off the joints, and don't use it for several days. Do you understand?"

At this point Anna found it easier to nod at every instruction. She'd do what she had to, and do the best she could. But honestly, how could she possibly not use her main arm? That would be damn near impossible.

Thankfully, the bullet hadn't hit a bone or artery, and it was a small injury compared to having a bullet tear through her organs. This was an inconvenience, but she would live with it.

It could have been a lot worse.

FLYNN CALLED ANNA. No answer. Had they remembered to grab her phone before they raced to the hospital? He could only presume that's where they were. It was where he'd have taken her. But since she wasn't answering her cell phone…

Quickly he dialed the number to the shelter and got the answering machine. Next he called Logan.

"She's fine," Logan said. "The bullet went through the soft tissue of her arm. She's got stitches, and it's bandaged. We're just heading to her car to drive home."

"Oh, thank God." Flynn pinched the bridge of his nose as he gave a silent prayer of thanks. "When I ran out like that, after the second barrage of bullets, I wasn't sure how badly hurt she was. I was just about to race to the hospital now to see if she was still there."

"We have to pick up a prescription, and that'll take at least ten minutes, so we should be home in half an hour. She's tired, still a little in shock, but fine and in fighting form, evidenced by the fact that she wouldn't stay in the hospital any longer."

"No, I don't think she likes hospitals." He could be wrong, but he didn't think so.

"I don't think anybody does. Anyway, can you meet us at her house? I want to get her into the vehicle and moving as fast as possible. She's looking a little on the pale side." Logan sighed.

In the background, Flynn could hear her snapping, "No, I'm not. Tell him I'm fine. He'll just worry."

And that—more than anything—made Flynn feel so much better. If she was in a feisty mood, then she was doing just fine. "I'll be home as soon as I can," he said. "The police have Brendan in custody. But I'm hanging here just in case they need me. I don't want the cops to come back to the place tonight. She's been through enough."

"This isn't your fault. Think forward."

When he ended the call, Flynn turned to study the area.

The cops were all over the place. Then again, this guy had been in several cop chases, and was a suspect of a drive-by shooting and murder. There should be a lot of attention to this property, the vehicle, and Brendan himself. Flynn wanted to go down to the police station and beat the shit out of Brendan to get some answers. But Flynn knew that wouldn't go down well. He walked over to a cop and asked, "Do you need me here?"

The cop studied him. "I want your statement. Give me a brief version now, and you can go down to the station later."

It took a little bit, but when he finally got through it all, the cop with his notepad said, "Okay, see you at the station tomorrow morning. We'll go through this place with a finetooth comb. We need proof he's the one who killed Jonas, and it would be nice to have proof he's the one responsible for the drive-by shooting and the attack on Anna."

That set up several more questions in Flynn's mind. By the time he was done and free to go, another half hour had passed. A half hour that really didn't matter because now he knew Brendan was caught and life could return to normal. They needed as much evidence as they could possibly get to pin it all on Brendan. Flynn didn't want to see the asshole get out for thirty plus years.

A part of him wanted to see Brendan go out in a blaze of gunfire so Flynn wouldn't have to worry about him anymore. But now that he was in police custody, Flynn was pretty sure they were in for a long-drawn-out court case. As long as Brendan didn't get a chance to be released on bail, then Flynn was good with that.

Speaking of which, he called Levi. "I guess there is no way we can stop Brendan from getting released on bail, is there? Not with murder charges against him, right?"

"Only if they can pin it on him," Levi said. "If he's cooperative and agrees to stay around, they may release him without bail. If they have evidence worth charging him with murder or attempted murder, they could still release him if he posts bail. Otherwise, they can hold him for twenty-four hours without charging him."

"We can't let him get bail," Flynn said. "I know his brother is local, but Brendan is a newcomer to this area, unemployed."

"Good point. I'll make a phone call to the DA. He owes us after last time. Maybe he can use his clout to influence bail."

Flynn had forgotten about Rhodes's problem with Sienna and the DA. Rhodes had saved the DA's life. It was always good to have friends in high places, especially to have them in cases like this. It was pretty major. It wasn't as if Flynn wanted anything illegal done, but if there were doors that could be closed, he didn't want Brendan getting out. If he came back after Flynn, it would be bad. But it was Anna who kept getting hurt. And that could not be allowed to continue.

By the time he made it to his truck and back out to the main road, driving toward Anna's place, he could feel some of his adrenaline draining away. It was amazing how good it was, keeping you going when everything was busy. But once that adrenaline shot drained out, it left you pretty empty.

He hoped some pizza was still left. He'd have some of that when he got there. But he knew the animals might be feeling the stress of these events too. Maybe tonight they all could finally get a good night's sleep for the first time in days.

As he pulled up into the driveway, Anna's car was already there. Which was a good thing. He hopped out, locked up the truck and walked to the front door. The security system was set. He punched in the code to let himself in the front door and called out, "Anna, you home?"

He closed the door, reset the alarm and turned to see Logan standing in the living room. A finger to his lips.

"She's just fallen asleep on the couch."

Flynn took a look. Sure enough, she was curled up with a pillow under her head and a blanket across her shoulders. Sleeping. But her face was pale, waxy. He leaned down and kissed her cheek gently and whispered, "I'm sorry. But it's all over now. You're safe."

She didn't shift, and he realized that, between the pain medication and stress, she was out cold. He turned back toward Logan. "You probably should have taken her to her bed before she crashed."

"I tried," Logan said. "But she was a mite too stubborn. She wanted to be down here when you came back."

"Like that'll help. Now I have to carry her upstairs," he joked.

"And you won't have a problem doing that," Logan said comfortably. "Chances are you'll stay in the bedroom beside her."

Flynn glanced back at her and said in a low voice, "I'd like nothing better."

"I'm damn glad they caught Brendan." Logan shook his head. "I wondered what it would take to bring down that asshole."

"And I'm still not sure he'll stay down. There's just too many ways he could get off. What if they don't have enough evidence to pin the murder on him? We can't prove it was a drive-by shooting if there are no eyewitness reports seeing the truck or him. It would be my word against his. There's just so much circumstantial evidence. And the fact that he has a brother close and he's ex-military too, a soft judge could let him go while they collect more evidence."

"What? Surely not."

Flynn shrugged. He turned a tired face toward Logan and said, "You and Levi both know it can happen. You've seen all kinds things occur in the courts. Honestly, I'd rather the guy was dead. But that's out of my hands."

"Make sure it's not by your hands," Logan warned. "It's tough in our business. We've had to kill. But we can't make it a choice to do so."

"I hear you. It doesn't mean I don't want to." He cast one more look at Anna. "I'd pound the shit right out of him if I could get my hands on him for what he did to Anna alone." He walked into the kitchen. "Any pizza left?"

"God, I hope so. I know there's beer."

Within minutes the two men sat down to warmed-up pizza and cold beer. Flynn stretched out his legs with a happy sigh after three pieces. He took a long swig of beer and said, "Goddamn, am I glad it's over with."

Logan nodded. "Do you think it's safe to leave you two alone tonight?"

Flynn gave his buddy a lopsided grin. "If she wasn't injured, I'd say get the hell out of here, but with her sleeping like she is, injured the way she was..." He shook his head. "It'll be sleep tonight."

Logan gave a good-natured laugh. "Understood. I'm really surprised, though I shouldn't be, as I'd heard about the two of you. But now that I see you together, I'm happy for you. You're really well-matched."

Flynn shrugged. "I'm not sure what that means anymore. But I know I found someone very special, and I want to hang on to her."

"Good. Then you won't do anything stupid. I doubt she'll be rushed into anything she's not ready for."

"No, but it's time for a change for her. She's contemplating selling and moving a little out of town. She's hoping she'll get more land for the animals. Then go bigger for the rescues. But that depends on all kinds of things, including money." He reached out with his beer bottle and tapped Logan's. "Your dad did a good thing with that check."

Logan's eyebrows shot up. "He sent one?"

Flynn nodded. "I saw the company name on it. She needed that money."

"Well, the old man's got it, and he donates hundreds of thousands a year to charities. There's no reason some of it can't filter here."

"That's a great way to look at it."

As Flynn finished his beer, he stood up and put his empty back into the case, grabbing another. As he did so, he heard an odd sound. He froze, turned and looked out to the backyard. The two dogs were in the pen; they needed to be brought into their cages. And it was already damn late. But he knew how Anna would worry. Yet he couldn't see what caused that sound. Still suspicious, he knew how easily normal night noises could be scary. "There are four cats and two dogs left to look after. I better get out there."

"Let me give you a hand."

Leaving the beer behind, the two walked out the back door. He led Jimbo and Duggy inside to their cages, gave them fresh water and food and both got a hug. They walked to the cats, made short work of the litter box, and with

Logan's help, dumped out a couple cans of cat food and gave them fresh water. He looked down the long rows of cages and said, "It's the least animals she's ever had."

"Well, there's certainly a need for her to do more. But after this crap..." Logan shook his head. "You're right. Maybe moving would be better."

"It'll be hard to recover from it here. I can't imagine too many charities will want to donate with all the bad publicity that'll hit the papers. I'd like to be wrong, bu ..."

"I could ask my dad to give a hand. Not so much with donating more money because I don't know what he's doing with that, but he could surely put out a good word. Also, she's got prime real estate here. Maybe she should move. If she can afford to, this is the best time because she doesn't have many animals. We can get the whole gang to give her a hand one day, get it done fast and simple."

"Do you think the guys would mind?"

Logan snorted. "You know how they love to be over the top, do it all at once and better than anyone else. They'd die for her, particularly if she's to be your ladylove." Logan waggled his eyebrows.

Flynn smiled. "I guess that's what families are all about."

Logan slapped him on the shoulder. "Remember you're part of the team now. You're one of us again. You are not out in the cold anymore."

Flynn glanced at Logan once more and smiled. "With you, buddy, I never have been. Thanks for always being there."

"That's what friends are for."

Chapter 16

ANNA WOKE TO a silence that was deep and unnerving. It took a long moment to figure out exactly where she was and why she was on her couch with a blanket over her. As soon as she jolted to a sitting position, she remembered. The pain in her arm kicked in. She leaned back and took several deep breaths, waiting for the throbbing to calm down. Her arm was in a sling, but some of that support had shifted. The bandage was solid and should do for the night. It was definitely dark out. And it sounded like she was alone. She got to her feet, made her way to the downstairs bathroom, used the facilities and washed her hands. She stared at her face in the mirror and saw drops of dried blood, her ashen complexion, and the great big bags under her eyes. "Wow, a beauty you are not."

With her left hand she awkwardly grabbed a washcloth, wet it and did a half-assed effort to wipe her face clean. She wasn't sure how the blood got up there. No way could she manage a shower tonight. She wasn't sure why she had awakened. That was one of the reasons she hated drugs as much as they did her. They never worked as well or as long as they should.

She opened the bathroom door and stepped out. Lights were on in the kitchen, but no sound came from there. As she walked into the brightly lit room, she noticed that half a pizza was gone, and several more beer bottles, opened and emptied, were on the table. So the guys were either out front at the vehicles or in back with the animals.

Dear God, she hadn't brought the dogs in. She opened the door and listened. But she couldn't hear anything. She wanted to call the dogs, but she'd been through enough scary shit lately and didn't want to bring any attention to herself. Then she heard voices, laughter and a door shutting. She sank back against the doorjamb, relieved, closing her eyelids as she realized Flynn and Logan were in with the cats. Her phone buzzed. She glanced at it and got her second good news of the day. The reptile center had room for her snake. She would contact them to arrange for the transfer.

She beamed at the guys as they walked toward her. "Thank you for looking after the animals. The snake has a new home as soon as I can make it happen."

"That's great news," Logan said.

"What the hell are you doing up and outside?" Flynn snapped. "You're injured. You should be back in bed—your own, not on the couch."

"Thank you, Flynn. How are you, Flynn? It's so nice of you to be concerned about my condition, Flynn. But please take it upon yourself to be anything but an asshole."

Logan howled with laughter. "Oh, my God, you two are so perfect for each other."

Both Flynn and Anna turned to glare at Logan. He snickered, but it subsided. Flynn motioned to her. She turned around and went back into the house. She decided she would follow his silent command because she felt tired enough that she needed to go sit down again, not because he told her to. She found a chair she assumed they hadn't been using at the kitchen table and collapsed into it. She eyed the pizza, wondering if she wanted a piece.

"You want some?" Logan asked, his gaze following hers.

She smiled. "Would you mind putting it in the microwave for a few seconds for me?"

"Not at all." He picked up two slices from the two different boxes, plunked them on a plate and popped it in the microwave.

She sat back as the aroma of pizza filled the room.

Flynn asked, "You want a beer? Although it's probably not a good idea with the painkillers."

"I'm not much of a beer drinker anyway. Thanks. Now if there was tea …"

Logan hit the button on the teakettle as he brought her the pizza. "Hot water coming up."

She stared down at the pizza, smiled brightly and said, "Thank you. Nice to know you're housetrained."

He chuckled. "I am. I don't know about this guy though."

She turned sideways, glancing at Flynn. "He's got more of the junkyard dog thing going on."

Logan howled again.

Flynn glared at him. "Enough already. Shut the hell up."

Logan subsided slightly, but his eyes twinkled as he looked from one to the other. "I guess now that you're safe, I can go home to my own house?"

"Do you have your own?" Anna asked in interest. "I thought you lived at the compound."

"I do. And my father is close by. He has a huge house with my own suite of rooms in it." He gave her a sheepish grin. "Seems silly to buy my own when he's got an apartment for me, plus, I do live at the compound."

"Nice, no bills anywhere." She shook her head. "Damn

nice."

He laughed. "There is just my father and me," he said. "I don't really want to move out and lose the relationship we have."

"I wouldn't either," she said softly. "If you have any relationship that you care about, you do what you need to nurture it."

"My thoughts exactly. Besides, I'm never around to look after a place, so thankfully people at both locations take care of things for me." He grinned. "And I'm a lousy cook."

"But you have Alfred. I would love to have an Alfred of my own," she said in a wistful tone. "My God, he's perfect. He does all the organizing, looking after the house. He cooks. He cleans…" She shook her head. "We should all have an Alfred."

"No argument there."

Flynn looked over at Logan. "Your dad has several Alfreds. And our counterpart in Africa, Bullard, has Dave, who's damn near a clone of Alfred. And in England, one of our friends we stay with, Charles, has a second Alfred clone. There's just something about that type of gentleman."

"*Gentleman.* Yes, Alfred's very much that. He's almost like an old butler."

"The compound does have staff members who come and handle things. It's well over 25,000 square feet. Way too big for any one person to clean."

"That's gotta be a nightmare," she said. "I understand the compound is high-security conscious."

"Absolutely."

Flynn's phone rang just then. He pulled it from his pocket, looked at the number and sighed. "Levi never sleeps."

"SHE'S FINE. SHE has stitches in her bicep, and the arm's in a sling. Still looking a little pale and chalky, but she's got antibiotics and painkillers. We're at her place. A good night's sleep and she'll be that much better tomorrow," Flynn said. "Any update on what the police found?"

"Not yet. We will touch base in the morning. Just wanted to hear Anna was safe. Katina's beside herself here."

"Tell her Anna is fine."

"She's gone to bed. I'll knock and let her know. They can touch base in the morning too."

After that Levi hung up.

Flynn turned back to Anna. "Just like Flynn here, you have a family you aren't even aware of. And over time, it'll just get bigger and stronger," Logan said. He pulled his long length to an upright position. "If you guys think you're good for the night, I'll head home and crash."

Anna got up and ran over, throwing her good arm around him.

Gently he hugged her back, dropping a kiss on her forehead. "Now you be good. I don't want to see you back in the hospital anytime soon."

She beamed up at him. "I plan to never go back. Of course I might end up having to send Flynn so he knows what it feels like."

Flynn spoke from behind her. "As if."

She stepped back and said to Logan, "Thanks for looking after me so well."

They followed him to the front door and stood on the porch until he got into the truck and drove away.

Flynn closed the door, reset the alarm and said, "Come on. Let's get you upstairs to bed."

She looked around her. "What about this mess?"

"Tomorrow's another day. I can do the dishes in the morning. Right now, you're ready to crash, and I can't say I'm very far away from that myself."

He waited for her to climb the stairs, making sure all the lights were out downstairs, and then trailed up behind her. At her bedroom he stopped in the doorway. "You'll be okay for the night?"

She scrubbed her face with her left hand. "I'm just realizing how awkward this will be. I can't get my shirt off with my arm like this."

He saw the tears in the corners of her eyes and felt like a heel. "Come on. Let's get you ready for bed." He pulled back the bedding, took off her shoes and socks in seconds, and helped her out of her pants.

She looked at him and said, "You are very experienced at this."

That startled a laugh out of him. "Not as much as you may think. Now let's get that shirt off." He studied the sling first, then gently lifted her arms so he could pull it over her head. As if dealing with a baby, he carefully pulled one arm out of her T-shirt, then over her head and off her injured arm.

"What do you want to sleep in?"

She pointed at the dresser. "I have an oversize cotton T-shirt I like to use."

It was lying on top of the dresser. He grabbed it and came back to her. "Honey, the bra has to go."

She glanced down and winced. "Yeah, it so does." She stood, turned her back to him and said, "Unhook it please."

He did, and as she leaned forward, it managed to drop off her arms. Then she put her good one in the air, and he dropped the big T-shirt down over it and her head, followed slowly by her right arm. Gently he eased her sore arm back through the sling.

She turned around. "Damn that hurts."

"It'll feel much better in the morning."

She shook her head. "I doubt it." She kicked her dirty clothes off to the side and sat down on the edge of the bed. "I should brush my teeth, but I'm so damn tired."

"But you'll feel better. Come on. Let's get it done, then you can go to bed."

She let him lead her to the bathroom, where he put toothpaste on her toothbrush, ran it under the water and gave it to her. Then he grabbed the washcloth, doused it with warm water, and while she was brushing her teeth, he gently dabbed at the dried blood in her hair. His goal was to let her sleep without having this pull and tug through the night. He rinsed the cloth in more warm water and some soap, and when she was done with the toothbrush, he gently washed her face.

She smiled. "I feel like a two-year-old."

Using the same washcloth, he finished the job by washing her injured arm and both hands. "Sometimes we all need to be looked after. Now into bed with you."

She made her way back to the bed, crawled underneath the covers and lay down. She looked up at him expectantly. She wasn't at all sure what she wanted, but he tucked the bedding up higher, bent down and kissed her on her forehead. Then he reached for the light.

"Wait."

He looked down at her. "What do you need?"

A flush stained her neck and cheeks a beautiful rose pink, but her eyes were direct and her voice clear when she answered, warm and lovingly, "You."

"Honey," he started to protest. He wanted her, but she was injured, so this was not a good idea.

She patted the side of the bed. "To sleep with me. Maybe just hold me until I fall asleep," she confessed. "It might hurt too much to do anything else. If you could see your way to sleeping beside me tonight …"

He lowered his head and kissed her passionately, thoroughly, just enough for her to know he was there any time she was ready. "Absolutely. Just give me a minute to grab my stuff in the other room."

She nodded and shifted more comfortably, her eyes closing.

He went to the spare bedroom, where he had always stayed, then returned to hers. Exhausted, he prepped for bed. He'd planned on a shower, but there really wasn't a need tonight. He washed his face, brushed his teeth, and when he went back into the bedroom, found her almost asleep. He crawled in on his side. She turned to him instinctively, and he wrapped his arm gently around her, tucking her ever-so-slightly closer. But she moved in like a homing pigeon, nestling close to his chest.

"Thank you," she whispered.

He reached up and stroked her back gently. "My pleasure. There's nowhere I'd rather be right now."

With a happy smile she fell asleep.

He followed soon after.

Chapter 17

THE NEXT MORNING, Anna woke, surrounded by the intense heat pouring off Flynn. There was such a sense of well-being inside, she couldn't resist snuggling closer. She moved her injured arm experimentally. It didn't feel too bad.

She shifted away from the sleeping man beside her and made her way to the bathroom. She wondered if she should risk a shower. She could probably get the T-shirt off by herself. If she left the bandage on, would that be better or worse?

When she realized she still had dried blood in her hair, even though Flynn had done his best last night to wash it out, she decided the shower was mandatory. She glanced out the window to see bright, strong sunlight. So it was morning. And the animals were waiting.

She turned on the water, closed the door and waited for the water to warm up. She stripped off her panties and the T-shirt, taking great care not to bang up her arm as she did so, then stepped under the spray, bandage on. She'd do her best to keep it out of the water, but she knew that wasn't possible. Just standing under the heat as the warm water pounded down on her head felt soothing. With soap and a washcloth, she gave herself a good scrub, then did her best to shampoo her hair, washing it twice in order to get all the blood out. When she was done, she turned to find a shadow outside the glass doors.

A shriek escaped her, and she fell.

The door opened immediately. "Anna? It's just me."

She stared at him as the fear slowly drained. And then she got mad. "You could at least call out to let me know you're there," she cried.

He apologized. "I woke up and found you were gone. I came right away to see if you were in here. I just got here when you shrieked."

He held out a hand, which she used to get herself to her feet carefully because everything was so wet. That's when she realized she was standing fully nude in the shower in front of him. And he was standing fully nude out of the shower in front of her.

She shook her head. "Well, you might as well come in and get cleaned up."

He glanced at her in surprise, then grinned. "I wouldn't say no to that invitation."

"I was washing my hair," she said, "but I can't reach places on the right side."

"Here, I'll do that." He grabbed the shampoo and proceeded to wash her hair gently. He massaged every inch of her scalp until she was melting and moaning in pleasure.

"Oh, my God, where did you learn to do that? That's wonderful."

He moved her gently back under the stream and let the warm water rinse away all the suds. "Do you have any conditioner?"

She pointed at the bottle on the shelf. He grabbed it and put some in his hand. Rubbing his hands together, he gently stroked it through her hair.

She smiled. "Obviously you've practiced." And oddly

enough it didn't bother her a bit. He'd had a life before her, as she'd had one before him. As long as their future was built together on truth and love.

"I've never done this before in my life."

Her eyes flew open. "Really?"

He nodded and smiled down at her. He dropped a kiss on her nose. "Never. But I can see I might be interested in doing it often from now on."

This time, when he lowered his head, his hands still massaging her scalp, he took her lips in a deep passionate kiss, but he was so in control. Giving her time to say yes, giving her time to say no. Lady's choice, and she appreciated that. But what she wanted was him.

She'd never wanted any other man like she did him. Heat surrounded her inside, outside—his steam, the water's steam, the steam enveloping them in the small stall. More than that, her body was softening, dampening, opening, readying for him.

She slipped her good arm up around his neck and pressed against him from her slippery soapy hips to breasts. Skin to skin. Heat to heat. She kissed him back like she'd always wanted to. Need clawed at her.

This was the first chance they'd had to be together without all the horror. Not ideal as she was injured. But if they were careful …

He raised his head and pulled back slightly, in case she wanted to let him go. Instead, she wrapped her good arm tighter around him. He reached up to stroke her wet hair back off her face, his fingers caressing, gently loving. "Are you sure?" he whispered.

Anna looked up at him and smiled. "I've never been surer of anything in my life."

He looked around her at the shower and said, "Here or in the bed?"

She laughed. "Your choice. But personally I have no intention of walking anywhere." Her eyes lit with humor as she confessed, "I don't think I can."

He chuckled, shut off the water and said, "Maybe not, but for the sake of your arm, we're probably better getting you into bed, just so you don't hurt yourself more."

He grabbed a towel, wrapped it around her, then got a second one for himself. He gently helped her out and taking the towel, dried her off. As in every single inch of her. His strokes warm, lazy, and teasing.

She whispered, when she finally could find her voice, "I said I couldn't walk before. How the hell do you expect me to now?"

He gave himself a brisk rub over, tossed both towels to the floor and swept her up into his arms. "I never intended for you to walk anywhere."

He carried her to the bed and laid her down. Then he dropped beside her. She turned and wrapped her legs around him.

"Now that you've done so much to stoke the fire," she whispered, "how about you put it out?"

He would've chuckled, but she reached up and kissed him, hard. Her teeth biting the inside of his lip gently and then harder, kissing, licking, tasting her own passion, rising, driving her forward.

When he finally pulled his head back, his voice was hoarse. "Jesus."

She dragged his head back down. "Sorry, he's not available. In fact, nobody can help you now."

He gave a muffled laugh, followed by a strangled moan

and positioned himself between her thighs. She wrapped her legs around him tight, high up on his hips, and rubbed up and down against the hard shaft between them.

Flynn grabbed her hips, pulling her back, but she fought, climbing all over his frame. He gave a half laugh. "Sweetie, I haven't actually gotten where I need to be."

She gave him a half-lidded look. "Are you sure about that?" She pushed on his shoulders, and he rolled over. She went with him and sat up on her knees, straddling him. Whether by luck or design, she was poised right above his erection.

He stared up at her, and a wonderful smile crossed his face. "Oh, my God, you are the most beautiful thing I have ever seen."

She threw her head back and slowly lowered herself on his shaft. She was so wet, ready, and damn hot that he slid right inside. He grabbed her hips and thrust himself upward, seating himself fully and as deeply as he could go. She cried out, and with her hand on his shoulders to brace herself, she rode like the inner Valkyrie she was. She set a fast tempo, as nothing else would do, and drove them to the edge of the cliff. He reached down between them, his fingers sliding between her curls, finding the nub, and with a cry she threw her head back and exploded. He cupped her shoulders and slowly moved within.

With a shudder, she opened her eyes again and stared back down at him, one eyebrow raised.

He grinned and said, "Round two?"

She groaned. "Oh, my God. Why do I think this is going to be a long session?"

He laughed and gently stroked the nub in her curls, sending her blood pressure roaring to maximum once again.

This time it was a slower ride to the cliff but just as fantastic. She didn't want to go alone. She stretched down behind her and gently caught the soft globes between his legs and gave a squeeze.

It was his turn to groan. So she did it again, then slowly lifted herself up as if to remove herself from him. He grabbed her hips, forced her down. This time he lost control and drove harder, higher, deeper, and faster, and shouted when his climax ripped through him, his seed pulsing deep inside, sending her crashing to the shores below.

She collapsed on top of him and whispered, "I knew my arm wouldn't be a problem."

He gave a great big shudder and held her close. "If this is what you're like when you're injured," he whispered, "I can't imagine what you're like when you're not."

"For that, you'll have to wait a few days." She closed her eyes and nodded off.

FLYNN WAITED UNTIL she was asleep. He slowly and carefully disentangled himself from her arms and slid off the bed on his side, got to his feet and went to use the bathroom. He collected the towels, straightened them over the railing and dressed. He needed to check in with Levi this morning. It was late already, but she needed the sleep.

He'd take care of the animals and get some coffee going too. By the time she woke, she'd be ready for a cup.

With a happy whistle, he made his way downstairs and put on the coffee first. He grabbed his phone and called Levi while waiting. No answer.

Fine, he'd call back in a few minutes. He'd take care of the animals. He moved Jimbo and Duggy out to the big dog run. If Anna was feeling up to it, maybe they could take them both for a walk later. The dogs certainly needed it, but the dog run was big and gave them lots of space to jump around, which was exactly what they were doing.

He gave them fresh water, refilled their food dishes and let them eat in the pen. He checked on the cats, but they appeared to be snoozing, although two walked over for a greeting as he stepped inside. He spent a few minutes cuddling them, realizing just how much he enjoyed being able to pick up an animal and snuggle with it. The cats had lots of dry food. He'd mix in some canned, and they'd be good to go.

When he was done, he went back toward the house, still whistling. He grabbed his phone and tried Levi again. When the other end was answered, he asked, "Levi, any update?"

"Yes, but not one you're gonna like. He's been released."

Flynn couldn't believe what Levi was telling him. He heard the words, but the concept was just not computing. "What do you mean, he's out already?" He glanced at his watch. "It's only been, what, ten hours at the most?"

"His lawyers. He answered all the questions reasonably and gave alibis the police have checked. And apparently the detective in charge, some new upshot, spunky asshole, said he was allowed to leave the station but to stay in town."

"I don't give a shit what kind of lawyers he's got ..." Flynn strode up and down the kitchen, his fury rising. "You do realize he is on his way here then, right? It's either that, or he'll disappear, and we'll never see him again. Except we'll always be watching our backs."

"I know. I hear you. The DA's on it. Apparently they've sent men to pick him up again." Levi's voice was just as frustrated and angry as Flynn felt.

Flynn calmed down; his mind kicked in, working fast. "I haven't seen any sign of him. I was just out with the animals. I'm back inside now. I've got to get her up. We have to be ready. You know we can't trust him."

He strode toward the living room to look out the big window. No sign of Brendan. Good thing. "They could have kept him for twenty-four hours with no problem," Flynn snapped. "No way in hell should he have been let out."

Levi was still talking in his ear. "Keep me posted if you see him."

"I'll go check out the rest of the house now," Flynn said, turning. And he froze. "Levi …"

Brendan stood in front of him, a gun pointed at his chest. "Say hello and good-bye to Levi for me."

And he fired.

Chapter 18

ANNA WOKE WITH a jolt, the harsh cold sound still zinging through her memories into full wakefulness. Instantly, she knew she was alone in the room—and nude—lying on top of the covers.

Awkwardly, but ignoring the pain, she slipped on the panties and T-shirt she'd slept in before the shower and crept to the bedroom door. Downstairs she could hear a door bang, followed by running footsteps. She raced to her bedroom window to look out.

And saw Brendan running. He threw something into the neighbor's garbage and darted for a small black car. Within seconds, he drove down the street.

Panicked, she grabbed her phone and raced downstairs. She couldn't see anything in the kitchen or office. She barreled into the living room.

And fell to her knees screaming, "Flynn! Oh, my God. Flynn."

Blood poured from his chest. He'd been shot. She dialed 9-1-1 and slapped her hand over the wound, keeping pressure to slow the bleeding. "Help, please. He's been shot. Dear God. He's been shot in the chest."

"Calm down, we need to know your address. Are you still in danger?"

"My God. No, he ran away. He took off in a small black

car. It was Brendan. I saw him."

"Just stay on the line and stay calm. I have to dispatch somebody to your address. Is the front door unlocked?"

Anna twisted to find the door was open. "Yes. They should be able to see me from the front porch."

"Please stay on the line until we get you some help. Are you sure nobody else is there? Are you sure you're not in danger?"

"No, no, no. He ran away. Please hurry. Please, he can't die. Oh, my God. There's just so much blood."

"There is always a lot of blood with any injury. Don't let that affect you. Stay calm, stay collected and talk to him. If you can get any kind of response, let me know."

"No, he's totally unconscious. The color from his face, I mean… Oh, my God. It's just so white."

"And that's normal. Don't panic. Help is on the way."

"I need to phone other people."

"I need you to stay on the line. We have to keep this communication open."

She fretted but understood. In the distance she could hear the sirens. "Oh, thank God. I hear sirens."

"That's right. They should be there any minute now."

Before the woman stopped talking, she heard a screech of brakes outside, and two EMTs ran into the house. They took one look and moved her out of the way.

Into the phone she said, "I'm hanging up now. They're here."

She wrapped her arms tightly around her chest. She could hardly breathe. It was bad. It was so goddamn bad.

She called Levi. Blubbering into the phone, she said, "He shot him. Brendan shot Flynn." The tears choked her throat and stopped her voice from coming through. "The ambulance is here right now. But I don't think he'll live through this."

"I was on the phone with him when it happened. How bad is it? Do you remember exactly what happened?"

"I just woke up. I heard the shot, looked out the window, and I saw Brendan leaving. He threw the gun into the neighbor's garbage bin." She stared around the room. "I should go get it. I'm not even dressed."

"Stay calm. Somebody'll be there. We're going to find him. Hold tight. Do what you need to do to keep Flynn alive. Stay in touch. But don't run out there right now."

"You don't understand … the gun. The gun that shot Flynn—I saw it. What if somebody grabs it? And I don't want to leave Flynn."

She stared down at her bare legs with his blood on them and his T-shirt in her hands. "There's just so much blood."

"We're in the vehicle already. Stay calm. We'll be there in a few minutes."

She gave a half laugh, one full of grief. "It's hardly minutes to get here."

"True, but Logan's on his way now too."

And she cried out, "Oh, my God. I should have called him first."

"It's not an issue. We called him. He's heading toward you right now."

Inside she wanted to feel relief. She wanted to know something would work out. But she knew it wouldn't. There was no way it could. "Levi, you have to see him. Oh, my God!"

And then she couldn't talk anymore for the tears clogging her throat. She sobbed quietly, deeply.

Levi's gentle voice whispered to her, "We've seen all of

us recover from some horrific injuries," he said. "I don't know how bad it is, but you have to hold on to faith. More than that, Flynn has to know you're there for him. He has to have something to fight for."

She nodded. It was the same with animals. She knew, when they gave up, it was all over. The spirit had to be there fighting, and it needed a reason. She wiped away her tears, taking several choking breaths and said, "I'm going upstairs to get dressed. I'll follow Flynn to the hospital. I don't want him to be alone right now."

In her bedroom, she dressed as quickly she could. She tossed the phone on the bed, not even knowing if she'd shut off the call. She quickly washed the blood off her hands and face, finished dressing, grabbed her phone and went back downstairs. She slipped on her shoes, grabbed her purse and headed outside. The EMTs were already loading Flynn into the back of the ambulance. She told the attendant, "Go. I'll follow."

She stood near her car, hugging her chest, watching as they took off. She didn't want him to go alone. But she also knew she would need wheels, and she would be damned if that Brendan asshole would get away with this. And for that she needed the gun.

She had a roll of poop bags in her pocket. She walked down to the garbage can where she'd seen Brendan throw the gun, opened the lid and looked inside. Sure enough it was here. She turned on the camera on her phone, took several pictures and then reached inside with the poop bag and grabbed it, carefully wrapping it inside.

As she turned around, Logan raced toward her. She started crying again. She held up the gun and said, "I saw him throw it in there. Oh, my God, I saw him throw it away."

Logan took her in his arms and held her close. "Did you actually see Brendan?"

She nodded. "From the back at first. Then he turned to look at the house as he threw the gun in the garbage." She motioned at the can where the gun had been. "And then he got into a small black car and took off. But it was too far away to get the license plate. I tried. I tried."

"Take it easy, sweetie. Take it easy. Let me take a quick look through the house and see if there's anything I need to do. Then we'll drive to the hospital."

Just then the cops came into the yard. Not one car, not two, but three. And she knew it wouldn't be easy to get out of her driveway now. Logan said in a low voice, "That's the same detective I spoke with earlier." The two men greeted each other. The gun was passed over.

Anna knew Logan was angry, but it was nothing compared to what she was feeling. She walked up to the cop and said, "The cops should never have let that asshole out. It's not enough that he shot me, but you had to wait until he actually killed somebody."

The cop didn't have anything to say. What could he anyway? It wasn't really his fault. It was the system's. He took the gun. "He's not dead yet. We'll do everything we can to ensure Brendan doesn't hurt anyone else. Can you show me the crime scene?"

Bitterly, she walked inside the front door of her house, following Logan. "Just put a bullet in his head. Save us all the trouble."

Inside she stopped and stared, tears flooding her eyes as she remembered the blood spurting out of Flynn. So much blood was in her living room. She knew that, whether Flynn survived or not, she was done with this house. She could not come into this living room ever again and not see the blood and the trauma she'd been through today. Nobody should have to. This place was going up for sale as soon as she could arrange it.

She turned to Logan. "I need to get to the hospital. Are you coming?"

"You're not driving."

She stared at him in determination. "I'm leaving now. With or without you."

He looked over at the cop and said, "You know what you have to do. You don't need us here."

The cop nodded. "Go. We'll catch you at the hospital."

She went with Logan to his truck, hopped inside and asked, "Should we tell Levi we're going?"

"Don't worry about it. I'll tell him."

She sat frozen, completely locked with fear as they drove to the hospital. It seemed like every mile they went, the fear grew worse. She just knew Flynn wouldn't make it.

"He'll make it. He's a fighter. You have to trust."

She stared at Logan blankly. "Trust what? They had him. They had Brendan, and they let him go."

"And they will get him again. This time they will throw away the key and forget he ever existed."

"It's too late for that. It's just way too late."

IT WAS CHAOS with lights, sirens, and screaming. Flynn lay caught in the dark cloud of confusion. But one thing he understood fully was the red fire that consumed his body from head to toe. So much pain. Everything hurt. Just to breathe hurt. He didn't dare move. He wasn't even sure he could. It seemed like so much weight was on his chest. Something was holding his legs and arms down. He struggled, trying to get to Anna. Danger was all around them. And he was fighting. He had to save her. He couldn't let her get hurt again. Not anymore.

And yet, he could do nothing. He struggled and struggled, but he knew nothing came of it. He wanted his arms and legs to move, but he couldn't get them to. As he fought against the heavy pain, with huge blackened hands reaching out for him, he knew he didn't want to go in that direction. He tried to get away from them. But they moved inexorably toward him.

He wanted to run. He wanted to cry out. In his mind was this endless long-drawn-out scream of "*Noooo.*" But nothing stopped the march of those hands. They latched on to his heart, mind, and soul. They dragged him back under into the murky depths of unconsciousness.

But he knew what they were. He knew they were really the fingers of death.

Chapter 19

THERE WAS NOTHING to do but wait. There was no update. There was no doctor coming in to give her a status. Flynn was in emergency surgery. Nobody knew anything.

Levi and Ice had arrived. Stone and Merk had gone to her house. Logan was at the hospital with her. Rhodes had gone down to the police headquarters. Apparently, he knew several cops and would raise Cain.

There wasn't enough Cain in this world for anybody to raise to make her happy. She had one goal now: to ensure Flynn survived. And if she had a secondary, it was: make certain Brendan didn't. But she had no idea how to get her hands on him.

Levi sat down next to her; Ice on the other side with her arm around Anna's shoulders. She said, "We need to hear your words. Exactly what you saw."

She stared at them, more tears burning her eyes, so hot with fear that nothing would cool them, and she once again explained what she'd seen. "I think it was the shot that woke me up." She shook her head. "After that it's all a blur. Just a painful, agonizing blur."

"At least it did wake you up. Flynn got attention as fast as possible. You have to hold on to that. Plus, you can confirm it was Brendan, and you found the weapon."

"I guess it proves Brendan was after Flynn all along. He could have come upstairs and shot me. I don't know that I would've been awake and aware enough to have avoided it."

Ice gripped her fingers. "Thank God he didn't."

Anna turned to look at Ice. "Did you guys find his car? Did the cops get the gun?"

"Yes and yes. You gave the gun to Logan, and he gave it to the cops."

Anna frowned. "Right. I remember that." She waved a hand. "Honestly, everything's a blur. I don't really understand the sequence of what happened."

"And you don't need to. The police are running the ballistics on the gun. We think the black car you saw at your house might've been Brendan's brother's."

At that Anna gave a half snort. "The brother who doesn't believe Brendan would do anything, right?"

"Well, he might be changing his mind now," Levi said coolly. "He's down at the police station. Rhodes is clueing him in."

"Good. He should be locked up too." Anna glared at Levi. "I suppose it's his damn lawyer connections that got his brother out in the first place."

"It's possible." Levi shrugged. "There's just no reason sometimes."

"Right now I know the reason. The best murderer is a dead one. I'm now a believer in the death sentence." She slumped back in the chair and leaned her head back.

Ice looked at her. "Did you have your arm checked out?"

Her head rolled over toward Ice, and she asked, "What's wrong with my arm?"

She could hear the heavy sigh from Ice and remembered her stitches from the bullet wound last night. She glanced down to see fresh blood all over the bandaged injury. She stared at it in surprise. "No idea how that happened. I can't feel it, so it can't be bad."

"You can't feel it because you're in shock. But those are stitches, and if you've ripped them, we need to get them looked at."

"I'm not leaving," she said firmly.

But Ice wasn't having anything to do with that. "There's stupidity, and then there is stupidity. We only deal with one kind. Right now Flynn's being taken care of. Now you need to be as well." And with a firm grip on her uninjured arm, Ice forced Anna to her feet and said, "Come with me now."

Ice, just like all the men in the company, was a force not to be ignored. Anna turned to look back at Levi as Ice dragged her toward the doorway.

"Don't let him be alone," Anna cried out.

"He'll be in surgery for several more hours. You'll be back before he comes out. If I hear anything, I'll let you know. And I promise, I won't leave him alone."

Sobbing quietly, Anna let Ice drag her down to the emergency area. It was full but not crazy. Ice walked over to one of the nurses and explained what happened. As it was, it was the same nurse she'd had the previous evening.

She took one look at Anna and asked, "Oh, my dear, you've had a terrible twenty-four hours, haven't you?"

Anna, hating to be the watering pot, turned and scrubbed her face. "It's probably nothing. Ice is just worrying over the blood."

"And she's right to." The nurse led Anna to a bed and made her sit down. She left a moment and came back with scissors, quickly cutting off the bandage. "It's not too bad though." She patted Anna on her good arm and said, "I'll let the doctor know in case he wants to see you too."

As her eyes went down to study the wound, Anna realized she probably needed to get it taken care of, but she hated to think about herself when Flynn had suffered so much.

"You have to consider your own health," Ice said. "The animals will need you, as will Flynn as soon as he wakes up."

Anna stared at her. "I didn't think about that."

And she hadn't. She'd been so locked into the immediate negativity, she hadn't seen that, if he did survive the surgery, somebody must take care of him. And she did have animals to look after. Therefore, she needed her dominant arm, which was the one that was injured.

She looked down at the blood. "You are right. I should've gotten it looked at. But I really didn't notice."

"Of course not," Ice said in a gentle voice. "But once you take care of the first emergency, it's very important to take a look around and see what needs to be dealt with next."

"That's your military training," Anna said. "Most people don't think like that."

"It's not just that training or even my medical training. But it is from a life lived on the edge all the time. Which we still are." Ice smiled at Anna. "You got the right stuff. Your instincts are strong and sound. But you have to learn to look after yourself. Because without that, it's almost impossible to do the same for those around us. And regardless of what happens, we're still females. We tend to be nurturers. So Flynn will need your help. If you aren't strong enough to help him, he won't get the care he deserves."

Anna nodded. She grabbed a tissue from the Kleenex box, wiped her eyes and blew her nose awkwardly with her left hand. She wasn't very good at looking after herself that way. She'd have to change that. Eventually.

Ice's phone rang. And the nurse returned. With her attention caught between what the nurse was doing and the phone conversation Ice was having with Rhodes at the police station, Anna couldn't keep track. By the time the nurse was done rebandaging her arm, it was on fire.

The nurse turned to her and asked, "Did you manage to bring any of your painkillers with you when you came to the hospital?"

"No. They're back at the house. And I probably won't be allowed in for a while. It's full of cops right now."

The nurse disappeared and returned a few minutes later with a small bottle. "There are enough here to get you through the day. Somebody should be allowed back into the house to at least get your medications."

She accepted them gratefully. "Thank you. I'm sure somebody will be able to." She managed to hop off the bed but hung on for a moment as the room swayed around her.

Ice looked at her sharply. "Have you eaten?"

She stared at Ice blankly. Then shook her head. "No, I haven't."

Ice nodded as if that was exactly what she figured. "Let me phone Levi to confirm there is no change, then I'm taking you to the cafeteria."

They waited in the hallway for Levi to confirm Flynn was still in surgery. At the cafeteria, they filled two trays and went to a table at the back of the room where they sat down and ate. Anna didn't want any juice, but Ice insisted. "I can't have you passing out."

Every time Ice opened her mouth, it was logical, reasonable, and made so much sense that Anna found herself following Ice's instructions without question. She poured the orange juice into a glass and drank half of it down. It didn't take long for her to start feeling better. As she looked at her omelet, she realized she really was hungry. It was just so hard to eat, knowing Flynn was upstairs.

Ice reached across the table and grabbed her hand. "Remember, you're eating for you, so you can be strong enough to look after him."

With a ghost of a smile, she teased Ice. "You get away with that line a lot."

Ice smiled. "I've been where you are."

She studied Ice, seeing the remembered pain and agony of almost losing somebody. Anna nodded. "I believe you." And she tackled her omelet. She made it almost all the way through before she slowed down. She stared at the last couple bites and shook her head. "I don't think I can do it."

"Finish your eggs—leave the toast."

Anna stuffed down the last of the omelet and pushed back her tray. A large hand reached over her shoulder, grabbing the toast off her plate, as the unmistakable Stone sat down beside them. She studied him. "You have any news?"

"I just came from your house. The cops are all over the place. It looks like Brendan walked in the front door and surprised Flynn or waited until he showed up. What I'm thinking is that Flynn put on coffee and went to look after the animals. When he came back in, Brendan was waiting for him." She could see it happen just like that in her head. It didn't make it any easier. "Why is it nobody has picked up Brendan?" She caught Ice and Stone exchanging glances. "What?"

"First, we have to find him. And second, he won't be picked up. He's likely to end up in a shootout to avoid capture."

"Good," she said in a hard voice. "As much as I like the idea of that man wasting away in a prison somewhere, I don't want to take the chance of him coming back out anytime in the future and ruining my life again. I want him dead. He deserves nothing less."

Stone grinned, studying her. "She's bloodthirsty. I like that." And he took a big bite out of her toast.

Just then both Ice and Stone's phones went off. They looked at the number. Ice said, "That's Levi. Surgery is over."

But they were talking to the air. She'd already bolted to her feet and raced back to Flynn.

MORE VOICES. MORE voices. And yet, more voices. Screaming, yelling, then quiet conversation. Between some kind of a mechanical scream in a weird tone, he couldn't quite make out what was being said. But once the machinery stopped, he heard the doctor say, "He's back."

Flynn wondered who'd gone and come back, and why anybody gave a shit. It was so hard to sort out the noises. But at least the pain was better. His chest didn't feel like it was closing in on him. He still couldn't move—a sense of being paralyzed. And he couldn't think of anything worse. It wasn't how he wanted to live his life. He tried to yell, "Help!"

But nobody answered.

"Hello."

He could hear the word in his mind, but he knew his lips weren't moving. He didn't think they could. He tried to open his eyes, turn his head. Nothing worked. The struggle was too much. The cotton batting around him closed in on him. But at least those long fingers of death weren't dragging him under. He wanted to roll over onto his side, but again he couldn't. He gave up the effort and let himself succumb to the clouds, willing them to carry him away.

Chapter 20

ANNA BURST INTO the waiting room to see Levi and the doctor's heads bent together. They both looked up at her as she made a mad dash into the room. Levi reached out to slow her pace. "He's alive. Take it easy. He's alive."

All the color washed out of her face as relief made her sway on her feet. She stared at the doctor, searching, looking for reassurance. "Will he be okay?"

"He's not out of hot water yet. He has a long road to recovery, but his prognosis is a whole lot better than it was. The bullet went into the chest cavity, nicked the heart at the top and went through, lodging into a rib in his back. We got the bullet out, and he's been stitched up. He's lost a lot of blood, and we had to give him several units." He sighed. "We lost him on the table."

"Lost him?" At that she gripped Levi's hands.

"His heart stopped while we were working on him. But we brought him back. He'll be just fine."

"Hold on to that thought," Levi told her.

She glanced toward the door. "When can I see him?"

The doctor shook his head. "Not until I get him settled in ICU. The next twenty-four hours are critical."

She nodded, biting her lower lip. Tears once again formed in her eyes. "Thank you so much for saving him."

He reached out and patted her shoulder. "He's a fighter.

Everybody deserves a chance to live, but when they fight, it makes our job so much easier." With a quiet smile he turned and walked off.

Anna walked to the bench against the wall and collapsed. "Oh, thank God," she whispered.

She didn't know what to do. All she could think about was that he'd survived the surgery and his chances were good. "We have to catch Brendan. Make sure he can never try this again."

"We will," Levi said. "Brendan's luck has run out."

She turned to study him. "Unless you know something I don't, I don't see how you can be so sure. That guy has been getting away with murder. Literally." She turned to study the double doors marked Surgery where Flynn still was. "Any way we can set a trap for him? Do you think he would go after Flynn again?"

Levi looked at her. "He might. He's gone through a lot of trouble already. What are you thinking?"

"Tell his brother how Brendan missed his mark, that Flynn will be home soon. There was some metal in his pocket, and the bullet was deflected. Brendan wasn't there long enough to see the blood that was everywhere. So he can't possibly know how good a shot he actually made. And then set up at my house and wait for him."

"You're assuming his brother will tell him."

"I'm assuming his brother has already gone overboard trying to protect him, and at some point the two will talk over the next few days." She shrugged. "Maybe even to just reassure Brendan he's not up for murder charges."

The others in the room looked at each other.

"That might work. But that's leaving a lot open to chance."

"Chance is all we have. He's made several attempts at my house. If he thought he'd missed, this time he might be so frustrated and enraged he would come back for one final move to kill Flynn for sure."

"She's right," Stone said. "Brendan's always been a bit of a wild card. But I'm not sure about his brother. He's a good guy. If he understands how out-of-control Brendan is right now, and the fact that he just shot Flynn in cold blood, I don't think he would protect him. I think he would help us catch Brendan before he hurts anybody else."

Just then the double doors opened, and Flynn was wheeled out. Anna dashed to his side, her hand over her mouth. He was unconscious, pure white, covered in tubes and blankets.

She turned to the others and said, "Set it up. I'll play my part. I don't want this to happen to anybody else ever again. I'm going in ICU with Flynn."

The nurse shook her head and said, "Only family can be in ICU."

Anna said, "I'm the only family he's got." She shot a hard glance at the three other medical personnel in scrubs, daring them to argue. Not one of them did. They smiled and gave her a nod.

In a low voice Ice called out, "Welcome to the family."

Anna grinned. It felt good to belong.

Following the nurses and orderly, she waited until Flynn was moved into recovery. Then she grabbed the visitor's chair and settled in for a long wait. She wasn't leaving his side. Not again.

FLYNN OPENED HIS eyes and slammed them shut again. The

light was so bright it hurt. He lay motionless for several long moments, then tried again. He opened them just enough so he could see he was in a room. Likely a hospital room from all the white around him.

Rolling his head to the side, he saw the IV line and machinery all around. Sure enough he was in a hospital bed. He remembered vaguely what happened. But it was disjointed and jumbled in his head. Until the name *Brendan* whispered through his mind. With a flash he was back in the living room, staring at Brendan as he raised a gun and fired. Flynn remembered the crushing pain as his body fell to the floor.

That answered how he got here. Moving carefully, he rolled his head to the other side and smiled. Curled up in the corner of the visitor's chair, feet tucked under her, her head resting on the back of the chair, was a sleeping Anna.

No wonder he'd survived. He had had his own guardian angel watching over him. He studied her pale skin and the bags under her eyes, realizing she'd probably been here since he'd been shot. She'd been sleeping upstairs at the time. He was just damn glad Brendan hadn't gone up and shot her too. He saw a fresh bandage on her arm. He hadn't been out so long that her arm had healed. That was good. A couple days he could deal with. He just didn't want to be coming out from weeks in a coma. Apparently that played havoc with the muscles.

Suddenly, as if realizing he was staring at her, her eyes flew open. She gazed at him for a long moment in disbelief, then bounded to her feet.

"Oh, my God. You're awake."

He smiled. "I am."

She reached down and gently picked up his hand. She brought it to her lips and kissed it. "I was so worried."

"I remember Brendan shooting me," he admitted. "What happened after that, I have no idea."

"I'll fill you in." And she did briefly. It was enough for him to get an idea.

"How long have I been out?"

"Your surgery was yesterday morning. You've surfaced and gone under a couple times but not really conscious."

"I suppose you've been sitting here, waiting all this time?"

She smiled. In a teasing voice she asked, "Are you telling me, if it was me in this hospital bed, you wouldn't be standing where I am?"

He squeezed her hand. "You know I would."

She glanced around and winced. "I did have to lie."

"Lie?"

"Yes. Only family is allowed in ICU."

And then he understood. His heart warmed, and his smile turned teasing. "Well, in truth that was just jumping the gun a little bit."

She sat down at the side of the bed and eyed him carefully. He stretched up a long finger and placed it across her lips. Immediately she kissed it. "You will be part of the family," he told her. "No way am I letting my guardian angel slip through my fingers." He watched the moisture well up in her eyes.

The door opened, letting in a nurse who scolded Anna. "You were supposed to let us know immediately when he woke up."

Anna jumped back and dropped his hand. "I'm so sorry. He just woke up though."

The nurse bustled around, brushing Anna out of the way. Flynn lay quietly as she ran him through a series of tests and questions. She then turned to Anna and said, "The doctor's on the way. When he comes, you'll need to step out."

Flynn watched as Anna collected her sweater, purse, several notepads, and a laptop. It looked like she'd planned to be here for a while. Just as she was about to exit, he called, "I love you, Anna."

She turned and gave him a special smile that made his heart warm.

The nurse stepped in between the two of them, and he never got to hear or see her reaction. Then the door was closed. It opened almost immediately as the doctor stepped in.

And his focus turned to the other people who'd saved his life.

Chapter 21

WHEN ANNA WAS finally allowed back into Flynn's room, he was ready to nod off again. They'd given him a sedative after changing the tubes and cleaning his wound. And he was in a great deal of pain, the nurse explained. While Anna had been outside waiting, she'd informed everybody Flynn was awake.

She sat back down in the visitor's chair, and Levi texted her.

Neil, Brendan's brother, has agreed to help. The word has already gone out to Brendan that Flynn wasn't badly hurt and is going home this afternoon.

She texted back:

Good. Do you want me to go home?

No. We'll handle this.

Perfect. She didn't want to leave Flynn, but if she must to keep him safe, then that was what she'd do.

Just make sure it works. I want to know that asshole can't get at us again.

Keep us updated on Flynn's condition. We'll let you know how it goes.

She put down her phone, curled up in the chair and closed her eyes. Now that Flynn had woken up, recognized her, and seemed to be improving, she could finally relax. Especially with Levi setting up a plan to take out Brendan. She wouldn't really be able to truly rest until he was, but everybody was doing their part, and she really appreciated that. She hadn't gotten any sleep last night, just drifted in and out. Every time she heard a sound, she woke up, thinking Flynn needed something. But now she yawned deeply, used her hand to cushion her cheek a little and drifted off to sleep.

She woke up a little bit later, seeing one of the doctors walking back into the room. She could expect a lot of that now. They would assess when to move him from ICU over to the main hospital. She hoped it wasn't too fast. She knew how quickly his condition could downgrade. She didn't want that for Flynn.

She closed her eyes again and then it hit her. She opened her eyes slowly to see the doctor walking to the IV line. He had a needle in his hand, about to inject something into Flynn's IV bag.

"What are you doing?"

The man turned to her, and she recognized him. Brendan.

"You." She bolted off the chair, racing toward him with her nails ready to scratch the hell out of him. She had no weapon, and he was a pro, but no way in hell was he getting close to Flynn.

She threw herself at him, sending him off balance, but still on his feet, knocking the needle from his hand. It skittered across the floor, and she was on him like a leech. He tried to drag her off, but she clung to him, dug her nails in his back and bit him hard in the neck, her teeth connecting with the soft tissue and going as deep as she could dig them in.

He roared in pain. She could feel his blood gush into her mouth, but she hung on. He tripped and fell to his knees, but she wouldn't let go. Suddenly she was wrenched off and flung clear. And then he was on top of her, both on the floor now.

"You stupid bitch."

He hit her hard in the face.

Pain slammed into her. She knew she'd lost the one chance of attack she had available to her. She reached for anything that could be used as a weapon. And her hand closed over the needle he'd dropped.

He struggled to his knees, his hand over the wound on his neck.

She sat up and stabbed him in the neck with the needle and plunged deep, shoving its contents into his body.

"No," he cried out. "You can't do that. He has to pay for what he did to me. He got me kicked out. Ruined my life."

"No," she yelled. "It wasn't him."

She hopped to her feet and backed away, spitting out his blood then wiping her mouth clean. "You did that all on your own." And she saw the truth slowly dawn even as his eyes started to glaze over.

She turned, opening the door between her and the nurses' station, screaming, "Help, please, help. He tried to murder the patient."

Several people ran toward her. With relief she saw one of them was a security guard. She turned to glance back at Brendan, but he was flat on the floor, his body jerking spasmodically.

"What happened to him?" the nurse asked.

Anna pointed at the needle in his neck. "He tried to inject that into Flynn's IV line. But I shoved it into him instead."

"You know for sure he was trying to kill him?" a different nurse asked.

Anna turned to face the security guard now on the scene. "He's the one who shot Flynn in the first place. He also shot me." She motioned at her arm. "I know for sure he killed another man too."

The security guard checked on Brendan, his weapon out and ready. But just as suddenly, Brendan stopped jerking. One of the nurses approached carefully, bent down and checked for a pulse. She looked up at Anna and said, "He's dead."

From the bed came a weak voice. "Good. And I concur with what Anna said. That's Brendan McAllister. He's the one who shot me."

The nurse straightened and said, "Well, he won't be shooting anybody else ever again."

Anna raced to Flynn's bedside and gently flung herself over him. She sobbed uncontrollably now.

Flynn wrapped an arm around her and held her close. "Easy, baby. Easy. You did good." He glanced at the other people in the room, then forgot all about them as he focused solely on Anna.

She sobbed even more. "Oh, my God. I couldn't believe it was him. Levi and the others are setting a trap right now at my house."

Flynn smiled. He reached up and wiped away the tears from her eyes. "That was always Brendan. Never doing the expected."

She stared at Flynn, then sat down heavily. "I killed him. Dear God. I killed a man."

Flynn nodded. "I'm so sorry you had to do that, honey."

She stared at him for a moment and then said defiantly, "I'm not. He was trying to kill you. For that, I would kill him all over again."

He gently stroked her lips and whispered, "So feisty. I like that."

She smiled down at him. "I love you. I never got a chance to say that before."

His hand slipped behind her neck, and he tugged her downward. When her lips were just above his, he whispered, "And I love you too."

She kissed him. Not hard, but with a sweetness that defined the moment in a way she had never expected.

When she lifted her head again, he said, "I believe I mentioned a position that might be of interest to you earlier."

She frowned, her eyebrows coming together as she studied his face to see a tiny smile playing at the corner of his mouth. "What position was that?" she whispered.

He tugged her gently forward until her head was just above his again. "The position of my wife."

She gasped in joy. "Do you mean it?"

He smiled. "Remember that part about not letting my guardian angel go?"

"You want to marry me because I saved your life, right?" she asked cautiously. "You'd be taking on the animals, the shelter, and me."

He chuckled. "Honey, I have a lot of reasons why I want to marry you. That just happens to be icing on top. I want to marry you because I want to wake up to you every morning.

I want to see you first thing when I open my eyes and know my days will turn out perfectly because you're there with me."

She sniffled back more tears. "That's a beautiful thing to say."

"And yet, you have not answered." His eyes lost some of the teasing.

"The answer is yes," she said softly. "There was never any doubt in my mind you were the one for me. I just didn't have an excuse to come back and see you again. But I was desperate to find one."

"Not to worry. I would've been there that same day if you hadn't come racing into the compound instead."

They smiled at each other in joy.

"Ice already welcomed me to the family," he said quietly, then chuckled. "She's very astute."

"She welcomed me to the family, here in the hospital," Anna said. "She's also a little scary."

"Agreed. But she's all heart."

"And you're mine. Truly you're my hero. And the hero for my animals." Anna smirked. "I think that makes you my Hero for the Homeless."

"Better not let Levi hear that," he warned. "Although Ice will love it."

With a misty smile, she whispered, "I didn't think I'd survive when I realized how badly hurt you were."

"I'm tough," he said. "Besides, I had the best thing in the world to live for."

When she raised an eyebrow in silent question, he pulled her head down once again for his kiss, and just before he claimed her lips, he whispered, "You."

Epilogue

LOGAN WALKED DOWN the hospital corridor. He couldn't believe the way the events had gone down. He was damn grateful but, at the same time, thought, *how typical of Brendan*. Logan shifted the roses in his arm. They were more for Anna than Flynn.

As he walked in, he saw lots of other flowers around the room. He laughed. "I guess you didn't need these." He handed them to Anna.

She accepted them, threw her arms around his neck and gave him a big hug.

He kissed her on her cheek. "Glad to see our warrior woman doing so well."

She laughed a little and put a smile on her face. "I don't know about the warrior-woman thing," she said, "but I'm doing just fine. Especially now that Flynn's doing okay."

Logan turned toward Flynn. "Not too bad, buddy. Get yourself shot and engaged at the same time."

Flynn gave him a lazy glance. "Recovery is a bitch," he said easily. "But I'm blessed with my own guardian angel." He reached out a hand, and Anna was there to grab hold of it.

Logan laughed. "I can see that. Too bad she doesn't have a sister. Maybe she could share some of that loving, healing light."

"You'll find your own light one day," Anna promised.

He looked at her, cocked his head to the side and said, "I'm not so sure about that."

She gave him a special smile and said, "I am."

He shook his head. "Maybe. But I doubt it."

Still, as he looked at how happy his friend was, he realized they truly were blessed. His time would come. But maybe not for a long while yet. Maybe. He was okay with that.

Hopefully.

LOGAN'S LIGHT

Heroes for Hire, Book 6

Dale Mayer

Chapter 1

LOGAN REDDING DRESSED quickly for the job he was heading out to this morning, but Levi had yet to give him any details. In fact, the text had come through just before midnight. Logan had grabbed as much sleep as he could, then showered, shaved, packed and now he was ready to go. He entered the dining room to find six other team members already in place. Conversation died when he approached. "Good morning."

With a full cup of coffee, he sat beside them. "Levi, what's the job?"

"You and Harrison are heading to Boston. Four men held on suspicion of human trafficking were released—not enough evidence to hold them—and disappeared underground. The detective who hauled them in knows Jackson, who then called me privately. He asked if we could take a day or two to consider the case. It'll be pro bono. Detective James Easterly says something was rotten with those men and is afraid it's a much bigger issue, but he can't find any proof. He's been pulled off the case due to budget concerns and manpower shortages. He doesn't know Jackson has called me."

"We've budgeted forty-eight hours for this," Ice said. "Hopefully that's more than enough to sort it out."

"It's basically an intel-gathering mission." Levi lifted the folder and added, "I have names, backgrounds, and pictures of the suspects' faces. Jason Markham, Lance Haverstock, Barry Ferguson, and Bill Morgan. All deemed to be leaders in a human trafficking ring."

Harrison nodded. "We'll check out the men, and we won't do anything major. I suppose in that folder you have a few addresses of friends, family, or businesses that they're known to frequent—or ideas about where these guys may have gone to ground—so we'll casually walk around and observe. See if we find anything of importance. If we don't, well, it is what it is." He shrugged. "We won't even be official. Hell, we both have friends and family there. Logan can visit his friends, and I'll go check on my sister-in-law," Harrison continued cheerfully. "Besides Logan and I are getting seriously housebound. We need to get out. The *love boat* is a little bit much to handle right now."

Levi glared at him.

But Harrison's good humor was irrepressible. He grinned at Levi and said, "You know what I mean, Levi. A whole lot of cooing and sexy stuff is going on around here."

Katina reached across the table, grabbed Harrison's hand and said, "That's okay. We understand you're feeling left out and lonely. Maybe you'll find somebody special on this trip."

Harrison pulled away his hand, groaning under everyone's laughter.

Logan lifted his hand to share a high five with Harrison. "Perfect. I'm ready to go."

Harrison jumped to his feet. "Give me two minutes, and I'll meet you in the garage."

Sienna walked in. "Seats are still available on the flights out of Houston later this morning," she said. "I've reserved two." She turned to Levi. "Who's going?"

Levi motioned at Harrison and Logan. "Book the tickets for these two. Returning three days from now."

Sienna smiled, filled her coffee and said, "Be back in a few minutes then." She walked out as Harrison bolted behind her, calling out, "Make mine the window seat. Logan gets the aisle."

Logan could hear the two of them wrangling as they left the dining room.

"Watch your backs," Levi warned Logan. "It might look like a bullshit mission, but these guys weren't picked up in the first place without good reason."

Logan looked at Levi and said, "Are we talking kidnapping? Murder? Human trafficking within US soil or being shipped overseas?"

"All of it," Levi said. "You both be careful. We can be in the air and at your side within six hours at most. But that's still six you have to handle on your own."

Logan nodded as he walked into the kitchen. Alfred was making breakfast, his usual sausage and bacon entrées. He glanced at Logan and said, "It'll be ready in about ten minutes."

Logan nodded. "We'll probably stick around then. But we'll have to eat and run."

Logan returned to the sidebar in the dining room, filled his coffee cup and sat again. He had more questions, but the conversation had already moved on. Levi shoved the folder toward him. Logan opened it to find files inside—damn slim ones, at that—for the four men they would be looking for. He quickly read all the documents, finding nothing there.

He closed the folder and shoved it toward Levi. "I gather we'll take a copy when we leave?"

"Sienna is putting that together."

Logan nodded.

Then Alfred came in with a platter of toast and hash browns. "Tell Harrison to get down here for breakfast."

Logan sent a quick text to Harrison.

By the time Alfred had dished out the rest of the food, and Logan's plate had been filled, Harrison showed up. He dropped the paperwork beside Logan and said, "These are our flights and bookings, plus our copy of the file." He glanced at Levi. "Considering this is a pro bono job, do you want us to bunk with friends and family?"

"We'll book you in a hotel so we're sure you have a place."

Logan finished eating, and with Harrison at his side, they made quick good-byes and hopped into one of the trucks.

By now Levi had quite a fleet of vehicles. They often used a small truck for quick trips in and out of town, although it'd be a forty-five-minute drive to the airport. They would leave this one at the long-term airport parking while they were gone for the next few days. No sense in tying up somebody else's time to drop them off and pick them up.

At the airport, they cleared security in time to board straight onto the plane.

When they landed in Boston four hours later, they stepped outside the airport and stood, gazing at a misty afternoon, gray and cloudy. Logan looked over at Harrison and said, "Let's grab the rental car and get to the hotel."

At the rental office, they completed the paperwork and walked to the parking lot to locate the midsize vehicle.

Logan sat in the driver's seat. "Does your sister-in-law live anywhere close to the hotel?"

Harrison shook his head. "No idea. I didn't have a

chance to confirm before now. I'll see once we're checked in."

"Did you tell her you were coming?"

Harrison shook his head.

Logan glanced at him and said, "Some history or problem there?"

"Not sure," Harrison said easily. "My parents have been asking me to check on her."

"What's the story?"

"My brother was killed in a car accident, and his wife lost the baby she was carrying shortly thereafter. Haven't heard a whole lot from her since."

"Wow, okay. That's a lot of really depressing news all at the same time." Logan thought about it and said, "She's probably moved on completely. I'm sorry about your brother and your niece or nephew."

"Tough times for all of us back then." Harrison glanced at him. "Have you contacted your friends?"

"Not yet." Logan winced. "I haven't stayed in touch, so not sure who's even still around. But for some reason, I really wanted to come to Boston."

"Were you close with any of them?"

"No. Not really. Just friends with the group. Still it might be nice to touch base. If it doesn't work out, that's fine too."

At the hotel, they checked into their room. Harrison sat down to figure out where his sister-in-law lived, comparing her location to the hotel's and to the addresses Levi had given them to check out.

Logan walked out onto the balcony to make his calls. Half an hour later he was no further ahead. One of the guys had laughed and said he wasn't even in Boston anymore.

Another got back to Logan and said he was on vacation in Hawaii. When Logan called Kandy, it never went through. Logan shrugged. That's what he got for not making plans ahead of time.

He went inside to see if Harrison had any more luck and found he'd already mapped out the known addresses for a quick drive-by. He'd also talked to his sister-in-law, who wasn't interested in a reunion. She'd moved on. Apparently that worked for Harrison too.

Logan checked his watch. "We have time this afternoon to check out a couple of those addresses."

They were back outside in the vehicle, the GPS on the rental already programmed. They hit the first one in a relatively wealthy section full of brownstone townhouses. Lots of parks, nice family area. They didn't drive around; instead they stopped and parked. They walked several blocks to a park and sat, studying the layout and address in question. The numbers on the house were clearly visible. It was a quiet, unassuming area—no sign of anybody coming or going. The curtains on the upstairs bedroom windows were closed. Logan studied the residence for a long moment and said, "I didn't get any hits on this. What about you?"

Harrison shrugged. "It looks deserted to me. I'm not getting any vibe off it at all."

They returned to the car to drive to the next address. On the way, Logan said, "Did you hear us? Talking about vibes and hits? How different is that from Terk and his warnings?"

"I'd like to think my vibes are more from years of experience looking for trouble."

"Absolutely. That's how I feel. But maybe that's what Terk feels too. Maybe he has a more developed instinct than we do. Perhaps that's what his insight is."

Harrison nodded. "Whatever it is, I'm not too bothered. If he doesn't start wearing a great big turban and carrying a glass ball, I'm good."

"I've never met the guy. Have you?"

Harrison laughed. "I haven't."

"Alfred appears to take Terk quite seriously too. He knew of him from the military as well."

Harrison turned to him in surprise. "Alfred?"

Logan nodded.

"Wow."

The second address appeared to be an apartment. They parked, then got out and walked the block, checking to see what the area was like. It looked middle-class family. No security system was on the main entrance, but as they stepped up, somebody unlocked the door and let them in. They headed toward the correct apartment, taking the stairs to the fourth floor.

They stepped into the hallway, found the apartment number but of course, saw no name or identification.

As they walked toward the elevator, one of the neighbors came out, and Logan spoke with her.

She smiled. "I've heard women at various times, but I don't know them and haven't seen one for months." With a shrug, she added, "I did hear some banging and noises the other day, but that's all. It's been damn quiet since." She beamed at them as she pushed a button to close the elevator door. "I did hear him yell at a woman this morning though, so maybe he has a new girlfriend."

As the door closed, Harrison asked, "I don't suppose you got anybody's name, did you?"

"Oh my, yes. This morning he called her Alina. I remember thinking that was such a pretty name." Then the double doors closed in front of her.

"Alina?" Logan asked as he glanced toward the apartment, his vibe triggering a strange feeling. "I'm definitely getting a hit on this place."

He walked to the apartment and pressed his ear against the door. No sign of anything. He gave a hard knock. Nobody answered. Harrison joined him as he knocked a second time. This time he thought he heard crying. "We have to check this out."

"We're going in?"

Logan already had his tools. The door opened in seconds. With a quick glance to make sure they were alone, he slipped inside with Harrison on his heels. This was not legal, and Levi certainly wouldn't sanction it, but they had to get in. Sometimes one had to follow instinct, and right now, Logan's was screaming at him.

Chapter 2

ALINA DROPPED HER head on the pillow, crying as that movement stretched her shoulders and twisted her neck, worsening the pain. How the hell had she gotten into this mess? And how would she get out? Colin was gone for a few hours—or so he said. It was the first time he'd left her alone. Therefore, her only window of opportunity. But that didn't help if she had no way to escape. She'd been here for two days. Two long days—as best she could remember. But the fate awaiting her was worse. The last thing she wanted was to be raped, but according to him, it was all she'd ever know after this. She shifted on the bed and once again tried to release the bindings on her wrists. Both were tied to one corner of the bed. Her ankles to the other bedpost kitty-corner.

She'd pleaded with him to not tie her up, but he hadn't listened. And she knew the longer she lay here, the more numb her body would get. That would almost be a gift right now. She had to get the hell out. But how?

Then she heard the door pop open. She froze. Colin hadn't been gone long enough yet. And if he was already back, she was out of time. And then what the hell would she do? She'd lost her one chance at freedom.

With hot tears in her eyes she couldn't wipe free, she listened for his footsteps. But she could not still the panic inside. She'd been in and out of a brain fog since she'd made the mistake of having coffee with him at the hospital cafeteria and found herself in deep trouble.

When she heard more footsteps than before, she froze in fear. Was the place being broken into or was it Colin? If it was him, and she cried out for help, he'd beat the crap out of her, like he had last time.

But what would an intruder do? Release her or laugh at her or … something much worse?

And then she remembered Colin's threat. He had guys looking for women. White women. Blondes. And they would pay a premium price. She shuddered. She couldn't imagine that any robber breaking into this apartment would be worse than Colin's buddies.

Her voice hoarse, she called out, "Help. Please help."

More silence.

And she waited. Please let that not be Colin sneaking in to test her. A man popped his face around the doorway. She heard his startled exclamation, followed by the appearance of a second man.

She didn't recognize either of them. She stared at both terrified and yet filled with hope. "Please untie me," she begged. "Help me get away before he gets back."

The men rushed to her side, one going to her hands, the other moving toward her feet. The man at her hands studied her face as he worked to untie her bindings and asked, "Who the hell did this to you?"

She stared up at him. "Colin Fisher. He's the man who tied me up."

He froze, then went back to her bindings.

She knew her mind was fuzzy, but it didn't make any sense that they had broken into an apartment and didn't know whose it was. Unless they were casing the joint. But then why stick around now? "Did you not know who lived here when you broke in?"

The first man shot her a hard glance and asked, "How do you know we broke in?"

She was about to answer, but her hands were freed then, and her arms fell to the bed. She cried out as pain screamed up them to her shoulders. The man grabbed her arms and gave them a good shake before massaging them.

"Take it easy," he said. "If your arms have been like this for a long time, it'll hurt like crazy to move them."

She gasped, unable to stop the tears in her eyes. "You're not kidding. I've been like this since this morning when he left. But he's kept me tied up off and on for two days now."

"Any idea where he's gone?"

"To meet his friends. The ones he keeps threatening me with."

The second man at her feet finally released her legs. He worked the bottom of her calves and the soles of her feet and ankles, massaging them as he slowly moved her legs up and down, bending her knees.

The pain coursing through her made it impossible to speak. When she could, she said, "Colin told me he knew men who would buy women like me."

"Like you?" the man nearest her asked.

She shot him a confused look. "I presumed he meant any women that crossed him because I wasn't giving him what he wanted."

The man stopped and stared down at her. "Did he rape you?"

She shook her head. "I've been out of it most of the time. I don't think so, but he gave me an ultimatum. He said if I didn't agree to submit, he'd sell me to these men."

"Still rape. No matter which way you cut it." He bent down and picked her up in his arms, carrying her out to the living room. "And he likely planned to sell you regardless. He would get something for himself and terrorize you even more."

She didn't know if she should clutch him or try to run away. Once he placed her in a chair, she realized how rubbery her legs were, as well as her arms.

He continued massaging her legs and feet, getting the blood moving once again.

She gave him a wobbly smile and said, "Thank you." She glanced at the door. "We really need to get the hell out of here."

"Tell us more about Colin," the first man said. "We can't let him do this again."

She shook her head, as if clearing it. "I'm a nurse. He said he worked part-time as an orderly. He kept asking me out, and I refused. After that it was just a nightmare, as if I was already his girlfriend and just being difficult. He kept stalking me. He finally caught me in the cafeteria, and I sat and had coffee with him."

"Did you call the police, report the stalking?" the second man asked.

She nodded and wrapped her arms around her shoulders. "I was hoping he'd stop then. But I don't remember anything after having coffee." She stared at the strangers. "Who the hell are you guys anyway? Not that I'm not grateful. I really want to get out of here." She glanced around, not even giving them a chance to answer and asked, "Is my purse here?"

"I'll look," the second man said.

The first man stopped massaging and gently put her foot on the floor.

"Thank you. I'm Alina Chambers," she whispered. "Who are you?"

"I'm Logan, and my buddy is Harrison. We work for a Texas private security company." He gave her a lopsided grin. "You're lucky we showed up to check out this apartment for a potential problem."

She stared at him blankly. "I'm sure this makes sense to you, but it doesn't to me." She pushed her hands down on the chair and struggled to her feet. "I have to leave before he gets back. Where are my shoes and purse? I can call the cops, but I'm afraid he'll get bail and be out on the streets after me in no time."

She took a couple steps and had to hang on to the wall for support. "How can I be so weak?"

"Did he give you any drugs?" Logan asked at her side, putting an arm around her shoulders to support her. He helped her to the front door and pointed to a set of women's boots on the floor. "Those yours?"

"Yes," she cried gratefully. He bent down and lifted first one foot and then the other. Using his back for support, she stepped into her boots.

She felt better already. What was it about having boots that gave her a little more security and self-confidence?

"Logan?" Harrison's voice came from the other room. "You need to see what I found."

Logan straightened and patted her on the shoulder. "Stay here at the door. Let me see what he discovered."

She leaned against the wall next to the front door, wondering if she could go outside. Surely it was a whole lot safer than being inside. But she really wanted her purse. She waited a long moment, then struggled toward where the men had disappeared. She found them in the kitchen.

At her arrival, Logan turned and asked, "Are any of these yours?" On the table was an assortment of purses.

Shocked, she could feel herself swaying. She clung to the counter as she studied the neat rows and counted fifteen of them. Her bones turned to rubber, and all the heat drained from her body. She whispered, "How many women has he done this to?" She took a deep breath and nodded to the purse on the far end. Even her joy at seeing it didn't begin to wipe out the enormity of what they'd found. "The burgundy leather one at the far end looks like mine."

Logan picked it up, opened it and gave it to her. "Your wallet is still in there."

"Where did you find these?" she cried out, going through her wallet and purse in relief.

Harrison pointed to cupboard above the fridge. "They were up there in a box."

Leaning against the kitchen counter, she quickly went through hers. "My apartment and car keys, wallet, money, and even credit cards are all still in here." She reached up a hand to wipe her forehead. "That's a relief. What do we do about all those?" She pointed to the remaining ones. "If a woman has gone missing for every purse here …"

The two men exchanged hard glances.

"We have to call the police," she said reluctantly. "He has to be stopped."

Logan glanced at her and asked, "Do you live in Boston?"

Her eyes grew wild. "Boston? I'm in Boston?" She shook her head. "No, I live in Somerville and work at the university hospital there."

"That's, what? A half hour from here?"

She gave a quick nod, then covered her mouth with her hands.

Logan lifted her arm.

She glanced down to see the swelling at the top of her arm. "So he did drug me." She watched his face as he nodded.

"Looks like it. And it doesn't look like your system appreciated it either." He glanced at Harrison. "She needs a hospital."

"And we should contact Levi."

"Who's Levi?" Alina asked, now suspicious about any newcomers in her life.

"Our boss," Logan told her.

"They were right about the trafficking ring," Harrison said.

"Crap," Alina said. "I thought he was just using that as a threat."

Logan pointed at the line of purses. "I highly doubt this is a purse-snatching problem."

She started to shake, and then tears sprang to her eyes. She turned and leaned on the counter, feeling her breath whooshing out of her body. "Oh, my God! How close did I come to ending up like these poor women?"

"Damn close I'd say." Logan stayed at her side, gently rubbing her shoulders and back. He turned to Harrison. "Want to call Levi from the other room?" He turned to her, bending down to study her face.

She gave him a wan smile and said, "I'm okay. Honest, I'll be fine."

He nodded. "You are now. Do you have any idea how long ago Colin left and when he's supposed to be back?"

"He said a couple hours." She closed her eyes, trying to think. Time seemed so unreal. "I'm not sure how long ago that was. I was lying there, figuring out how to get free. This is the first time he's ever left me alone."

"You sure he didn't touch you?"

She stared at him with tears growing in her eyes. "How am I supposed to know? If he drugged me, how would I even…" And she started to cry.

He turned her into his arms and held her close. "Take it easy. You've been through a huge ordeal, but you're safe now."

She shook her head, her tears dripping onto his shirt, and mumbled, "How can you say that? We're still in this place where I was held captive. You haven't caught the bad guy yet. And I highly doubt you'll do so now. But I can't let him go free."

"You don't have much trust in the legal system, do you?"

She shook her head. "I'm a nurse, and had worked in one of the poorer areas in town. It was incredible the amount of repeat people we saw. Abused women, gang fights, and rape victims." She shook her head. "The world's a mess out there."

For Alina, snuggling in close to the big and strong man at her side for the moment was a heady experience. She slowly wrapped her arms around him and clung.

He held her tighter. "It's going to be okay. Harrison and I won't let anything happen to you."

She lifted her head and stared up at him. He dwarfed her five foott four; she guessed he had to be at least six foot four. She was small-boned and lean, and he was the opposite—an easy 240 pounds. She shook her head.

"Let me take you to the hospital," he said. "Get you

checked over."

"Then I'll be in the system, and that's not a happy place to be."

"*Trust*," he said firmly. "You need to trust."

She gave him a weak smile. "For all I know, you are two of the men Colin was talking about."

Logan shifted and grabbed his wallet from his back pocket. "I can fix that right now. He pulled out his Legendary Security ID for her to see. "I was also in the military for ten years. I'm not into beating, hurting, or trafficking women." He smiled. "And I like teddy bears, birthday cake, and suntanning by the pool."

She blinked. "What does any of that have to do with trafficking?"

"All I'm saying is, I have a much softer side. Just a normal man. I'm not a monster."

She understood. That was exactly what Colin was—a monster. She glanced at the purses. "Why would he keep these? Should I see if I know any of the women he may have taken before me?"

Hope was in his voice when he said, "Actually that's not a bad idea." He led her to the kitchen table and helped her to sit down on one of the chairs. "We'll do this methodically."

He opened the first purse, pulled out a driver's license, took a good look at the name and face, then snapped a picture with his phone, before handing it to her. "Looks like the money is gone and so are the credit cards. Just driver's licenses left inside."

"Laura Resnick," she said out loud. "No, I don't know her." She put the ID into the wallet, back into the purse, closed it and set it off to the side. They went through the others, and she didn't know anybody; neither did he recognize any faces or names. When it came to the last purse, he opened it up and said, "This is Cecily."

"Cecily Turner?" She snatched it out of his hand. "Oh, my God! I know her. She works at the same hospital I do. She worked in the kitchen area. She delivered all the meals to the patients."

He glanced over at her and said, "Two of you from the same hospital?"

She looked up and winced. "Hunting ground?"

"None of the other names mean anything to you from the hospital?"

She shook her head. "No, but that doesn't mean much. Typically hundreds of people staff a hospital. The fact that I even know Cecily is mostly because her name is so unique."

Then Harrison walked into the kitchen and said, "Levi wants confirmation the purses are fifteen separate women. He wants copies of the IDs."

Logan held up his phone and said, "I got photos of all of them. I'll send them right now."

Harrison nodded. "Good. He said to wait to see if this Colin guy returns. If he does, call the cops. And if he doesn't, after a few hours call them anyway."

She listened to the conversation, her gaze going from one to the other.

Harrison explained, "This is only one of five addresses we have for the four men we're tracking. No way to know what else we might find at this point."

"Four men," Alina asked cautiously. "Not even sure I want to know about that. Any chance those are the same ones Colin threatened me with?"

"Do you know their names?"

She shook her head. "He didn't say."

LOGAN STUDIED HER face, still shocked at finding her when they broke into the apartment. He could easily cover his tracks for making the illegal entry as he would tell the police they heard something very suspicious, like her crying for help. No doubt she had been a victim in all this. And she was still damn shaky, but they had to determine what she might know that could be of help, anything she had to offer. He shook his head. "This address is obviously of some importance. Did you hear him mention any names? Addresses? Dates? Anything to help track down these men?"

"No, he hardly spoke." She stared up at him, her light-blue eyes gone dark. "All part of the same trafficking ring." She glanced around and wrapped her arms around herself. "I'm getting a real chill, so please can I leave now?"

"Where would you go?"

"Home," she said.

"How do you expect to get there? I presume your vehicle is still at the hospital as that's the last place you remember."

Harrison spoke up. "I'll see if a missing report has been filed for you."

"I doubt it. I live alone. My rent's paid up, and I was due for four days off anyway." She turned toward them. "I wonder if Colin knew that."

"We have to assume he had inside information, like your schedule."

"In the hospital, lots of people talk," she said.

Logan heard a sound. He put his finger to his lips, motioned to Harrison, who raced quietly to the front door and stepped behind it, in case it was Colin. Logan motioned for Alina to duck behind the end of the counter, giving Colin a second or two before seeing her. Allowing Logan and

Harrison time to nab him.

Alina closed her eyes and held her breath.

Logan stood just inside the bedroom, out of sight.

A key was put into the lock, then the door popped open. "Goddammit," the stranger said. "I know I locked this stupid door." He stepped in and slammed the door hard, glancing at the kitchen and froze when he caught sight of Alina. "Goddamn bitch. How the hell did you get free?"

When he started toward her, Harrison grabbed him from behind, put him in a choke hold and dropped him to his knees.

Logan stepped in front of the man, putting up a barrier between him and Alina, his fist out and ready.

"I got him," Harrison said with a snarl. "A nasty piece of shit, trafficking young women."

Colin glared at Logan, but he deliberately closed his mouth and kept it shut.

Harrison forced Colin to his feet, and Logan grabbed the wire strips from his back pocket, tying Colin's hands together and twisting the wire extra tight. It wouldn't stop him from running away, but it would from getting his hands free. Logan pointed to the purses on the table and said, "Care to explain?"

Colin glared at him, a snarl on his lips, that look in his eye … and the tensing of his neck muscles, like a bulldog ready to attack—only held back against his will.

The man's attitude held something vicious, yet he was an average-looking male with short brown hair and nothing assuming about his features. Logan could have walked past him on the street and would never have known he was anything other than normal. Which was exactly what made him so easy to hide from the authorities. Women wouldn't recognize the monster within. Neither would they remember him when asked.

Harrison dropped him on a kitchen chair where Alina still stood. She gasped and backed away to the other side of the room.

Colin sneered. "Stupid bitch. Do you think this will let you off the hook? Like hell! I already handed over your details. They'll get you whether it's here or in your house."

Logan reached over and grabbed Alina before she went to pieces. He tucked her up close and said, "Don't listen to him. He's just trying to scare you."

She turned terrified eyes to Logan and murmured, "But what if he's right?"

Logan turned to study the man. Harrison fished through Colin's pockets, pulling out his phone and ID.

Colin didn't fight. He sat there nonchalantly, as if he had some sort of a security system, and the men didn't know what surprise he had planned for them.

And shit like that always worried Logan. Because too often these assholes did have tricks up their sleeves. He reached for Colin's cell and checked through the contacts from the recent phone calls. He pulled out his own phone and called Levi.

When Levi answered, Logan said, "We have Colin Fisher here. I got a cell, and a bunch of names and numbers." He ran through the man's contacts. "The last two calls were to a Roma Chandler."

"Okay, I got it. Anything else on the phone?"

"Yes, a bunch of text messages here. One mentions having picked up a new product. I'm scanning through it now." By the time he worked his way through them, Logan wanted to shower. It wasn't just dirty; it was pure nasty. "Levi, we need to find this Chandler asshole. He's after Alina."

Beside him Colin sneered again. "I told her. She's done no matter what you do to me."

Logan exchanged a hard glance with Harrison. Then he asked, "Anything in the wallet?"

Harrison nodded. "Let me talk to Levi."

Logan handed over the phone and stepped closer to Colin in case he tried anything funny. Harrison went over the contents of the guy's wallet with Levi. Logan half listened. It didn't appear to be anything too important—his driver's license and credit cards. If they could trace his activities through the cards, it would give some idea where he'd been and who he was potentially meeting. It all depended on if he paid or if somebody else had.

As he studied Colin, Logan saw a pack of cigarettes in his top pocket. He pulled it out, and Colin laughed.

"You lighting one up for me?"

Logan opened the pack and saw only six inside. He dumped them on the table and checked the box. He'd seen all kinds of stuff hidden inside cigarette packs. But this one appeared to be empty. He tossed it on the table and faced Colin. "You realize the trouble you're in, right?" He could feel Alina hiding behind him, obviously shaking, and with good reason. "You're into raping and drugging women so they can't resist, and then turning them over to your guys to put in the sex trade."

Colin shrugged. "It sure beats wining and dining them and getting dumped all the time."

"Hardly. But whatever excuses work for you."

Colin ignored him and turned to stare at the window.

Harrison came back then. He handed the phone to Logan and said, "Help him stand. I haven't checked all his pockets."

They stood Colin up, first checking the inside of his socks and shoes to make sure. In his back pocket, he had a small notebook. When they pulled that out, Colin's gaze hardened.

Logan smiled. "So this is interesting." He flipped it open and studied it. Names and numbers. "Looks like a bookie list." It wasn't, but he watched for any reaction from Colin.

Then he saw a couple names he recognized. Beside the names, first only, were dollar amounts. When he hit Laura Resnick, the first name Alina had read out loud, $14,000 was written next to it.

"How long ago did you get paid for Laura Resnick?"

Colin slumped in his chair, closed his eyes and pretended to fall asleep.

Harrison stepped in front of Colin, blocking Alina's view, and reached down.

Colin screamed.

Logan worried about Alina's reaction, but no way in hell would he stop Harrison for making this asshole talk.

When Harrison backed away, Colin whimpered like a little girl. "You can't do that," he managed between broken cries. "That's police brutality."

"Oh, we're not the police," Harrison said. "And you're nothing but a trafficker, so you don't deserve any rights. Besides"—he turned to look around at Logan and Alina—"I don't think either of them saw anything."

Alina shook her head. "No, but a second demonstration would be nice to see," she said bitterly. "This asshole needs to pay for what he's done to those women."

Logan grinned at that. "Nothing like a little bit of payback to make a victim feel better."

"So talk, asshole," Harrison snapped. "How many women are still in Boston? Where is the exchange happening and when? If we're lucky, some of them, if not all, might still be on American soil."

"Oh, my God!" Alina stared at him. "Do you think that's possible? Can we find them? Save them?"

Chapter 3

JUST THE THOUGHT of helping the other women made Alina feel so much better. Having seen the purses had been like a death sentence. To think this asshole had been responsible for the torment of so many others… she couldn't bear thinking about it. And she'd been saved by a fluke. Maybe these guys could help the other women. They weren't the police, but were private security—whatever the hell that meant. Yet she knew they'd broken into the apartment and saved her and captured Colin.

As far as she was concerned, these guys were heroes.

"I want to help," she said.

Harrison glanced from her to Colin. "Tell us everything you know about the others in your ring—where they worked, what they did and how they tracked down the women. Where the women came from as well."

"How can finding out where he took them help us?" Alina asked.

Logan wrapped an arm around her and walked her into the next room.

Finding it something she already missed, she wrapped hers around him and snuggled close. "Thank you so much for saving me," she whispered.

"You're welcome," he said. "And any information we can find out about him will lead us to his connections and hopefully to where the women are."

"But you guys have a job to do, don't you? Can you help with this?"

"Yes, we do, and this is it. But we're not officially here. The problem is, once we bring in the police, they will ask us not-so-politely to butt out."

She nodded in understanding. "I get that, but any information we find on our own to hand over to them will still move their case forward, right? We have an obvious time issue here. I don't know when I was supposed to be moved to the other guys, but they are still after me—which is a nightmarish thought." She shook her head and squeezed him tighter. "But what if they had a quota to fill? Maybe they're moving all the women at once?"

With a tilt of Logan's head, he moved them closer to Harrison and Colin.

Harrison exchanged a glance with Logan, then focused on Colin. "Feel like talking now?"

"Fuck you."

Harrison reached forward once more. Before he even made contact, Colin screamed again at the top of his lungs, "Don't hurt me. Don't hurt me."

"Then talk," Harrison said. "I don't give a shit if I have to rip each body part off you one at a time. I've got absolutely no patience with rapists and murderers, or child and women traffickers. You are scum. And once you go to jail, I have inside connections to make sure everybody in that place knows exactly what kind of piece of shit you are. I'll make sure your life is nasty. You'll spend the rest of it on your knees in that prison cell with your ass up in the air. So, talk now or forever hold your peace."

Colin whimpered. "Don't you understand they will kill

me?"

Harrison smiled. "If you make me lay hands on you one more time, I might kill you myself. And, if I don't, I can guarantee one of the guys in the prison will, but only after you've been everybody's little girlfriend for a while."

It wasn't easy for Alina to watch Harrison. On the other hand, if ever a man deserved to be terrorized, it was this one. This was the asshole who had drugged and beaten her and who-knew-how-many other women. She stepped forward and said, "All these purses belong to women. How many more are there?"

He glared at her. "I don't talk to bitches."

Harrison reached forward.

"No!" Colin screamed.

Harrison straightened up, giving Colin a hard look. "Answer the lady."

"I don't know." He shook his head. "I've been doing this for a long time."

"How long?" Alina snapped. "And how many did you kidnap from my hospital alone?"

He glared at her. "It was one of the locations where we found women."

Logan stepped closer, standing on the other side of Alina. "Where are you taking them? Are these women alive?" Logan pointed to the purses lined up. "Have they been taken off American soil?"

He shook his head and said, "The exchange is in two days." He groaned. "Shit. If I say anything more, I'm done."

"You're done anyway," Harrison snapped. "Talk."

"And while you're at it, explain why you have the purses."

Colin glared and pinched his lips together.

Harrison took a step forward.

"Leave me alone," Colin cried out. He glared at Harrison for a long moment, but, as if seeing no weakening in the man before him, his shoulders slumped. "Ah, hell." Colin stared at the men, then shook his head. "I wasn't to keep 'em. They're like my trophies—of what I've done. I could keep the cash but had to hand over the credit cards. I was supposed to dispose of the rest …"

"Well, I'm glad you didn't," Logan said calmly. "That proves your involvement in all these women's disappearances."

"Just these ones," Colin protested. "I didn't have anything to do with the others. I wasn't organizing this. I took orders. Not too many, not too fast. All by the numbers. But I don't know what those are."

The apartment phone rang three times and stopped.

"If you don't let me answer that, there'll be hell to pay," Colin warned, eyeing the phone with fear. "These are not people to mess around with."

Logan and Harrison both shook their heads. At Alina's confused expression, Logan explained, "He'll give away his current situation."

"Someone called this morning," Alina said calmly. "I'm not even sure anybody was at the end of it. It could be a checkup call. Plus, it doesn't make sense to have a landline and cell if only one person lives here."

"That's not true," Colin said. "Lots of people have both."

"The only reason to have both," she snapped, "is if you want certain people to use the landline and others to call the cell."

Logan picked up the house phone, checked the last

number dialed, wrote it down, then walked a few steps away.

She could hear him calling somebody. "If you hadn't wanted anybody to know who you are," she told Colin, "you idiot, you should have one of those ancient rotary dial phones. Not a digital that lets you read the call display."

He glared at her but didn't say anything. Logan walked back a few moments later, putting his phone in his pocket. "Where are the women?"

Colin smiled and said, "You might beat me, but I can't give you information I don't have. I meet somebody in the mall, and that's it. We make the exchanges in the parking lot from my vehicle to theirs. The earlier women are lost. Some of them were taken years ago. I'm not the only collector. It's a cross-country system. I'm just responsible for my corner. Hell, I wasn't going to stay here, but we lost someone a while back and are now trying out a new guy. They said when I run low on prospects, they'd move me to another area."

Harrison snorted. "A mall? Not likely. No way in hell you can get somebody like Alina willingly out of your vehicle, and then into a public parking lot at a mall and not cause havoc. And if she's unconscious, with you carrying her, that's even more trouble."

She thought about that. "He has a really large suitcase in the bedroom," she said quietly. "Any chance he's been using that to transport the women?"

Logan turned to her. "Show me."

She led the way to the bedroom. "I only thought about it now when you were talking about transporting the women. Because Harrison's right. No way would they have gone willingly."

Sure enough, a large wheeled black hardcase piece of luggage sat in the closet. Logan laid it down and quickly flipped it open. He frowned. "Not a whole lot of space in here."

"I could get in there and see if I fit," she offered.

He shook his head. "No, because you'll leave a DNA trace. If he's had women in here, we'll find out another way. The case comes with us." He took some snapshots of it, inside and out.

She stood beside it and said, "If you close it, I can lie on top of it. And scrunch up."

As a rudimentary test, it wasn't a bad idea. He closed it, and she curled up on the top of the hard metal, and she'd fit without too much trouble. He took a few photos with her on top of the case. As she got to her feet, she said, "That'll certainly narrow down the women he chooses."

"So he's looking for petite women." Logan nodded to himself and carried the suitcase to the front hall. As they returned to the kitchen, sirens could be heard.

She walked to the window and saw two cop cars and an ambulance pull up outside the apartment. She looked at Logan and Harrison. "Did you guys call them?"

Both shook their heads and joined Alina at the window. Logan lowered his voice and said, "Levi would've." He glanced at Harrison. "We still don't have all the information."

Harrison nodded. "After this," he said, "we'll lose access."

He raced back to Colin. "How many women have been picked up right now?"

Colin shrugged. "Alina was the fourth, moving out in the next two days. I was waiting for instructions." He sneered. "But you won't find them. We couldn't do this since forever without some inside help."

"Cops?"

"You could tell us their names," Alina said quietly. "You'll never be released from jail. Why not take the cops down too?"

Colin turned to look out the window, some of the starch taken out of him. "Two cops. But I don't know who. I never saw or met them. That connection is higher than me."

"Not quite," Logan said. "We have his tally book, which I'll finish taking pictures of right now." He stepped into the bedroom, opened the little notebook with the money and first names, then quickly took pictures of everything. "We'll access the apartment building cameras, see if they have underground parking lot with security down there and find out how many times he's taken the suitcase in and out of here."

"What a horrible thought," Alina said.

"Let's go meet the locals," Harrison said, as they all moved into the main room.

She stared at the suitcase near the door. She turned on Colin. "Is that how you got me into the apartment?"

He gave her a flat stare.

"That's what you did, didn't you?" She glared at the suitcase with loathing. "I guess this can already be traced to me," she said to Logan.

Logan nodded. "Most likely. I saw blood inside that will help with IDs as well."

She could feel the color washing out of her face at the sound of that. She turned, knowing time was running out. "Did you kill any of those women?" She shoved her face into his and snapped, "Did you?"

He shook his head. "I didn't kill anyone," he protested. "My boss wanted these women. It was my job to collect them, then move them out."

"What was all that bullshit about wanting something from me first?"

"I'm not allowed to rape you," he said. "Damaged goods aren't worth as much. But if you were willing, then I was allowed."

Her hand went to her mouth. "So those women had sex with you, thinking it might get them out of here and that you might treat them better? Instead, you used them and then handed them over, didn't you?"

But he dropped his gaze to the floor.

At the pounding on the front door, Harrison opened it, and the police flooded inside. Logan, Harrison, and Alina explained what was going on. It didn't take the police long to grasp who was in charge and who was the criminal.

When Logan turned and said, "We found Alina tied up in the bedroom," all attention turned to her.

She tried to smile but was suddenly intimidated by that many men crowding around her. She wrapped her arms tight against her chest and said, "I'm okay. Outside of the fact he tied me up for a couple days and beat me up as much as he wanted to, I don't think I have any broken bones or anything. I don't need medical attention."

"That's not quite true," Logan said. "She was drugged, and we don't know what she's been given, but her arm is quite puffy and raw." He lifted her T-shirt sleeve so the police could see her arm.

The paramedics out in the hallway moved inside. She was led to the living room where she was given a quick once-over.

"I still think you should go to the hospital," one of the paramedics said. "This arm doesn't look very happy at all."

"It's been like that for a couple days," she confessed. "It's getting better."

"And yet, you noticed it with all the other stuff going on," Logan pointed out.

They looked at the lacerations on her ankles and wrists, and the EMT said, "You should go in so we can take photographs to document all this too."

She bit her bottom lip, completely loathing to do so. Yet she was a nurse, and she had no reason not to trust the hospital. But she didn't know these men, and right now going with anybody anywhere was not a good idea.

Logan stepped in front of her. "Go with them. It's important they get whatever trace evidence they can from your body, and you should have a rape kit done. You can't trust this asshole to say he didn't touch you. You were drugged and unconscious for however long."

She stared at him, fear in her eyes, and shuddered.

He rubbed his hands along her arms, giving her a little squeeze. "I didn't mean to come across so harsh. But the facts are the facts. Until we know them, we won't have the right answers."

Tears filled her eyes as she stared up at him. She tried to nod, but instead she started to shake.

He glanced at the two paramedics. "Give us a minute."

They backed off, and he wrapped her in his arms and held her close. "I know you're terrified," he whispered against her ears. "But there will be no repeat grabbing and bringing you here."

She drew a deep breath, reminding her how much her body hurt, and with a brave face, she said, "I'll be fine."

With the paramedics at her side and Logan behind her, she let them lead her downstairs, out to the ambulance. She was grateful no stretcher had been brought in. That would be the last thing she wanted, to be strapped down again. She sat inside the ambulance, waited as one of the policemen got in, and then she stared at Logan.

"You contact me and let me know what happens." He pulled out a card and tucked it into her purse, then handed it to her, which she had already forgotten about. She reached for it gratefully. "Your phone is in there too. If you're worried at the hospital, you give me a call."

She clutched the purse against her chest and nodded. The door shut in front of her, and she tried to settle herself, knowing a very unpleasant process would begin soon.

LOGAN HATED TO leave Alina, seeing the lost look on her face. If she'd been happy to go, it would've been a different story. He couldn't imagine a rape kit would be anything other than incredibly violating. But he didn't know what had happened to her while she'd been here. This place would also be gone over with a fine-tooth comb, including the bed. They would have to look for bodily fluids there as well. She was dressed when found, but that didn't mean jack when it came to being violated. He quickly retraced his steps to the apartment. He phoned Levi while in the elevator and asked, "What excuse did you give the police for us entering the apartment?"

Levi said, "You could hear her calling for help."

"Good enough." He hung up and realized it was nothing but the truth. He might not have heard it clearly on a physical level, but his intuition certainly had. He was damn glad he had come anyway. Who knew where the hell Alina would've ended up if they hadn't gone in then?

Organized chaos ensued in the apartment. Colin was led out in handcuffs. Harrison stood off to the side in the hallway outside the apartment. He nodded at Logan when he returned and said, "They want a statement from us, and then we're free to go."

"That's to be expected. Can we do it here or do we have to go to the station?"

One of the detectives said, "We can talk right now if you want. We've already spoken with your boss."

"Good. Thanks."

"He told us everything about why you came here in the first place." The detective pulled a card out of his shirt pocket and handed it them. "I'm James Easterly. If you find out anything new while you're working on your own job that pertains to Alina's situation, I'd appreciate it if you'd call me. Our budget is very tight, and our officers are overworked. I'm not against accepting help if any is coming."

Surprised at the man's attitude but happy to hear it, Logan accepted the card. "In that case, fire away and let's get through this. We have a lot of work still to do on our end." He waited a moment, then added, "By the way, Jackson says 'hi.'"

Easterly gave a start of surprise, then his eyes lit up. "Now that is good news. I'm glad he asked you to come."

It took about an hour to go through the full retelling of information while the detectives taped the entire process. Logan wished he had a copy of it himself. Still, he hadn't lied, and, if Alina was going to be okay now, it was all in the hands of the Boston police.

When they took their leave and were in their rental car, Harrison said, "It's not a good idea to split up or go alone to the other addresses."

Logan gave a laugh. "Isn't that the truth?" He shook his head. "We've done a lot of missions but have never come across something like this. Our focus now needs to be finding the other three women before they are moved out of the country."

The police still hung around, standing outside the apartment with Colin beside them.

A sharp noise echoed as they watched a red streak cross Colin's head as he collapsed to the city street.

"Oh, shit." Logan unbuckled his seat belt, opened the vehicle door and bolted toward where the circle of men had been. They were scattered at this point, squatting on the ground, weapons out. Logan kept behind the police vehicles until he got to the side. They all waited. But no second shot came. The gunman had done exactly what he had intended to do—and had left.

Chapter 4

ALINA WAS GIVEN a small hospital room where she waited until somebody could see her. When the nurse arrived, she said, "We're waiting on the detective to come and take photographs of the evidence. Please strip down and put on this hospital gown."

And then it started. How horrible to go through something like this to find out if she'd been molested while she'd been unconscious. Did she really want to know? Then she decided she did. Ignorance was bliss in a lot of ways, but it would forever haunt her to wonder *what if.*

She stripped down to her skin, folded her clothes, setting them on the side of the small bed, and put on her hospital gown. Chilled, she sat up in the bed and pulled the blankets over her. Seeing herself naked had been an eye-opener.

She was scratched, with bruises all over her body; and her hands, wrists, and ankles were chafed as well as sore, bloody, and scarred—already turning colors from being restrained. She didn't even know how long she had been out.

It seemed like forever before a female detective came in. She had a gentle smile when she explained she would take photographs. She wasn't the one administering the rape kit—that would be a nurse or doctor—but Alina had to lie still while her injuries were photographed. And that was when she realized there were more than she even knew.

Including bruises around her neck.

When she was asked to roll over to show her back, Alina asked the woman, "Does it look that bad?"

"It's bad, but I've seen a lot worse," the policewoman said quietly. "Let's hope he didn't rape you at the same time." When she was done, she left her card. "If you ever need anything, call me."

Even if it was a platitude, it was still nice to hear. After this had happened, it certainly made her reassess how she felt about human nature.

Then the nurse came in with a package. She calmly explained it was a rape kit. And, although the process might be uncomfortable, it was necessary. It would be done as fast as possible. As a nurse, Alina had seen the kits but had never administered one.

She'd gone to her doctor for her regular yearly checkups, so the internal exam was something she was accustomed to. When it was over, she lay there for a long moment and asked, "Can I leave now?"

The nurse looked at her in surprise. "The doctor hasn't seen you yet."

"Oh," she said. For all she knew it could be another several hours. "How long until I get the results on the rape kit?"

"A day or two if I can get a rush on it. Otherwise it could take weeks."

While she lay there, she considered how the hell she was supposed to get home, wondering if her vehicle had been towed or if it was still at work. She also should contact her supervisor. She wasn't sure when they expected her again because she didn't know what day it was. Her memory seemed to be quite trashed. She pulled out her phone and called her supervisor. When Selena answered, Alina explained what happened. Between the woman's cries of distress, Alina got the answers she needed. But she wasn't allowed to return to work.

"No, no, no."

In general, Selena was fair but could be a bit of a hard ass. But right now, she was all soft.

"You should take a few days off. I also don't know where your vehicle might be. I'll call security and see if it's still in the parking lot." A pause followed while she scratched out notes. After noting Alina's license plate, Selena said, "I'll call you right back. Are you sure you will be okay?"

"I'll be fine. I'm in the hospital right now, waiting for the doctor to see me."

"I've got you down for four days off, starting today. Call me if you need longer."

Then she hung up. "Well, four days off right now would be nice," she whispered to the empty room. But this wasn't going to be a vacation, so she'd rather be working.

Selena phoned a few moments later. "I've given your license plate number to security. They're looking for your vehicle. Please take care of yourself." She hung up.

While Alina waited for security to call her back, the doctor walked in. He took one look at her and said, "I hear you've been through an ordeal, young lady."

Something about the father figure and his gentle tone brought tears to her eyes.

He reached down and gently patted her on the hand. "You're going to feel this way for quite a while. You should take it easy and give yourself some time. Getting over shock and trauma is hard. There is no real way to make it easier on yourself. But you have to do it if you want to feel safe and secure again."

She stared up at him. "How does one do that? And, when I do feel better, I'll return to work—where I was kidnapped. I don't even remember the hours before it happened. I woke, tied up in a strange apartment."

He nodded. "Some people are never able to really relax in the same environment again. If that's where you were taken from, that makes a lot of sense. However, since you were kidnapped from work, it would help if you could piece together those hours before your kidnapping." He shook his head. "The trauma will often cause short-term memory lapse, but those memories will return. Do you have somebody you can stay with?"

She shook her head. "No, not really."

"It would be good for you if you weren't alone. Particularly in the beginning. You can expect nightmares and a general sense of not feeling safe."

She nodded, but she had no idea who she should call. It wasn't like she had a lot of friends in her life. Mostly coworkers. She didn't have a boyfriend, hadn't for a long time. And, although she wanted to go home, she wasn't looking forward to being alone there either. He was right; it would take time.

He gave her a thorough physical exam and said, "I'll have some blood tests run to see what drug they gave you." He looked at the injection site. "If you don't have any other symptoms, we are probably dealing with an allergic reaction here. I'll get the nurse to give it a good cleaning, as well as your wrists and any other lacerations and put ointment on them." He wrote his notes on his tablet and added, "After that you should be good to go."

As he turned to walk away, he stopped and looked at her. "Do you have any way to get home?"

She shook her head. "I'm from Somerville. Security at the hospital is checking to see if my car is still there."

He glanced at her and asked, "You work in a hospital?"

She smiled. "I'm a nurse."

He nodded. "Good. Then I don't have to worry about you looking after yourself because you know how important it is." And yet behind his words was a question.

With a nod, she said, "I promise I'll take care of myself."

"Good to hear. You've been given a huge second chance at life. I can't imagine what would have happened if you hadn't been rescued. Talk about having a guardian angel …"

She smiled. "Yes, he'll always be a hero to me."

Then the doctor was gone, and the nurse returned. And like Alina had done many times herself, the nurse washed her wrists, back, neck, and all her bruises and lacerations. When she was done, she said, "Okay, you can get dressed now." As the nurse walked out, she joked, "And I'd dress fast if I were you, as a man is here to get you, and he's"—her voice dropped to a low whisper—"gorgeous."

Alina's instinctive reaction was fear. "I don't have anybody taking me home." She could feel it trembling right through her. She grabbed her pants and the rest of her clothes, and quickly dressed.

When she put her boots on and straightened, the nurse returned, saying, "He's definitely here to pick you up. He said to tell you his name's Logan."

Instantly the fear inside her drained, and she sank onto the bed. "Oh, my God. He's the man who rescued me."

The nurse leaned closer. "He looks like a hero."

As Alina walked outside to meet Logan, the nurse's words rolled inside her head. She caught sight of him standing there, on the phone, waiting for her, and she realized the nurse had been quite correct about one thing. *Damn, he's gorgeous.* It said much about her life that she hadn't noticed this before. She plastered a smile on her face and strode forward, already feeling like she wasn't quite so alone.

AS LOGAN FINISHED the call to Levi, Alina appeared in front of him. With a big smile on her face.

He grinned at her. How was he supposed to explain that Colin was shot dead in front of a yardful of cops? He decided to put that off for now. Besides, he didn't want her stuck in town when they could drive her home or to her workplace to get her car. Not like they needed anything else on their job list, but maybe they could get a little more information from her.

Harrison had been on the same wavelength. Neither of them wanted to see a woman who'd already been victimized left alone, stuck at the hospital, looking at a half-hour taxi ride to get to her vehicle.

"Hey," he said. "You look great."

She snorted. "Great? I hardly think so. On the other hand, I'm done here, and that makes it a lot easier to face the rest of my day." She took a deep breath and asked, "Any news on the kidnapped women?"

He shook his head, then wrapped an arm around her shoulders and asked, "Are you ready to leave?"

She let her arm drape around his back, as she nodded. "Yes. So the nurse was right? You're here to take me home?"

"Yeah. Harrison and I didn't feel good about leaving you here alone."

She squeezed his waist and gave him a grin. "I don't

know how to thank you," she confessed. "I wasn't looking forward to figuring out how to get home. I could take a cab, but I would worry about sitting in a stranger's vehicle, wondering where the hell he was driving me. I don't know this area well …" She shook her head. "This is much nicer. I really appreciate it."

He gave her a gentle hug. "Come on then. Harrison's waiting outside." He glanced at the cuts and bruises on her face and neck. "Do you need a prescription filled?"

"No, I don't think so. He didn't give me one, and the nurse said I could go."

He gave a chuckle. "Meaning you think you can take care of yourself after this?"

"If it wasn't for the rape kit, I probably wouldn't have come at all," she admitted. "But it was a good idea to run some blood tests to see what injection he gave me."

The double doors opened in front of them, and they took two steps outside. She stopped and lifted her nose to smell the air. It was cloudy and smelled like rain was due any moment.

"Remember to enjoy every day after this. Nothing like surviving a horrible event to make you realize how good some things are in your world."

He led her toward Harrison, leaning against the car waiting for them. She smiled and let her arm drop from Logan to reach up and hug Harrison.

He gave her a gentle hug in return and said, "Glad to see you looking so good. Let's get you home." He opened the back door and waited until she slipped inside. He closed it and asked Logan, "You want to drive, or you want me to?"

"I'll drive," Logan said. He'd do better with something to keep his mind occupied instead of the warm feeling of having Alina in his arms. He wasn't sure what to think about her hugging Harrison too. He was hoping she was leaning more toward him. On the other hand, he wasn't in Boston for very long, and the last thing she needed was a relationship that wasn't going anywhere. Right now, she needed a man who would be around, one she could trust. And even then, it would take her a while to get to that point.

But she was a sweetheart. And he really admired her gumption. What was not to love about a woman who could stand up after what she'd been through and get feisty with her attacker?

As he got inside the vehicle and turned on the engine, he checked the area—heavy multiple-lane traffic. He turned and asked Alina, "Any idea how to get to where we're going?"

"Not a clue," she said. "I'll give you the address of the hospital where I work. Your GPS can give you the rest."

She quickly rattled off the address, and Harrison punched it into the car's navigation system. Logan followed the directions, getting on the main freeway. "It's not very far away, is it?"

"My apartment is closer than my work," she said. "But my vehicle should still be in the hospital parking lot. I'm waiting on the security guard to call me when he finds it."

"Smart to have somebody check that it's still there."

"I spoke to my supervisor. She gave me four days off to start," she confessed. "But I can't decide if I'd be better at work, where at least I'll have something else to think about, or if I should never go back, because I'll always be looking over my shoulder, terrified of being kidnapped again."

"There are two sides to every coin. You must be ready to face people and questions, and anybody who might know anything about this in their prying looks and intrusiveness.

But you also don't want to stay home where your own thoughts are running around in circles."

She settled into the vehicle and said, "True enough." Alina stared out at the traffic.

Logan kept an eye on her, checking the rearview mirror as he followed the directions.

After being quiet for a long time, she said, "You know? It's bad enough this happened, but I almost feel like work will be a bigger issue. Because I can't remember anything outside of having a cup of coffee with Colin in the lunchroom. So …"

Harrison turned to look at her. "He likely drugged your coffee. You probably got up, headed toward your car, and he caught you as the drug took effect."

She frowned. "But how do I return to work knowing I was taken from there?" She shook her head. "I don't know if I'll feel safe at home either, but at least I wasn't kidnapped there."

Logan could understand how confused she felt, but that wouldn't change the fact she had to adjust to both. "Are you independently wealthy?" he asked in a calm voice. "If not, you have to return to work and face that demon."

"I was prepared to," she admitted. "Until I spoke to my supervisor, who told me to take time off. But her words hit me sideways, and I'm not sure I could ever go back. I'm so confused right now." Her voice darkened in pain. "But I am *not* independently wealthy. Although I do have some savings, I don't have enough to retire."

Harrison chuckled at that. "Few of us do. Logan and I work for the same reason."

"And because we love the job," Logan added.

"Have you ever been attacked or kidnapped yourselves?"

"Many times," Logan said quietly. "We can't talk about most of our military years. But now, working for Legendary Security, we continue to do similar kinds of work."

She shook her head and whispered, "I can't imagine."

"It's not something you ever get used to, but it's what we're trained for."

"I'm trained to save lives, to help people. But when I saw Harrison going a few rounds with Colin, … all I could think about was how I wanted to get my hands on him too."

Bloodthirsty. He really liked that. "It's natural that you'd want some payback. But mostly it's an outpouring of rage because of all the fear he put you through. Given a few days, you will probably be very grateful you didn't follow through on that first urge." He pulled into the hospital parking lot. "What vehicle are we looking for? Did you ever hear from the security guard?"

"Oh, my goodness. I didn't even know we were here already," she cried out.

He watched as she looked around the parking lot and frowned.

"I can't remember where I parked," she said in despair. "How the hell does that work?"

"Short-term memory loss is extremely common with any trauma. It's the body's way of healing without adding more stress to your system."

"You have a designated parking spot here?" Harrison asked.

"That'd be too easy." She ran her fingers over her face and rubbed her eyes. "I'm trying to remember what kind of vehicle it is."

"You had to give something to the security guard to look for," Harrison said.

She brightened. "The license plate," and she quickly spouted it off.

Harrison punched it into the laptop they always carried with them. "Your vehicle is a Volkswagen Beetle. Black."

"Yes, it is," she said warmly. "I remember that now."

Chapter 5

THEY DROVE AROUND the parking lot but there was no sign of her vehicle. Harrison said, "Alina, the keys."

She took them from her purse and handed them to him.

Harrison said to Logan, "Park and we'll walk around to see what we can find with the alarm on her system."

"Good idea." He pulled into a visitor parking spot.

With the three of them looking, they strategically stopped at one corner and started walking with Harrison pressing the button off and on to see if any vehicle alarm shot off. There was nothing in the front of the parking lot, nor on the side. As they went around to the back they found a single black Volkswagen Beetle. Harrison clicked on the button and the lights flashed. As they got close to it, they confirmed the license plate.

Harrison handed the keys back to her and said, "This is yours."

She clapped her hands in delight and raced forward. She quickly unlocked it and looked inside. "It doesn't appear to be damaged in any way."

"Were you expecting it to be?" Logan asked.

She noted the odd tone in his voice, but with her excitement at having found her wheels and part of her life restored, she didn't think anything of it. She popped the trunk. It was empty. She didn't know if it was supposed to be or not. She turned to the guys. "Thank you so much. Just getting this back is huge for me."

"How far away do you live?"

"Just a few miles. I'll be fine from here."

Logan stepped in front of the vehicle and said, "Have you forgotten something?"

She looked up at him. "What?"

"Remember what Colin said. They already know where you live, and you're going to get picked up regardless."

She grabbed a hold of the open car door and roof of the Volkswagen and stared at him. All the color drained from her face. "Still? I figured once the police arrived it was safe." She looked over at Harrison. They were both shaking their heads.

"There is no way to know," Logan said quietly. "I suggest we check your house and see if anybody's been there."

She stared at him nonplussed. But inside, she was starting to shake. In a bad way. She turned to look at the hospital. "They know where I work. If they know where I live, I'm not safe anywhere."

Logan could see her start to buckle in a faint. He bolted to her side and grabbed her around the waist, tucking her close. When that didn't work and she started to fall, he picked her up and carried her around to the other side of the vehicle.

Logan opened the passenger door and sat her down in the seat. "You're not in any shape to drive," he snapped. "Let me buckle you in. I'll drive and Harrison will follow us. We'll go to your place to make sure it's okay."

"Make sure of what?" she cried softly. "If they haven't been there yet, that doesn't mean they aren't going to be coming in the next hour, or ten. Until this is over there's no way I'm going to be safe. How the hell do I come to terms with that?" In fact, she had no idea if that was even possible.

Logan grabbed the keys from Harrison, got in the car and turned on the engine. "Give us your address."

She rattled it off but stared at him, almost blind. "What's the point of going there? We can lead them right to it."

"And that means you think you're actually being watched right now." He gave her a hard stare. "Are you?"

She stared at him in shock. "Oh, my God! I have no idea." She slid down in her seat until she was hidden beneath the window.

"If you are, it's already too late. Sit back up again properly. We'll drive to your house and check it out." He closed the door, rolled the window down and said to Harrison, "You lead with the GPS."

Harrison nodded, hopped into the car and pulled out of the lot.

She looked over at him. "I could drive."

Logan snorted. "Sweetheart, you're not driving anywhere."

She sagged back gratefully. It was one thing to make the offer, but she'd be much happier not driving. Now if only the men could solve the rest of her problems. She stared out the window, not really seeing the scenery as it passed. They made several turns and she recognized her neighborhood.

"Does this look right?" Logan pointed to the building in front of her.

She nodded. "Yes. That's my place."

He got out of the vehicle, went around to her side, and opened the door. As she stood, she murmured, "I really am feeling okay, you know."

"Good. Glad to hear that. It doesn't change the fact you were held captive for several days. And you've got to be feeling rough. So instead of having to stand on your own two feet, accept the help you have."

He held out his hand. She slipped her much smaller one into it and smiled up at him. "Are you always this protective?"

He looked surprised and then contemplative. "Maybe?"

She chuckled. "Maybe that's why you're so good at it. You didn't do it because you're supposed to." Her smile widened. "But because you're a natural at it."

Together they walked to the front door. Harrison met them at the sidewalk. His gaze drifted from their joined hands to Logan's face. There was a twinkle in his eye when he said, "You're looking much brighter."

She shook her head. "No reason why I shouldn't. I'm away from the hospital."

She led them inside, pulling her apartment keys out. There was a code to get into the building, which she punched in, then headed straight for the elevator. "My place is on the third floor."

They took the elevator up and then made a right turn. "The apartment building is bigger than I thought it would be," Logan said.

Harrison nodded. "And obviously extends quite a bit down the back. We didn't drive that direction."

At her apartment, she hesitantly stuck the key in the lock. Logan stepped forward and moved her back to Harrison. Relieved, she let him open the door.

As she went to follow him, Harrison grabbed her arm and whispered, "Wait."

She saw the hard look on his face and felt her heart drop.

Please let the apartment be *empty*.

Logan appeared again at the door. "It's all clear."

Her breath let out with a whoosh. "Thank heavens," she murmured. "I don't want to think about being attacked here. Is no place safe?"

"I doubt it. They paid for you and have all your details. In their minds, it's an easy snatch and grab. He does the work finding the women that fit what they're looking for, grabs you, arranges a meet, does the delivery, and he's free and clear. On their part, he hasn't delivered, so they have the full prerogative to go and collect what is owed."

She shook her head. "You guys live in a dark world."

Logan spun on his heels, looking at her. "And now so do you."

She stared at him, all the color draining from her face. And it hit her that was the reality she was facing. If these men were right, then she was likely to be hunted. She hadn't seen it coming the first time, how the hell was she going to see it a second?

LOGAN DIDN'T WANT her terrified, but he did want her on guard. She couldn't possibly be thinking straight yet. She'd been a captive, freed, checked over, and was now facing the enormity of knowing it wasn't necessarily over.

He needed her to get that message. Loud and clear. And yet, at the same time not be paralyzed by it because that was the worst thing any victim could be. He searched the apartment, not liking very much about it. There was just a standard lock on the door he could pop in seconds, and though it was on the third floor, there was a fire escape to the apartment next door, easy enough to climb up, go to the window, which also had no alarm, get in and come around.

The front door alarm was literally no issue. In fact, it could be disabled with a couple snips. This was a mid-level moderate income type of apartment. There were probably a hundred or so people in here, all of them busy, rushing out to their day jobs, not seeing what was really happening in the much wider world around them. He walked through and checked the bedroom window to see it had a screen and was half open. He looked out, thankful to see the three-story drop.

There was only one bedroom, no spare. The living room had a tiny balcony he'd seen earlier. And again, not much of an issue. He could easily put an eight foot plank between apartment balconies and make that crossing without any trouble. People never thought about that, but with time and effort it was damn easy to cross any of these. He turned around, studied the small apartment, glanced up at Harrison and raised an eyebrow.

Harrison shrugged. "Can't say I like it, but what do you want to do about it?"

And there lay the problem. They were here on the job. Already their personal reasons for coming had been tossed out the window. There was nothing like finding a trafficking ring and freeing one woman to completely upturn your plans. And then there were three more addresses to check out. And now just as many women to rescue—and fast.

In a low voice he said, "I can't in good conscience leave her here alone."

Harrison winced. "I hear you, buddy. Well, I hope you have some kind of a good idea because we'll need an explanation for Levi."

Then he considered how Levi really was inside, and how

he felt about Ice. "You know, I think he might actually understand. I'm just not sure how we're supposed to move ahead. We can hardly take her home with us." Even adding that last bit made him grin. "Although I think she'd blend in just fine."

Harrison chuckled. "Then Levi really would have a fit. It's not like we're running a home for the hunted."

"That's not bad. That's not bad at all."

Harrison rolled his eyes and turned, wandering around the small apartment. Alina had gone into the washroom. She should be out any time. They didn't have much chance to discuss this turn of events while she wasn't in the room.

"We should call Levi."

Harrison glanced back at him. "Good idea. You do it."

Logan frowned. "You call him."

Harrison grinned. "No way, man. This is your deal."

"What the hell do you mean by that?" Logan stared at his friend.

Harrison just rolled his eyes again. "Surely you can see."

Logan shook his head. "I don't see dick shit."

"Obviously," Harrison retorted.

The bathroom door opened just then and Alina walked out. She smiled brightly at the two men. "Can I offer you coffee or a bite to eat before you leave?"

Logan studied her, smiled and a gentle voice settled deep inside. A certain truth. "We're not leaving."

Harrison chuckled.

Alina stared at both in shock. "What are you talking about? You have a job to do and I'm certainly not it." She ran her hand up the side of her temple and added, "I can't say I am feeling up to entertaining. I'd like to go to bed," she confessed, her gaze turning toward her bedroom. And that was exactly what she should do. Logan motioned at her to head into her room. “Go to bed. We’ll stand guard.”

She swayed on her feet, but still, even though her body was demanding down time, her mind was grappling with the idea of sleeping with strangers in the house.

Logan gently took her in his arms, giving her a quick hug. Against her ear, he whispered, “Take the offer, go and sleep. We promise when you wake you’ll still be here.” She glanced at him gratefully and he realized he’d guessed correctly. He lowered his head, dropped a kiss on her temple and said, “Go.”

She shot him a disgruntled look and said, “Who said you could kiss and order me around at the same time.”

He knew she didn’t mean it quite the way it came out. It was a sign of the fatigue eating at her. He pushed her gently in the direction of the bedroom. “And if you need help getting into bed, let me know.”

She shot him a look, walked into her bedroom and slammed the door.

Logan chuckled. “I guess that was a no?” He turned to Harrison and saw a wicked grin on his face.

“And another one has fallen.”

Understanding wiped the smile right off Logan’s face. “Hell no. I’m being a nice guy.”

Harrison arched an eyebrow, but his grin widened. “Nice guy? Hugging and kissing her? Teasing her, flirting with her? Yeah, it’s a whole lot more than that.”

“Of course I treat her nicely. You forget about any of that *fallen* shit. Damn you for even being at the bloody compound. That attitude has already gotten ingrained in you. Not everybody’s going to hook up, you know.”

Harrison nodded his head slowly, sagely. “Of course not.

Just the fact that we have already, what? Five couples now?" He shook his head. "Damn good thing I'm doing mostly away jobs. Otherwise the bug might get me too."

"If you think it's biting me, I'll make damn sure it gets you." Logan shook his head. "Stupid conversation. What the hell are we going to do about this place, and do our job from here?"

"I'll get our bags and laptop. The hotel is prepaid, so nothing we can do about that."

"Levi won't give a damn about that minor cost. He'll be more upset if we don't get these addresses checked out." Logan turned to face the bedroom and then Harrison. "How do you feel about checking out some of those addresses alone? I don't think we should leave her. Not only was she hurt, but she could be on somebody's list."

"It's also very late. Chances are we'd be better off starting fresh in the morning anyway." Harrison contemplated the living room. "Well, I'll take the floor. That leaves you with the couch."

Logan studied the minuscule living room. For Harrison to sleep on the floor, they'd have to move the coffee table into the kitchen. And the couch was a love seat, too small to sleep on.

He groaned, glanced around at the rest of the kitchen and hallway. "Guess I'll sleep on the kitchen floor."

Harrison chuckled. "What about food?" He checked his watch. "It's past eleven." He shook his head. "We didn't get dinner, and I doubt she's eaten anything in a long time."

"Pizzas are about the only thing at this hour." Logan walked to the fridge and opened it to find a lot of green vegetables but not much of anything else. "I wonder if she's a vegetarian."

"She probably eats healthy. She's a nurse, remember?"

"Still we have to eat. Let's find anything close by."

Harrison held up his phone. "I've checked. Two pizza joints within a couple miles. I'll call and place an order and then go pick it up. We don't want to have any delivery coming here, bringing attention to the fact she's home."

Logan nodded. "I'll stay and keep watch."

Harrison ordered two full-size pizzas, one with everything and the other just vegetables. Once he left, Logan locked the door behind him. He walked over to the kitchen window and stared down, waiting until Harrison got into the car and drove away.

And that's where he kept watch until he returned twenty minutes later. Logan hadn't seen or heard anything in the meantime.

He let Harrison inside. Placing the pizzas on the table, Logan realized Harrison had brought the laptop up too. Good thing because, right now, they had a lot of research to do.

The two of them sat at the kitchen table and ate.

After a couple pieces, Logan's mind working away on the issues they'd found, he said, "I was going to call Levi but decided it was too late."

"He already knows where we are, so unless we have something new to share, we're better off leaving it until morning."

"Plan of attack for then?"

"We have three addresses left to check out. Three women to find. So not much hope of seeing your friends."

"They weren't available anyway. I'm sorry it didn't work out with your sister-in-law." Logan asked, "Your brother's been gone for years?"

Harrison nodded slowly. "And she didn't have much to do with the family back then. I'm assuming she's moved on with her life. But I know for my parents, she's a piece of their son's life they were hoping to stay connected with."

"Sorry about your brother. That must have been a really tough time for you."

"You don't know the half of it."

Logan raised an eyebrow, studied his friend's face and said, "Tell me."

Harrison gave him a look. "His wife was my fiancée."

Logan froze, his pizza in midair. "Oh, shit." He slowly lowered the food, seeing the pain in his friend's eyes. "So, you lost your fiancée to your brother, and then you lost your brother."

"Not quite that fast, but … you know. Not much fun for anybody. My parents were pretty upset with her and my brother when they married. I had no choice but to make peace with it. But now …" He shrugged. "Honestly, I'm happy to walk away from it. I was hoping my parents were equally happy to also. Maybe they'll be able to now."

Logan winced. "That can't be easy."

"No."

"Did you break up with her, or did she do it?"

"Finding her and my brother in bed made it mutual." Harrison leaned back in the chair. "Hence my relationship issues."

Logan stared down at the pizza, hating to think what his friend had gone through. "Did your brother ever say anything to you about it?"

Harrison snorted. "You mean in between me pounding the hell out of him?" He shook his head. "He never did defend himself, never said anything about it. They got married six months later. I showed up for my parents' sake, walked away and never saw them again." He stared off in the distance. "No way to come back from that."

Shit. Logan felt terrible. Not only had his fiancée dumped Harrison to be with his brother, but she had killed the relationship between Harrison and his brother at the same time, and now he had no way to make amends. Not that he had any to make. That was on his brother's head. And his parents had to watch the fallout in horror. "Given all that, I'm surprised they still wanted anything to do with your sister-in-law."

"I don't think they will now. But it's hard to lose a child. I don't blame them for wanting to cling to bits of his life. She was part of the family for years, and they worry about her. She was never terribly friendly." Harrison tossed his last crust into the box. "I'm done. In more ways than one. Not going to be a great night on the floor, but honestly, I'm ready to hit it."

He got up, went to the bathroom, came out, then moved the coffee table out of the way. He grabbed a pillow off the couch, then stretched out on the carpet in the small room.

Logan watched him, almost jealous. Harrison had always been able to sleep anyplace.

Logan was a lot fussier. He didn't mean to be, but it seemed like the minute he lay down on a hard surface, all the pressure points felt wrong, and they hurt. Each shift to get comfortable just added new ones.

The other guys seemed to block it out. Logan felt like such a wuss, so he'd learned to not listen to the pressure points. Then when he woke up the next morning, his body would hurt. Often they were on the move, and he couldn't afford things like that. Still, Harrison was right about one thing they needed to do, and that was to get some sleep. It was necessary, and they would have an early morning.

They also had no guarantee they would sleep tonight. He closed the pizza boxes, placed the leftovers in the fridge, left the garbage on the table and did a quick security check to make sure nobody was out there and that everything was locked up as tight as it could be. Then he went to the bathroom and took a quick wash. On his way to the couch, he heard a sound in the bedroom.

He walked over to crack open her door. He wanted to make sure she was sleeping. Her window was wide open, and a chill was in the air. He closed it about halfway and then turned to check on her. She slept but restlessly, her body twitching. He wasn't sure if she was caught in a nightmare or having a dream.

And suddenly her eyes flew open, and she screamed. He rushed to her side and said, "It's okay, Alina. It's all right. You're just having a dream."

She gripped his fingers and gasped as she caught her breath. "It's Colin," she said. "I saw you in my bedroom and …" She shook her head. "I wonder how long I'll keep seeing his face."

"Possibly on and off for the rest your life," he said quietly. "I don't mean that to scare you. But our subconscious often has ways of undermining us by bringing up some of our worst fears and nightmares under times of stress."

She let go of his fingers and relaxed onto the bed, pulling up the blankets. "Why did you come in here?"

"I'm heading to bed. I peeked in to check on you, realized the window was wide open and closed it some. And that's when you saw me."

She nodded. "My couch is hardly big enough for you."

He chuckled. "It will be fine. Try to get some sleep. I'll leave the bedroom door open, okay?"

But she had already drifted back to sleep. He watched for a moment and pushed the door wide. When he didn't hear any sound from her, he headed to the couch and reassessed. Maybe it would work. He stretched out. His knees draped over the side of the arm, and his head was kinked up against the other. Floor or couch? What the hell. He was here already. He closed his eyes, determined to make the best of it, and finally drifted off.

Chapter 6

THE NEXT MORNING Alina lay in bed for a long time, acclimating to the change in her reality. She was home, no longer tied up, and in her own bed, alone. The last part she would do differently. Like inviting Logan maybe. But it was too early for that. Besides, he wasn't sticking around.

Hearing sounds from her living room, she froze and then recognized Logan's voice. How comfortable she felt around him and Harrison. Maybe because she knew those men weren't Colin.

She slowly got out of bed, walked to the kitchen in her pajamas and found they'd made coffee and were sitting at the kitchen table, eating pizza. "For breakfast?"

Logan bounced to his feet, his arms outstretched.

Like a homing pigeon, she snuggled right into his hug. It had certainly taken away a lot of the awkwardness, worrying about how she would react to another man after Colin. She stepped back and smiled into his worried face. "I'm fine."

But he wasn't content with her words. He studied her face, then how she moved.

She shook her head and laughed. "Don't fuss," she teased. "Honest, I'm fine."

He nodded, motioning at the pizza. "We ordered some last night. Harrison went and picked it up, and this is our breakfast." He gave her a lopsided grin. "I'm sure it's not your definition of healthy, but we were hungry."

She smiled at Harrison as he munched through another piece. "Not to mention you're big guys, and I highly doubt a little bit of yogurt and some seeds would do you much good."

Harrison froze, the look in his eyes one of horror.

She laughed. "Like I said …" She lifted her nose in appreciation. "And you guys are house-trained." She wandered over and poured herself a cup of coffee. "I'm going to take a shower. Seems like I haven't been clean for days." With that reminder, she took her coffee, headed to her bedroom, grabbed some clean clothes and went into the bathroom.

Her coffee was too hot to drink now, but by the time she was done, it should be about right.

When she stepped under the hot water, she held in her cry. Not only did it sting, but it was in places she hadn't been aware she'd been hurt. When she turned her back to the hot water, she realized why they'd taken so many pictures at the hospital. She had no idea what Colin had done to her. But she hurt everywhere. It was mind-boggling how lifting an arm that had been tied and held in an awkward position made every muscle ache. She knew it would ease up. But for the next few days, she'd be lucky if she didn't need muscle relaxants on a continuous basis.

She stood, letting the heat flow over her body. That little bit should help make her joints move easier. When she was done, she stepped out, cautiously dried off and carefully got dressed. She took several sips of coffee before realizing it didn't taste right. She picked up her toothbrush and toothpaste and brushed her teeth. When she was done, she tried the coffee again and smiled. "That's much better."

She hung up her wet towels and grabbed her pajamas. In

her bedroom, she put away her clothes and made up the bed.

When she headed to the kitchen, she found three pieces of pizza left on the plate. She laughed. "Are you trying to be polite, or are you really full?"

Logan grinned. "We are your guests. It would be very unkind of us to eat all the pizza without offering you some."

She studied it and realized how hungry she really was. "I don't remember him feeding me. My stomach is pretty touchy right now."

"Probably the drugs," Harrison said. "I hope you get the results from that soon."

"I hope the police follow up in some way," she said. "But honestly, I have no idea what their procedure is. I've never been kidnapped before."

She sat down to the pizza. It was so good, she had a second slice, and by the end of that, she was done. Logan looked at her, and she shoved the plate toward him. "Finish it." She watched in fascination as it disappeared in about four bites.

"How can you possibly eat such a large mouthful at one time?"

"Lots of practice." Logan's face was deadpan as he delivered the line.

She smiled. "Glad to see you guys have a sense of humor, considering the work you do."

She glanced around her small apartment. "And it's nice to know we had a solid night's sleep. I didn't wake up until the sun was up." She cast a curious glance at the men and asked, "I presume there were no intruders?"

Logan shook his head. "A quiet night."

She nodded. "You guys can go. I should be safe here."

Harrison snorted. "What universe do you live in? Because you were safe for one night doesn't mean you are for the next ones."

She leaned back in her chair and sighed. Once again she looked around her home. "I've only been here for a couple years. It still doesn't seem like I've moved in since I work so many shifts. But it's the only home I have." She opened her arms and waved them around the small space. "It's not like I can just pack up and move."

"And you'd have to do it without anybody knowing, so no moving truck, no assistance and no sign of anybody helping you."

"Like that's going to happen." She gasped. "Do I look like I can lift the couch on my own?" She picked up her coffee mug, taking a sip while she thought about it. "It's not like I can stay with somebody. At least not any more."

The men looked at her in question.

She shook her head. "My best friend moved away a couple months ago. She's the only one I knew well enough to be able to bunk at her place. I came here for work, and she followed within a few months. We often did sleepovers at each other's house if we were drinking and partying. And no, I don't have a boyfriend, nor any close family or friends here. Although I do have some money. I could go to a hotel for a night or two, but that's obviously not a long-term answer."

"That would be someone catching these guys before they come after you."

"I'm all for that," she snapped. "I have to stay here. I don't have anywhere else to go."

LOGAN HAD BEEN afraid of that. He and Harrison had had that discussion this morning. They'd also talked to Levi. She could stay at their hotel, but, like she said, that was a short-term answer. Still, it was something.

"We have a solution for the next couple days," he said quietly. "We have a hotel room that's paid for in Boston. You have days off anyway so you could come and stay with us."

She raised her eyebrows in surprise. "That's very generous of you. But what do I do when you leave?"

"We don't have an answer yet for you. Hopefully the police are on this, and there is a fast resolution. If not, potentially we can arrange for somebody to move your stuff. Help you find another apartment. But we can't stay. We have jobs in Texas."

"Texas? Any chance close to Houston?"

Both men frowned at her. "Yes, why?"

"Because my best friend moved there. She's been telling me to join her because the weather is so much nicer. The hospitals are always hiring." She shook her head and laughed. "But I couldn't see myself making a move like that. I was happy here. I quite liked my job."

Logan took note of her past-tense usage: *was*, *liked*.

"You might want to give that some further consideration due to the situation you find yourself in now," Harrison said, then nudged Logan.

Logan ignored him. He knew exactly what Harrison was thinking. But no way in hell would Logan bring up the subject about how he'd love to have her living a whole lot closer. He had to stay focused, otherwise his mind tended to wrap around this beautiful woman sitting close enough for him to hug her all over again.

When she'd walked out of the kitchen, rubbing the sleep from her eyes, he'd never seen a sweeter sight. He wanted to bundle her up and take her to bed. Honestly, he hadn't expected to meet anybody like her. And it wasn't like they had a relationship. But if she did move to Texas, they might have a chance.

"The trouble is, I'm not sure I want to get locked away in a hotel room either," she said. "You guys have things to do, so you'll be gone all day."

"True enough, but at least there you'll be safe. And think about it, the police will likely contact you again. And you'll be nice and handy to talk to them if needed."

"That's a good point."

Logan reached over and placed his hand on hers. "Honestly, you don't have much choice."

She stared at him in surprise. "Yes, I do. I can stay here and take my chances."

He sat back, a smile playing around his lips.

She stared at him suspiciously.

Finally, he grinned and said, "You could, if I gave you a choice. But something about having saved your life once makes me feel like I must continue doing so. Which means you are coming to the hotel with us."

She opened her mouth in outrage, then snapped it shut. Her gaze went from Logan to Harrison, who was of zero help to her because he was laughing.

"You guys look good together," he said with a big grin. He stood and grabbed the cardboard boxes from the pizza. "I'll take this down the hall to the garbage chute." He let himself out of the apartment.

Alina turned and blasted Logan. "I can't move into a hotel with you two."

"Why not?"

"Because I have a life."

"I'm trying to keep you safe."

She sat back and winced. Colin's voice echoed through her head. He had said she wouldn't be safe. They had her phone number and address, and they would collect, no matter what. She shook her head in defeat. "I need a few minutes to pack."

"You've got fifteen," he said cheerfully. He stood and moved to the front door to let Harrison in. He took one look at the two of them and said, "Did you settle your differences?"

She sniffed, turned on her heels and walked into the bedroom.

Logan laughed. "Absolutely. She's packing and coming with us."

"Good. Levi called. He wants her with us anyway." In a lower voice, barely above a whisper, he added, "And to keep an eye out in case someone comes after her, whether to kidnap her or to kill us. The cops are working on finding the other women. With Colin dead, there isn't much in the way of leads. But they are dissecting his life to find some. Levi wants them all taken down if we get the chance."

He gave Harrison a hard nod. "I'm on it." He knew he had to watch out; he was getting too involved. This was one of those cases that could go south very fast. He had to make sure he kept his heart safe.

Chapter 7

THEY QUICKLY LOADED her overnight bag into their rented car. Logan drove them all to their Boston hotel.

Once inside, they settled her on a bed. "This is yours for the next couple nights," Logan said as he placed her bag by the window. "We'll share the other."

She glanced from one bed to the other. They were both huge. In theory, they could easily share the bed.

But then so could she.

She turned to face the men. "Now what?"

Logan walked to the door and said, "Now you watch TV or something, and we'll be back in a few hours."

She frowned as they headed out. "Bring lunch then," she called out. She gave him a bright smile, but she didn't feel it. She felt lost already. How very female of her. She sagged on the bed as the door shut behind the men. Damn. She glanced around the room. What the hell was she doing here?

Then the door opened, and Logan stood glaring at her. "I can't leave you here alone." And the wattage in his glare grew stronger.

She raised her eyebrows. "Okay, I'm confused. You just left."

"And I came back." He gave his head a shake. "My mind says you should be safe here, but my instincts say you shouldn't be alone."

She brightened. "Glad to hear that. I was feeling at a loss by myself here."

"Being alone is one thing, but doing so while being hunted is a completely different issue."

She hopped off the bed, grabbed her shoes, slipped them on and picked up a sweater. "So where are we going?"

He still hadn't moved. Now he was positively growling. "That's the problem. We have addresses to check out."

"So, am I in more danger going with you guys?"

"Harrison and I have been standing in the hallway, arguing." He glanced toward the door. "Trying to figure out the best way forward."

"Well, the only way anybody would know I'm here is if they followed us."

"Unless your apartment was bugged."

She stared at him as her jaw dropped. In a strangled voice, she said, "I didn't think about that."

"No, but we did. We didn't have anything with us to check the apartment, and honestly we didn't think they'd be that fast. But we have no way to know for sure."

"But they don't know what hotel we are in, and they don't know what room."

He gave her a lopsided grin. "I know all that. I understand all the reasoning. My mind is completely on board with all the logical answers. However, my instincts can't be ignored."

She considered that for a long moment, thinking of all the times she'd returned to a patient's room because she'd felt like they were either in distress or heading into a major issue she could stave off. She stepped forward and said in a low voice, "I'm prepared to listen to that. I'm okay to sit in the vehicle the whole time."

"You have to do exactly what we tell you when we tell you. No hesitation."

And with that, her eyebrows rose. "I do work in a hospital," she said to make him feel better. "I do follow orders and deal with emergencies."

He studied her carefully.

When he relaxed, she realized she had passed some sort of test. "Good." She led the way to the door. "What route do we take, and when can we have lunch?"

He laughed. "You should have had more than two pieces of pizza for breakfast."

"I've been trying to lose ten pounds," she confessed.

"You've been what?"

At the shock in his tone, she turned to face him. "My last boyfriend said I wasn't slim enough. I guess I hung on to some of that."

With the door locked, they stood in front of the elevator as Logan viciously punched the button to call it. "That's ridiculous," he said. "If you lose any more weight, you'll disappear on us." And then his voice turned crafty as he gave her a sideways glance. "Just think, if you lose it, you could be kidnapped and stuffed into a smaller suitcase."

"That's not funny," she snapped, as they both got on the elevator.

"No, it's not. But now you can think about that if you try to take off more weight. You're perfect as you are, so leave it alone." Logan shook his head. "What is it about women and weight anyway?"

"You don't understand. I like to eat. *I really* like to."

Logan stared at her and shook his head. "The universe is laughing at me right now."

She stared at him in confusion as the elevator landed and

the double doors opened. "Why? Because you don't like to see women eat?" she challenged.

He grabbed her arm, pulled it through his and led her to the vehicle out front. "No," he said with a chuckle. "The exact opposite. I am suddenly surrounded by tiny women who can eat like crazy. I swear they outeat all my male friends."

Harrison twisted around in the driver's seat as they both got in the car. "Hi. Are you okay to come with us today?"

"I was actually quite lost in the room and wondered what the hell I was doing there."

He nodded. "We're still not sure this is the right thing to do, but it seemed wrong to leave you."

"I'm good with that," she said.

They drove away, and she sat in the back with her tablet. She'd be fine to sit here and watch. She was safe; she had the men with her. Although they were strangers in many ways, she knew who they were inside. Heroes.

As she listened, she could hear the men discussing every detail. With the first address up on the GPS, they followed the directions, taking them to an old residential area, with money from the looks of it.

"Wow, look at some of these houses," she whispered. She didn't know if this counted as big money anymore with all the billionaires in the world, but it certainly counted as it in hers.

"They are something." Logan tapped the GPS. "It's the right address." Harrison slowed, and they drove past a big-gated property. It was a majestic brick-and-stone house. A mixed siding that should've been at odds with each other, but somehow it all pulled together into a beautiful facade with even rooftop decks all the way around.

Harrison pulled the vehicle past the house, made a U-turn at the next intersection when traffic allowed and slowly drove past again. "I guess these places have no alleyway?"

She stared at the huge circular driveway in the front yard but also saw an entrance toward the rear. "How do they even get municipal service here? Garbage pickup, all that stuff. Surely that's at the back. I can't imagine anything this gorgeous having anything so disgusting in front," she said with a laugh.

Harrison turned left at the next street and went around the block. "No alleyway but a road." *Interesting.* And because the house appeared to take up the block, it didn't abut another house but a back entrance used for servicing.

At the front, Harrison parked and hopped out. "Back in a moment."

They watched as he strode up to the security gates. Instantly a uniformed guard stepped out to meet him. Harrison spoke with him for a moment, then was ushered toward the car.

"That's what I expected," he said when back inside. "No information and no leeway. Security is tight."

"It's owned by an Italian company. The owner is Dorian Mutually," Logan said.

"I don't know that name." Harrison glanced at Logan. "And this one we'll give the cops to check out. Otherwise, we'll need to make a night trip to check it out."

Alina could see the two men taking notes, texting information back and forth with someone. They must have quite the headquarters they sent details to. It was a fascinating concept to think of the type of work they did.

When they drove past the block and didn't turn around again, she asked, "Aren't you going to check this place out?"

"There is security front and back. We have no reason to approach. But if we wanted to get inside, we would, just not during daylight."

Her eyes widened as she considered them breaking and entering a property like that. But then she remembered them doing the same where she'd been held. "If you had probable cause? Then we can call the cops."

Logan turned and flashed her a smile. "Like we did with you."

"You didn't have that with me." She sank back in her seat. "I just realized how much of a risk you took, breaking and entering into that place, and how damned grateful I am you listened to your instincts."

"In our business instincts are very important," Harrison said quietly. "We don't take anything like that lightly." He pulled out into the main traffic and headed toward an intersection. He took a left onto a main road, and they drove around for another twenty minutes.

She realized they were heading to the next address. "What exactly are you looking for here?"

"Anything and everything." Logan settled back against the seat. "We're after information."

She digested that slowly. "Is that the work you do?"

"Not often," he said cheerfully. "But I'm not against this type."

"And these addresses?"

"Supplied by a street informant. We've been asked to check them out."

"Wow, and you found me at one of them." She stared out the window. "So the big fancy house we just saw would have enough room to house the other women."

"Possibly. I've got an email in to Detective Easterly to

check it out. He has more police resources now that the priorities have changed. We need to find the three women. They can get a warrant to check out this house based on what we have so far."

HARRISON SPOKE UP. "We'll be at the next address in another couple blocks. Look lively, people."

Logan settled back in, understanding exactly what Harrison meant. It had nothing to do with glancing around as much as it did with being alert and listening to his instincts. If they had gotten Colin to talk, they might have had something more to go on. That reminded Logan to check in with the police in the next couple hours. Detective Easterly hadn't been in this morning when Logan had called. And he could use an update on the case.

At this point, they came up to a series of townhouses and a large family-oriented complex of at least eighty units. It was one of those subdivisions where every house was a cookie cutter copy of the next. About ten were sandwiched together in a single block.

"Looking for number fourteen," he said.

Harrison slowed ever-so-slightly as they drove past the fourth house on the first block. It faced the main street and was scrunched in the middle of several others. The only thing different was the curtains were closed upstairs. He drove to the back, finding more complexes. Finally, he went around to the beginning and entered through the main entranceway. No security gate was here; he drove in and past number fourteen. On the side was a single carport, empty. Harrison pulled into the guest parking space. The guys looked at each other.

"We can take a walk," Harrison said.

From the back Alina said, "Let me go with Logan to make it look like we're a couple thinking about buying, and you sit here."

Logan looked at her. "It's a good idea."

When she stepped from the vehicle, he reached for her hand. When she placed hers in it, they walked together around the complex. Alina talked about the nice playground for children and the common building in the center for birthday parties and meeting rooms.

He looked at the security—or complete lack of it. Although a lot of people and families were here, too much coming and going would be ignored. Unless they found a talkative nosy neighbor who kept watch. Still, number fourteen looked innocuous and innocent. Back at the car Logan asked Harrison, "You want to knock?"

Harrison nodded. He walked straight through the carport to the back door. At the kitchen, he knocked several times.

When he did it again, Logan watched if anybody peered through the windows to see who was at the door. But there was no answer or movement inside. The place appeared to be empty.

Harrison turned to Logan, making a hand motion. Harrison grabbed the knob and turned it. The door opened. Seconds later Harrison grimaced, and he hurriedly closed the door again.

Logan turned to Alina. "I want you to sit in the back of the vehicle and lock the door behind you. Do not get out of the car, and do not come into the condo."

She glanced at him with worry. "What is it? What's wrong? Are the women in there?"

Unable to help himself, he gave her a kiss on the temple. "I'm not sure yet. I have to go look."

He led her to the vehicle and unlocked it. Before she sat, she asked, "Somebody's dead inside that house, aren't they?"

He stared at her in surprise. "I don't know, but from the look on Harrison's face, maybe." He shut the door, heard the lock click and walked over to Harrison.

Harrison was on the phone with Levi. He opened the door again and stepped inside.

Logan followed. The smell of decay was rampant. Not only did it smell of death, but it was one that had been here for a while. Whoever or whatever had died had been so for a couple of days.

They did a quick search of the downstairs—small, cramped rooms, nice enough for maybe two people though not Logan's style at all—but it was empty. They did a quick dash up the stairs, calling out in case anybody was still here. They did a walk-through of the first bedroom and headed to the master. At the door, Logan nudged it open with his boot, just in case. There on the bed lay a dead man.

More to the point, it was one of the four missing human traffickers—Jason Markham. Logan turned to look at Harrison. "And once again things have gone to shit."

Chapter 8

ALINA SAT IN the car, her body twisted so she could look out the rear window. It seemed forever before Logan and Harrison reappeared. She wasn't sure what to make of that. They stood outside, their faces grim, and she knew it was worse than they had expected. She felt sorry for whoever was in the house. Hopefully only one dead body was involved. Still, as a reminder of how grim her own reality was, it was effective.

She didn't know if this was connected with her abduction, but she did know Logan had saved her. She wanted to get out and put her arms around him, as much for her own security as to give him comfort. He was a good man.

Logan walked toward her, his steps measured, quick, and determined. So much power radiated from him right now, but anger was also there, like a red wave washed ahead of him as he strode toward her. Harrison was on the phone. She could imagine the calls that had to be made now. The two men who came to only check out some places found a whole lot more than they were looking for. On the other hand, she couldn't imagine what life would have been like if they hadn't come on this fact-finding mission.

She rolled down the window and looked up at him. He crouched down beside her. She said in a low voice, "It's bad, isn't it?"

He nodded. "It's one of the four human traffickers who disappeared. But no women."

She cupped a hand over her mouth. "Oh, my God!"

"Murdered," he added gently. "This changes things again."

She shook her head. "Does it really? You already knew this was a bad deal when you found me, and this is only the fourth address. You still have one more to check."

He took her hand. "After the ambulance took you to the hospital, a sniper took out Colin on the front yard, standing among all those policemen."

Her mouth trembled, slightly opened.

"So this is now the second murder." He gauged her expression, watching for shock or denial to set in. He patted her hand again. "The police are on the way," he said. "We'll wait here for them. I'll try to keep you out of the report as much as possible."

She frowned at him, her gaze a little distant. "I didn't have anything to do with it. Why would I be in the report?"

He gave her a sideways glance. "You came with us, and we drove here. So I would have to explain why we came here, therefore, anybody with us will be a part of it."

She sagged back and winced. "The last thing I want to do is see any cops right now."

"Understood. Just not an option. However, you didn't go into the house. You haven't seen anything. You don't know anything. You're sticking close to me because I'm the one who rescued you."

She brightened. "Now that much I can do. And you should get a medal for saving me from that asshole, Colin."

She was back to bloodthirsty, so he was glad about that. "Like an Alina medal?"

She wrinkled up her face, then she realized what this would mean. "I guess lunch is delayed?"

He chuckled. "Not so much. Harrison and I will search the house, see if we can find out anything before the police get here. You have to stay here out of sight and don't leave the vehicle. Otherwise, I'll have to explain what you were doing."

"I'm totally fine here." She shook her head. "I'm playing games on my tablet," she confessed. "Anything to pass the time and take my mind off…life."

He leaned in and gave her a hard kiss on the top of her head. "Understood." And he turned and walked away.

She wondered how the hell their relationship had progressed to him feeling comfortable enough to kiss her like that and her to accept it. Not only that, but hate the fact he was walking away without having pulled her into his arms and given her a hug first. She'd started to really crave those. She never thought of herself as much of a hugger. She'd always been more physically distant with people, but with him, all she wanted was to stay in his arms.

She leaned her head back and let her thoughts run free. She was sorry for the murdered man in the house. That added another nasty element to this whole scenario, but he was a trafficker and maybe got his just desserts.

Those missing bad guys had a lot to answer for. She understood the men would turn over every rock to get to the bottom of this mess. She wished now she could get her hands on them. But she wanted to find the missing women first—before it was too late.

But surely the Boston police were already on that aspect. She didn't know how much time had passed before she heard the arrival of the police cruisers without sirens. She sat up straight and watched as three pulled in. One parked beside the car she sat in; another in the carport of the house, and the last behind him. The officers got out and headed to the house.

She hoped Logan and Harrison were aware of the cops' arrival, as they'd been inside for a good twenty minutes. Then both stepped out on the small deck and spoke with the officers. She watched nervously until Logan and Harrison walked toward the car.

"It's all good," Logan said. "We gave the cops our names, numbers, and the boss's contact info, as well as a statement for why we were checking here. And when the door opened, we could smell something wrong inside. We do have a solid history and a background for stuff like this, so when we walked in and took a quick look, it wasn't out of the ordinary."

"Do they still need to talk to you two?" she asked. "Or to me?"

Both men shook their heads, and Logan said, "If they want to, they'll call us."

"And me?"

Harrison chuckled. "Nope, you're off the hook too."

She sat back with relief. "Thank heavens for that. Personally, I've had more than enough of the police in the last day."

On that note, Harrison started the vehicle and slowly drove out of the driveway.

As they left, Alina saw the coroner's vehicle drive in and was reminded that somebody had lost their life here. And, although she might not be delighted to be called to deal with the police, somebody else would love that opportunity, if it meant he was still alive.

"Where to now?" she asked quietly.

Harrison answered, "As much as I would like to finish for the day, we still have one more address to drive by. Then we need to check in with the police."

"Let's do it then," she said. "So far this outing really sucks." She settled into the back seat of the car and watched as the scenery went by. She'd never spent much time in Boston, so the area was new to her.

Once again, they followed the GPS, which took them to a small residential area outside of the main city. Small houses and yards, with playground equipment in the backyards and small children running around.

"This is really a family area, isn't it?"

"Playgrounds everywhere," Logan said.

They made several turns and ended up on a small side street lined with beautiful poplars on both sides. Harrison drove to the second-to-last house on the left and said, "That's it. Number 211."

They looked at the nondescript two-story family home, painted a soft blue with white shutters and a white door. A tricycle was in the front yard. There was no garden but a small picket fence with a gate to keep children inside. Bright cheerful curtains were pulled back at the windows and tied.

She could see no basement. "If there was ever a less likely looking house to find trouble, I'd want to see it."

Logan laughed. "That's almost enough to make me suspicious."

She understood what he meant—almost too much complacency and niceness about it. Then the back door opened, and a woman holding the hand of a toddler and a baby in her arms stepped out onto the porch, then walked down to the grass. She stopped a little bit ahead, easily seen through the wire fence as she let the toddler walk a few steps in the grass before he fell. She laughed, picked him up and stood him on his feet again.

"Still think it's suspicious?" she asked.

"We've seen a lot worse things in our lives," Harrison said. "We never take the surface at face value. But I'm not getting a hit on my instincts on this one at all."

"Neither am I. I think it's exactly what it looks like it is. But it'd be interesting to know who owns it." He bent his head and worked on his laptop.

She figured he got the name, phone number, and probably everything down to the type of food the family ate within minutes.

"The names aren't connected to any of the four that I can see," he said. "The owner is Richard Noble. He and his wife, Tabitha, bought the house three years ago."

They watched as the toddler went up the stairs and back down, joined by the mother with the baby.

"That'll be why they bought the house. Family time. She was probably pregnant with the one and had the second since." Alina hoped to hell they weren't involved. The last thing she wanted to think of was the mother and two kids involved in something as scary as the murder at the last house or human trafficking, like her situation.

Harrison drove around to the front again and parked not too close to the picket fence. He studied the small house, a frown on his face.

Finally Logan asked, "What's bugging you?"

"It's not that house, but the one beside it that has me off."

"Why is that?"

She hadn't even considered that maybe they had a wrong

house number, and they wanted the neighbor instead. But when she saw the curtains twitch in the main living room, and a face look out only to jerk back again, she realized he was completely right. "Did somebody give you the wrong address on purpose?"

"Informants can give you all kinds of shit for numerous reasons," Logan said calmly. "Just like you. It could be simply the fact that somebody knew Colin was up to this or had seen something suspicious." He shook his head. "Unless the intel is three years old, I don't see this house being involved. But the house beside it, yes, it's all too possible."

Harrison looked over at him. "I'll talk to the mother on the other property. Stay here. This is one time when a single male is better than two."

Logan nodded. Together Alina and he watched Harrison exit the car, walk across the road to the front yard and enter the side gate. He called out, and a few moments later the woman appeared around the side of the house with the baby in her arms. Logan and Alina were too far away to hear the conversation, but it lasted several minutes. Apparently, Harrison was getting some information.

When he came back to the car, it was hard to read his face, unlike when Logan had left the condo after finding the dead man. It had been easy to see he was pissed off. She struggled to read Harrison's body language.

When he got back in the car, he said, "The family moved in three years ago. A single male lived there originally. The property was owned by their neighbor, Lingam, and his brother was living in the house."

Silence reigned in the vehicle.

A moment later Harrison added, "She hasn't had anything to do with the neighbor since they moved in. He's a loner, no family, not friendly at all. Keeps a big dog in the backyard most of the time."

"Did you see a dog?" Alina asked.

Logan answered, "I bet if we drive around back now, we'll find the dog is outside. The brother's been watching us from the front window."

"True, but I've seen all kinds of people in my life as a nurse," Alina said. "A lot are plain paranoid and not necessarily for any valid reason."

Logan brought up the information on the neighbor's house. "Lingam. He owned both properties until the one was sold three years ago. He also owns another in the Melville District."

She waited a few minutes for him to come up with more information.

"Doesn't have gainful employment and appears to be forty-four years old. One brother deceased a year ago."

"The trouble is he seems too suspicious," Alina said.

Harrison gave a chuckle. "In our business, everybody seems suspicious, so too suspicious? … Is it really a thing?"

"But you know what I mean. It's almost textbook. Some guy peeking out behind the curtains of the windows, watching everything. Doesn't work, is a hermit."

"I'm not sure he's the bad guy at all," Logan said. "But you've got to consider if he isn't, the way he watches everything going on, he might very well know something."

Logan looked at Harrison. "My turn?"

Harrison nodded.

Logan opened the car door, slammed it closed, then knocked on Alina's window as he walked around the vehicle. She watched him approach the second house, go up to the front door and knock. He waited and waited, and then he knocked again. Finally, the door opened just a hair.

And Logan stepped forward to talk to the occupant.

Alina sat in the car and wondered what the hell he was asking the man?

LOGAN SMILED AT the tall, stocky man and introduced himself, holding out one of his cards. "Good afternoon. Are you John Lingam?" At the man's suspicious nod, Logan added, "We were looking for the previous owner of the neighbor's house. And I understand from her that she bought it from you."

Lingam stared at him with anger and a hint of fear. "Yes, it's mine…was mine," he corrected. "I needed the money, so I sold it off."

Lingam walked with a cane. Maybe that was why he didn't hold a job anymore. And it would make sense as to why he had sold the property.

"What do you want to know about that house?" Lingam stared at him. "I don't know nothing. I mind my own business and stay out of trouble."

"What kind of trouble?" Logan said quietly. "Is there any with that address?"

Lingam stiffened. "Nothing's going on there now. When my brother, Joe, lived there, it was a different story. He was no good. He was supposed to pay rent, but every month I had to fight him to get something. He never understood money, that I still had a mortgage to pay. Every month he gave me a fraction of what he owed me. He was bad news."

"Was?"

Lingam nodded. "Yes, he's dead now."

"How did he die?"

"The way most do in his world." Lingam shook his head. "He ran with some bad people." He stared out at the car. "I don't even know or want to know how bad. But he was shot one day on his front doorstep. I found him."

Logan nodded. "I'm sorry for your loss."

"Don't be. He was an idiot. He got hooked up with all kinds of nasty stuff."

"Drugs?"

Lingam shrugged. "He took several of his own. But I don't think he was dealing. It was way worse than that."

Logan studied him carefully. "Human trafficking by any chance?"

Lingam's face went white, and his gaze darted anywhere but to Logan's. His voice rose. "I don't know anything about that. And I don't want to. If he was involved, then he deserved what he got."

Lingam backed up and tried to shut the door.

Logan didn't argue with him. He said, "We need to find the truth. We're trying to break up a ring. If you have any information that can help these women, I would appreciate it."

Lingam shook his head. "I don't know anything about any women. That's all over with." But he stopped shutting the door. He looked hopeful as if Logan would confirm his words.

"No, it isn't. Not at all. We saved a woman yesterday. But we're missing fourteen right now."

Lingam's eyes opened in horror. "I don't know anything about that."

"Did you ever see any women come through that place?"

Lingam snorted. "You kidding? My brother had women coming and going all the time."

"Did he travel much? Did he have a large suitcase?"

A frown appeared on Lingam's face. "He did buy a really large one, saying he was going to travel. But he never went anywhere. He was too drugged and drunk, lying around the house all the time. He never worked, never did anything. It was hell to get my damn rent money."

"Interesting. I must ask, when he died, did you inherit anything? And if you did, was there any cash?"

Lingam nodded. "That was the weird thing. About sixty thousand dollars was in his account. And I found several more in the house when I cleaned out the place. He lied to me the whole time and refused to pay what he owed, yet he was stacking it up." He shook his head. "That's no way to treat family. And hell, I don't even know how he earned that money, and I don't want to. Good riddance to him."

"Do you know any of his friends? Remember any names? Men or women? Anything that would help us? And when he died, what did you do with his belongings? Was he living there alone? Or was there any evidence of someone else there?"

"He was living alone, but, yes, I cleaned out his crap." Lingam nodded. "It's all in the back shed. I don't want any of it. And if he's got anything to do with that human trafficking garbage, I really don't want."

Bingo. Logan gave him a slow smile. "How about I take it all off your hands?"

Lingam looked at him suspiciously. Logan nodded at the card in Lingam's hand. "Our company is working with the Boston Police Department. We'll see if anything in your brother's belongings connects to the current case. I can take it all now." If he had room. He glanced at the rental car and realized it depended on how much there was. "Or I can let the cops know it's here."

Lingam's face shut down. "No cops. I won't talk to them. I don't want to have anything to do with them. If you want it, you can take it now. I sold and got rid of whatever I could. The rest is sitting there. I didn't know what to do with it. Drive around to the back alley. A gate's there. I'll show you, but you have to forget my name. No cops coming around."

"I'll try to keep you out of it," Logan said. "But you understand, they may come back to confirm all the stuff came from you."

Lingam shook his head. "You drive to the side. I'll unlock the gate and show you the boxes. While you load, I'll write you a letter giving you permission. But no cops. I won't even open the door." And at that, he slammed the door in Logan's face.

Still, as far as gaining something valuable from the encounter, this could potentially be huge. He walked back to the vehicle and got in.

After relaying the info to Harrison, they drove around the block, parking behind the house in the alley.

Lingam was waiting for them and had opened the gate. They drove toward the shed. Logan hopped out and swung open the door.

A half-dozen boxes were stacked on one side. "This is all of it?"

Lingam nodded. "That's it. Take it all. Good riddance to him and this crap."

Harrison stepped in and grabbed two boxes, taking them to the car. Logan grabbed the next two. By the time he reached the car, the trunk was open. Then the last two were loaded in beside Alina.

Lingam locked the gate behind them, calling out, "And don't come back."

With letter in hand, signed by John Lingam, they drove away.

Chapter 9

BACK ON THE road again, Alina studied the boxes. They were dusty, old, and she couldn't imagine what was inside. She understood the theory that everything was important and any detail could lead to another, but it was hard to imagine these dirty, busted boxes held anything of value to the case. "Are we going back to the hotel now?"

"Yes." Logan added, "We're about fifteen minutes away."

"Can we pick up some lunch to take back with us first? Or do you want to eat at the hotel?"

"I saw a deli around the corner from the hotel on the same block. How about we try that?"

"It sounds good to me." She settled back, happy to know they hadn't forgotten about food.

At the hotel a few minutes later, the men got out with the boxes and carried them upstairs. Once inside the room, they put everything down on the floor.

"I'll get the food," Harrison said, "and we can go through all this stuff while we eat."

"Okay."

While Harrison was gone, Logan and Alina picked up the first box and opened it, carefully laying the contents across the bed. With the empty box on the floor, Logan went through every item of clothing, checking all pockets to see if anything was in them. He also made note of the sizes for each article.

She felt useless as she watched. "Is there anything I can do?"

He nodded. "Sure. Go through the clothing, check the pockets, see if anything's of interest."

She walked to the far side of the bed and stared at what appeared to be a sack of socks. She was sure it wouldn't have anything of interest. As she looked closer, the socks looked more dirty than clean. She said, "You might want to use a pair of gloves."

He laughed and threw her a pair of gloves from his pocket.

She was surprised, shook her head, and said, "If you'd seen all the things I've seen …" She put on the gloves and went through all the dirty socks, finding a few pairs of underwear, also not looking extremely clean. "Where do we put the stuff that has nothing in it?"

"Back in the box," he said.

Methodically they went through everything. When they came to the last shirt, he picked it up, checked it out and then put it in the box. Before they could open a second box, a rap was at the door as Harrison called from the outside.

"Logan, my hands are full."

Logan opened the door and let Harrison in. He carried a tray of paper coffee cups and two bags of food.

Placing the food down on the small dresser, he handed out the coffee. Then he opened the bags and handed Alina a large sandwich. They didn't make very much conversation while they ate. She settled back with her coffee as the men rose to start again.

Logan opened the second box, repeating the process with

everything. This box was also full of clothing, including shoes. But nothing else of interest was found.

When they opened the third box and repeated the process, she wondered if this was worth the trouble or if it was all junk.

By the time Harrison opened the fourth box, she could see from his face that he wondered about it too.

He glanced over at Logan and smiled. "We'll have a ton of garbage to get rid of. Hope they have a bin downstairs."

"Me too," Logan said. "I don't know why Lingam didn't do that in the first place."

Alina put down her coffee and said, "Let's do a trip now. It will give us more space."

The men looked at each other, glanced at the two boxes on the floor, and Logan asked, "Do you think you can lift it?"

She laughed as she stood. "Well, only one way to find out." She picked up a box and nodded. "This one's light enough."

Logan picked up the other. "I'll come with you."

She shot him a look. "I am pretty sure it's safe to walk to the garbage area."

He grinned. "But what if it's not?"

Together they walked downstairs and outside to find the dumpsters to get rid of their loads.

Motioning back to the hotel room, he said, "Let's go. After this, I really want a shower."

"Yeah, you and me both," she said. "Sitting in the shed for a year. It's gross."

"More than that, it's probably the way the man lived."

She winced. "That doesn't sound like fun either."

Back in the hotel room they found Harrison had filled

the fourth box back up again. Making a sudden decision, they picked up the two newly searched boxes and headed back out for another trip.

Afterward, Logan grabbed his coffee and sat for a moment. Harrison was laying out everything from the fifth box on the bed.

She really appreciated the methodical way they handled this, although it was frustrating. But still, she likely would've dumped this box upside down, gone through each piece and tossed it as useless.

However, this box appeared to have more knickknacks, books, notebooks, and the odd pair of shoes. She grabbed what looked like a small journal, flipping through it. Every page was blank. She set it off to one side and reached for a stack of papers, pulling it toward her, studying the scribbles on each. She didn't know if the men would throw this out because it was almost impossible to make heads or tails of any of it. She went through a dozen pages and found nothing legible. She placed them with the journal.

Logan was helping Harrison again. They went through the easy stuff—the rest of the shoes, the ties, and towels—until they only had what could be the most interesting of all of it so far. They each reached for a book, carefully checked out the spine, the front and back covers, held the book upside down to see if anything floated out free. One book was a paperback novel. The other a hardback. Neither yielded anything. After close examination, both ended up back in the box. Another twenty minutes, and they finally came to the end of that box's contents. The only thing she'd found were the odd pages with crisscrosses over them, as if they'd been grabbed to jot down notes at odd times, reusing the paper over and over. She held them out. "I don't know if anything is useable in this."

Harrison took the papers from her and sat, slowly studying the notes. He picked up the last pages and handed them to Logan.

Logan snatched them up and said, "Okay."

She lifted her head and studied him. "What?"

He held up the four pages so she could see them. Some of them had stains, like coffee had been sloshed over them. But the last entry was clearly legible, easily recognizable. And why wouldn't it be. It was her name.

LOGAN WATCHED HER face as she read her name on the sheet. Curiosity became horror.

She glanced back at all the stuff on the bed and the boxes on the floor. "He knew me?" She shook her head. "I can tell you that I didn't know him."

"And the question now is, why was your name on a piece of paper in his room a year ago?"

She slumped back in position. "I don't know," she cried in horror. She raised a trembling hand to her temple. "Unless he knows Colin, and they predetermined I was on the list of possible people to get kidnapped." She shuddered. "How horrible is that? To think people were plotting to kidnap me for over a year."

The stack of papers was set off to the side. Harrison, after determining nothing else of value was on the bed, removed everything else, putting it back in the box and opened the last one. And this appeared to be all notes, papers, journals, and books.

Logan said to Alina, "Hopefully this one will yield a little more information."

Once again, with everything spread out on the bed, the three stood and stared at the stack.

She shook her head. "Is this all that remains of a man's life?"

"That and sixty thousand dollars," Logan said. "Let's start with the books, and then we'll go through those loose pages."

Each took a book, and following the same procedure as before, carefully checked for notes or paper stuffed inside, something used as a bookmark that might be of interest, and if it had a jacket flap, anything that might be tucked underneath. Logan picked up a dog-eared journal.

He flipped through several pages; the beginning had been ripped out. Handwriting appeared on the next few pages, but it was very difficult to read. The rest of the book was empty. He checked the very last page, as he had a habit of doing so to write notes sometimes if he had nothing else handy. But it too was empty. He looked at the notes in the front again, not able to determine if they were of value or not. He set it off to one side and reached for another notebook. By the time they'd gone through everything, they found nothing else of value. Now they had all the loose pages they'd set aside.

Harrison picked up a stack. "Looks like a set of accounts scratched onto loose leaf pages but stapled together." He glanced through them. "Not a lot of accounting here. Whether that's him trying to keep a budget for himself or for the kidnapped women, who knows?"

"Do we know when these women were kidnapped?" Alina asked.

"No," Logan said. "So after all that, his address and your name is the connection. I wish we'd found more."

"But that connection is damn strong," she snapped. "I can't say I like seeing my name on any of these sheets."

Harrison was still flipping through lines of accounting entries.

Logan glanced around to see what else there was and found several crumpled-up pages. He opened each and spread them flat on top of the bed. Several contained numbers but had nothing to identify what they were. It looked like somebody doing simple accounting. He set them off to one side and kept going.

At the end of the stack he found another set of stapled sheets. He pulled it up and studied the entries. "And here's a connection to Colin." He tapped the paper and read out loud, "'Colin's asking for more money. He's getting paid enough.' And the word 'enough' has been heavily underlined." He glanced up to see Harrison studying him and said, "Since Joe is in cahoots with Colin, we have to assume he was part of this trafficking ring. Likely one of the minions below the four ringleaders. Joe either was paying Colin or negotiating, so he was caught in the middle between what Colin wanted and what the buyers wanted. Joe was not happy, but he's the one who ends up dead."

"Why would that be?" Alina asked. "It doesn't make any sense."

"It does if Colin cut out the middleman."

Looking ill, Alina sat on the chair, hugging her empty coffee cup. Logan glanced at Harrison and motioned toward her.

Harrison nodded. "Let's finish the rest of this," he said. "We'll have a box of whatever that we'll keep track of. The rest can go."

Although they went through the rest of the pages, they

didn't find anything of value aside from the stack they put aside. This time Harrison grabbed the boxes to toss in the dumpster.

Logan nodded. "I'll take this comforter outside. It's your bed, and we didn't consider all the dirt in those boxes." He rolled up the top cover so the dirt and dust would be contained. Then he stepped outside into the hallway, tossing the comforter into a laundry hamper. He returned and asked, "Do you think you need a cover? I can go find another one."

She looked up at him, confused, then looked at the blankets on the bed. "I'll be fine with what's here, thanks." She smiled. "Truly, I wasn't too impressed with the idea of having all that happening on the bed I was sleeping in."

"We should have had put a protective cover over it first."

He laid all the pages out on the bed again, and with his phone carefully took close-up images of everything. He did the same with the accounting sheets Harrison had. When he was done, he sat and sent the whole lot to Levi, quickly dialing and waiting for him to answer.

"A hell of lot of paperwork you sent us," Levi said.

"Yeah, but it also has Colin's name in there and Alina's."

He heard a low whistle on the other end. "Nice work. That certainly connects the three of them."

"Plus to a couple of the addresses you were sent," he said. "We didn't find anything at the house where we found the dead man." Logan cast a quick glance to Alina, but she didn't appear to be listening. "You have any update from the property?"

"He's one of the four men we were looking for. It's not evident yet why or who he might've known living at the property or even why he was there. The police are on it.

They suspect that the address was a holding property where the kidnapped women were kept and is now too 'hot' to be used again."

"You've told Jackson, I presume?"

"Yes. He's also very interested in the information you found. I'm waiting to hear further instructions from him."

Logan nodded. "Are we to stay here on location?"

"For the moment. I'll call back when I know something more. Still hoping to hear the police have something." Levi hesitated, then asked, "Where's Alina?"

"Right here," Logan said. "I have to admit that my instincts told me not to leave her alone."

"Right," Levi said, concern lacing his tone. "Am I to arrange for a spare bed here for her?"

Logan's eyebrows shot up. He glanced over at Alina. "That would be a long commute. She has a job here and is expected back at work in a couple days."

"Right," Levi said in a brisk tone. "Did you leave anything behind at her apartment?"

"I set the doors to trip so we'd know if anybody went in, and I left a bug in the living room." At that Alina glanced at him. He turned and smiled at her reassuringly. "So far nothing's been triggered on the bug."

"Okay, keep me posted."

Logan hung up, pocketed the phone and turned to face her. "It's the only way we could know if your apartment had been accessed." He crouched down in front of her and grabbed her hand. "Trust us. We know what we're doing and keeping you safe."

Chapter 10

SHE STARED AT him in shock. "It never occurred to me to figure out if somebody had gone into my apartment when I wasn't there," she whispered. She shook her head. "This is a nightmare that just won't end."

He hesitated, glanced over at Harrison, and then back at her.

She leaned forward, her hands gripping his hand. "What?"

"Our time here could be very short," he said. "That was my boss. We're to stay for the moment, but we can't forever. And you may have to face the fact that if this isn't solved, people could still be after you."

She shook her head. "What are you saying? That I should pack up my life and move because of this? How is it I can be safe in another location other than here? Wouldn't they track me?"

"It's possible, but at the same time, if you move out of their reach, it'll cost them that much more to go after you. They might want to cut their losses and walk away. A lot is going on behind the scenes. But at some point, our plug will get pulled, and we'll have to return to Texas."

She gently disentangled her hands and sat back, crossed her arms over her chest and contemplated what she was supposed to do. She didn't have any answers. What kind of a nightmare was this? "What if I took a leave of absence and went for a vacation?" She cast her eyes around the room, as if seeing her apartment, the few belongings she had. "To uproot my life and make a move like this with no job, place to live, or security…" She shook her head. "That's extreme."

"Is it?" Harrison asked. "Consider what the other option is. You stay home. You get relaxed, figure it's all over with and wake again tied up in another bedroom."

Her hand went to her chest at the reminder. She straightened against the chair back, fished her phone out of her pocket, opened her contacts and called Caroline. When the phone was answered, she said, "Caroline, it's Alina."

"Alina!" Her friend, overjoyed to hear from her, bubbled with good news. When she finally calmed down, she asked, "But you called me for a reason, right?"

Alina filled in her friend as much as she could, with an awful unpleasant silence greeting her on the other end. After a quiet pause of her own, Alina said, "The police haven't told me very much at all." She glanced at her watch. "I should've called them earlier to get an update. I don't know if I have to be here for a court case or what, but according to the two guys who rescued me, I'm still in danger."

"Of course, you're still in danger," Caroline cried out. "And that rat who kidnapped you said they would come after you. The chances are very good they will. That's it. You're coming down here."

"What good does that do?" Alina asked wearily. "I'm working and likely would be coming back and forth for the stupid trial."

"Are you kidding? That could be two years from now." Caroline let out a gust of breath. "I've tried to get you to move here anyway, so this is perfect."

Alina sat back, happy to hear her friend's voice, realizing how much she had missed her. "I don't have a job there or a place to live. And I don't have a ton of money. I can't be out of work forever." And yet, even she knew those were weak excuses.

"You're just afraid. You're afraid to make the move, like you were when I did. But surely the fear of being taken again must supersede the one of changing jobs and locations. I have a home. You can stay here with me until you're on your feet. And the hospitals here are screaming for nurses. You can move here." Caroline's voice was firm and adamant. "I'll even pay for your plane fare."

"And my furniture? What do I do with that? Am I supposed to sell it?" she asked, her voice rising at the end. "How does that make any sense when I'll need furniture at a new place?"

"It makes more sense than to ship it. All of it was secondhand when we bought it. We can do that all over again here."

"I can't walk away from my apartment, leave everything behind." She made a slow 360 turn, mentally calculating the contents of her place. "I have the couch, tables, and my bed."

"Put an ad for free in the newspaper," her friend suggested. "Everything will go on the first day. I'm not taking no for an answer."

"I'll call you back as soon as I talk to the police." Alina hung up the phone. She stared at Logan blindly. "She's pretty insistent that I move to Houston."

"Maybe the real question you must ask right now," Harrison said, "is why you wouldn't?"

And just like that she saw the enormity of the situation she was in. "I need a few minutes to lie down," she murmured. She sagged on the now-clean bed and curled up with her head on the pillow. She'd been holding on decently for most of the day, pushing back all the memories, all her fears under control because she had these two men standing by her. No way would she be kidnapped with her two bodyguards. But they had to leave soon. Then what?

Her eyes were wide open and completely dry, like the issue was too big for tears. The chasm between her old and new life was so vast, so wide and impossible to cross, she had no emotion other than shock.

She recognized his touch instinctively. Logan quickly scooped her up, pulled the blankets back and tucked her under, pulling them close to her shoulders. Harrison was a nice guy, but he was not the touchy-feely person Logan was. That touch wasn't irritable or cranky; it was easy, calming. Logan was holding her hand, giving her a hug, stroking her arms or cheek, or in some other way making contact with her most of the time. It helped her stay grounded in this crazy new reality.

But as she heard the men's voices whispering behind her, it was as if she had been fooling herself all this time.

She couldn't imagine going back to her place now. And if she didn't, where else could she go? She had slept there last night. But she'd had the two men with her. Now she was in their hotel room, strangers but not. She'd never felt safer. Yet it would only last if she was with them, and that wouldn't continue for long. They'd check out as soon they were told to. She didn't know if more was on their itinerary, but they were waiting for orders. They'd been here one night and were supposed to leave the next day. And that meant she had to return to her life. Without them.

When the shaking started, she didn't know how to stop

it. Maybe if she could sleep, it would do her good.

She heard a muffled exclamation before she was suddenly picked up, blankets and all, and tucked up against Logan's chest. The lights were turned down, and she didn't know if it was still daylight. The curtains were closed and she heard Harrison mumble something.

She whispered against Logan's chest, "I'm sorry, so sorry."

He held her close, rubbing her back. "You have nothing to be sorry about," he said quietly. "I've been expecting a reaction like this the whole time. I didn't quite understand how you were so composed."

"I'm not. When I finally realized what I could be facing forever, I understood then how much trouble I could be in."

"Or maybe you were in denial," he said. "It's our instinctive nature to look at things in a positive light."

She nodded her head. She wanted to convince him that she was okay, but the words wouldn't come. Instead, she turned her head into his chest and clung to him. He didn't talk or bother her with questions. He just held her close and rubbed her back. Some of his calm, his compassion, finally slipped into her consciousness, and she could feel the shaking ease. She took several deep breaths, and, lying against his chest, whispered, "Thank you."

"I have hardly done anything," he murmured. "I wish I could've saved you those couple days tied like that, panicking and afraid, worried about where you would end up. I haven't done anything. The problem is, I can't guarantee your safety if you stay here. We could put you in protective custody, but we know all too well how easy it is for somebody to get at the victim if they truly want to." He squeezed her tight against his chest. "I'm not saying that to scare you, but it is the reality. The criminal world has ways, means, and manpower that is almost impossible to beat sometimes."

She lifted her head and looked up at him. "What if you catch the bad guys?"

His gaze was hard and yet soft, determined and yet weary, as if he held too much knowledge of the world.

"We hope we catch all the bad guys, but you know how very slim the chances are, so we must focus on catching all who were after you."

"The only way to do that is… Surely the police will track down all Colin's associates." She was terrified for the fourteen women who had been kidnapped, still caught in that bad situation. "That big house. The expensive one. What are the chances the missing women are in there?"

He shook his said. "We don't know. All I can tell you is we're awaiting orders. We've done what we were supposed to, and I don't know what's coming next."

She glanced around the room. "Harrison left. Did I scare him away?"

"No. He went for a breath of fresh air and to make more phone calls. He'll be back in a little bit. You haven't had much time to yourself. We've needed to stay close to make sure you were okay."

She stared around the small room that had become home so very quickly. "I don't know what to do."

"I'm sorry that picking up stakes and moving is a hard thing for you because it would be so much easier if you disappeared from the grid. The men wouldn't have a clue where you were, and they wouldn't be able to track you."

She glanced at him and asked, "Can you make that happen?"

He looked down at her in surprise. "Make what?"

"Help me disappear. To get away from the city. From my apartment. From that world. Find a job somewhere, somehow." She paused. "It seems so real suddenly. Like the last forty-eight hours wasn't—like I pushed it away into the recesses of my mind—but now I can see how dangerous my situation is. I'm terrified of getting caught again."

"When you say *that world*, you mean your life? Your normal home and job?" Logan kept her tucked close and gently rocked her on the bed. "Well, it's probably a good thing you are more aware now. As to making you disappear…" He leaned back to consider it. "I'm sure we can help you. Not sure of the time frame." He glanced down at her. "How much of this is a passing whim on your part? You could change your mind tomorrow. Or a week from now. If we help you relocate to a new city, and you find a new job, are you going to regret it?"

She pushed herself off his chest and stared at him. "Will I be alive? Will I not be a sex slave or slave labor, or God-knows-what they had in mind for me? I might always wonder if this was a necessary step, but then the nightmares will remind me how bad it was being tied up in that bed, panicking to escape." With that line, she shook her head. "If I have to move, I want to go to Houston. At least that's where Caroline lives. She's been bugging me to move there as it is."

"Oh, I agree. But that's no guarantee they can't track you."

She nodded. "But it's about as good as I can get. It must happen quietly, like you and Harrison said. I don't know how much trouble it would be to change my name. Or if that's even necessary," she confessed. "I make decent money, and I have some saved, but I can't be out of work for six months."

She studied him as she pushed the blankets off her shoulders, realizing she was now sitting in his lap, a new situation for her but she liked it. He looked a little preoccupied, as if contemplating the logistics of making her disappear.

"What about the police?" she asked Logan. "We must tell them something. But it's hard to imagine rings like this operating within the city without some law enforcement knowing."

He tilted his head, his mouth in a grim line.

She hated the thought of the police being involved or at least knowing and turning a blind eye. She wanted to believe they were honest and doing the most beneficial things they could for the citizens of the city.

She stared around the hotel room. "Why Boston? I thought trafficking would be in places like Florida, Texas, or California."

He nodded. "They are. The fact is, human trafficking rings are operating in most states."

With that statement, she slumped back against his chest, not wanting to move away from the contact, his presence being so soothing, reassuring. He was big, strong, and indomitable that she couldn't imagine someone like Colin even thinking about kidnapping her from Logan. No one would want to provoke Logan's wrath.

Colin had been a weasel. He'd sneaked around behind people. She still found it hard to believe she'd been carried out in a suitcase. Her mom used to laugh at her when she was growing up, because she'd said she could take her traveling around the world whenever and wherever in a suitcase. It had been a joke at the time. Only now Alina realized how much of one it wasn't. It was an eye-opener to the world around her, showing her how shady it could be.

For the first time, she considered how very vulnerable every single female was. That didn't exclude married women from being victimized, but the former were much easier, particularly when they lived alone. And that was another reason to consider Caroline's offer. At least then Alina wouldn't be living alone, not for a while.

Although she didn't want to give up her independence out of fear. She could see how that was a step down a path she didn't want to take. She wished she could shrink Logan to a pocket-size elf to keep him with her forever—as if needing that security blanket he'd so generously supplied up to now. One part of her knew it was wrong. But the part that had been kidnapped and tied to a bed for several days didn't give a damn. She'd do a lot to keep this man around. He saved her once. The question was, could he again?

LOGAN COULD IMAGINE Levi's reaction. Particularly given his earlier comment about making a spare room available in the house. It wasn't what he'd intended at all. But at the same time, a disappearing act in this case would not be a bad idea. Was it something they could pull off? Hell, he knew they could. It certainly wasn't all that difficult. They could hire a company to come in and clean out her place, donate the furniture she left behind. It would be a simple matter of taking her back with them on a one-way ticket to Texas. That she was looking to move there was something he would call a coincidence, but he knew the rest of his friends would say it was Levi's hero magic happening all over again. Mason, if he ever found out, would be howling with laughter. But then he also would pat Logan on the shoulder.

He wasn't against running with the idea. He was with leaving these assholes behind to take off with her. She shouldn't have to spend the rest of her life looking over her shoulder. He pulled Detective Easterly's card from his pocket and sent a text. "Hopefully Easterly is closer to finding the other three men involved and the missing women. Then Harrison and I want to be involved when they take down this ring and fast."

She stared at him. "Here I am safe and snug, warm and well fed. They could be hurt right now. Or dead."

He rubbed her shoulders. "At least now we know there are other women. For the ones Colin was responsible for, the police have their IDs to track them down. Somebody knows where these women are."

She settled back somewhat, wrapping her arms around her chest. "Part of me wants this whole nightmare to go away. I want to run and never be reminded of it again."

"Understandable, but it's not just about you."

She frowned. "But can't we do something more about it?"

He smiled. "Harrison's outside right now, checking in with Levi, seeing what our next move should be. We'll do what we can while we are here."

When the door opened, Harrison walked back inside, his face serious and determined. "Levi sent a link and access to the documentation on the server." He motioned at the laptop sitting beside Logan. "Bring it up. They've mapped the women's locations, jobs, and given us a JPEG of all their faces. According to Ice all the women run the same type."

Logan set her gently aside as he stood. She sat up to ask, "Who is Ice?"

"Blonde Amazon woman. Hell of an ex-marine helicopter pilot we work with," Harrison said without even looking at Alina, but watching Logan boot up the laptop and login to the server.

Using the code Levi had sent, Logan brought up the files. Once he was in, he opened the map, and they could see Colin had been hunting locally. He tapped the monitor and said to Alina, "Come look."

She came nearer, looking over his shoulder. "Oh, my God! It looks so scary when you see it like that."

"Red dots are where the women lived. Blue are where they worked. The red are scattered around, but still all within the Boston area. But the blues were gathered in four specific areas." The hospital where Alina worked had dots. The university had several. A large assisted-living home had several more. And then the last one appeared to be another medical center of some kind.

She sat beside Logan. "Presuming Colin had some association with these places, it gave him access to roam freely to pick out his victims."

"Yes." Logan opened his email and sent the map to Detective Easterly. Anything they could do to help with the investigation was a good thing. He glanced at Harrison and asked, "Did they find any connection between the women, other than places where they worked, lived, and their general appearance?"

"No. But the workplace is how they were found."

Harrison put on a small pot of coffee in the room, then said, "Another folder in there has the missing person files for each of the women. Ice also made a time line, so we can see how long they've been missing and how much time elapsed between taking each one. Even though they had Colin, that doesn't mean they don't have other people scoping out women. Somebody else, like the dead brother, may be collecting women too."

"We need to contact Easterly or Levi. Find out if the police have any leads on how Joe Lingam died."

"But we know he was shot," Alina said. "Maybe by the same people who shot Colin?"

"Maybe, but it could be completely unrelated. It's hard to say."

"It will be," Harrison said. "I'm sending Levi a text to find out."

Logan opened the other folders. One had the case files. Another one with a time line, which he checked first. They were taking one woman every three to four months. Which meant many had been missing for years. He glanced at the time line. "The first one went back about four years."

Alina let out a shuddering gasp and dropped back down on the bed. She threw her arm over her eyes. "I don't think I want to see any more."

Logan reached across the bed and grabbed her hand, giving it a squeeze. When he went to pull free, she wouldn't let go. "We need to read the missing persons file for every one of these women."

Harrison shrugged. "Send them to me on my phone. Then we can both go over them." Within seconds they were settled in, reading the histories of the missing women.

Logan grabbed a notebook, one left behind from the brother but completely empty, flipped it open to the first page and jotted down notes as he read.

Chapter 11

ALINA OPENED HER eyes to realize she must've dozed off. She rolled over to see Logan still sitting beside her, reading the files on the computer. She yawned, sat up and slipped off the bed.

"How are you feeling?" he asked.

She smiled. "I'm fine. I hadn't even realized I was so tired."

Harrison spoke from behind her. "You'll probably do that for a few days. Shock and trauma sneak up on you. Your body needs to recover, and it'll take some time."

"And thanks to you guys, I have that," she added seriously. She made her way to the bathroom, and after using the facilities, washed her hands and took a careful look at her face. She still had scratches and bruises, blooming deep yellows and greens now.

Her phone rang on the night table, and she returned to the bedroom to answer it. It was her boss. "Hi, Selena." She smiled.

"How are you doing?" her boss asked. "I couldn't sleep thinking about you. I can't imagine what you're going through still. Are you back home? Are you sure you shouldn't be in the hospital still?"

"No, I don't belong in the hospital," she assured Selena. "But I have to admit I'm not adjusting as well as I'd hoped."

"If you need more time off, say so. You certainly have cause," Selena said. "Now when anyone misses work, I'm immediately worried. Take Tracy Evans. She didn't show up today. I'm sure she's fine. But knowing what happened to you, well, it's making me a bit paranoid."

"I'm sure she's not feeling well. She calls off almost once a month, remember?"

Selena sounded better by the end of the call.

When Alina put her phone away, she turned, Logan still reading files. "Did you guys find anything interesting in the women's files?"

Logan looked up. "Some basic similarities. Size and age, body type—the fact that ten of the women were taken either going to or coming from work helps, but not in any big way. They were likely stalked, picked out. The men probably tried to get close to the women, and, depending on the women's reactions, the kidnappers would know whether they would take the women from home or work. Every three to four months one goes missing."

Alina shook her head. "So, because you saved me, it means they're out looking for another one right now?"

"It's quite possible. No way to know who else would be targeted. Colin's friends could have any number of scouts out looking for potential victims."

Harrison spoke from the far side. "And yet, they'd keep the ring fairly small, tight-knit, and very well paid. Too many men means trouble. And the ringleaders will have proof of the girls they've kidnapped, in case anyone decides they want out. A job like this, there is no quitting. Which brings us around to Joe Lingam's file. Levi talked to Easterly. They have no leads. They believe it was a drug deal gone bad."

She nodded. "I presume the police are forming a task force, now that they know these cases are all connected."

"That would be the most likely prospect. But it'll be hard to warn every woman with this body type to watch out."

Alina frowned, her mind returning to her recent conversation with Selena. "Or they may already have the next one." Quickly she filled them in on her phone call.

Logan brought up Tracy Evans on Google and searched for an image. Alina leaned over his shoulder. "That's her. She's my height and body shape," Alina added painfully. "But how could they have grabbed someone so fast?"

"Probably because she fits the profile. It is definitely worrisome." Logan brought up his phone and called the detective. He explained about the woman, adding, "Normally this wouldn't be of such high concern, but she is five feet, four inches tall with a tiny frame."

She watched the relief on Logan's face. "He'll check on her," Logan assured Alina.

She nodded. "Then considering the hour, is anyone else hungry?"

Both men checked their watches.

Harrison laughed. "She's going to fit right in with the rest of them."

Alina turned to Logan. "The rest of who?"

"Other women we know. I mentioned them to you before." He laughed. "Let's get dinner. A break is a great idea right now."

"Maybe it's because you didn't feed me, or it's the stress, but I am hungry." She stood and picked up her sweater. "To go or can we go to a restaurant?"

"We should be totally fine to sit in a restaurant."

"Good. Where?"

The men rose and grabbed their jackets. Logan asked, "What do you want?"

She linked her arm through his. "I don't care, as long as there is lots of it."

He gave a bark of laughter and opened the hotel door. The three of them walked outside.

At the car, Alina asked, "Do you think Tracy might have been kidnapped? By the same people? And if so, how would they even know about her? Unless they scouted her out earlier like they did me."

Logan was silent, but Harrison spoke up. "If Tracy was taken according to some quota after you were freed, the kidnappers have a deadline to make. Or alternatively, if they already accepted payment for her …"

Alina felt that punch to her gut. "It's a hard thing to consider that because I was saved, somebody else is going to suffer." Glancing out the window, she realized she had no idea where they were. "How far away is Colin's place?"

Logan turned and looked at her. "Only a few minutes, why?"

"Did you search it?"

They shook their heads, and Logan said, "Not in-depth. The police arrived too quickly for us to do that."

She settled back in her seat. "Although I'm starving, we should check it out. He had to have a list of names of his prospective victims. If there's any chance it's still in his apartment, we should look for it."

The two men exchanged glances and shrugged. Harrison turned the vehicle on the next side street as he said, "We'll give it a half hour."

"I'll contact the detective to get permission," Logan said,

pulling out his phone.

She smiled, pleased with this turn of events. She could hear Logan talking in the front seat but not clear enough to understand the conversation.

At Colin's apartment building no sign remained that the police had been there. On the sidewalk, she forced herself forward. She didn't want to be here, but they had to look. At the apartment door, Harrison knocked. Although they had permission to enter, that didn't mean someone else wasn't inside.

Standing behind the men, she found herself hyperventilating. She'd been a fool to think she could do this.

As Harrison brought out a small tool and quickly opened the door, she slipped her hand into Logan's. When he squeezed her fingers, she immediately felt better. She might be back to the place where she'd been held captive, but she was no longer alone, and the circumstances were very different.

Inside the apartment, Harrison made a quick sweep to ensure they were alone, then they spread out. She headed to the kitchen first. Colin had coffee and food. But only for himself. Why waste spending money on her needs?

She could see signs where the police had been through the place, but she didn't know if they'd found anything helpful.

She started with the bottom cupboard. She went through every shelf and its contents very carefully. She couldn't imagine him going to too much trouble to hide something. He was lazy. This was easy money for him. The bottom shelves were empty. She went through every drawer. One for junk was of interest, specifically because something was jammed in the back. She took it out, carried it to the kitchen table, and returned the drawer to its slot. In the back was a small notebook. Black and a couple inches wide.

She pulled it out to take a look. It was hard to make sense out of most of it until she came to her own name. It wasn't her full name, just her first two initials and last. Her address was there, where she worked and a date—from like six months ago.

At the check mark below, her blood ran cold. Obviously she'd been on a list and had been checked off as accomplished. But below her name were several more marks. She got up and ran to Logan. He turned when she came in, holding out the notebook for him to look at.

"Where did you find this?" he asked.

"It was jammed in the back of the kitchen drawer. I took the drawer completely out to get at it."

Harrison came over and read the name below hers. "Do you know any of the names below yours?"

She read the rest of the page and shook her head. "No, I don't."

Logan said, "We should get this to the police right away. They'll contact these women and see if they are still safe." He turned the page and found four more names.

Alina's finger shot out and stabbed the last one on the list. "Tracy Evans." She gasped. "I can't believe her name is here."

The men exchanged looks as they both pulled out their phones. Once again, she felt useless. Scared of what she'd found. Hoping beyond hope that maybe the other women were safe. She returned to the kitchen to finish going through that drawer, then started opening the rest of the cupboards.

She found one with a boxful of keys and a satchel tossed

inside. The police would've gone through the bag for anything damaging. She pulled it out and checked. Too small to hold a laptop, but she'd seen kids at the university carry similar type bags. She did a quick glance through it, but it was empty. Which was why it was still here obviously. She went through the rest of the kitchen and didn't find anything more.

She went to the hall closet and opened it. More junk, a mop and brooms. Which really surprised her because he didn't seem to be doing any cleaning when he was here. On the upper shelf was cleanser, and above that had more cleaning supplies.

With nothing left to check, she went back into the living room. The men were still on their phones. She headed to the bathroom and gave it a very thorough check, then went to the bedroom. She remembered all of Colin's movements when he ignored her. He'd opened the night table and dresser drawers, plus the closet while she lay here. She checked out both tables, but there was nothing. She looked in the closet; nothing there. She knew there shouldn't be anything left to find. After all, the police would've been through this apartment.

The bed had been picked up, checked over thoroughly and obviously dropped again. It was on its frame on the box spring but askew. She got down on her hands and knees and checked underneath, but couldn't see anything. The bed was on wheels, so she grabbed the frame at the back and pulled it toward the doorway, to look behind the headboard. A part of it fell. As she reached for it, it fell all the way to the floor. An envelope was taped to the back.

She ran back to the living room. Logan had finished his call. "Come see what I found." Back in the bedroom, she pointed at the headboard.

He glanced around the bedroom. "Did you move the bed?"

She nodded. "I pulled it away from the wall. The police had obviously moved the mattresses and already dusted the headboard. We can see fingerprint dust all over it anyway. When I pulled the bed away from the wall, the headboard fell off." She pointed to the floor. "And this envelope was taped behind it."

He pulled out his phone and took several photos and then removed the 9x12 envelope. He walked back into the living room and held it so Harrison could see.

Harrison spoke into the phone. "I'll call you back. Looks like we found a hidden envelope too." He put his phone away. "Let's clear off the coffee table and empty the contents onto a smooth surface."

They were photographs. Lots of them. Most were of the women. All held in the bedroom, or in the suitcase, evidence that Colin had been the one who had taken them. Those who were tied up were bloodied, bruised.

None were of Alina. She sat back and said, "I'm so damn grateful I'm not among that nasty collection." She hung her head. "What's wrong with me? I should be feeling bad for the other women instead."

"All these women are unconscious. These are reprints. And if you aren't here, we have hope that, while you were unconscious, he wasn't up to other stuff." He held up one photo with a woman nude, obviously tied and unconscious.

Alina clapped her hand over her mouth and shook her head. "Oh, my God." She wrapped her arms around her stomach and paced the small apartment.

Logan lined up the photos, recognizing most of the faces

from the files Levi had gotten access to. Logan looked inside the envelope and found one more picture. He pulled it out and dropped it to the table on top of the others. This one was of men.

Harrison picked it up, studied it. "And why the heck does he have this here?"

Logan looked. "Blackmail. In case anything ever went wrong, he had this photo along with all the women."

"So, if we can identify the men in this photo …"

Alina walked back over to them. "How many are there?"

"Four in the photo. And if I'm not mistaken, they look familiar. As in the ringleaders who were released and disappeared. But the photo is older, so we'd have to confirm my ID."

Harrison looked over at her with respect. "This was a really good find."

She nodded, but didn't feel like smiling. "It's also horrible. A couple of those women don't even look like they're alive."

Logan picked up several and turned them over. "Names and dates. Likely the time he picked them up."

"And something else. A number. This one says sixteen," Harrison said.

"Is that victim number sixteen?" she asked. "Or was he paid sixteen thousand?"

Logan shook his head. "It's too hard to tell what the number represents." He checked them all. They were all numbered. "The first couple have more information though. This one says, 'eight thousand, Jason.' The second, 'ten thousand, Lance.' Two of the first names of the four suspected traffickers. It's quite possible in the early days these are the men who paid Colin directly. All in all, there are four different men's names, matching the four we're looking into. The rest don't include names. There are fourteen photos, each one of a different woman. At least we know that's how many we're looking for. I was afraid fourteen purses were actually just the most recent missing women."

"Again it's more proof that he was involved. But hopefully these photos are the ones we really can use." Harrison then lined them up carefully, took pictures and then returned them to the envelope. "We should take these to the police." He stopped and looked at Alina. "Do you feel like you've had a good look, found everything there is to find?"

She shook her head. "I never checked his dresser." She ran back to the bedroom, buoyed by the two things she had found. In both cases, they would be hugely useful. They went through all the drawers, pulling every one out, checking inside, around, and behind them, but there was nothing more.

At the end, she asked the men to pull the dresser away from the wall, saying, "I found the envelope when moving the headboard, and the back panel fell off. Maybe the back of this comes off too."

The men did that and then carefully pried off the back. It matched the headboard, so they had to check. With the back removed, they found nothing more.

Still not ready to leave, she headed to the night table, took off the stuff on top and turned it upside down to lie on its side on the bed. She checked it over but found nothing.

Harrison grabbed the other one and did the same. She went back to the headboard, still on the floor, and checked to make sure they hadn't missed anything. Finally, she stood in the room and said, "I don't think anything else is here."

Both men nodded, and Harrison said, "And we would

agree with that."

Logan reached out a hand to grasp hers. "Let's go. We'll drop these off at the police station, then get that food we promised you."

She gave him a grateful smile. "At least now I feel like I earned a meal. I couldn't stand the thought that another woman might be missing, and here I was warm, free, and being fed while she was likely tied to a bed. She probably still is, but maybe now we can track her."

"What we can confirm is she's been taken by the same group of assholes. And her time will run out—soon."

AT THE POLICE station, Logan kept his arm around Alina. It was either that or let her pace until her shoes had holes in the bottoms.

Coming into the police station was unnerving for a lot of people. In her case, it was very understandable. But he thought it was more the realization that another woman had been taken in her place. She'd been amazingly resilient so far. He wanted her to hold on a little longer.

They had to meet with the police, and Logan would keep it as short as possible. After that they'd head off to a restaurant, feed her and then take her back to the hotel. He was hoping she'd go to sleep easily. But he wasn't sure if it was possible tonight.

Last night she'd slept, but that was more about physical exhaustion. He knew she was still feeling incredibly sore, but apparently she was the kind who never complained. And she had no prescription to be filled, so she was handling her injuries without painkillers. That made him respect her even more.

After asking for Detective Easterly by name, they were escorted to a table in a small room. They all took seats on one side and waited. The detective came in quickly with a notepad. When they showed him all the stuff they'd found, he shook his head.

"I can't believe any of this was missed."

But when they explained where the stuff had been found, it helped to mollify his anger.

As they handed it all over, Logan said, tapping the picture with the males, "We think this picture of the four guys is connected to all these women individually photographed. That this is the group of kidnappers and these were their victims. We need to find proof of that though." He spread out the women's photos. "The early ones have men's names on the back. We're really hoping that has something to do with these male faces. If we're lucky, that might be the names to help identify them. A lot of photos have no male names written on the backs."

Detective Easterly quickly went through the photos, then looked at Alina. "None are of you." He looked at each man with a hard glare, as if thinking they had stolen it to protect her.

"I don't remember him ever taking any. I never saw him with a camera." She shook her head. "Chances are he takes his photos and then gets them printed. He didn't have time with me."

The detective dropped his gaze to the pictures and nodded. "That's possible." He picked up the notebook and shook his head. "So many women."

"And under my name is a check mark," she said bitterly. "Nice to know he was keeping track."

Logan leaned forward and tapped the name at the very

end. "This woman is the one I called you about. She didn't show up for her shift at the hospital. Unfortunately, we're afraid she's been taken in Alina's place."

The cop nodded. "Given her physical stature and similar size…it's all too likely. Forensics are all over the suitcase, and they've found hair and in some cases blood. There are also epithelial cells. It's gonna take a while, but we will get to the bottom of it." He glanced over at her. "Where are you staying? And are you back at work?"

She shook her head a little too violently for the occasion, Logan thought. He reached over and grabbed her hand to help her calm down. She took a deep breath. "I stayed the first night at my place. The guys were with me to make sure I could actually get some sleep, but I can't stay there anymore," she said. "Look what they just did. Colin threatened they would come after me. But now that they've taken Tracy, I don't know if they're still after me or not. I want to leave. I want all this to go away."

The cop's face softened. "I'm sorry this happened to you. We're doing our best to solve it."

She reached out with both hands and clung to Logan. "Can I leave town? Go to Texas and stay with a friend there?" She looked at the cop hopefully. "I'm just so scared. I don't want to be alone anymore. I have nobody here."

The cop frowned. "As much as I understand you need to get away …"

Logan butted in. "Unless, of course, you can do a round-the-clock detail for her?" There was no budget for such a thing. "Otherwise we can escort her to Texas and see her settled with her friend there. She should be able to build a new life and hopefully forget this one. She can fly back for the court case."

Detective Easterly frowned, staring at the new evidence in front of him.

Alina squeezed Logan's fingers hard as if to say thank you.

Harrison added smoothly, "Of course we won't be leaving just yet."

Detective Easterly looked up and nodded. "You guys came up with a lot of very helpful information. Not everybody here is very happy about that. But we must find these missing women, and fast. Worrying about egos is not my department right now."

Logan grinned. "It's all right. We understand. We'll do what we can while we're here."

"I had Artie track down the woman's address. We had a black-and-white go over there, but she's not answering her door. Now that I see Ms. Evans's name here, we'll assume the worst. We'll get officers inside her apartment."

Logan lifted that piercing gaze of his and stared at her. "Can you think of anybody else who might've been involved? Any chance somebody you work with might have been helping Colin?"

She shook her head. "I can't imagine. It never occurred to me what Colin had been doing. I never liked him, but still didn't think he was capable …"

The cop's gaze narrowed with interest. "How often would you see him, and how did he try to approach you?"

"He kept asking me for dates, but I kept saying no. Then the day I was kidnapped, I went the cafeteria to get coffee. It was after my shift, and he was there, so I sat down with him." She shrugged. "Honestly, I don't remember anything after that."

The cop nodded. "Chances are he drugged your coffee."

"Because I was snatched from the hospital where I worked," she said in a trembling voice, "I don't want to go back there. All I'll ever do is look over my shoulder."

Logan wanted to add something, but knew it wouldn't help. It wouldn't matter if she went to this hospital or not ever again. It would take a long time to stop looking over her shoulder regardless. He'd known several people who had been kidnapped, and one thing they always felt was that sensation of heading into danger again. They always carried that feeling of having to watch their back to make sure they were safe.

She glanced at the other two men. "But I'll feel so much better when all these missing women are found, especially Tracy. She's the most recent and should be easiest to track, right?"

At that, the detective's phone rang. He answered it; the others waited while he finished the call. "That was the black-and-white. They're at the apartment right now. The door was open. The lock showed signs of forced entry. No sign of her in the apartment."

With that Alina sank back with a cry. Logan reached out and held her in his arms. "Calm down. This is not your fault."

"But if you hadn't rescued me, she would have been safe."

Harrison shook his head. "You can't think like that. For all you know, they were planning on snatching her too. Her name is in the book."

She stared, her mouth open. "What kind of a world do we live in where they'd take women from their homes and put them in suitcases to sell to the highest bidder?"

Logan looked at the cop, but he was phoning someone

again.

"Does the apartment building have security cameras?" he asked Easterly.

He smiled at Logan and said, "Give me a couple minutes. I'm checking." While they waited, Easterly rose and excused himself. When he came back, he said, "Yes, they do. Getting the videos right now to look." He turned to Alina. "I'd like you to watch, see if you recognize the person taking her out of her apartment. Of course, I can't guarantee any decent imagery. But, just in case, would you mind waiting until we can look?"

She bolted to her feet. "No, I don't mind. Yes, I'll definitely look at the video. Anything to help find her."

Easterly took them to another area, where several monitors were set up. He asked her to take a seat, and with Harrison and Logan standing behind, they watched the camera feed. And sure enough, sometime earlier today, a large male, tall, his back to the camera, popped the outside door open and in seconds was inside Tracy's apartment. The recording came with no audio, so they couldn't hear what went on. They fast-forwarded, waiting for the man to come out. When he did, he pulled away a large suitcase on wheels.

"Where did he get that from?" Alina asked.

Logan said, "He probably delivered it to her apartment earlier."

The cameras followed him to the elevators. But he was very careful to keep his face out of sight. He disappeared into an elevator. They switched to a camera inside it, but again, he kept his face out of view. They followed him outside, but it never once caught a glimpse of his face.

He was tall though. And large. She tried to place a physique like that but didn't really see a resemblance to anyone she knew.

He stopped outside on the street, turned toward the first intersection. He looked up, then crossed the street.

Logan asked, "Can you patch into the city cameras from here?"

Detective Easterly called over a different police officer. He sat, shifted programs and on the screen on the right brought up the camera at the intersection. Sure enough, it caught the full face of the man hauling the suitcase.

Logan yelled, "That's it. I know who that is."

Detective Easterly asked, "Who?"

Logan turned to Harrison. "Do you recognize him? From this morning?"

Harrison nodded. "Oh, yeah. That's the asshole who gave us the boxes he had kept after his brother's death." He snorted. "That's John Lingam, terrified to talk to the police, brother of Joe, whose address was linked to the four traffickers."

Chapter 12

LEAVING THE POLICE station and heading for the nearest restaurant that looked good to them all, Alina asked Logan, "Did you mention it to Levi?" This time she was in the passenger seat while Logan drove.

He obviously understood her cryptic question. "Why?"

She shrugged. "I guess I'm wondering when you're leaving. And what your response is to my earlier request." She shot a sideways glance toward Harrison; he was stretched out in the back seat, his legs up, listening. She frowned at him. "Did Logan tell you?"

Harrison nodded. "I can't say I'm surprised."

Her eyebrows rose. "Why?"

"Because in this situation, I'd want to get a hell of a distance away too. And disappearing is something I can do. It would be a lot harder for you without help."

Then Logan's phone rang. "Levi, what's up?"

"One of the four traffickers has turned himself in—Lance Haverstock. He says he and the two other men killed Colin Fisher and Jason Markham, the man you found. The other two are still in the wind. But Haverstock's spinning quite a tale."

Logan stood. "That makes sense. Taking care of any weak links now after being arrested, making sure the cops can't make a case stick."

"We can't afford to assume anything at this point." Levi paused for a moment and then said, "How is she holding up?"

"Scared. Feeling guilty. Otherwise she's doing fine. She's healing, but it'll take time. She wants to disappear in case they should try again."

"Smart of her. Where does she want to go?"

Logan winced. This wouldn't be good. "She has a friend in Houston." He could hear Harrison chuckle from the back seat. And also the stark silence on Levi's end of the phone.

Then Levi laughed. "I guess my intuition was right on when I asked if I'm supposed to make room for her here."

"That shouldn't be necessary. Her friend moved away from Boston a few months ago. I guess they've been very close since they were kids, only Alina wasn't prepared to make such a drastic move."

"And how about now?" Levi's tone was dry. "What should we do to make it happen?" His tone turned brisk. "I presume she has furniture to be disposed of, and the place needs to be emptied, and the lease canceled. What about her job?"

"She's been given several days off, but she's considering telling them she can't handle returning to work after what happened. I'm sure they'd understand and let her walk without any penalty."

"Right. Let me call you back."

Alina watched as he put his phone away.

He shrugged and said, "He'll get back to me."

She leaned over and kissed him on the cheek. "Thanks for taking the chance."

He raised his eyebrow. "What chance?"

"To help. Even if Levi can't do anything about it, I appreciate the thought."

They chose a restaurant and quickly ordered, Logan aware of Alina's need to eat. After they finished their dinner and ordered coffee, Harrison contacted Detective Easterly for an update on Tracy's fate. He hit speaker and laid the phone down on the table so they could all hear the conversation.

"The men went through the place but found nothing. No sign of him or her." The cop was frustrated and angry. "We followed the city cameras, but he must have another hideaway where he can take her, or he delivered her right away. We're still tracking down where he went from his last position."

Logan spoke up. "Make sure you check any properties under Joe's name. The brothers felt a great deal of animosity for each other. Although Joe rented the house next door from John, Joe still might have had another place. He had a lot more cash than his brother knew about too. Also, John had a second property in the Melville District."

"If we can believe anything he said," Easterly added.

"Right." Harrison leaned forward. "Let us know what we can do."

The detective rang off, and the three of them stared at each other. Logan was worried about Alina. The color had washed out of her face. Though she had just eaten, she looked like she was ready to pass out. He covered her hand with his. She barely moved. He glanced at Harrison and raised an eyebrow. Harrison nodded. Not a whole lot they could do but get back to the hotel and keep her safe. They asked for the check.

When they cleared the bill, Logan helped Alina to her feet. Keeping an arm around her shoulders, he led her out the front door. "We have to trust they'll find her."

"I trust that *you* will," she corrected. "I'm not sure about anyone else."

He tucked her closer and held her. When Harrison walked out of the restaurant, the three proceeded to the car, Harrison driving this time. They were only a couple blocks from the hotel.

In the car, Alina asked, "Can we drive past John's place?"

Logan winced. "That's not likely to help."

She stared at him, and the dark wells of emotion in her eyes made it hard for him to argue.

Harrison shrugged. "Why not? Maybe we can figure out where she is. Joe had a place of his own even when he lived at his brother's house. John might have inherited property from his brother or used the cash he got after his brother's death to buy the Melville District property."

"You think he kept it?

"Why not? It's not like the market has been very good for sellers. And if he had any connection to the business his brother was in, then maybe this was a good opportunity for him to step into his brother's place."

"It's only three women in a year for Colin. We don't know that this brother wasn't also procuring several in that time. Or maybe his brother was a trial run? Or they worked together. We know it was connected. Maybe one was the scout, and then they switched off who got to kidnap the women."

She shook her head. Her voice low, hard, and painful. "I know several women are suffering right now, and I'd like to do anything I can to help them."

Logan had the laptop open, already running properties under both brothers' names. "If it's that obvious, the police would've been there already though."

"I don't think he's a hardened criminal. His brother, yes," Alina said. "I'm hoping he will go home and take his prize with him. What if he had to go somewhere first? And what if he hadn't quite made it home? What if, once he got close, he was worried, remembering you guys had found him, wondering if the cops might come too? What if he then made a sudden decision to go somewhere else? Can they track down his vehicle? Perhaps he knows a citywide search for him has begun. But what about hotels? Has anybody checked them, particularly ones between his place and where he was last seen on the cameras? There's more than a couple, I'm sure."

"Joe did have a small apartment, but it was sold about six months after his death. Apparently, he had rented it from time to time and used the income to live off while staying in his brother's house with various friends. Let me check some of the names out." A moment later Logan spoke again as he read the information flashing on the screen. "Found another property listed to Lingam with the names reversed. So instead of John Lingam, it's Lingam John, and it's only a couple blocks from the house we were at. We're less than two minutes from that property anyway." Logan quickly gave Harrison directions, and within minutes, they pulled in front of a rundown house that looked to be deserted. Several other similar-looking residences were in the neighborhood—ready for demolition or just unkempt, like renters hadn't given a damn. The front lawn wasn't mowed, the front door needed paint, and to have the roof shingles replaced. Maybe it wasn't just the tenants, but also the owners. He studied the property and then drove past and parked.

Logan turned to look at Alina in the back seat. "You want to come or stay here?"

"I'm coming," she said. She opened the door and hopped out.

Logan did the same beside her. He reached out, grabbing her arm. "You stay at my side then." He infused his voice with enough power for her to understand she had to listen to what he said.

She glanced at him and nodded.

HARRISON WALKED AHEAD as if not together with them in any way. He walked to the front and rang the doorbell. The two of them kept well back. When no answer came, Harrison walked around to the back of the house.

Logan's phone buzzed. He pulled it out.

The text from Harrison read **Come to the back**.

With a quick survey of his surroundings, Logan led Alina on the sidewalk that went all around the house. At the back, he saw a fenced yard. The fence itself seemed to be in better shape than the rest of the property.

Harrison stood at the back door and said softly, "Door's open."

The two men frowned, staring at each other, assessing the odds. Logan glanced down at Alina, wishing she wasn't with them now.

As if catching his train of thought, she glared at him. "I'll be fine. Go in and check. Make sure the place is safe."

"Stay here."

She stepped to the corner, out of sight from almost every angle. "Good idea. Go search. See if she's in there."

He ran up the porch steps, and together he and Harrison entered the house. The place was dark and empty. They did a sweep of the first and second floors, but found nothing. No one had been here in a long while.

As they were ready to leave the house, a vehicle pulled around to the side of it. Harrison grabbed Logan's arm. "Go to Alina and get her out of here. I'll stay and see who it is."

Because of the position of this new car, they couldn't leave from the back door anymore. They both slipped out the front, and Logan raced around to the back, grabbed hold of Alina and took her to the side of the property where she couldn't be seen.

She was trembling in shock. "Did you find her?"

"No. A vehicle just drove up, and we have to get you away safely."

She dug her feet in. "It's probably him. We have to see if she's here."

"Cops are on the way." His voice hardened when he added, "I have to make sure you're safe."

She shoved her chin up and forward. "You can't make my safety a priority over another woman's."

He glared down at her. "And that's where you're wrong. I will do everything I can to keep you safe. I will also do the same for her. But we don't even know for sure she's here."

"So, find out," she cried in exasperation. "Stash me somewhere safe and then go."

He gave her a lopsided grin. "And where do you think you're safe?"

And she realized she'd have to go to the car. She rolled her eyes. "I'll lie down in the back seat. I promise I won't sit up, so nobody will know I'm there."

He shook his head. "If anybody's watching, they already know you're here." He opened the back door to the rental and helped her get inside. "Stay out of sight."

He closed the door and then turned to study the house.

Harrison bolted toward him. “Move. He’s backing up. Let’s go.”

“Go, go, go!” Logan raced to the driver’s side of the car, hitting the unlock seconds before Harrison dove in the passenger seat, and Logan hit the road at top speed. They weren’t about staying hidden anymore; they were focused on following John. This was about making sure the asshole didn’t shake them.

Logan could hear Harrison’s call to the cops, but he didn’t take his attention off driving through traffic ahead of them. “Hang on. Make sure your seat belt is buckled,” he tossed back to Alina.

“It is,” she said in an almost panicked voice. “Don’t let him get away.”

“I’ve no intention of it.”

Harrison said, “The cops are setting up a roadblock. Helicopter will be in the air in ten. At the rate he’s driving, we might have a major car crash.”

He could hear the panic in Alina’s cry behind him. He reassured her. “Not from us. That guy is driving incredibly recklessly. He’s desperate to get free right now. When we catch him, he’s looking at twenty years in jail.”

“Hopefully more,” Harrison snapped. His phone rang.

Once again Logan could hear him talking—he presumed to the cops.

“We’ve taken two rights,” Harrison relayed the directions into the phone. “They got us on satellite now. The request is to stay on him, hoping to direct him toward the freeway, where they are setting up a roadblock on the on-ramp.”

Logan watched the getaway vehicle speed through a red light. He was forced to put on the brakes as the cross traffic picked up between them.

Behind them Alina cried out, "He's getting away."

"No, he's not," Logan snapped. "I can still see him ahead of us."

Although this guy was smart, making several turns to lose Logan, no way in hell would Logan let this asshole get away. As soon as the light turned green, he jumped forward, picked up speed past the turning traffic and caught sight of the vehicle ahead. Keeping an eye out, he completely disregarded traffic signs. He pushed the small car to top speed as he slowly gained on the kidnapper.

"The cops don't want you to be right on his tail. If you can, they're asking that you stay back a little." Harrison was back to talking to whoever was on the other end of his phone.

Logan nodded to say he understood. That wasn't quite so easy. He let up on the gas. At a distance he saw an opening between vehicles and moved over a couple lanes. "I think he's headed toward the highway."

"Looks like it," Harrison said. He tapped the laptop. "Stay straight. If we can push this guy to the right-hand turn, a roadblock will be waiting for him."

"Looks like he's about to take the right turn…"

The getaway car, at the very last moment, took a hard right and spun onto the on-ramp. Logan, farther behind, turned easier. They were headed into a roadblock.

"He's not slowing down," Logan's voice rose as he watched the car speed up, racing straight for it. The car clipped the police and kept on going as men dove out of the way.

Logan leaned on the horn, letting the cops know he was coming through as well. Only remnants of the blockade were left. Driving the vehicle hard, Logan went full speed ahead, thankful for a small opening to let them inside the flow of traffic. He was two cars behind. Now he could hear the helicopter.

Alina called out, "It's above us."

"Good. They should keep track of where he's going," Harrison snapped. "If he's fully tanked up, he can go a hell of a long way."

"We have to hope he runs out of gas."

The vehicles between Logan and the runaway transferred over to the center lane, and Logan moved up.

"Several fields are up ahead, all bordered by heavy woods," Harrison said.

Logan barely had a chance to notice the surrounding countryside when the getaway vehicle ahead took a hard right and drove straight off the road into the fields and dropped into a bit of a ditch. But then it bounced down and right up over the ditch and ripped into the high grass, heading for the trees on the far side.

"Hang on," Logan yelled.

He took the angle slightly better down into the ditch and back up on the other side, then turned the wheel and straightened. The other car stopped ahead. As they reached the vehicle, they saw Lingam disappear into the wooded area, showing no sign of a limp.

Harrison called back. "Check the car for the girl." And he was gone after Lingam. Two more police vehicles pulled behind them. Logan told them to start searching the woods. Two men took off on the manhunt; another came over toward the car, and together they popped the trunk and sure enough found the suitcase.

Alina stood bedside them. "Hurry, hurry, hurry. How

much air could possibly be in there?"

The men glanced at each other as they carefully lifted the heavy suitcase out. Logan was surprised at the actual weight. It also gave him hope. They laid it on the ground, struggling to unclip the locks on the suitcase.

"Hurry, open it," Alina cried, dancing impatiently.

Finally the locks gave way, and they threw the lid back.

Inside lay a small woman, curled up tight. Logan shook his head. "Damn, that's a tight fit." And worse, her skin tone was lax, white.

"Let me see her," Alina said. "Move out of the way."

She squeezed in front of the cop and reached down for the woman, searching for a pulse, any sign of life.

The cop protested until Logan said, "She's a nurse."

Then he stepped back and pulled out his phone. "I'll get an ambulance for her."

Alina lifted her face, tears in her eyes, and whispered, "She's alive. Oh, my God! We made it in time. She's alive."

Chapter 13

ALINA CAREFULLY DIRECTED the men to lift Tracy out of the suitcase. That was a delicate operation. She was in so tight, they had to move her joints individually to ease out each limb. When they finally had her free and stretched out on the grass, Alina could work much better. She didn't have any equipment, but she was bound and determined to see if Tracy had any further injuries. Behind her she could hear the men's voices.

The cop said, "The ambulance is on the way."

It was a damn good thing because Tracy's color and heartbeat were incredibly erratic. Alina also found the injection site which pretty much matched hers. As she checked over the woman's body, she was relieved to find no broken bones. She sat back on her heels and stared at Logan. "With any luck, she'll sleep through this whole thing, and not remember any of it."

Sitting down beside her, the cop asked, "She's drugged?"

She pointed to the injection site.

"Yes," Logan said. "She didn't have the same bad reaction you did."

Alina nodded. "Looks like they only injected once. He didn't have her long enough to do much more than that." Under her breath, she added in a heartfelt whisper, "Thank God."

Logan straightened her up and pulled her into a hug. "You did well. We found her, and she'll be okay. Now, you're not to blame, you hear me?"

She nodded, her gaze still on her coworker. "I know that. At least a part of me does. But …"

He gave her a little shake. "Stop. That's enough. Forget about these guys and go about living your life again."

Alina looked at him and smiled. "Live my life where?"

He motioned to Tracy. "Has finding her changed how you feel about not returning to your job? Do you feel better about your decision?"

She glanced down at the ground. "It helps me leave with a clean conscience," she replied, adding, "but it doesn't change the fact that I went through what I did. And that experience is now tattooed in my brain. I don't know if I'll ever feel comfortable at my place or work, but in some ways, it feels like a chapter closing. No"—she shook her head—"let me rephrase that. It feels like one has slammed shut. Even if I could go back to those two places, I don't want to." She turned in his arms.

"Good enough. I didn't want to unfairly persuade you to move to Texas," he said. "But I'm really hoping you do."

She pushed back slightly, looking at him. In a low voice, very aware of the cops milling around and the ambulance quickly turning off the highway, racing toward them, she asked, "Seriously?"

He leaned forward and kissed her gently on the forehead. "Seriously."

She slipped her arms around his waist and leaned in. Her heart swelled with joy when his went securely around her. She didn't want to feel dependent on him; neither did she want to view him as an escape. Because those things weren't good long-term. And to think she may have found somebody through this maelstrom of horror, well, that made up for a lot. He was a good man.

"We'll get the asshole who kidnapped her," Logan said.

With the ambulance moving toward them, they stepped out of the way. When the men loaded Tracy onto the gurney, Alina turned to Logan and said, "I should go with her to the hospital. I don't want her to wake up alone."

He nodded in understanding. "You've got your phone. Let us know when you're ready to leave."

She nodded and walked toward the ambulance, stopped and turned to look back at Logan. "You'll call me if I can't get through to you, right?" She hated the fear and tremor in her voice, but this wasn't the time to hide her worries. She needed to know if he would be there.

His grin flashed bright. "You're not getting rid of me that fast." But he did ask that a policeman ride with her and Tracy.

She gave him the sweetest smile she could, then turned and climbed into the ambulance. She knew the hospital's policies. She might not be allowed at the woman's side, not being family. But since Alina was there at the time of Tracy's rescue, and Alina had already gone through the same experience, she was hoping the hospital personnel might make an exception for her.

They weren't far from the hospital. She was grateful she wasn't on the gurney this time.

She could see Tracy's vitals as the EMTs checked them. Her heart rate was very slow. Who knew what or how many drugs she'd been given?

The ambulance kicked on its sirens and drove as fast as it could back to the hospital. Alina realized the attendant shared her concerns too.

At the ambulance bay in the emergency area, Alina hopped out first to get out of the way while the EMTs unloaded Tracy. She was rushed into the emergency room, and Alina was left to mill around, feeling left out. She wasn't a nurse in that department, but she'd done several stints there, so she understood the process and procedures. But she'd never been on the other side, waiting for a victim to receive treatment.

She didn't like it one bit. It was unnerving to sit and wait, trusting in others to get the job done correctly. Part of her wanted to race in there, make sure they were doing everything they should be, and another knew she did not have the right. That was their domain. She could say she was a nurse until she was blue in the face. But she wasn't in charge. Finally, when she didn't hear anything, she asked a nurse who had come out of Tracy's room, "How is she? May I sit with her?"

The woman frowned, opening her mouth.

Alina explained how she had been in the ambulance with Tracy, had been there on the spot when she was rescued, and in the same kidnapped situation as the patient. "I don't want her to wake up alone with that nightmare in her head. Please let me sit with her." Then she added, "I don't know if makes any difference, but I am a nurse. I work out of University Hospital."

The woman nodded. "The doctor is about done. When he is, you can come in a few minutes later."

Grateful, Alina said, "Thank you. I appreciate that."

The woman turned to look at her. "You were kidnapped as well?"

"The same human trafficking ring, different kidnapper."

The woman shook her head. "Who'd have thought there'd be such a problem in Boston?"

Alina went in a few minutes later and sat beside Tracy's bed. She reached out and covered her coworker's hand with her own. She knew how important it was for people in a drug-induced state to believe they had a purpose to return, a reason to live. And she wanted to make sure the kidnapper couldn't claim another victim.

"Hi, Tracy. I'm Alina. I was there when the police found you," she said. "Just know that you're safe here in the hospital, and you'll be fine now."

There was no response, but then Alina hadn't expected one.

She stayed where she was, occasionally talking to the comatose woman. A nurse came in to check on Tracy and asked, "Any change?"

Alina shook her head. "No, not yet."

"Let me know if there is." The nurse left her alone again.

That happened several more times. And finally, after the silence shifted in some almost imperceptible way, Alina looked to see Tracy opening her eyes.

"Tracy," she exclaimed. She leaned over and explained once again why Tracy was here. Then Alina said, "I'll be right back." She raced to the curtains and called to one of the nurses, "She's awake."

Within minutes a nurse and doctor walked in.

With a smile the nurse said to Alina, "I need you to step out into the waiting room."

Alina understood what was coming next. She still wasn't prepared to separate from Tracy. She smiled at Tracy and said, "I'll be right outside."

The doctor was with Tracy for a lot longer this time.

When he came out, he walked over to Alina. "She's still confused and doesn't comprehend what happened. I understand from the nurse that you are also a victim. Maybe you can help clarify things. She wants to speak with you."

She smiled at the doctor. "She will be all right?"

The doctor nodded. "Do you have any idea how long she was held for?"

Alina gave him the time line she knew. "A police officer rode in the ambulance with us," she said. "I'm sure he can fill you in with any further details."

The doctor nodded. "She's lucky. There doesn't appear to be any trauma to the body, so we'll take that as a good sign."

"That's good news, indeed." With a smile, she walked past him and went in to speak with Tracy.

Tracy appeared a little more alert. And a whole lot more confused. Alina sat and carefully shared the details of what she knew. The two women had seen each other in the hospital before. Enough to recognize each other's faces, but they weren't friends. And Tracy likely hadn't heard what had happened to Alina.

By the time Alina was done, Tracy shook her head and whispered, "Oh, my God. Oh, my God. Oh, my God."

"The thing to remember is, you're safe. We found you, but I don't know if they caught the man who kidnapped you yet," Alina said. "I know the manhunt was underway when I came in the ambulance with you to the hospital."

And just like that, Tracy wept. She cried and cried. Partly from the drugs, Alina knew; but also from the shock. Alina understood so much of her crying was the sheer relief of having been rescued. And that Alina remembered all too well.

She stayed with Tracy for a long moment. And then Alina's phone went off. She looked at Tracy, patted her hand and said, "I have to take this call. I'll be right back." She stepped out into the hall to see by the caller ID it was Logan. Her grin brightened, and she raced out of the hospital to answer it. "Hey, did you catch him?"

"No, not yet. With the helicopters and about twenty police officers here, he can't get too far."

She groaned. "Damn, I was so hoping. I can't wait to put this to rest."

"It'll happen. How is Tracy?"

"She's awake now. Shocked and grateful to be alive." Alina shook her head as she stared at the setting light outside. "It's going to be dark soon. If he can stay hidden until then, he could get clean away." She wanted to scream in frustration.

"We'll get him. You sit tight. Don't leave the hospital."

She froze, turned around and said, "I'm actually outside right now," she admitted. "I had to take your phone call."

"Get back inside and stay there," he ordered. "I'll text next time."

"Why?" she asked, her fear making her nervous. "You expect him to come back after Tracy arrived at the hospital? How would he know?"

"How can he not? It's all over the news—although the details are sketchy. They said an unidentified woman has been rescued from an apparent kidnapping. She's in the hospital, in the emergency room. Make sure you stand at her side so she can't be taken again. I don't know what the hell's going on. I imagine they must find you and Tracy to make their quota or do it some other way. Losing both of you, they're desperate. They'll be after her, and if they're lucky, they'll find you too."

And just like that, Logan hung up. She cast a nervous glance around and bolted for the relative safety of the hospital. As she walked back to Tracy's side, she realized what he meant. Not only could Tracy be snatched from the hospital, but with both of them here, they could be taken together.

LOGAN TURNED HIS back to the chaos around him. Harrison was still in the woods, tracking down Lingam. The cops were out there too. At the getaway car, Logan looked for any information that would lead to Lingam's associates.

It still bugged him that nobody connected all these missing women. He understood it took several cases before anyone had any inkling something was going on, but to consider the number of women who'd been kidnapped over the last four years, and the cops didn't know? That thought made him view the men around him in a slightly more analytical way.

Logan and one policeman had looked over the car from top to bottom; and forensics was on their way. They'd gone through the glove box where they'd found an old satchel bag, like the one they'd discovered inside Colin's apartment. Once he explained who and what he'd been involved with, the other detectives showing up on the spot had allowed him to take part, if he shared all information. He was thankful because this was a police case, and he really had no business there.

They were currently going through the bag, emptying the contents on the hood of the car, including one smelly sweatshirt. Detective Easterly showed up and told Logan how they had cops working this from various angles all throughout the city. One at Lingam's house, where Logan had collected the boxes. Another at the second residence, where John had driven Tracy but had left in a hurry, as if he knew Logan had been there. The question was, now where would John go? To ground?

Logan really wished they could've gotten this fool before he hit the tree line. But that wasn't to be, and it was pissing Logan off.

He kept glancing around, wondering if the man was hiding in the long brush up ahead, laughing at them. He knew that, if Lingam was smart, he'd be long gone. No way he was getting his car back. And that was just another thing.

"We should check to see if he has a second vehicle registered," Logan said. "Or whether his brother did. He'll need more wheels to carry on from here."

One of the cops stepped out of the way, phone to his ear. That was the good thing about having so many men about. Somebody was always available to track down information. This was the manhunt that didn't dare accept anything less than success. Not if they planned to keep the city safe. They needed to know who was involved in this.

What he really wanted was Lingam's cell phone. "Can we track down his calls?"

"It's in progress. I was hoping something useful would be in the damn bag."

A pocket was in the front. Logan reached in and pulled out a crumpled piece of paper on the bottom. It looked like a hamburger wrapper. But as he spread it out and held up his cell phone to use for light, he could see some notations on it. "A phone number's here," he said.

He quickly turned his phone around and dialed the

number. With the men listening, the phone rang and rang; then a man's voice snapped, "Where the fuck are you? Better get your ass here. You're going to be in deep shit if you can't get that damn girl here fast."

Logan coughed several times, then in a gruff tone, deliberately masking his voice, he said, "Sorry," and coughed again.

"Goddammit, you sick again?"

Logan held the cop's gaze with his as he said, "Just a little."

The man's voice was disgusted. "You better not be on the goddamn drug again. Your brother was a loser that way too. If you want to keep working for us, you'll keep your nose clean and not stuffed with powder."

Holding his shirt half over his mouth, Logan continued to mask his voice as he said, "Be there soon."

The other man snorted. "I don't have time for shit. Things have blown up here. The exchange is tonight. I need the girl, and now. Tell me where you are, and Bill or I will come pick her up."

Logan smiled at the name. This was likely Barry Ferguson. One of the four ringleaders they'd come to check out. The cop held up the name of the mall around the corner. "At the mall. Had to get air in a tire."

"Goddammit, I'll be there in twenty minutes. I don't care how flat your tires are. Make sure you're at the rear right-hand corner where the restaurant is. A gas station is off the main street." Then the line went dead.

Logan held out his phone and said, "Well, that changes things. See if you can track that number." He looked at the car. "We need the suitcase back in the trunk, and we need the car at the rendezvous spot, so he recognizes it."

At that the police galvanized into action.

"It would also be damn good if we had a policewoman inside the stupid suitcase," Detective Easterly said in irritation. "But I doubt I can find one that size that fast."

One of the men said, "Iris. She's small."

Detective Easterly looked at him. "Can you call her?" Then he shook his head. "We don't have time. I have to go through official channels to get this set up."

But the cop was already talking to Iris on the phone. He came back and said, "She's calling her supervisor. We're trying to get this organized. She's on the way in case it's a go."

The men quickly put the car back together again.

Logan realized he was certainly not the physique of the driver. He motioned to one of the cops. "Can you get out of uniform and take the driver's place? You're about the same build as the man we're looking for in the woods."

The cop's gaze shot up, but he nodded and said, "Can't take off my uniform."

"Grab this guy's sweatshirt and pull it over your shirt. Hopefully it's dark enough it won't matter. Besides, we're planning to be there before he shows up anyway. If we're lucky, we'll get more than just him and capture the rest of his network."

The cop did as instructed and turned toward Logan.

Logan nodded. "Rough up your hair and try to look like you've been on coke for the last twenty-four hours."

The guy rolled his eyes. "Great. Just what I need. To copy a drugged-out kidnapper."

"He was angry and pissed at life. Looking to score. Mad that his brother seemed to have found a way to make easy money and took his place from what I can gather. This may be the first time he's taken a woman, and they only used him because Colin was killed."

The cop nodded.

"Let's get going, everyone," Logan said. "I'll take my car to pick up my partner, and we'll meet you there." He pulled out his phone and called Harrison. "Where are you?"

"Heading back to the car. I can see a lot of activity. What's happening?"

Logan quickly brought him up to date.

Harrison whistled. "I'll be there in five. Warm up the car so we can get moving."

Logan ran back to the car and fired it up. They'd been driving through a lot of long grass. The last thing he needed was to have it not run. It was only a rental, not exactly the Jeep and trucks he was used to driving. He turned on the headlights and saw Harrison racing toward him while the other men spread out and combed the woods. Logan urged Harrison to go faster. He had the car turned around and his foot on the gas pedal, ready when Harrison bolted into the front seat.

"Let's go."

Logan took off, following the cops. He punched in the location on the GPS. He figured they had about three minutes to get there so nobody saw them arrive. At the same time, he wanted to make sure they wrapped this up tight.

Levi hadn't exactly known what they would get into on this case. Sometimes life wasn't so easy.

Besides, if Logan ended up having a relationship with Alina, well, he'd be more than happy to take her home with him. So he'd considered this an extremely good trip. He knew the guys would bug him constantly, but that was life. He was okay with it.

Up ahead was the turnoff to the mall. He slowed down and headed toward the restaurant. The gas station was at the back, and he made sure they were in position.

The last thing he wanted was to get involved in any more wild car chases tonight with his rental.

Chapter 14

BACK IN THE hospital emergency room, Alina walked into Tracy's room.

Tracy looked up in relief. She reached out a hand and said, "I have to admit, I'm really grateful you're here."

Alina grabbed her hand. She sat on the edge of the bed. "I checked in with Logan, and so far, the man who kidnapped you hasn't been caught. There is quite a manhunt for him right now. But they want us to stay alert, and hopefully they can catch him and the ringleaders before anybody notices you are here in this hospital."

Tracy's eyes widened as she realized the implications. She lowered her voice, looking around hurriedly. "You really think he would try to attack us here?"

"It's always possible, "Alina said. "But why would they at this point? Surely the game is up. They should be cutting their losses and running."

Tracy frowned. "He said something about they were out of time." She shook her head. "He actually apologized."

Alina nodded. "That would make sense. After I was rescued, you were snatched to take my place. You weren't exactly on their list for this go-round." She leaned forward and said, "Is there anything else? Some information that would help the cops find the rest of this ring?"

Tracy lay back on the bed and stared at the ceiling, as if

trying to remember. "So much of it is all a blur."

"I know. If we had a location, a house, if he referred to anything, it would be huge."

"He said something about a truck. As in, we have to catch the truck."

Alina sat back and considered that. "A truck. Like a big transporter? Like they must move you? Moving into Mexico, Canada, or to a private airplane?"

Tracy shook her head. "I can't imagine. I'm so grateful not to be there."

"I know how you feel. I hurt for the other women. They've been gone a long time. The last one was taken three months ago." Alina winced at the concept, but it made a lot more sense. "Then they just put you in a truck and meet up with the others. That could be anywhere from California to Florida. It wouldn't take that long, and traveling by land in a private vehicle, it would be much harder to see a woman either sleeping in the passenger side or tied up in the back of a truck—even a normal pickup with a canopy."

Tracy nodded. "He was quite insistent about the time frame. He said I was his big break."

"That's because his brother, Joe, had been involved before but was killed a year ago. If John had any idea how to get in touch with these people, then he'd have a chance to step into his brother's shoes. Joe was making anywhere from ten to fifteen thousand for each woman. So was Colin."

Tracy looked at her and said something surprising. "Am I worth so little?"

"You're worth an awful lot. And they are paying that much just to one leg of this ring. Imagine what both of us would have been sold off for at the end."

Tracy said, her voice low, "Honestly I don't want to find

out."

Alina shook her head. "Neither do I." Then she turned and stared off. "I was actually held for several days. Although I live in Somerville, I was taken from the hospital where we worked. I don't think I can go back there. It's bad enough to be looking over your shoulder, but to think that I was actually snatched from the cafeteria there …" She shook her head. "Truthfully, I don't think I can stay."

Tracy nodded. "Right about now, all I can think about is going home to my family in Salem." She shook her head and added, "My mom was right. Big cities are dangerous."

"I think it happens everywhere. We just got very unlucky."

"Why us?"

"Whether they were looking for small women to begin with, I'm not sure. But, being our size, we fit into the suitcases the men moved us around in."

"I didn't think such a thing was possible."

"Well, I was there when they opened the suitcase and found you. And it was quite a job to get you extricated."

Tracy let her breath out. "I'm definitely going home now."

"Did you call your parents?"

"The hospital did. My mom's on her way here."

"Good for you. That'll help you get over this. I'm sure your local town has a hospital too. Apply there."

"That's what my mom said." She cast a glance over at Alina and said, "I'm only twenty-two. To think that my life would have ended in such a horrendous manner…"

"I don't think they were looking to kill us. They were selling us as slaves."

Tracy shuddered. "How can this even exist in today's

world? Things like that shouldn't be allowed."

Adding a note of humor, Alina said, "It's not. But not everybody follows the rules."

Tracy stared at the phone in Alina's hand. "I hope they catch him."

"I hope they catch all of them." Alina glanced around nervously. "I'm constantly looking over my shoulder." She shook her head. "I wonder how long it will take for that to go away?"

"How long has this been going on? How could the police not know?"

Alina leaned forward and whispered, "I was thinking about that. But I don't want to consider that some cops might be involved. Still…it's hard not to wonder."

Tracy curled up in a ball as if that concept was too much for her.

Alina realized Tracy was correct. She really needed to go back home and live with her parents. Return to a life where there had been innocence. She would likely never feel that way again, but at least she missed the couple of days tied up like Alina was.

She settled back in the chair and said, "Just sleep. I'll watch over you."

With a grateful smile, the two women still holding hands, Tracy let her eyes drift closed. Alina wished she could sleep away the next few hours too. But her stomach was knotted, and her nerves were frayed. Every second she kept checking her phone for an update. Of course, they were all busy doing whatever they needed to. She wanted this to be over with. But what she wanted most was to make sure the bad guys were caught.

She settled into her chair, resting her head against the

back, her mind free-floating on the concept that a cop was involved. Most were good honest, upright citizens. But often all it took was one bad apple. And in a position like that, he would have access to so much information. Including the list of names to research. The cop could've found where she lived, who she loved, where she'd worked, how long she'd been employed there, any tickets or arrests. Including the fact she lived alone. If nobody would really note her absence, then she'd be one more missing person. And there were literally thousands of those in every big city.

As she sat thinking about how many of the missing women might be due to human trafficking rings, she was overwhelmed. Then a nurse came and checked on Tracy. She gave Alina a smile and said, "Would you like a cup of coffee? We have some here at the nurses' station. I can get you one if you'd like."

Alina smiled at her gratefully. "Thank you. That would be lovely."

The nurse came back with a cup and handed it to her. "We will be moving her down to a different room on the other end. There has been a large multicar pileup. We need all the beds in emergency we can get. It's a couple doors down on the far side, so expect an orderly to come in and move her soon. Okay?" And she left.

The thought of a multicar pileup made her cringe. That car chase she'd already been in earlier had been bad enough. She hoped Logan and Harrison weren't part of it. That none of the cops involved in this case were. Everyone was trying so hard to catch this guy; it would be terrible if something happened.

To think they had met John face-to-face, and he'd handed over his brother's crap. Playing the innocent … And it had worked.

Now she waited for the orderly to move Tracy. Alina didn't want Tracy waking up on her own. Alina sipped her coffee and waited. Still no update from Logan. She itched to text him and ask how things were, but if he hadn't turned his phone off, she didn't want to be the one who got him in trouble when it rang and gave away his position or something. Not the time for her to be pushing things. He would call when he could.

Then two orderlies came in, smiled at her and pulled up the side rails on Tracy's bed.

She nodded to them, set her cup of coffee down and stood. "I'm coming with you."

The orderly smiled and nodded. "We're only going down a few doors."

"Good. I don't want her to wake up alone."

They took Tracy to a big open room and set her up on the far side against the wall. Alina paced the room until they were done. No chair was here for her, so she leaned against the window and waited.

When nobody came along with furniture, she walked toward a nurse, asking if she could take a chair from the outside hallway into the room. The nurse smiled and told her to go ahead. She grabbed it, walked back to the room and found Tracy still sleeping.

She slipped out into the hallway again and saw a public washroom a few feet down the hall. When she was done, she washed her hands and looked in the mirror. Using a brush from her purse, she gave her hair a quick taming, put it into a braid, tied it off, and gave her face a wash, then headed back to Tracy's room.

Before she stepped back into the large room, one of the

nurses called to her. "Tracy's mother arrived. They want a few moments."

Right. That made sense. She glanced around and decided she should probably go to the waiting room outside emergency then. "If you see either of them, let them know I'm in the waiting room. I don't want to intrude."

The nurse smiled and nodded, then said, "Good idea."

Alina went to the waiting room and sat. Now she wasn't connected to Tracy or Logan. Surely she could do something.

With that thought, she rose and paced. Then decided to walk the hallways. She'd never been in this hospital, but most of them were of a similar construction.

She walked the corridor, determined to wear off some of the festering energy inside. When she came back around to Tracy's room, the door was partially open. She peeked inside to see if her mom was still there but found both Tracy and her mom gone. Her mom hadn't wasted any time in taking Tracy away. Alina didn't blame her, but she'd hoped she'd be able to say good-bye. Dispirited she walked to the nurses' station and said, "I see they left. I was hoping to say good-bye."

The nurse looked up. Only it was a different nurse. She gave Alina a distracted look and said, "Sorry, people are coming and going all the time."

She heard the sirens, and the nurse bolted. Coming in were the multicar pileup victims. Now quite perturbed, Alina walked back to the waiting room and slid down in a chair, the only one left. The waiting room had filled abruptly. She could do nothing to help; all she could do was wait for Logan to contact her. With Tracy gone, she was at loose ends. She pulled out her phone, studied it and wondered if it was worth taking a chance, then decided what the hell. She sent a text to Logan.

> **Tracy's gone home with her mom. I'm stuck at the hospital. Any idea when you'll be done?** After she sent the text, she settled back to wait.

Logan sat behind the gas station, waiting to see if the vehicle arrived to meet up with the cop pretending to be Lingam. The suitcase, now filled with rocks for weight, was stashed in the back of the car. They never did get clearance for the female cop to be part of the sting. Hopefully they wouldn't need her.

So far, the vehicle hadn't shown up. The police hadn't been given much time to get their people organized. They had cops spread out all over the end of the mall. Also, a couple ghost cars were hidden throughout. Too many black-and-whites and people get nervous. Then a vehicle drove up. It looked like a work truck, but it didn't have a canopy over the back. Instead it had what looked like foot lockers. As he eyed the size of them, he realized it was a little too easy to imagine one of these women stuffed into them.

He shook his head, thinking that nobody would even think to check something like that. As the truck drove up and parked on the side, a man hopped out and walked around to the back while another went behind the truck cab to unlock on one of the big storage tool chests. Logan recognized him from the photos. It was one of the four men: Barry Ferguson. That was three down and one to go. The man popped open the lid and lifted out a toolbox tray. A full-size truck and that toolbox was at least five feet long, if not six. They could easily fit a woman inside and cover her up. Well, it wasn't happening this time.

He could see Harrison approach from the far side, walking casually, as if heading to the stores on the other end. He stepped within sight of a couple of the guys looking in his direction, but they didn't appear to notice much. The two guys walked over to the car, slammed on it hard and yelled, "Come on. Open up. We don't have time for this shit."

The cop lowered the window and popped the trunk. The men carefully brought out the suitcase and carried it to the truck.

From Logan's position, he imagined they were ready to open the suitcase. But Harrison came up behind them with the cop on the far side and said in calm low voices, "Get on your knees. Hands over your head."

The men froze. Logan raced toward them. He knew they wouldn't lie down quietly. They were facing lifetimes in prison for what they'd done. No way they'd give up easily.

One of the men pulled a gun. Logan fired first and so did Harrison. Other shots were fired from various angles. Logan hid behind the truck to get out of range. Harrison remained with the two bad guys, now wounded and lying on the ground, but they were still alive, swearing fast and furiously.

Logan came around the side of the truck, only to see another gunman running toward the car. He was afraid for the cop. It was not exactly a good place to get caught. He creeped around the front of the truck and looked, but he was on the far side of the getaway car now.

The cop had the driver's door open and was hiding behind it. But he probably didn't know the guy was on the other side. As Logan raced toward them, the gunman stood, leaned over the car and lined up for his shot. Logan shot him first.

Logan raced to the cop, sighed and asked, "You okay?"

The cop nodded. "Yes, I'm fine, but that was damned close."

Logan walked over to the man. He'd shot him high in the chest and didn't know if he would make it or not. He checked for a pulse. "We need an ambulance here. Three of them at least." He glanced around as the other cops started to come out. "Did we get them all?"

But he could see another policeman peeling off, racing after yet another man. Another cop gave chase from a different angle. Even as he watched, the last man went down under one of them.

Logan walked over to the truck with the large foot lockers. With several cops at his side, he hopped up in the bed. All three foot lockers were padlocked. Hard to tell if any had breathing holes without more light. Grabbing a hammer from the toolbox, Logan broke off all the padlocks. Then raised the lid on each locker. With a flashlight, he shone the light inside.

And found terrified eyes staring at him. In each trunk. A total of three sets.

He heard the cops around him cry out and two policemen joined him in the truck bed. One leaned down and carefully lifted a woman up. He called out, "We need an ambulance. Looks like we found the missing women."

Cheers rang out. The other two were lifted free and lowered to the ground as the men carefully removed the gags from their mouths, untied their bonds, then massaged their joints to get the blood circulating again until the ambulances arrived.

Logan sat on the tailgate of the truck, staring at the ugly spaces where they'd been imprisoned. The thought of Alina transported in a locker made his heart ache.

A cop walked over, holding up a phone, then said, "It's for you."

Logan grabbed it then held it to his ear to hear Detective Easterly saying, "We found him. He went back into his old house. He was ready to jump ship. But we got him."

"That's damn good news." Logan laughed. "Actually, that's the best news I've heard in a long time. We've got three bad guys down here and one on the run. Your men are after him. So, with any luck we can get him too." His gave a happy sigh. "And, as I'm sure you've heard, we've found the missing women, so today has been a great day."

Chapter 15

ALINA, ONCE AGAIN back in the waiting room, heard her phone buzz. She clicked on it to see a text message from Logan.

> **We've got three bad guys, including Lingam, looking for one more. Found the missing women—all alive and well. Looks like we're wrapping up. I'll call you in about ten minutes.**

She smiled. She wished Tracy was still here so she could send her the good news. Maybe she still could. Maybe the nurses had her phone number. She rose and walked to the nurses' station. "I know Tracy left with her mom, and you probably can't give me any personal information, but I forgot to get her phone number, and I heard from the police they caught three of the men involved in the human trafficking ring. I wanted to give her the good news."

The nurses exchanged glances and said, "We can't give out any personal information."

Alina nodded. "That's what I thought. Okay, I'll call my supervisor and see if I can get it from her."

She walked down the hallway to the exit. Once outside she put a call through to Selena. When she answered, Alina quickly filled her in. Selena was shocked at the news. When she calmed down enough to understand, Alina filled her in on the rest of the details, explaining how the cops had picked up the rest of the ring but one, and they were tracking that one down now.

"Tracy was just here. She left with her mom, and I forgot to get a phone number from her. I wanted to tell her they've caught a lot of people, so she'll hopefully feel safer now. Do you have a cell I can send a text to?"

Selena muttered, "I shouldn't. You know that."

"I spent three hours sitting at her bedside talking to her. It was my fault I forgot to get it. But honestly I don't think anybody would mind."

"Fine. But you can't tell her where you got it from." Selena rattled off the number.

Alina wrote it down on the receipt she found inside her purse. "Okay, got it." When she hung up, she added Tracy's number to her contact list, then sent her a text explaining in short form that three of the ringleaders were accounted for, and the cops were chasing down the fourth. Then remembered to shoot her another text regarding Lingam's capture and that it looked like things were wrapping up today.

She wasn't expecting an answer quickly, but when she didn't get one, she fretted. Maybe Tracy was sleeping, or she wasn't even looking at her phone. Having a hard time letting it lie, Alina picked up the phone and dialed. No answer. She let it ring. Finally, a woman's voice came on the line and said, "Shut the fuck up." And hung up.

Alina froze. That couldn't be Tracy's mom. So who the hell answered Tracy's phone? Then the panic hit. She quickly phoned Logan. "I called Tracy to let her know the good news, but a woman answered. All she said was 'Shut the fuck up.'"

She could hear the silence harden on the other end.

"What's the number?"

She read it off for him.

"I'll call you back."

She sat in the waiting room with her cell clenched in her fist, hating that once again she was stuck doing nothing to help. Then she worried. What if Tracy hadn't been taken away by her mom? What if her mom had nothing to do with this? Who the hell said it was even her mom?

She got up, walked to the room where Tracy's bed had been placed and opened the door. The bed was still there, and it wasn't even made yet, but the linens were right there. How could they have moved her? She wouldn't have gone willingly. It would be easy enough to give her a shot, put her in a wheelchair and take her out. But then again, why? Still confused, she kept sorting through the bedding and then froze. On top of one of the sheets, under the blanket, was a needle. She took a picture of it and sent it to Logan, then a text.

I think they got Tracy.

His response was instant.

Stay there. Stay safe.

She'd walked away from Tracy, gone to the bathroom, only to find out Tracy and her mom had gone. How long ago had that been?

She sent Logan another message.

Contact Tracy's mom. Find out if she was at the hospital. Because if she wasn't, then a woman is involved, because a nurse told me her mom was with her. I didn't see or meet her.

She wandered to the window, searching for any sign of Tracy, her fists clenching and unclenching in a rhythmic motion as she waited for somebody to get back to her.

Finally, her phone rang. She raced out of the hospital at the rear parking lot and answered it.

"Her mom is on the way," Logan said, "but she hasn't arrived in Boston yet. It wasn't Tracy's mother."

Alina flopped down on one of the benches. "Oh, dear God. I didn't get a chance to see who was with her."

"The hospital has video cameras. We'll get a visual on her within minutes. The police are already patching it through."

"Thank God for that. I'm such a fool. When I came out of the bathroom, I heard her mom was in with her, and I should leave them alone for a few minutes as they needed privacy, so I went for a walk—I wasn't gone ten minutes."

"You are not responsible," he snapped in her ear. "Got that?"

She nodded. "I got that. I'm not, but somehow I feel I am." Of course she understood that was the same refrain she'd already said several times over. She shook her head. "Are the kidnappers' lives actually on the line if they don't deliver somebody? And is she the easiest replacement they know of?"

"It could be any number of things. But we've got the truck with the driver and somebody else. There was a backup vehicle too. We got it. The last man isn't getting away either."

"And who the hell was the woman?"

"The missing link."

He rang off, and Alina sat still for a long moment. Then she went back to the nurses' station and said, "The police are going to be here any minute, but that woman who said she was Tracy's mother has effectively kidnapped her. The police have contacted Tracy's real mother, and she is enroute, but she is not in Boston yet."

The nurses stared at her in shock; no one knew what to say. Or dare not say anything.

Alina could understand. They'd let a patient be kidnapped. The PR storm over this would be horrific. Their jobs could even be on the line. She leaned forward and said, "Please, do you remember what she looked like? I wasn't here when she arrived, and a nurse told me not to go in, so I didn't get a chance to see her. The police will look at the video cameras, or maybe they can do that from the station." She shook her head. "I don't know, but can you give me a description of her—anything to tell me what she looked like?"

One of the nurses lifted her cell phone and said, "I can do better than that. I took a picture of the chaos when the big accident came in," she confessed. "My boyfriend doesn't think it ever gets crazy here. I'm not actually in the ER on duty, but I wanted him to see."

She pulled up the photo, and sure enough, it was a full-on nightmare at the hospital. Paramedics were everywhere, and beds were moved all over the place. And jammed up against the reception counter was a woman, her hair pulled back in a bun at the nape. She was well dressed, a stranger.

"Can you send me that image please?"

The nurse nodded. Alina brought it up on her phone and sent it to Logan.

This is her. Accidentally caught in a photograph in the hallway.

She headed out the back exit with the woman's image strong in her mind. There was a huge parking lot. But how would the woman have gotten an unconscious Tracy into a vehicle? That couldn't have been easy. Unless she had help. Had the woman managed to get Tracy straight out of the hospital, or was the woman hiding somewhere inside?

Amid this much chaos, she could have done any number of things.

Alina raced to the parking lot. "Dammit, where are you, Tracy?"

Of course there was no answer. Her phone rang. It was Logan. "The woman's well-known to the police. They sent out an alert looking for her and Tracy. We also have a vehicle registered to her. With any luck, we'll get her."

"I'm not feeling the luck very much now," Alina said. "She can't have left the hospital more than twenty minutes ago. The cops need somebody in the air looking for the vehicle."

"I'm sure they'd like to. It doesn't mean they have the manpower."

She shook her head. "This is ridiculous. That woman came in and walked away with Tracy, with absolutely nothing and nobody stopping her."

"Hospital administration will have to look at that. But because you got the face, we now know who we're looking for."

Tracy walked to the far side of the parking lot, her rage so extreme her footsteps gave off a staccato sound. "She could still be here, you know? How could the woman get Tracy into the vehicle on her own? Tracy's small, but she's still a dead weight if she's unconscious. And it's obvious she's been drugged again, so what the hell?" she cried out in her frustration.

"Look for a black Honda Civic." He rattled off the license plate. "We're only minutes away."

She heard the letter *C*, but the rest of it went over her head. She spun around looking for black cars. "Do you have any idea how many black cars are here?"

"She'll likely be driving carefully to not bring attention to herself. It wouldn't have been easy to get Tracy out of the hospital and into the car, so she's probably still there. Cops are on the way."

As she turned around, she said, "A black car, a Honda, is heading to the exit. I'm running toward her. I must confirm Tracy is in there."

There was a lot of traffic, and no one would let her vehicle in.

"She's trying to make a left turn onto the main road here but can't cross."

Coming alongside the car, Alina saw Tracy collapsed on the back seat. "It's her. Goddammit, it's her." She opened the passenger door.

The woman hit the brakes and shouted, "Get out. Get out."

Instead, Alina jumped inside and came up fast, slamming the woman against the glass of the driver's side window. The steering wheel jerked to the side, sending the small car to the curb. Alina didn't have any fighting skills except for her pure rage at watching this goddamn woman stealing poor Tracy all over again. Her ire knew no bounds. She kept hitting and hitting and hitting. The woman screamed, fought back, but Alina was like a bedeviled animal.

She could hear Logan in the background, shouting at her

from her cell. Yet, she couldn't say anything. The outlet for all her rage, fear, and torment was to keep hitting the woman. When Alina finally drew a shuddering breath, she realized the woman's face was bleeding, and blood was all over the side window. Alina could hardly breathe.

With her left hand, she picked up her phone and gasped. "Oh, my God, I killed her. I think I killed her."

"Stay calm. Where are you?"

She gave him the details.

"Is the vehicle still running?"

Realizing they were sitting in an idling vehicle, she reached over and pulled the keys free. At his instruction, she pulled up the emergency brake to stop them from moving.

"Stay right where you are. We're on the way."

She shook her head. "We're blocking traffic. Oh, my God. What have I done?"

"You've done exactly what you needed to do to save Tracy. Now stop thinking about it. Do not leave the vehicle. Do not leave Tracy. And if that woman gets up, hit her again. Do you hear me?"

She gave a shuddering breath and broke down. "Oh, my God! What am I?"

"You're an animal in pain, sweetie, that's all. You did what you had to. I'm already on the way toward you. I am not very far away. Give us five minutes. Hold on for five more minutes, and we'll be there."

She stared almost blind out at the traffic. Vehicles were going around them. She couldn't look at anybody. She couldn't even begin to lift her face. And then some of her training took over. She reached out with her bloody hand and touched the woman on the neck. Relief flowed through her as she felt a pulse. "She's alive." And she burst into tears.

LOGAN SWORE UNDER his breath. The cops drove ahead, leading the way as fast as possible. Harrison drove their car with Logan as a passenger. And like him, Harrison was having a hard time keeping behind the cops, wanting to race ahead. "She found Tracy lying in the back of the vehicle. She's beaten the woman driver to a pulp."

Harrison raised an eyebrow and said, "Holy shit."

Logan leaned back and closed his eyes. "Yeah, that's an understatement."

"Is the woman dead?"

"Alina said she is still alive. She's pretty unnerved over what she's done."

"I understand that. I've seen women do some pretty scary things when they're afraid. We're all capable of killing in the right circumstances."

They pulled up to the hospital, coming in through a different entrance, Logan exiting the car before Harrison rolled to a stop. The cop ahead of them drove to the far corner where he could see the black Honda Civic parked. Two other cop cars came in behind them. Others were driving around the stalled car, merging into the traffic on the main lane. Not sure what he would find, Logan raced forward, his hands out to the cops. "Let me talk to her."

Sure enough, Alina sat in the front seat, covered in blood. A woman sat in the driver's seat, her head against the driver-side window, bloodied from top to bottom, moaning.

He opened the passenger door. "Alina, take it easy."

She turned, and he could see the shock in her face, the deadness in her eyes.

Finally, she registered who he was, and lifted her arms like a two-year-old. He wrapped his arms around her and picked her up, taking her out of the vehicle. The cops surged in with a doctor and several orderlies pushing a stretcher from the hospital. With her in his arms, the two of them watched as Tracy was carefully removed from the back seat, and the woman driver was carried on another stretcher that arrived soon afterward.

Alina whispered, "I hope she's gonna be okay."

"I hope she is too. So she can spend a lot of years locked up in prison. Come on. I'm taking you inside to get that hand looked at."

She gave him a broken smile and held up her bruised, bloodied hand. "I guess I'm not going back to work for a while."

"Honey, you're not going back to work until you find a new job in Texas."

She glanced at him. "How could you want to possibly help me after this?"

He leaned down and gave her a kiss on the temple. "Not only do I want to, I don't have any intention of letting you go. Not often do we see people with the character willing to go the distance and do what needs to be done to save others. You jumped into my heart when I first met you. You were so valiant and strong. Nothing that has happened since has changed my mind."

Laying her head against his shoulder, she whispered, "So you only want to be with me because I'm some honorable Amazon woman?"

Logan grinned. "Because you're sexy, and the sweetest girl I've ever met. Because I really want to take you to meet my Dad and all my friends." His grin widened. "And because you're some honorable Amazon woman."

She cast him glance, and her eyes were huge. "Really?"

He heard the hope and fear in her voice. He shifted her in his arms and kissed her full on the lips. "Absolutely."

Chapter 16

THE REST OF the day and evening was awash in chaos. Not only did she have to be treated again, but the police were all over her. And through the entire process, she held a deep hidden fear that she'd beaten up an innocent woman. Yet, in her mind, she kept seeing Tracy stretched out unconscious on the back seat. If that woman was innocent, why was she moving an unconscious woman?

Since finding her in the car, Logan hadn't left her alone. He was either carrying her or had his hand in hers. Making sure there was physical contact between them. And she was just as bad. Anytime he made a move, she reached for him. Thankfully, he'd always reached back. She didn't understand this bond.

That it was born through danger was one thing she'd like to think would strengthen as they discovered who each other was. She wanted to believe what they had was something to grow, build, and nurture. She knew he felt the same way, but this was new. And as such, it was like a young sapling springing roots. Something to be protected. To be watered and given sunshine and nutrients. Something that would grow strong, straight, and true over time.

That's what she wanted for their relationship. She wasn't sure how to give him exactly what he needed. She'd never made it that far. All her previous ones had broken up after a few months. Never had she felt about the men the way she did about Logan. He'd been her hero and had been there for her every step of the way. She knew she'd make that move to Texas now, without any qualms. Just to be close to him. Just to give this, whatever *this* was, a chance.

At the same time, she had a lot of nightmares to deal with. Not the least of which was finding out that, within her own inner core, was a savage animal determined to protect somebody so much less fortunate when needed.

She'd seen women, mothers, do the same thing when protecting their children. So she shouldn't have been surprised. But she'd never seen that in herself before. Tracy certainly hadn't been her child, but she felt responsible. And seeing her taken once again, had been too much.

The police were all over the damn hospital. She was sure the staff was waiting for them to get the hell out of their lives. She'd had evenings like that. The hospital was overwhelmed with patients from the multicar pileup. Some were taken to surgery, and others were moved in, registered and taken to different floors and specialty areas.

Once again, she was here. Her hand was looked at, and the doctor sent her for an X-ray. So far nobody mentioned the woman. And she was terrified she'd hurt her permanently. With Logan holding her left hand, he led her toward the X-ray room. She sat on the chair and waited. He held the paperwork in his hand, and they sat in silence. When Alina couldn't stand it any longer, she asked, "How bad is she hurt?"

He didn't pretend to misunderstand. "I don't know. They're working on her."

She let her breath slowly escape. "That could mean anything."

He squeezed her fingers. "Yes, it could."

"Am I going to get charged?" She rolled her head to look at him, to see his beautiful green eyes staring at her. "How is it I haven't even noticed what color your eyes were before?"

He shook his head. "No reason why you should. You were protecting yourself and saving Tracy from a human trafficking ring, of which you had already been a victim." He smiled. "And no judge in this country would convict you for beating up the kidnapper to save the victim."

But that was his version. Until she heard that from the cops, she knew she wouldn't relax. Finally, she was taken in, her fingers very carefully spread out into various positions as they took numerous pictures, and she was led back into the waiting room. Logan was there. She sat, and her hand started to really hurt. She'd tried hard not to cry as they had positioned her fingers for the best pictures, but it had hurt. She looked down at her hand and said, "I'm pretty sure a couple of my fingers are broken."

He nodded. "If they are, they are."

She tossed him a smile. "It's my right hand. I do everything with it."

"Especially punching," he teased. "That means no more for you."

She rolled her eyes. "If I knew how to punch properly, I wouldn't have broken my fingers."

He chuckled. "I was going to mention that, but I figured I'd save it for another time."

"I wouldn't mind learning self-defense," she admitted. "When I was tied up on the bed, you can bet that's one of the things I regretted not having learned."

"We can work on that too. Everybody at the compound is high up in martial arts of one kind or another. We do hand-to-hand combat because of our work. We're all trained with various weapons."

She stared at him. "Compound?"

"Where me, Harrison, and the others live and work."

She nodded. "It seems like such a different world to what I know. You kill people, and I heal them."

He smiled. "Then we're a perfect fit."

She sagged against him as they waited for the results of the X-rays. "I hope you mean that."

The radiologist walked out of his office and said with a smile, "You did quite a number on your hand and wrist, my dear. A cast is definitely required. You broke two fingers, fractured your wrist and a couple small bones in the base of your hand."

She winced, glanced down at her hand and said, "I knew it hurt but hadn't realized how bad."

"It'll take a few minutes, but we'll get it taken care of. So you won't be going home anytime soon. Hand this to someone at the nurses' station."

She winced. "I understand the drill. Thanks very much, Doctor."

He nodded as Logan led her back to the main reception room and handed one of the nurses the X-ray report. The woman nodded and said, "Figured it was broken. Okay, let's get you down to one of the treatment rooms. Not sure how long you'll have to wait. It's still really crazy."

"Thank you," Alina said giving him a small smile.

Logan looked at her as she sat on the stool in the treatment room. "You want me to get you coffee or something to eat?"

She shook her head. "I want this over with. We'll talk about food afterward. Now I'm feeling a little bit on the queasy side. The pain from having the X-rays is… Wow. I hadn't really thought about it before, but rearranging broken fingers so they can take pictures is… not fun."

He leaned down and kissed her on top of her head. "But you were so valiant."

She shot him a look. But he appeared perfectly serious. "You got it bad," she muttered, "if you think that."

"I do think that." When his phone went off, he pulled it out. "It's Harrison. I need to take this."

She nodded, already feeling the pain of separation. "That means you have to go outside the hospital."

As he stepped toward the door, he turned and looked at her. "You going to be okay?"

"Did you get all the bad guys?" she countered.

He nodded and said, "You should be safe now."

"Safe. I hope so. Especially if it will prevent anybody else from being kidnapped again." She lifted her broken hand. "This is going to stop me from doing a whole lot."

He chuckled. "Actually, it won't. Once that has a cast on it, it'll really be a weapon."

She brightened. "Then send the doctor in here and get this sucker fixed."

It'd been a shaky couple of days. But he was a hell of a light at the end of the long, dark tunnel. Then she smiled at that. Did he even know what her name meant? *Alina* meant *light*. She'd asked her mom about it a long time ago, and she said her birth had been a light after their journey.

That's how she felt about Logan. He was her light. She'd have to tell him about it later.

And she had no idea what *later* would mean. Were they going back to the same hotel? Were they flying out? With this stupid hand, she'd have an even worse time moving. She didn't even know where to start.

First, she needed to hand in her notice. And cancel her lease. Her mind filled with all the logistics of moving. At the same time, she needed to relax. It was her right hand. While she waited, she tried, with her left, to send a text to Caroline. It was a bit garbled. But Caroline appeared to understand. And her demands were clear, something along the line of **Get your ass over here**.

Alina smiled. She put her cell away as the door opened to let in the same doctor who had examined her earlier. She asked, "You can put the cast on now?"

He smiled. "Sure, if you're ready. It's been a hell of a night so far."

The next few minutes were spent getting her arm bundled up in fiberglass.

"I understand you're a nurse. So, you know how to take care of this, what to watch for, should a problem arise."

She nodded. "And hopefully I won't be alone overnight, so I'll have someone to watch over me, to make sure I'm doing okay."

"If the man pacing outside the door right now is yours, he won't be leaving you to sleep alone. That's for sure."

She felt a smile climb her face. She couldn't think of anything she wanted more than to be sleeping with Logan tonight. Even if it meant Harrison was in the hotel bed beside them. She just wanted to be held. To wake up and know she was safe and sound, and, even more important, that he held her close because he wanted to.

LOGAN WAITED UNTIL the doctor opened the door again, saying, "She can go home now. She needs to keep an eye on those fingers for swelling. The next forty-eight hours are important." And he turned and walked away.

Logan got his first look at her standing there. She sported a bright purple cast on her right arm and over the bulk of her fingers—just the tips were showing.

She straightened and smiled at him. "I don't know where we're going from here, but food and a place to crash would be awesome."

He nodded. "Coming right up."

"The doctor had more good news," she added as he held her left hand, walking her outside. "They put a rush on the rape kit and apparently it came back negative. Also, the drug Colin gave me was a common date rape drug. No long-term side effects, thank heavens."

Logan wrapped an arm around her and held her for a long moment. "That is good news, indeed."

Stepping back, she looked around. "What vehicle are we driving?"

He pointed. "I have the rental car. Harrison came with me, then took a cab to the airport. He's heading to another job. As this has concluded, Levi's ordered us both home."

He watched as her face fell. Helping her into the car, he reached around and got her buckled up. He knew that, for quite a while, she would need help. She was also prickly and stubborn and wouldn't take kindly to being looked after.

"I guess we knew that time was coming," she said sadly. She sank back against the seat and closed her eyes.

He drove back to the hotel and helped her into the same room they'd been in before. Only this time it was just the two of them.

"What about you? Are you going back tonight too?"

He chuckled. "No. I'm staying here for three days.

That's as long as I've got."

"Why do you have that?" she asked cautiously.

He gave her a grin. "Because I asked for them. I figure that's how long it'll take to deal with the contents of your apartment, get you packed up, purchase your airline ticket and, if you have anything to ship, get that done too. We'll have to work our asses off though, if you plan on flying home with me. Alternatively," he added, "we could drive your car. It will take us a while, but we'll get there that way too."

She grinned. "I really could use my car in Texas," she admitted. "And I don't know if we can make all that happen in three days, but I'd sure like to give it a good try."

"Good. First things first—food. I placed an order with room service, and then it's crash time. You need sleep."

She nodded. A knock came at the door. "That was fast."

He laughed. "I called it in from the hospital. Once I realized you were getting a cast, I could give them a time frame."

He opened the door, accepted the trays on the trolley, paid the man a tip, closed it and turned, saying, "I wanted it to be ready. And then you get some sleep. Because tomorrow will be a long day."

While Logan brought the tray over, she sat on the bed and thought about all she had to do. "It doesn't have to be. I'm not caught up by having tons of possessions I must keep. Besides, it's limited to what the car can hold. As for my furniture, it can go to someone else." Taking in the aroma of their meal, she felt her stomach protest its emptiness. "The food smells wonderful."

She readjusted her position on the bed, propping herself against the headboard. He brought her a plateful of food. By the time she had eaten, the effects of shock were wearing off. She excused herself and went to the washroom.

She let out a small gasp at her face in the mirror. She opened the door. "You let me walk around in public like this?"

He took one look at her and smiled. "You're beautiful no matter what."

He went into the small room, grabbed a washcloth, soaped it up in warm water and carefully washed her face. He took a minute to clean the strands of hair along her face, still covered in dried blood. Then he turned her to look in the mirror. "Better?"

She smiled and said, "Yes. I'd love to do these fingers now."

He turned the warm water on to run over the tips as she let them soak underneath the tap for a few minutes. They were still so sore that she didn't want him to dry them. She let them hang to drip-dry and said, "That'll do." When they went back into the main room, he put their dishes on the tray, took it outside the room and left it on the floor in the hallway. Then he came back and said, "Bedtime for you." He pulled back the covers and looked at her. "What do you want to sleep in?"

She winced and stared down at her clothes. "This is easiest."

"You can't sleep in those." He picked up her bag and put it on the spare bed, quickly opened it and pulled out the nightgown she'd worn the previous night. "You up for getting into this?"

She nodded.

Gently, treating her like a little child, he undressed her with complete tenderness.

When the nightgown dropped over her head, she smiled at him. "You'd make a great father."

He shook his head. "Now that's a long way in the future."

She crawled under the covers. He bundled up all her dirty clothes, tucked them into the side pocket of her bag and reached for his laptop, placing it on the spare bed.

She looked at him and said, "Can you turn the lights"—she snuggled farther under the covers—"off?"

HE WATCHED AS she drifted under sleep's embrace. It had only taken seconds. He watched her eyes slowly close. She was exhausted. Shock was like that, and so was injury and pain. He grabbed his laptop and phone to check up on the world, to see if he had any messages. He found an email from Detective Easterly.

Instead of responding the same way, Logan dialed Easterly's number and waited for him to answer.

"Logan, glad you called. I heard about Alina. How is she doing?"

Logan gave Detective Easterly an update on her condition, explaining she was fast asleep right now with her cast elevated. He stood, walked over to her.

"She really went to town on the woman."

"Yeah. How bad?"

"Broken nose and cheekbone, plus a concussion. But she'll survive."

"I have to ask this next question for Alina's sake. Can you confirm that this woman was involved in the trafficking?" Logan reached over and gently stroked Alina's shoulder while she slept. "She was really concerned she'd attacked the wrong woman."

"You can definitely put her mind at ease on that point. It appears she was one of the coordinators in the group. We also picked up the last man, Bill Morgan. The woman is talking, so with any luck, we'll pick up the entire network when we do a full sweep."

Logan reached up and pinched the bridge of his nose. "I sure as hell hope you can track down that system and help recover the missing women."

"The superintendent is setting that up right now. The female coordinator's name as it was on Colin's cell is Roma Chandler. She is giving names, dates, places, and the whole line up. She was originally trafficked herself. So on one hand you can kind of understand, but on the other, well, it's like the worst thing possible. With any luck, we'll find these women. But you know it won't be a fast solution. A warrant has been issued on the house you asked me to look into. We're hoping it's involved in this mess, but it's too early to tell. Also…" He lowered his voice. "A couple names from Roma indicate a law enforcement connection—confirming Colin's mention of two bad cops. That will take even longer to sort out."

"Have to admit, we wondered about that last bit," Logan said. "No, it's never fast tying up something like this. I know my boss would want me to extend all the help we can give. We have connections around the world."

Detective Easterly's voice was light. "That's really good to know, because it looks like this is going all the way around the world. I've asked to be assigned to the task force. Watching how they move those women, that was scary. My sister is about the same size. And thinking of Tracy Evans curled up inside that suitcase is terrifying."

Logan nodded. "At least we saved the ones we could."

"There is that. John also confessed to killing his brother. He was pissed about Joe not paying rent," Easterly said. "Goes to show that you should never piss off family. Speaking of, are you heading out tonight?"

"I'm helping move Alina to Texas. She's got a friend there she'll stay with. She doesn't think she can handle being here anymore. She's not running away from you though, so if you need her for court or deposition testimony, then we'll send you the address once we get her relocated."

"I'm glad to hear that. That woman's got a lot of grit. And that is never a bad thing." The detective ended the call.

Logan thought about that and said quietly to himself, "Grit, that's exactly what she's got."

Beside him Alina murmured, "That's what my grandma used to say."

He laid his cell on the bedside table, sat gently on the bed, wrapping his arm around her, tucking her against him. "You're supposed to be asleep."

"I had a power nap," she said with a half smile.

But her voice was drowsy, as if she was still looking at going back under. He gave her a gentle hug. "Go right back to sleep."

"Not sure I want to," she whispered. "It was really nice to hear you say you are helping move me to my friend in Texas. Clearing the pathway so I could start over."

"I'm a nice guy."

She rolled over under the blankets and wrapped her good arm around him. Holding up her injured arm, she said, "I knew that the moment I laid eyes on you." She pulled his head down and kissed him. "Thank you for the rest of my life."

He placed his fingers on her lips, gently teasing her. "I was hoping you'd be willing to spend the rest of your life with me."

She smiled, tears coming to the corner of her eyes. "Are you sure? We hardly even know each other."

He slid his hand up her body, gently cupping her breasts, his hand still over the blanket. "True, but I know what counts. I know you have heart. I know you'll stand up for the underdog and will defend our children to the death. You're adorable when you're riled. And I admire the honesty I see inside you. What is there not to love?"

A tear sparkled on her eyelashes. She slid her finger across his lips and then pulled him down closer, gently kissing him, dropping little ones on his upper lip, then his bottom and square jaw. As if she didn't know what to say but wanted to show him instead.

And he was willing to accept a demonstration. With a smile, he let her gently explore his face, running her fingers through his hair, stroking down the side of his cheek with her fingertips.

She whispered something across his ear, and he chuckled. "Now that tickles."

She opened her eyes, raised her eyebrow and smiled. "You think that tickles? I might be handicapped because of my bum arm, but that doesn't mean, down the road, I might not take full advantage of you when you're helpless and see how ticklish you are everywhere."

He gave her a wicked grin. "One day down the road," he promised, "you can do what you want. But right now, you look after that arm."

It was her turn to flash a wicked smile. "So, are you going to lie here and let me do my worst?" she teased.

He chuckled. "Well, I don't know about just lying here."

With her good arm, she pulled him down. "I don't think that's possible. Something about you makes me ache to have you deep inside."

At her words his head lowered, and he crushed his lips against hers. He couldn't imagine not wanting this woman in the future. So much about her was perfect. But even if she wasn't, it was like his body knew her, and his heart already recognized her. His soul opened, enjoying her, as if seeing somebody he had already known and was reacquainting himself with. He didn't even know how to explain it.

But thankfully, no words were necessary. When he ripped the blankets off the bed and turned to face her, she shook her head at him and held up her hand. "Oh, no, you don't. You're not coming back to bed unless you strip down."

He gave her grin. "What about you? You're still wearing a nightgown."

She grinned back. "And it's gonna take you to get it off me too."

At that he laughed out loud and quickly divested himself of his shirt and pants. By the time he kicked off his shoes and peeled away his socks and stood before her in his birthday suit, she was on her knees, trying to hike the nightgown over her waist.

He chuckled. "Let me."

Obediently she put her arms up, and gently he worked her bad hand and arm out of the nightgown, then threw it over the side of the bed.

When she was again kneeling before him, he said, "If I'd realized this is what you wanted, I wouldn't have put you in the nightgown in the first place."

"I thought about it," she said, "but I was a little too tired."

"Thank God for power naps," he said in a fervent whisper.

And knowing she was still sore and banged up from her own captivity, not to mention the beating she'd given the poor woman today, Logan stretched out beside her and gently caressed and teased her until she was writhing with passion. Honest in her response. Open in her joy. And he loved every second of it.

His fingers stroked and caressed, teased and delved, and he found he couldn't get enough. He leaned over, his lips and tongue leaving wet trails over her ribs, up to her beautifully plump breasts. When he took one nipple in his mouth and suckled hard, she cried out, her body arching under him.

"God, you're so beautiful." He turned his attention to the other, not wanting either to feel left out. At the same time, he slipped one hand to the curls at the juncture of her thighs, finding the moistness from within. He groaned, sliding higher up her body to take her lips with his. "So responsive," he whispered again.

She wrapped her good arm around him. The cast was cold on his back, but he didn't notice for the fever burning through him. He slid a hand down her back to one cheek, spreading her thighs wide, hooking her legs over his hips in position. He looked down at her and whispered, "Ready?"

Alina smiled and pulled him closer. "I am," she whispered, "I was born ready—for you."

He surged deep inside, closing his eyes as she held him tight within her. She cried out as he seated himself right at her core. And he stayed still, frozen, inhaling the moment. Her muscles eased and then clamped tight around him. He groaned hard. And she did it again.

"You're killing me."

She chuckled. "How about we kill each other—with love."

He lowered his head and whispered, "Absolutely." He took her. His hands slid down to hold her hips firmly in position as he slowly raised and lowered, driving them both to the precipice they each wanted. Higher and higher as the coils twisted within them.

Finally feeling his own lack of control splintering around him, he slid a finger between the crevice of her cheeks and squeezed while gently stroking the soft tissue beneath. She arched up high and cried out as her body clenched tight around him, milking him of everything he had to give her. His groan erupted from deep inside as his body shuddered and shook with his own orgasm.

Then he collapsed beside her, careful of her arm, and gently tugged her close.

She lifted her fingers to stroke his cheek. "Now I'm tired." She closed her eyes.

He leaned over and kissed her eyelids and whispered, "Sleep. I'll watch over you."

And she believed him. If anything were to happen, Logan would be there for her. She stretched her arm up around him and whispered, "You have been the light that kept me going through all this. But I wanted to tell you that *Alina* means *light*."

"And that's perfect," he whispered. "Because you're my Alina. You're my light." With her wrapped in his arms, they both fell asleep.

Ready to take the next step of their lives together forever.

Epilogue

HARRISON WAITED FOR Logan to arrive. He was needed for a job. Harrison had been in Mexico for the last two days but had flown in to Houston this morning. It had worked out well, leaving Alina and Logan in Boston. Harrison hoped they'd cemented their relationship. It also gave her a little longer to heal after all she'd been through. He was damn sure Alina would fit right in at the compound. But having Caroline's apartment as a go-between for the moment was even better. At least until Alina had a chance to meet everybody, get to know their people and see how she liked the idea.

Except Logan was not likely to wait.

Some things Logan was possessive about. And this woman was one of them. It amazed Harrison to see how quickly the relationship had solidified between those two. Logan had always had a way with women. Something Harrison didn't. But Logan's relationships had always been lighthearted. This one was different.

That was good. He was happy for his friend.

LOGAN HAD PROMISED to explain all about the compound to Alina so she wasn't completely overwhelmed on arrival. They had arrived at Caroline's place early this morning, helped Alina unpack, and then he would drive Alina out to the compound, so she could meet everyone. He admired her guts. It wouldn't be easy to come into a place like this and be introduced to everyone. They were all good people, but it would still be daunting on her part. She'd been reluctant to accept change, and this would be a huge one.

Harrison was outside in the garage when he heard his name called.

"Harrison, they came around the bend."

He grinned. Everybody was watching. No way they weren't. He crossed his arms and leaned against the open garage bay doors as Logan drove in—in the same car Alina had picked up in the hospital parking lot a few days ago. He could see the two of them talking. Stone and Levi came out and stood beside him. Of course it would be the men first.

Logan grinned sheepishly as he parked the car. A possessive look in his eyes. And pride shone on his face. He got out of the car, and the passenger door opened too.

Harrison took one look at Alina, saw the purple cast and couldn't help but tease her. "Did you really have to beat the poor woman up?"

She slapped her good hand over her mouth to hold back a cry. Then she raced toward him, calling out, "Harrison." She flung herself into his arms.

He had to brace himself to catch her. The little whirlwind didn't weigh more than 110 pounds. He caught her midair and wrapped his arms around her, spinning her into a big hug.

She laughed when he finally put her down and reached up to kiss him on the cheek. "Trust you to get away from all the work," she teased him right back.

He groaned. "I'm not housebroken. Logan is."

She patted him on the cheek. "You're more so than you would like to admit." Instead of being shy or waiting for Logan, she turned to the two men beside him. "Well, you're Stone, and you must be Levi." She held out her left hand to them. "I'd love to give you a hug as thanks, but I really don't know you, so maybe a left-handed shake is better."

Levi chuckled. "Hell no." He opened his arms.

She grinned and walked right into them. Logan stood beside them as she stepped backed. "Thank you so much for sending these two men to save my life."

Levi said, "If we had known, we would've been there two days earlier."

Her smile fell away, and shadows deepened her eyes. "And that would've been much easier on me. But you sent me my own hero, and for that, I will always be grateful."

Levi winced at the term *hero.*

Harrison chuckled. "Yep, that's what everybody here is," he said unhelpfully. "Heroes for Hire. That's the nickname for the company."

Levi gave him a hard look. "Legendary Security is our company name."

She turned to face Stone. "Logan's told me so much about you." She gave him a gentle smile. "And I understand Lissa has found her own hero with you too."

And damned if Stone didn't blush.

She reached up her arms, and in a move so damn careful, Stone put his arms around her waist, picked her up and gave her a hug.

Harrison glanced at Logan to see the surprise on his face too. "Not only is she an icebreaker but she is definitely a heartbreaker." He didn't realize he'd said that out loud until she turned to him.

"Heartbreaker? Me? No." She shook her head and reached a hand out to Logan. "He's my heartbreaker. My Heartbreaker Hero." She turned to Logan and kissed him on the cheek. "And if this is Texas, I'm absolutely loving it."

She froze as she caught sight of somebody behind Harrison.

Harrison pivoted and grinned. Alina stepped forward, holding out her left hand again. In a more formal voice, she said, "I'm Alina. You must be Ice."

Ice's cool voice warmed. "Welcome, Alina. From what I've heard, you've been through the grind already."

Tears sparkled on her eyelashes. Alina brushed them away impatiently. "I keep telling myself not to cry anymore. And then it hits at the oddest times."

She turned as several other women came to join them. Lissa wrapped her arms around Stone and said, "You're not alone there. Stone saved me from a kidnapping too."

Ice walked over to stand beside Levi. Then the rest of the gang showed up. Merk with Katina, even Rhodes was here with Sienna. The only ones missing were Flynn and Anna.

Logan asked, "Where's Flynn? Everybody is here but him."

"Not too far from here. He and Anna went into town to sign the purchase documents today," Ice said. "You'll see them tonight."

Alina turned to look at all the couples. "Harrison, where's your girl?"

There were muffled chuckles. He narrowed his gaze to shut them all up and said, "I'm the only sane man here. I'm single and intend to stay that way."

She gave him the sweetest, gentlest smile and said, "Not happening. You're definitely hero material too."

He shook his head and turned to leave. "To hell with that."

"Okay, run then," she called to his back. "But remember, you are a *hero*, and you will find a partner one day."

He turned to face her and give her a hard glare, hoping to cut back some of the sunshine and roses in her voice. Instead, her smile brightened, and she laughed, the musical sound flying easily as it rolled through the garage. How could anybody be upset with so much sunshine? Still, he wasn't giving in without a fight. "You are getting into so much trouble if you say that damn word one more time."

She stepped over the threshold and said, "Hero."

He fisted his hands on his hips and said, "I warned you."

She shoved her face in his and said, "Hero, hero, hero, hero."

He threw his hands in the air. "Logan, control your woman."

Logan responded with a great belly laugh that rippled across the nearby hills. "Hell, no. I haven't found a way to do that yet."

She spun and looked at him. "And you're not going to either."

The other women cheered. They all linked arms together and took Alina inside.

As Ice walked away, she said, "Logan, we're keeping this one."

As Katina passed Harrison, she whispered, "You're next."

He stomped his foot and said, "Forget it. Not happening."

But nobody was listening—maybe not even Harrison. He gave a loud snort, adding for emphasis, "Never."

This concludes Heroes for Hire, Books 4–6.

Read about Harrison's Heart: Heroes for Hire, Book 7

Heroes for Hire: Harrison's Heart (Book #7)

When a call for help comes from the father of his boss Levi's partner Ice, Harrison answers. A senator has been shot, his wife beaten and the man's kids are in the wind. With a press-conference's-worth of questions needing answers, Harrison has his job cut out for him. Unfortunately, that's not all that's expected of him. The senator's adult daughter is also missing. She's ex-military and apparently has a grudge against the world. She doesn't want to be found, and, even after Harrison locates her, she refuses to have a single blessed thing to do with him. If only he felt the same…

Zoe's on a mission that doesn't leave room in her worldview for heroes, especially a gorgeous badass warrior like Harrison, whom she considers little more than a mercenary for hire. Good thing Harrison has never been the type to take 'no' for an answer because the situation—and their relationship—has all the ingredients of a powder keg requiring one small spark to ignite it. Zoe has angered exactly the wrong people…and they're plotting to put an end to her meddling…and *her*…permanently.

Books 7–9 are available now!

To find out more visit Dale Mayer's website.

https://geni.us/DMSHfH7-9

Author's Note

Thank you for reading Heroes for Hire, Books 4–6! If you enjoyed the book, please take a moment and leave a short review.

Dear reader,

I love to hear from readers, and you can contact me at my website: www.dalemayer.com or at my Facebook author page. To be informed of new releases and special offers, sign up for my newsletter or follow me on BookBub. And if you are interested in joining Dale Mayer's Reader Group, here is the Facebook sign up page.
http://geni.us/DaleMayerFBGroup

Cheers,
Dale Mayer

Your THREE Free Books Are Waiting!

Grab your copy of SEALs of Honor Books 1 – 3 for free!

Meet Mason, Hawk and Dane. *Brave, badass warriors who serve their country with honor and love their women to the limits of life and death.*

DOWNLOAD your copy right now! Just tell me where to send it.

dalemayer.com/seals-honor-free-bundle

About the Author

Dale Mayer is a *USA Today* best-selling author, best known for her SEALs military romances, her Psychic Visions series, and her Lovely Lethal Garden cozy series. Her contemporary romances are raw and full of passion and emotion (Broken But … Mending, Hathaway House series). Her thrillers will keep you guessing (Kate Morgan, By Death series), and her romantic comedies will keep you giggling (*It's a Dog's Life*, a stand-alone novella; and the Broken Protocols series, starring Charming Marvin, the cat).

Dale honors the stories that come to her—and some of them are crazy, break all the rules and cross multiple genres!

To go with her fiction, she also writes nonfiction in many different fields, with books available on résumé writing, companion gardening, and the US mortgage system. All her books are available in print and ebook format.

Connect with Dale Mayer Online

Dale's Website – www.dalemayer.com

Twitter – @DaleMayer

Facebook Page – geni.us/DaleMayerFBFanPage

Facebook Group – geni.us/DaleMayerFBGroup

BookBub – geni.us/DaleMayerBookbub

Instagram – geni.us/DaleMayerInstagram

Goodreads – geni.us/DaleMayerGoodreads

Newsletter – geni.us/DaleNews

Also by Dale Mayer

Published Adult Books:

The K9 Files

Ethan, Book 1

Pierce, Book 2

Lovely Lethal Gardens

Arsenic in the Azaleas, Book 1

Bones in the Begonias, Book 2

Corpse in the Carnations, Book 3

Daggers in the Dahlias, Book 4

Evidence in the Echinacea, Book 5

Footprints in the Ferns, Book 6

Psychic Vision Series

Tuesday's Child

Hide 'n Go Seek

Maddy's Floor

Garden of Sorrow

Knock Knock…

Rare Find

Eyes to the Soul

Now You See Her

Shattered

Into the Abyss

Seeds of Malice

Eye of the Falcon

Itsy-Bitsy Spider

Unmasked

Deep Beneath

Psychic Visions Books 1–3

Psychic Visions Books 4–6

Psychic Visions Books 7–9

By Death Series

Touched by Death

Haunted by Death

Chilled by Death

By Death Books 1–3

Broken Protocols – Romantic Comedy Series

Cat's Meow

Cat's Pajamas

Cat's Cradle

Cat's Claus

Broken Protocols 1-4

Broken and... Mending

Skin

Scars

Scales (of Justice)

Broken but… Mending 1-3

Glory

Genesis

Tori

Celeste

Glory Trilogy

Biker Blues

Morgan: Biker Blues, Volume 1

Cash: Biker Blues, Volume 2

SEALs of Honor

Mason: SEALs of Honor, Book 1

Hawk: SEALs of Honor, Book 2

Dane: SEALs of Honor, Book 3

Swede: SEALs of Honor, Book 4

Shadow: SEALs of Honor, Book 5

Cooper: SEALs of Honor, Book 6

Markus: SEALs of Honor, Book 7

Evan: SEALs of Honor, Book 8

Mason's Wish: SEALs of Honor, Book 9

Chase: SEALs of Honor, Book 10

Brett: SEALs of Honor, Book 11

Devlin: SEALs of Honor, Book 12

Easton: SEALs of Honor, Book 13

Ryder: SEALs of Honor, Book 14

Macklin: SEALs of Honor, Book 15

Corey: SEALs of Honor, Book 16

Warrick: SEALs of Honor, Book 17

Tanner: SEALs of Honor, Book 18

Jackson: SEALs of Honor, Book 19

Kanen: SEALs of Honor, Book 20

Nelson: SEALs of Honor, Book 21

SEALs of Honor, Books 1–3

SEALs of Honor, Books 4–6

SEALs of Honor, Books 7–10

SEALs of Honor, Books 11–13

SEALs of Honor, Books 14–16

SEALs of Honor, Books 17–19

Heroes for Hire

Levi's Legend: Heroes for Hire, Book 1

Stone's Surrender: Heroes for Hire, Book 2

Merk's Mistake: Heroes for Hire, Book 3

Rhodes's Reward: Heroes for Hire, Book 4

Flynn's Firecracker: Heroes for Hire, Book 5

Logan's Light: Heroes for Hire, Book 6

Harrison's Heart: Heroes for Hire, Book 7

Saul's Sweetheart: Heroes for Hire, Book 8

Dakota's Delight: Heroes for Hire, Book 9

Michael's Mercy (Part of Sleeper SEAL Series)

Tyson's Treasure: Heroes for Hire, Book 10

Jace's Jewel: Heroes for Hire, Book 11

Rory's Rose: Heroes for Hire, Book 12

Brandon's Bliss: Heroes for Hire, Book 13

Liam's Lily: Heroes for Hire, Book 14

North's Nikki: Heroes for Hire, Book 15

Anders's Angel: Heroes for Hire, Book 16

Reyes's Raina: Heroes for Hire, Book 17

Dezi's Diamond: Heroes for Hire, Book 18

Vince's Vixen: Heroes for Hire, Book 19

Heroes for Hire, Books 1–3

Heroes for Hire, Books 4–6

Heroes for Hire, Books 7–9

Heroes for Hire, Books 10–12

Heroes for Hire, Books 13–15

SEALs of Steel

Badger: SEALs of Steel, Book 1

Erick: SEALs of Steel, Book 2

Cade: SEALs of Steel, Book 3

Talon: SEALs of Steel, Book 4

Laszlo: SEALs of Steel, Book 5

Geir: SEALs of Steel, Book 6

Jager: SEALs of Steel, Book 7

The Final Reveal: SEALs of Steel, Book 8

SEALs of Steel, Books 1–4

SEALs of Steel, Books 5–8

SEALs of Steel, Books 1–8

Collections

Dare to Be You…

Dare to Love…

Dare to be Strong…

RomanceX3

Standalone Novellas

It's a Dog's Life

Riana's Revenge

Second Chances

Published Young Adult Books:

Family Blood Ties Series

Vampire in Denial

Vampire in Distress

Vampire in Design

Vampire in Deceit

Vampire in Defiance

Vampire in Conflict

Vampire in Chaos

Vampire in Crisis

Vampire in Control

Vampire in Charge

Family Blood Ties Set 1–3

Family Blood Ties Set 1–5

Family Blood Ties Set 4–6

Family Blood Ties Set 7–9

Sian's Solution, A Family Blood Ties Series Prequel Novelette

Design series

Dangerous Designs

Deadly Designs

Darkest Designs

Design Series Trilogy

Standalone

In Cassie's Corner

Gem Stone (a Gemma Stone Mystery)

Time Thieves

Published Non-Fiction Books:

Career Essentials

Career Essentials: The Résumé

Career Essentials: The Cover Letter

Career Essentials: The Interview

Career Essentials: 3 in 1

Ingram Content Group UK Ltd.
Milton Keynes UK
UKHW020824200323
418838UK00011B/1674